the
COLLECTOR

BY NORA ROBERTS

Hot Ice	Hidden Riches	Birthright
Sacred Sins	True Betrayals	Northern Lights
Brazen Virtue	Montana Sky	Blue Smoke
Sweet Revenge	Sanctuary	Angels Fall
Public Secrets	Homeport	High Noon
Genuine Lies	The Reef	Tribute
Carnal Innocence	River's End	Black Hills
	Carolina Moon	The Search
Divine Evil	The Villa	Chasing Fire
Honest Illusions	Midnight Bayou	The Witness
Private Scandals	Three Fates	Whiskey Beach

SERIES

IRISH BORN TRILOGY

Born in Fire
Born in Ice
Born in Shame

DREAM TRILOGY

Daring to Dream
Holding the Dream
Finding the Dream

CHESAPEAKE BAY SAGA

Sea Swept
Rising Tides
Inner Harbor
Chesapeake Blue

GALLAGHERS OF ARDMORE TRILOGY

Jewels of the Sun
Tears of the Moon
Heart of the Sea

THREE SISTERS ISLAND TRILOGY

Dance Upon the Air
Heaven and Earth
Face the Fire

KEY TRILOGY

Key of Light
Key of Knowledge
Key of Valor

E-BOOKS BY NORA ROBERTS

The MacGregor Brides

The MacGregor Grooms

Rebellion / In from the Cold

For Now, Forever

THE CALHOUNS

Suzanna's Surrender

Megan's Mate

Courting Catherine

A Man for Amanda

For the Love of Lilah

IRISH LEGACY

Irish Rose

Irish Rebel

Irish Thoroughbred

Best Laid Plans

Loving Jack

Lawless

Summer Love

Boundary Lines

Dual Image

First Impressions

The Law Is a Lady

Local Hero

This Magic Moment

The Name of the Game

Partners

Temptation

The Welcoming

Opposites Attract

Time Was

Times Change

Gabriel's Angel

Holiday Wishes

The Heart's Victory

The Right Path

Rules of the Game

Search for Love

Blithe Images

From This Day

Song of the West

Island of Flowers

Her Mother's Keeper

Untamed

Sullivan's Woman

Less of a Stranger

Reflections

Dance of Dreams

Storm Warning

Once More With Feeling

Endings and Beginnings

Tonight and Always

A Matter of Choice

BY NORA ROBERTS AND J. D. ROBB

Remember When

BY J. D. ROBB

Naked in Death
Glory in Death
Immortal in Death
Rapture in Death
Ceremony in Death
Vengeance in Death
Holiday in Death
Conspiracy in Death
Loyalty in Death
Witness in Death
Judgment in Death
Betrayal in Death
Seduction in Death

Reunion in Death
Purity in Death
Portrait in Death
Imitation in Death
Divided in Death
Visions in Death
Survivor in Death
Origin in Death
Memory in Death
Born in Death
Innocent in Death
Creation in Death
Strangers in Death
Salvation in Death

Promises in Death
Kindred in Death
Fantasy in Death
Indulgence in Death
Treachery in Death
New York to Dallas
Celebrity in Death
Delusion in Death
Calculated in Death
Thankless in Death
Concealed in Death

ANTHOLOGIES

From the Heart
A Little Magic
A Little Fate

Moon Shadows

(with Jill Gregory, Ruth Ryan Langan,
and Marianne Willman)

THE ONCE UPON SERIES

(with Jill Gregory, Ruth Ryan Langan,
and Marianne Willman)

Once Upon a Castle
Once Upon a Star
Once Upon a Dream
Once Upon a Rose
Once Upon a Kiss
Once Upon a Midnight

Silent Night

(with Susan Plunkett, Dee Holmes, and Claire Cross)

Out of This World

(with Laurell K. Hamilton, Susan Krinard,
and Maggie Shayne)

Bump in the Night

(with Mary Blayney, Ruth Ryan Langan,
and Mary Kay McComas)

Dead of Night

(with Mary Blayney, Ruth Ryan Langan,
and Mary Kay McComas)

the

COLLECTOR

NORA ROBERTS

**Doubleday Large Print
Home Library Edition**

G. P. PUTNAM'S SONS | New York

This Large Print Edition, prepared especially for
Doubleday Large Print Home Library, contains
the complete, unabridged text of the original
Publisher's Edition.

G. P. PUTNAM'S SONS
Publishers Since 1838
Published by the Penguin Group
Penguin Group (USA) LLC
375 Hudson Street
New York, New York 10014

USA • Canada • UK • Ireland • Australia
New Zealand • India • South Africa • China

A Penguin Random House Company

ISBN 978-1-61129-200-8

Printed in the United States of America

**This Large Print Book carries the
Seal of Approval of N.A.V.H.**

In memory of my mother,
who collected everything,

and my father,
who always made room.

PART ONE

Any place I hang my hat is home.

JOHNNY MERCER

One

She thought they'd never leave. Clients, especially new ones, tended to fuss and delay, revolving on the same loop of instructions, contacts, comments before finally heading out the door. She sympathized because when they walked out the door they left their home, their belongings, and in this case their cat, in someone else's hands.

As their house-sitter, Lila Emerson did everything she could to send them off relaxed, and confident those hands were competent ones.

For the next three weeks, while Jason

and Macey Kilderbrand enjoyed the south of France with friends and family, Lila would live in their most excellent apartment in Chelsea, water their plants, feed, water and play with their cat, collect their mail—and forward anything of import.

She'd tend Macey's pretty terrace garden, pamper the cat, take messages and act as a burglary deterrent simply by her presence.

While she did, she'd enjoy living in New York's tony London Terrace just as she'd enjoyed living in the charming flat in Rome—where for an additional fee she'd painted the kitchen—and the sprawling house in Brooklyn—with its frisky golden retriever, sweet and aging Boston terrier and aquarium of colorful tropical fish.

She'd seen a lot of New York in her six years as a professional house-sitter, and in the last four had expanded to see quite a bit of the world as well.

Nice work if you can get it, she thought—and she could get it.

"Come on, Thomas." She gave the cat's long, sleek body one head-to-tail stroke. "Let's go unpack."

She liked the settling in and, since the

spacious apartment boasted a second bed-room, unpacked the first of her two suit-cases, tucking her clothes in the mirrored bureau or hanging them in the tidy walk-in closet. She'd been warned Thomas would likely insist on sharing the bed with her, and she'd deal with that. And she appreci-ated that the clients—likely Macey—had arranged a pretty bouquet of freesia on the nightstand.

Lila was big on little personal touches, the giving and the getting.

She'd already decided to make use of the master bath with its roomy steam shower and deep jet tub.

"Never waste or abuse the amenities," she told Thomas as she put her toiletries away.

As the two suitcases held nearly every-thing she owned, she took some care in distributing them where it suited her best.

After some consideration she set up her office in the dining area, arranging her lap-top so she could look up and out at the view of New York. In a smaller space she'd have happily worked where she slept, but since she had room, she'd make use of it.

She'd been given instructions on all the

kitchen appliances, the remotes, the security system—the place boasted an array of gadgets that appealed to her nerdy soul.

In the kitchen she found a bottle of wine, a pretty bowl of fresh fruit, an array of fancy cheeses with a note handwritten on Macey's monogrammed stationery.

Enjoy our home!
Jason, Macey and Thomas

Sweet, Lila thought, and she absolutely would enjoy it.

She opened the wine, poured a glass, sipped and approved. Grabbing her binoculars, she carried the glass out on the terrace to admire the view.

The clients made good use of the space, she thought, with a couple of cushy chairs, a rough stone bench, a glass table—and the pots of thriving flowers, the pretty drops of cherry tomatoes, the fragrant herbs, all of which she'd been encouraged to harvest and use.

She sat, with Thomas in her lap, sipping wine, stroking his silky fur.

"I bet they sit out here a lot, having a drink, or coffee. They look happy together.

And their place has a good feel to it. You can tell." She tickled Thomas under the chin and had his bright green eyes going dreamy. "She's going to call and e-mail a lot in the first couple days, so we're going to take some pictures of you, baby, and send them to her so she can see you're just fine."

Setting the wine aside, she lifted the binoculars, scanned the buildings. The apartment complex hugged an entire city block, and that offered little glimpses into other lives.

Other lives just fascinated her.

A woman about her age wore a little black dress that fit her tall, model-thin body like a second skin. She paced as she talked on her cell phone. She didn't look happy, Lila thought. Broken date. He has to work late—he says, Lila added, winding the plot in her head. She's fed up with that.

A couple floors above, two couples sat in a living room—art-covered walls, sleek, contemporary furnishings—and laughed over what looked like martinis.

Obviously they didn't like the summer heat as much as she and Thomas or they'd have sat outside on their little terrace.

Old friends, she decided, who get together often, sometimes take vacations together.

Another window opened the world to a little boy rolling around on the floor with a white puppy. The absolute joy of both zinged right through the air and had Lila laughing.

"He's wanted a puppy forever—forever being probably a few months at that age—and today his parents surprised him. He'll remember today his whole life, and one day he'll surprise his little boy or girl the same way."

Pleased to end on that note, Lila lowered the glasses. "Okay, Thomas, we're going to get a couple hours of work in. I know, I know," she continued, setting him down, picking up the half glass of wine. "Most people are done with work for the day. They're going out to dinner, meeting friends—or in the case of the killer blonde in the black dress, bitching about not going out. But the thing is . . ." She waited until he strolled into the apartment ahead of her. "I set my own hours. It's one of the perks."

She chose a ball—motion-activated—

from the basket of cat toys in the kitchen closet, gave it a roll across the floor.

Thomas immediately pounced, wrestled, batted, chased.

"If I were a cat," she speculated, "I'd go crazy for that, too."

With Thomas happily occupied, she picked up the remote, ordered music. She made a note of which station played so she could be sure she returned it to their house music before the Kilderbrands came home. She moved away from the jazz to contemporary pop.

House-sitting provided lodging, interest, even adventure. But writing paid the freight. Freelance writing—and waiting tables— had kept her head just above water her first two years in New York. After she'd fallen into house-sitting, initially doing favors for friends, and friends of friends, she'd had the real time and opportunity to work on her novel.

Then the luck or serendipity of house-sitting for an editor who'd taken an interest. Her first, **Moon Rise**, had sold decently. No bust-out best seller, but steady, and with a nice little following in the fourteen-to-eighteen set she'd aimed for. The second would hit the stores in October, so her fingers were crossed.

But more to the moment, she needed to focus on book three of the series.

She bundled up her long brown hair with a quick twist, scoop and the clamp of a chunky tortoiseshell hinge clip. While Thomas gleefully chased the ball, she settled in with her half glass of wine, a tall glass of ice water and the music she imagined her central character, Kaylee, listened to.

As a junior in high school, Kaylee dealt with all the ups and downs—the romance, the homework, the mean girls, the bullies, the politics, the heartbreaks and triumphs that crowded into the short, intense high school years.

A sticky road, especially for the new girl—as she'd been in the first book. And more, of course, as Kaylee's family were lycans.

It wasn't easy to finish a school assignment or go to the prom with a full moon rising when a girl was a werewolf.

Now, in book three, Kaylee and her family were at war with a rival pack, a pack who preyed on humans. Maybe a little bloodthirsty for some of the younger readers, she thought, but this was where the path of the story led. Where it had to go.

She picked it up where Kaylee dealt with the betrayal of the boy she thought she loved, an overdue assignment on the Napoleonic Wars and the fact that her blond, beautiful nemesis had locked her in the science lab.

The moon would rise in twenty minutes—just about the same time the Science Club would arrive for their meeting.

She had to find a way out before the change.

Lila dived in, happily sliding into Kaylee, into the fear of exposure, the pain of a broken heart, the fury with the cheerleading, homecoming queening, man-eating (literally) Sasha.

By the time she'd gotten Kaylee out, and in the nick, courtesy of a smoke bomb that brought the vice principal, another thorn in Kaylee's side, dealt with the lecture, the detention, the streaking home as the change came on her heroine, Lila had put in three solid hours.

Pleased with herself, she surfaced from the story, glanced around.

Thomas, exhausted from play, lay curled on the chair beside her, and the lights of the city glittered and gleamed out the window.

She fixed Thomas's dinner precisely as instructed. While he ate she got her Leatherman, used the screwdriver of the multi-tool to tighten some screws in the pantry.

Loose screws, to her thinking, were a gateway to disaster. In people and in things.

She noticed a couple of wire baskets on runners, still in their boxes. Probably for potatoes or onions. Crouching, she read the description, the assurance of easy install. She made a mental note to e-mail Macey, ask if she wanted them put in.

It would be a quick, satisfying little project.

She poured a second glass of wine and made a late dinner out of the fruit, cheese and crackers. Sitting cross-legged in the dining room, Thomas in her lap, she ate while she checked e-mail, sent e-mail, scanned her blog—made a note for a new entry.

"Getting on to bedtime, Thomas."

He just yawned when she picked up the

remote to shut off the music, then lifted him up and away so she could deal with her dishes and bask in the quiet of her first night in a new space.

After changing into cotton pants and a tank, she checked the security, then revisited her neighbors through the binoculars.

It looked like Blondie had gone out after all, leaving the living room light on low. The pair of couples had gone out as well. Maybe to dinner, or a show, Lila thought.

The little boy would be fast asleep, hopefully with the puppy curled up with him. She could see the shimmer of a television, imagined Mom and Dad relaxing together.

Another window showed a party going on. A crowd of people—well-dressed, cocktail attire—mixed and mingled, drinks or small plates in hand.

She watched for a while, imagined conversations, including a whispered one between the brunette in the short red dress and the bronzed god in the pearl-gray suit who, in Lila's imagination, were having a hot affair under the noses of his long-suffering wife and her clueless husband.

She scanned over, stopped, lowered the glasses a moment, then looked again.

No, the really built guy on the . . . twelfth floor wasn't completely naked. He wore a thong as he did an impressive bump and grind, a spin, drop.

He was working up a nice sweat, she noted, as he repeated moves or added to them.

Obviously an actor/dancer moonlighting as a stripper until he caught his big Broadway break.

She enjoyed him. A lot.

The window show kept her entertained for a half hour before she made herself a nest in the bed—and was indeed joined by Thomas. She switched on the TV for company, settled on an **NCIS** rerun where she could literally recite the dialogue before the characters. Comforted by that, she picked up her iPad, found the thriller she'd started on the plane from Rome, and snuggled in.

Over the next week, she developed a routine. Thomas would wake her more accurately than any alarm clock at seven precisely, when he begged, vocally, for his breakfast.

She'd feed the cat, make coffee, water the plants indoors and out, have a little breakfast while she visited the neighbors.

Blondie and her live-in lover—they didn't have the married vibe—argued a lot. Blondie tended to throw breakables. Mr. Slick, and he was great to look at, had good reflexes, and a whole basket of charm. Fights, pretty much daily, ended in seduction or wild bursts of passion.

They suited each other, in her estimation. For the moment. Neither of them struck Lila as long-haul people with her throwing dishes or articles of clothing, him ducking, smiling and seducing.

Game players, she thought. Hot, sexy game players, and if he didn't have something going on, on the side, she'd be very surprised.

The little boy and the puppy continued their love affair, with Mom, Dad or nanny patiently cleaning up little accidents. Mom and Dad left together most mornings garbed in a way that said high-powered careers to Lila.

The Martinis, as she thought of them,

rarely used their little terrace. She was definitely one of the ladies-who-lunch, leaving the apartment every day, late morning, returning late afternoon usually with a shopping bag.

The Partiers rarely spent an evening at home, seemed to revel in a frantic sort of lifestyle.

And the Body practiced his bump and grind regularly—to her unabashed pleasure.

She treated herself to the show, and the stories she created every morning. She'd work into the afternoon, break to amuse the cat before she dressed and went out to buy what she thought she might like for dinner, to see the neighborhood.

She sent pictures of a happy Thomas to her clients, picked tomatoes, sorted mail, composed a vicious lycan battle, updated her blog. And installed the two baskets in the pantry.

On the first day of week two, she bought a good bottle of Barolo, filled in the fancy cheese selections, added some mini cupcakes from an amazing neighborhood bakery.

Just after seven in the evening, she

opened the door to the party pack that was her closest friend.

"There you are." Julie, wine bottle in one hand, a fragrant bouquet of star lilies in the other, still managed to enfold her.

Six feet of curves and tumbled red hair, Julie Bryant struck the opposite end of Lila's average height, slim build, straight brown hair.

"You brought a tan back from Rome. God, I'd be wearing 500 SPF and still end up going lobster in the Italian sun. You look just great."

"Who wouldn't after two weeks in Rome? The pasta alone. I told you I'd get the wine," Lila added when Julie shoved the bottle into her hand.

"Now we have two. And welcome home."

"Thanks." Lila took the flowers.

"Wow, some place. It's huge, and the view's a killer. What do these people do?"

"Start with family money."

"Oh, don't I wish I had."

"Let's detour to the kitchen so I can fix the flowers, then I'll give you a tour. He works in finance, and I don't understand any of it. He loves his work and prefers tennis to golf. She does some interior design, and you can see she's good at it from the way the apartment looks. She's thinking about going pro, but they're talking about starting a family, so she's not sure it's the right time to start her own business."

"They're new clients, right? And they still tell you that kind of personal detail?"

"What can I say? I have a face that says tell me all about it. Say hello to Thomas."

Julie crouched to greet the cat. "What a handsome face he has."

"He's a sweetheart." Lila's deep brown eyes went soft as Julie and Thomas made friends. "Pets aren't always a plus on the job, but Thomas is."

She selected a motorized mouse out of Thomas's toy basket, enjoyed Julie's easy laugh as the cat pounced.

"Oh, he's a killer." Straightening, Julie leaned back on the stone-gray counter while Lila fussed the lilies into a clear glass vase.

"Rome was fabulous?"

"It really was."

"And did you find a gorgeous Italian to have mad sex with?"

"Sadly no, but I think the proprietor of the local market fell for me. He was about eighty, give or take. He called me **una bella donna** and gave me the most beautiful peaches."

"Not as good as sex, but something. I can't believe I missed you when you got back."

"I appreciate the overnight at your place between jobs."

"Anytime, you know that. I only wish I'd been there."

"How was the wedding?"

"I definitely need wine before I get started on Cousin Melly's Hamptons Wedding Week From Hell, and why I've officially retired as a bridesmaid."

"Your texts were fun for me. I especially liked the one . . . 'Crazy Bride Bitch says rose petals wrong shade of pink. Hysteria ensues. Must destroy CBB for the good of womankind.'"

"It almost came to that. Oh no! Sobs, tremors, despair. The petals are pink-pink! They have to be rose-pink. Julie! Fix it, Julie! I came close to fixing her."

"Did she really have a half-ton truckload of petals?"

"Just about."

"You should have buried her in them. Bride smothered by rose petals. Everyone would think it was an ironic, if tragic, mishap."

"If only I'd thought of it. I really missed you. I like it better when you're working in New York, and I can come see your digs and hang out with you."

Lila studied her friend as she opened the wine. "You should come with me sometime—when it's someplace fabulous."

"I know, you keep saying." Julie wandered as she spoke. "I'm just not sure I wouldn't feel weird, actually staying in— Oh my God, look at this china. It has to be antique, and just amazing."

"Her great-grandmother's. And if you don't feel weird coming over and spending an evening with me wherever, you wouldn't feel weird staying. You stay in hotels."

"People don't live there."

"Some people do. Eloise and Nanny did."

Julie gave Lila's long tail of hair a tug. "Eloise and Nanny are fictional."

"Fictional people are people, too, otherwise why would we care what happens to them? Here, let's have this on the little terrace. Wait until you see Macey's container garden. Her family started in France—vineyards."

Lila scooped up the tray with the ease of the waitress she'd once been. "They met five years ago when she was over there visiting her grandparents—like they are now—and he was on vacation and came to their winery. Love at first sight, they both claim."

"It's the best. First sight."

"I'd say fictional, but I just made a case for fictional." She led the way to the terrace. "Turned out they both lived in New York. He called her, they went out. And were exchanging 'I dos' about eighteen months later."

"Like a fairy tale."

"Which I'd also say fictional, except I love fairy tales. And they look really happy together. And as you'll see, she's got a seriously green thumb."

Julie tapped the binoculars as they started out. "Still spying?"

Lila's wide, top-heavy mouth moved into a pout. "It's not spying. It's observing. If people don't want you looking in, they should close the curtains, pull down the shades."

"Uh-huh. Wow." Julie set her hands on her hips as she scanned the terrace. "You're right about the green thumb."

Everything lush and colorful and thriving in simple terra-cotta pots made the urban space a creative oasis. "She's growing tomatoes?"

"They're wonderful, and the herbs? She started them from seeds."

"Can you do that?"

"Macey can. I—as they told me I could and should—harvested some. I had a big, beautiful salad for dinner last night. Ate it out here, with a glass of wine, and watched the window show."

"You have the oddest life. Tell me about the window people."

Lila poured wine, then reached inside for the binoculars—just in case.

"We have the family on the tenth floor—they just got the little boy a puppy. The kid and the pup are both incredibly pretty and adorable. It's true love, and fun to watch. There's a sexy blonde on fourteen who lives with a very hot guy—both could be

Is it me? Why couldn't I make it work? Who will I have dinner with?

When you lived in a culture of couples, it could make you feel less when you were flying solo.

"I don't," Lila assured the cat, who'd curled up in his own little bed sometime between the last kabob and the first cupcake. "I'm okay being single. It means I can go where I want when I want, take any job that works for me. I'm seeing the world, Thomas, and okay, talking to cats, but I'm okay with that, too."

Still, she wished she'd been able to talk Julie into staying over. Not just for the company, but to help deal with the hangover her friend was bound to have come morning.

Mini cupcakes were Satan, she decided as she readied for bed. So cute and tiny, oh, they're like eating nothing, that's what you tell yourself, until you've eaten half a dozen.

Now she was wired up on alcohol and sugar, and she'd never get to sleep.

She picked up the binoculars. Still some lights on, she noted. She wasn't the only one still up at . . . Jesus, one-forty in the morning.

Sweaty Naked Guy was still up, and in the company of an equally hot-looking guy. Smug, Lila made a mental note to tell Julie her gaydar **was** like Superman.

Party couple hadn't made it to bed yet; in fact it looked as though they'd just gotten in. Another swank deal, from their attire. Lila admired the woman's shimmery orange dress, and wished she could see the shoes. Then was rewarded when the woman reached down, balancing a hand on the man's shoulder, and removed one strappy, sky-high gold sandal with a red sole.

Mmm, Louboutins.

Lila scanned down.

Blondie hadn't turned in yet either. She wore black again—snug and short—with her hair tumbling out of an updo. Been out on the town, Lila speculated, and it didn't go very well.

She's crying, Lila realized, catching the way the woman swiped at her face as she spoke. Talking fast. Urgently. Big fight with the boyfriend.

And where is he?

But even changing angles she couldn't bring him into view.

Dump him, Lila advised. Nobody should be allowed to make you so unhappy. You're gorgeous, and I bet you're smart, and certainly worth more than—

Lila jerked as the woman's head snapped back from a blow.

"Oh my God. He hit her. You bastard. Don't—"

She cried out herself as the woman tried to cover her face, cringed back as she was struck again.

And the woman wept, begged.

Lila made one leap to the bedside table and her phone, grabbed it, leaped back.

She couldn't see him, just couldn't see him in the dim light, but now the woman was plastered back against the window.

"That's enough, that's enough," Lila murmured, preparing to call 911.

Then everything froze.

The glass shattered. The woman exploded out. Arms spread wide, legs kicking, hair flying like golden wings, she dropped fourteen stories to the brutal sidewalk.

"Oh God, God, God." Shaking, Lila fumbled with the phone.

"Nine-one-one, what is your emergency?"

"He pushed her. He pushed her, and she fell out the window."

"Ma'am—"

"Wait. Wait." She closed her eyes a moment, forced herself to breathe in and out three times. Be clear, she ordered herself, give the details.

"This is Lila Emerson. I just witnessed a murder. A woman was pushed out a fourteenth-story window. I'm staying at . . ." It took her a moment to remember before she came to the Kilderbrands' address. "It's the building across from me. Ah, to the, to the west of me. I think. I'm sorry, I can't think. She's dead. She has to be dead."

"I'm dispatching a unit now. Will you hold the line?"

"Yes. Yes. I'll stay here."

Shuddering, she looked out again, but now the room beyond the broken window was dark.

Two

She dressed, caught herself actually debating over jeans or capris. Shock, she told herself. She was in a little bit of shock, but it was all right. She'd be all right.

She was alive.

She pulled on jeans, a T-shirt, then paced around the apartment carrying a confused but willing Thomas.

She'd seen the police arrive, and the small crowd that gathered even at nearly two in the morning. But she couldn't watch.

It wasn't like **CSI** or **SVU** or **NCIS** or any of the initial shows on TV. It was real. The beautiful blonde who favored short black dresses lay broken and bloodied on the sidewalk. The man with wavy brown hair, the man she'd lived with, had sex with, talked with, laughed with, fought with, had pushed her to her death.

So she needed to be calm. To get calm and stay calm so she could tell the police just what she'd seen. Coherently. Though she hated reliving it, she made herself see it again. The tear-streaked face, the tumbling hair, the blows. She made herself see the man as she'd seen him through the window—laughing, ducking, arguing. In her mind, she sketched that face, etched it there so she could describe him to the police.

The police were coming, she reminded herself. Then jumped at the sound of the buzzer.

"It's okay," she murmured to Thomas. "Everything's okay."

She checked the security peep, saw the two uniformed officers, read their name plates carefully.

Fitzhugh and Morelli, she repeated to herself as she opened the door.

"Ms. Emerson?"

"Yes. Yes. Come in." She stepped back,

trying to think of what to do, what to say. "The woman, she . . . she couldn't have survived the fall."

"No, ma'am." Fitzhugh—older, more seasoned to her eye, took the lead. "Can you tell us what you saw?"

"Yes. I . . . We should sit down. Can we sit down? I should've made coffee. I could make coffee."

"Don't worry about that. This is a nice apartment," he said conversationally. "Are you staying with the Kilderbrands?"

"What? Oh, no. No, they're away. In France. I'm the house-sitter. I'm staying here while they're away. I don't live here. Should I call them? It's . . ." She stared blankly at her watch. "What time is it there? I can't think."

"Don't worry about that," he repeated, and led her to a chair.

"I'm sorry. It was so awful. He was hitting her, then he must've pushed her because the window broke, and she just—just flew out."

"You witnessed someone strike the victim?"

"Yes. I . . ." She clutched at Thomas another moment, then put him down. Instantly he jogged over to the younger cop, jumped straight into his lap.

"Sorry. I can put him in the other room."

"It's okay. Nice cat."

"He is. He's really sweet. Sometimes a client will have a cat who's aloof or just plain nasty, and then . . . sorry." She caught herself, took a shaky breath. "Let me start at the top. I was getting ready for bed."

She told them what she'd seen, took them into the bedroom to show them her view. When Fitzhugh stepped out, she made coffee, gave Thomas an early breakfast as she talked to Morelli.

She learned he'd been married a year and a half, and his wife was expecting their first child in January. He liked cats, but was more a dog person, came from a big Italian-American family. His brother owned a pizzeria in Little Italy, and he played basketball in his downtime.

"You'd make a good cop," he told her.

"I would?"

"You get information. I'm halfway to telling you my life story."

"I ask questions—I can't help myself. People interest me. Which is why I was looking out the window. God, she must have family, parents, siblings, someone who loves her. She was just gorgeous, and tall—maybe a model."

"Tall?"

"Oh, the window, where she stood in it." Lila held her hands out, palms facing to indicate height. "She had to be about five-nine or -ten."

"Yeah, a pretty good cop. I'll get that," he told her when the buzzer sounded again.

Moments later he walked back in with a weary-looking man of about forty and a sharp-looking woman a decade younger. "Detectives Waterstone and Fine. They're going to talk to you now. You take care, Ms. Emerson."

"Oh, you're leaving? Thanks for . . . well, thanks. Maybe I'll grab a slice in your brother's restaurant."

"You do that. Detectives."

When he left her alone with them the nerves he'd calmed sprang back.

"I have coffee."

"Wouldn't mind that," Fine said. She crouched down to pet the cat. "Pretty cat."

"Yeah. Um, how do you take the cof-fee?"

"Black's fine for both of us. You're staying here while the Kilderbrands are in France?"

"That's right." Better, Lila thought, with her hands busy. "I'm a house-sitter."

"You stay in other people's houses for a living?" Waterstone asked.

"Not so much for a living—it's more an adventure. I write for a living. Enough of a living."

"How long have you been staying here?" Waterstone asked.

"A week. Sorry, a week and two days now since it's today. I'm here three weeks altogether while they're visiting friends and family in France."

"Have you stayed here before?"

"No, first-time clients."

"And your address?"

"I don't have one, really. I bunk with a friend if I'm not working, but that's rare. I stay busy."

"You don't have a place of your own?" Fine qualified.

"No. Low overhead. But I use my friend Julie Bryant's address for official things, for mail." She gave them another address in Chelsea. "I stay there sometimes, between jobs."

"Huh. Why don't you show us where you were when you witnessed the incident?"

"This way. I was getting ready for bed, but a little wired up. I should tell you I had a friend over—Julie, actually—and we had some wine. A lot of wine, to be honest about it, and I was wired up some, so I picked up my binoculars and looked out to see the window show."

"Binoculars," Waterstone repeated.

"These." She stepped over to the bedroom window, picked them up. "I take them with me everywhere. I stay in different neighborhoods in New York and, well, everywhere. I travel. Just got back from a job in Rome."

"Somebody in Rome hired you to watch their house?"

"Flat in this case," she told Fine. "Yeah. It's a lot of word of mouth, client recommendation, and I have a blog. I like to watch people, think up stories about them. It's spying," she said flatly. "I don't think of it that way, honestly don't mean it that way, but it's spying. It's just . . . all those windows are like little worlds."

Waterstone took the glasses, held them up as he studied the building. "You've got a pretty good eye line."

"They fought a lot, or had intense conversations, made up a lot."

"Who?" Fine asked.

"Blondie and Mr. Slick. I named them that. It was her place because, well, it had a female vibe to it, but he stayed there every night—since I've been here anyway."

"Can you describe him?"

She nodded at Waterstone. "A little taller than her—maybe six-one? Solid build— buff, so probably about one-ninety—brown hair, wavy. Dimples that popped out when he smiled. Late twenties, maybe. Very attractive."

"What exactly did you see tonight?"

"I could see her—great little black dress, her hair falling out of an updo. She was crying. It looked like she was crying, and wiping at the tears, and talking fast. Pleading. That's how it looked to me. Then I saw him hit her."

"You saw the man who hit her?"

"No. I saw someone hit her. He was to

the left of the window. All I saw was the hit—kind of a flash. A dark sleeve. And the way her head snapped back. She tried to cover her face, and he hit her again. I grabbed my phone. It was right on the nightstand, with the charger. I was going to call the police, and I looked out again, and she was against the window—her back against the window. It blocked out everything else. Then the glass broke, and she fell. She fell, so fast. I didn't see anything but her for a minute. I called the police, and when I looked back up at the window, the light was off. I couldn't see anything."

"You never saw her assailant?"

"No. Just her. I just saw her. But someone over there, in the building, someone must know him. Or some of her friends, her family. Someone must know him. He pushed her. Or maybe he didn't mean to, but hit her again so hard it broke the glass and she fell. It doesn't matter. He killed her, and someone knows him."

"What time did you first see her tonight?" Waterstone set the binoculars aside.

"It was right around one-forty. I looked at the time when I went to the window, thinking it was so late to be up, so I know it was one-forty, only a minute or so after when I saw her."

"After you called nine-one-one," Fine began, "did you see anyone leave the building?"

"No, but I wasn't looking. When she fell, I just froze for a minute."

"Your nine-one-one call came in at one-forty-four," Fine told her. "How long after you saw her was she struck?"

"It had to be under a minute. I saw the couple two floors up come in—dressed up like for a fancy dinner party, and the . . ." Don't say sexy naked gay guy. "The man on the twelfth floor had a friend over, then I saw her, so it was probably about one-forty-two or -three anyway when I saw her. If my watch is on the mark."

Fine took out her phone, swiped, held it out. "Do you recognize this man?"

Lila studied the driver's license photo. "That's him! That's the boyfriend. I'm sure of it. Ninety-nine percent—no, ninety-six percent—sure. You've already caught him. I'll testify."

Sympathetic tears stung her eyes. "Whatever you need. He had no right to hurt her that way. I'll do whatever you need me to do."

"We appreciate that, Ms. Emerson, but we won't need you to testify against this individual."

"But he . . . Did he confess?"

"Not exactly." Fine put her phone away. "He's on his way to the morgue."

"I don't understand."

"It appears the man you've seen with the victim pushed her out the window then sat down on the couch, put the barrel of a .32 in his mouth and pulled the trigger."

"Oh. Oh God." Staggering back, Lila dropped to the foot of the bed. "Oh God. He killed her, then himself."

"It appears."

"Why? Why would he do that?"

"That's a question," Fine said. "Let's go over this again."

By the time the police left, she'd been up for nearly twenty-four hours. She wanted to call Julie but stopped herself. Why start her best friend's day off so horribly?

She considered calling her mother—always a rock in a crisis—then ran through how it would go.

After being supportive, sympathetic, there would come:

Why do you live in New York, Lila-Lou? It's so dangerous. Come live with me and your father (the Lieutenant Colonel, retired) in Juneau. As in Alaska.

I don't want to talk about it again anyway. Just can't say it all over again right now.

Instead she flopped down on the bed, still in her clothes, cuddled Thomas when he joined her.

And to her surprise, dropped into sleep in seconds.

She woke with her heart pounding, her hands clutching at the bed as the sensation of falling rocked her.

Reaction, she told herself. Just a projection reaction. She rolled herself up, saw she'd slept until noon.

Enough. She needed a shower, a change of clothes and to get the hell out. She'd done everything she could do, told the police everything she'd seen. Mr. Slick killed

Blondie and himself, ripping away two lives, and nothing could change it, especially obsessing over it.

Instead, obsessing, she grabbed her iPad, went on a search for any stories about the murder.

"Runway model falls to her death," she read. "I knew it. She was built for it."

Grabbing the last cupcake—knowing better but grabbing it anyway—she ate while reading the sketchy story about the two deaths. Sage Kendall. She even had a model's name, Lila thought. "And Oliver Archer. Mr. Slick had a name, too. She was only twenty-four, Thomas. Four years younger than me. She did some commercials. I wonder if I've seen her. And why does that make it worse somehow?"

No, she had to stop, do what she'd just told herself to do. Clean herself up and get out for a while.

The shower helped, as did pulling on a light summer dress and sandals. Makeup helped more, she admitted, as she was still pale and hollow-eyed.

She'd walk out of the neighborhood— away from her own thoughts, maybe find somewhere for a quick, decent lunch. Then she could call Julie, maybe ask her to come over again so she could just dump all this out on a sympathetic, nonjudgmental ear.

"I'll be back in a couple hours, Thomas."

She started out, walked back, picked up the card Detective Fine had given her. She couldn't reasonably stop obsessing until she'd finished obsessing, she told herself. And there was nothing wrong with an eyewitness to the murder portion of a murder/suicide asking the investigating detective if they'd closed the case.

In any case, it would be a short, pleasant walk. Maybe she'd use the pool when she got back. She wasn't technically supposed to have use of the complex's pool or gym as a non-resident, but the most considerate Macey had wheedled around that block.

She could swim off the dregs of fatigue, stress, upset, then end the day with a whine session to her best friend.

Tomorrow, she'd go back to work. Life had to go on. Death reminded everyone life had to go on.

∝≫

Ash emptied the contents of the bag. "Effects," they called them, he thought. Personal effects. The watch, the ring, the wallet—with too much cash, the card case with too many credit cards. The silver key ring from Tiffany's. The watch, the ring, had likely come from there—or Cartier's, or somewhere Oliver had deemed important enough. The slim silver lighter, too.

All the shiny pocket debris his brother had gathered up on the last day of his life.

Oliver, always on the edge of the next big thing, the next big score, the next big anything. Charming, careless Oliver.

Dead.

"He had an iPhone, we're still processing it."

"What?" He looked up at the detective—Fine, he remembered. Detective Fine, with the soft blue eyes full of secrets. "I'm sorry, what?"

"We're still processing his phone, and when we've cleared the apartment, we'll need you to go through with us, identify his possessions. As I said, his license lists an address in the West Village, but our information is he moved out three months ago."

"Yeah, you said. I don't know."

"You hadn't seen him for . . . ?"

He'd told her, told her and her hard-faced partner all of it when they'd come to his loft. Notification, that's what they called it. Personal effects, notification. The stuff of novels and series television. Not his life.

"A couple of months. Three or four months, I guess."

"But you spoke with him a few days ago."

"He called, talked about meeting for a drink, catching up. I was busy, I put him off, told him we'd make it next week. Jesus." Ash pressed his fingers to his eyes.

"I know this is hard. You said you hadn't met the woman he'd been living with for the past three months, almost four months now."

"No. He mentioned her when he called. Bragging some—hot model. I didn't pay much attention. Oliver brags, it's his default."

"He didn't mention any trouble between him and the hot model?"

"Just the opposite. She was great, they were great, everything was great." He looked down at his hands, noticed a smudge of cerulean blue on the side of his thumb.

He'd been painting when they'd come

to his loft. He'd been annoyed by the interruption—then the world changed.

It all changed with a few words.

"Mr. Archer?"

"Yeah. Yeah. Everything was fucking great. That's how Oliver works. Everything's great unless it's . . ."

"Unless?"

Ash dragged his hands through his mop of black hair. "Look, he's family, and now he's dead, and I'm trying to get my head around that. I'm not going to punch at him."

"It's not punching at him, Mr. Archer. The better picture I have of him, the better I can resolve what happened."

Maybe that was true, maybe it was. Who was he to judge?

"Okay, Oliver ran hot. Hot deals, hot women, hot clubs. He liked to party."

"Live large."

"Yeah, you could say. He liked to consider himself a player, but God, he wasn't. Always the high-stakes table for Oliver, and if he won—gambling, a business deal, a woman—he'd lose it and more in the next round. So everything was great, until it wasn't and he needed somebody to pull him out. He's charming and clever and . . . was."

The single word slashed through him. Oliver would never be charming and clever again.

"He's his mother's youngest, her only son, and basically? He was overindulged."

"You said he wasn't violent."

"No." Ash pulled himself back from the grief—that was for later—but he let the quick flash of temper come through. "I didn't say Oliver wasn't violent, I said he was the opposite of violent." It stuck in his gut like a knife, the accusation that his brother had killed. "He'd talk himself out of a bad situation, or run from it. If he couldn't talk himself out of it—and that was rare—or run from it, he'd hide from it."

"Yet we have a witness claiming he struck his girlfriend multiple times before shoving her out a fourteenth-story window."

"The witness is wrong," Ash said flatly. "Oliver's more full of bullshit and delusions of grandeur than anyone I know, but he'd never hit a woman. And he sure as hell wouldn't kill one. Over and above? He'd never kill himself."

"There was a lot of alcohol and drugs

in the apartment. Oxy, coke, marijuana, Vicodin."

As she spoke, cop-cool, Ash imagined her as a Valkyrie—dispassionate in her power. He'd paint her astride a horse, her wings folded, overlooking a battlefield, face carved like stone as she decided who lived, who died.

"We're still waiting on the tox screens, but there were pills and a half-empty bottle of Maker's Mark, a glass still holding a finger of it, on the table beside your brother's body."

Drugs, alcohol, murder, suicide. The family, he thought, would suffer. He had to pull this knife out of his gut, had to make them see they were wrong.

"Drugs, bourbon, no argument. Oliver was no Boy Scout, but the rest? I don't believe it. The witness is either lying or mistaken."

"The witness has no reason to lie." Even as she said it, Fine spotted Lila, visitor's badge clipped to the strap of her dress, walking into the squad room. "Excuse me a minute."

She rose, headed Lila off. "Ms. Emerson. Did you remember something else?"

"No, sorry. I can't get it out of my head. I keep seeing her falling. Keep seeing her begging before he— Sorry. I needed to get out, and I thought I'd come in just to see if you've finished . . . closed it. If you know for certain what happened."

"It's still an open investigation. We're waiting on some reports, conducting other interviews. It takes a little time."

"I know. I'm sorry. Will you tell me when it's done?"

"I'll take care of that. You've been helpful."

"And now I'm in the way. I should go, get back. You're busy." She scanned the room. Desks, phones, computers, stacks of files and a handful of men and women working.

And a man in a black T-shirt and jeans carefully sliding a watch into a padded bag.

"Everyone's busy."

"We appreciate the help." Fine waited until Lila started out, then walked back to her desk and Ash.

"Look, I've told you everything I can think of," he began, and got to his feet. "Gone over it a couple times now. I need to contact his mother, my family. I need a little time to deal with this."

"I understand. We may need to talk to

you again, and we'll contact you when it's clear for you to enter the apartment. I am sorry for your loss, Mr. Archer."

He only nodded, walked out.

And immediately scanned for the brunette in the thin summer dress. He caught a glimpse—grass-green skirt, long, straight tail of hair the color of a strong mocha—as she took the stairs down.

He hadn't caught much of her conversation with the girl cop, but enough to be fairly certain she'd seen something that had to do with Oliver's death.

Though the stairs were nearly as busy as the hallways, the squad room, he caught up with her, touched her arm.

"Excuse me, Miss . . . Sorry, I didn't quite catch your name up there."

"Oh. Lila. Lila Emerson."

"Right. I'd like to talk to you if you've got a few minutes."

"Okay. You're working with Detectives Fine and Waterstone?"

"In a way."

On the main level, with cops coming and going, with visitors working their way through security, she unpinned her badge, set it on the sergeant's counter. After the briefest hesitation, he took his own out of his pocket, did the same.

"I'm Oliver's brother."

"Oliver?" It took her a moment, which told him she hadn't known Oliver personally. Then her eyes widened. "Oh. Oh, I'm sorry. I'm so sorry."

"Thanks. If you'd talk to me about this, it might—"

"I'm not sure I should, that I'm supposed to." She looked around, gauged her ground. Then looked back into his face, into the grief. "I don't know."

"A cup of coffee. Let me buy you a cup of coffee. Public place. There's got to be a coffee shop around here, and it's probably full of cops. Please."

He had eyes like Thomas's—sharp and green—but she could see sadness in them. Sharp features, too, she thought, as if someone had carved them out with a keen and clever blade. The stubble gave him an intriguingly dangerous look, but the eyes . . .

He'd just lost his brother, and more, his brother had taken two lives. Death alone was hard enough, but murder, and suicide, had to be brutal on the family left behind.

"Sure. There's a place just across the street."

"Thanks. Ash," he said, holding out his hand. "Ashton Archer."

Something tickled the back of her brain at the name, but she offered her hand in turn. "Lila."

He led her out, nodded when she gestured to the coffee shop across the street.

"I really am sorry," she said as they waited for the light beside a woman who was arguing bitterly on her cell phone. "I can't imagine losing a brother. I don't have one, but I can't imagine losing him if I did. Do you have other family?"

"Other siblings?"

"Yes."

He glanced down at her as they started across the street, washing along in the surge of pedestrian traffic. "There are fourteen of us. Thirteen," he corrected. "Thirteen now. Unlucky number," he said half to himself.

The woman on the phone marched beside Lila, her voice pitched high and shrill. A couple of teenage girls pranced just ahead, chirping and giggling over someone named Brad. A couple of horns blasted as the light changed.

Surely she'd misheard him. "I'm sorry, what?"

"Thirteen's unlucky."

"No, I meant . . . Did you say you have thirteen brothers and sisters?"

"Twelve. I make thirteen." When he pulled open the door to the coffee shop, the smell of coffee, sugary baked goods and a wall of noise greeted them.

"Your mother must be . . ." "Insane" crossed her mind. "Amazing."

"I like to think so. That's step-sibs, half sibs," he added, grabbing an empty two-top booth. "My father's been married five times. My mother's on her third."

"That's—wow."

"Yeah, modern American family."

"Christmas must be a madhouse. Do they all live in New York?"

"Not exactly. Coffee?" he asked her as a waitress stepped up.

"Actually, can I get a lemonade? I'm coffee'd out."

"Coffee for me. Just black."

He sat back a moment, studied her. A good face, he decided, something fresh and open about it, though he could see signs of stress and fatigue, especially in her eyes—deep, dark brown as rich as her hair with a thin line of gold around the iris. Gypsy eyes, he thought, and though there was nothing exotic about her, he immediately saw her in red—red bodice with a full skirt, and many colorful flounces. In a dance, mid-spin, hair flying. Laughing while the campfire blazed behind her.

"Are you all right? Stupid question," she said immediately. "Of course you're not."

"No. Sorry." Not the time, not the place, not the woman, he told himself, and leaned forward again. "You didn't know Oliver?"

"No."

"The woman, then. What was it? Rosemary?"

"Sage. Wrong herb. No, I didn't know either of them. I'm staying in the same complex, and I was looking out the window. I saw . . ."

"What did you see?" He closed his hand over hers, removed it quickly when he felt her stiffen. "Will you tell me what you saw?"

"I saw her. Upset, crying, and someone hit her."

"Someone?"

"I couldn't see him. But I'd seen your brother before. I'd seen them in the apartment together, several times. Arguing, talking, making up. You know."

"I'm not sure I do. Your apartment looks right out into hers? Theirs," he corrected. "The police said he was living there."

"Not exactly. It's not my apartment. I'm staying there." She took a moment when the waitress brought the lemonade and coffee. "Thanks," she said, offering the waitress a quick smile. "I'm staying there for a few weeks while the tenants are on vacation, and I . . . I know it sounds nosy and invasive, but I like to watch people. I stay in a lot of interesting places, and I take binoculars, so I was . . ."

"Doing a Jimmy Stewart."

"Yes!" Relief and laughter mixed in the word. "Yes, like **Rear Window**. Only you don't expect to see Raymond Burr loading up the pieces of his dead wife into a big chest and hauling it out. Or was it suitcases? Anyway. I don't think of it as spying, or didn't until this happened. It's like theater. All the world really is a stage, and I like being in the audience."

He waded his way through that to the

key. "But you didn't see Oliver. You didn't see him hit her? Push her?"

"No. I told the police. I saw someone hit her, but it was the wrong angle to see him. She was crying and scared and pleading—I could see all that on her face. I got my phone to call nine-one-one, and then . . . She came flying out the window. The glass shattered, and she just flew through it and fell."

This time he put his hand over hers, left it there because it trembled. "Take it easy."

"I keep seeing it. Keep seeing the glass breaking, and her flying out, the way her arms went wide, and her feet kicked at the air. I hear her scream, but that's in my head. I didn't hear her. I'm sorry about your brother, but—"

"He didn't do this."

For a moment she said nothing, just lifted her glass, sipped quietly at the lemonade.

"He wasn't capable of doing this," Ash said.

When she lifted her gaze to his, sympathy and compassion radiated.

She was no Valkyrie, he thought. She felt too much.

"It's terrible what happened."

"You think I can't accept my brother could kill, then kill himself. It's not that. It's that I **know** he couldn't. We weren't close. I hadn't seen him in months, and then only briefly. He was tighter with Giselle, they're closer in age. But she's in . . ."

Sorrow fell into him again like stones. "I'm not entirely sure. Maybe Paris. I need to find out. He was a pain in the ass," Ash continued. "An operator without the killer instinct it takes to be an operator. A lot of charm, a lot of bullshit, and a lot of big ideas without any practical sense of how to bring them around. But he wouldn't hit a woman."

She'd watched them, he remembered. "You said they argued a lot. Did you ever see him hit her, push her?"

"No, but . . ."

"I don't care if he was stoned or drunk or both, he wouldn't hit a woman. He wouldn't kill a woman. He'd never kill himself. He'd believe whatever he'd gotten sucked into, someone would pull him out again. An eternal optimist, that was Oliver."

She wanted to be careful; she wanted to be kind. "Sometimes we don't know people as well as we think."

"You're right. He was in love. Oliver was either in love or looking for it. He was in it. Whenever he's ready to be out of it, he wiggles out, takes off awhile, sends the woman an expensive gift and a note of regret. 'It's not you, it's me,' that kind of thing. Too many drama-filled divorces, so he went for the clean, callous break. And I know he was too damn vain to stick a gun in his mouth and pull the trigger. If he was going to kill himself—and he'd never hit that much despair—he'd've gone for pills."

"I think it was an accident—her fall. I mean all in the heat of the moment. He must've been out of his mind in those moments after."

Ash shook his head. "He'd have called me, or come running. He's his mother's youngest and her only son, so he was indulged. When there was trouble, he'd call somebody to help him get out of it. That's his knee-jerk. 'Ash, I'm in some trouble here. You have to fix things.'"

"He usually called you."

"For big trouble, it would've been me. And he'd never mix pills with his bourbon," Ash added. "He had an ex who went that way, and it scared him. One or the other, not that he wouldn't go too far with either, but one at a time.

"It doesn't hold. It doesn't," he insisted. "You said you'd seen them together over there, watched them."

Uncomfortable with the truth of that, she shifted. "I did. It's a terrible habit. I need to stop."

"You saw them fight, but he never got physical with her."

"No . . . No, she was more physical. Threw things, mostly breakables. She threw her shoe at him once."

"What did he do?"

"Ducked." Lila smiled a little, and he caught the tiny dimple—a happy little wink—at the right corner of her mouth. "Good reflexes. My take was she yelled— and she shoved him once. He did a lot of fast talking, gestures, smooth. That's why I called him Mr. Slick."

The big, dark eyes widened in distress. "Oh God, I'm sorry."

"No, that's accurate. He was slick. He didn't get mad, threaten her, get violent? Shove her back?"

"No. He said something that made her laugh. I could see, sense, she didn't want to, but she turned away, tossed her hair. And he came over and . . . they got physical together. People should close the curtains if they don't want an audience."

"She threw something at him, yelled at him, pushed him. And he talked his way out of it, talked his way into sex. That's Oliver."

He never responded with violence, Lila considered. They'd had some sort of argument or fight every day, some disagreement every day, but he never struck her. Never touched her unless it was a prelude to sex.

And yet. "But the fact is she was pushed out the window, and he shot himself."

"She was pushed out the window, but he didn't push her—and he didn't shoot himself. So, someone else was in the apartment. Someone else was there," he said again, "and killed both of them. The questions are who, and why."

It sounded plausible when he said it, just that way. It seemed . . . logical, and the logic of it made her doubt. "But isn't there another question? How?"

"You're right. Three questions. Answer one, maybe answer all."

He kept his eyes on hers. He saw more than sympathy now. He saw the beginning of interest. "Can I see your apartment?"

"What?"

"The cops aren't going to let me into Oliver's place yet. I want to see it from the perspective you had that night. And you don't know me," he said before she could speak. "Have you got somebody who could be there with you so you wouldn't be alone with me?"

"Maybe. I can see if I can work that out."

"Great. Let me give you my number. Work it out, call me. I just need to see . . . I need to be able to see."

She took out her phone, keyed in the number he gave her. "I have to get back. I've been gone longer than I meant to be."

"I appreciate you talking to me. Listening."

"I'm sorry about what happened." She slid out of the booth, touched a hand to his shoulder. "For you, his mom, your family. I hope whatever the answers are, you get them. If I can work things out, I'll call you."

"Thanks."

She left him sitting in the narrow booth, staring into the coffee he'd never touched.

Three

She called Julie, and dumped the entire story while she tended the plants, harvested tomatoes, entertained the cat.

Julie's gasps, amazement and sympathy would've been enough, but there was more.

"I heard about this when I was getting ready for work this morning, and it was the Big Talk at the gallery today. We knew her a little."

"You knew Blondie?" Wincing—the nickname seemed so wrong now. "I mean Sage Kendall."

"A little. She came into the gallery a few

times. Actually bought a couple of very nice pieces. Not my sale—I didn't work with her, but I was introduced. I didn't put it together. Even when they mentioned West Chelsea. I didn't hear the specific apartment building, if they released that."

"I don't know. They have by now. I can see people down there, taking pictures. And some TV crews have done stand-ups in front of the building."

"It's awful. A terrible thing to happen, and awful for you, sweetie. They hadn't released the name of the guy who pushed her, then killed himself, not this morning. I haven't checked since."

"Oliver Archer, aka Mr. Slick. I met his brother at the police station."

"Well, that's . . . awkward."

"It probably should've been, but it wasn't." She sat on the floor of the bathroom, carefully sanding some shiny spots on the runners of one of the vanity drawers. It kept sticking, but she could fix that.

"He bought me a lemonade," she continued, "and I told him what I'd seen."

"You . . . you had a drink with him? For God's sake, Lila, for all you know he and his brother are both homicidal maniacs or made men, or serial killers who worked as a team. Or—"

"We had the drink at the coffee shop across from the police station, and there were at least five cops in there while we did. I felt terrible for him, Julie. You could see him struggling to come to grips with it, just trying to make some sense out of what's just not sensible. He doesn't believe his brother killed Sage, or himself, and he actually made a pretty good case against."

"Lila, nobody wants to believe their brother's capable of this."

"I get that, I do." She blew lightly on the runners to clear off the dust from the sanding. "And that was my first reaction, but like I said, he made a pretty good case."

She slid the drawer back in, out, in. Nodded in satisfaction. Everything should be so easy.

"He wants to come over here, see his brother's apartment from this perspective."

"Have you lost your mind?"

"Just wait. He suggested I have somebody here with me, and I wouldn't consider it otherwise. But before I decide anything, I'm going to Google him. Just make sure he doesn't have any nefarious deeds in his past, any wives who died under mysterious circumstances, or other siblings—he said he had twelve, half and step."

"Seriously?"

"I know. I can't imagine. But I should make sure none of them have a shady past or whatever."

"Tell me you didn't give him the address where you're staying."

"No, I didn't give him the address, or my number." Her brows drew together as she reloaded her makeup in the drawer. "I'm not stupid, Julie."

"No, but you're too trusting. What's his name—if he gave you his **real** name. I'll Google him right now."

"Of course he gave me his real name. Ashton Archer. It does sound a little made up, but—"

"Wait a minute. You said Ashton Archer? Tall, rangy, blow-up-your-skirt gorgeous? Green eyes, a lot of wavy black hair?"

"Yes. How do you know that?"

"Because I know him. He's an artist, Lila, a good one. I manage an art gallery, a good one—and we're his main venue in New York. Our paths have crossed a number of times."

"I knew the name was familiar, but I thought it was because I had the brother's name on my mind. He's the one who did that painting of the woman in the meadow playing the violin—ruined castle, full moon in the background. The one I said I'd buy if I actually owned a wall to hang it on."

"That's the one."

"Does he have any wives who died under mysterious circumstances?"

"Not to my knowledge. Unmarried, but was linked with Kelsy Nunn—American Ballet prima ballerina—for a while. Maybe he still is, I can find out. He's got a solid professional reputation, doesn't appear to be completely neurotic, as many of them can be. Enjoys his work, apparently. There's family money, both sides. I'm doing the Google just to fill in the blanks. Father's side real estate and development, mother's shipping. Blah blah. Do you want more?"

He hadn't **looked** like big money. The brother had, she decided. But the man who'd sat across from her in the coffee shop hadn't looked like money. He'd looked like grief and temper.

"I can check for myself. Basically, you're

saying he's not going to throw me out the window."

"I'd say chances are slim. I like him, personally and professionally, and now I'm sorry about his brother. Even though his brother killed one of our clients."

"I'm going to let him come over, then. He has the Julie Bryant seal of approval."

"Don't rush this, Lila."

"No, tomorrow. I'm too tired for all this tonight. I was going to beg you to come over again, but I'm just tired."

"Take a long soak in that fabulous tub. Light some candles, read a book. Then put on your pj's, order a pizza, watch a romantic comedy on TV, then cuddle up with the cat and sleep."

"That sounds like the perfect date."

"Do it, and call if you change your mind and just need the company. Otherwise, I'm going to do a little more checking on Ashton Archer. I know people who know people. If I'm satisfied, **then** he gets the Julie Bryant seal of approval. I'll talk to you tomorrow."

"That's a deal."

Before she took that long soak, she went back out on the terrace. She stood in the late afternoon heat, looking over at the window, now boarded up, that had once opened into a private world.

Jai Maddok watched Lila walk into the building—after the skinny brunette stopped for a brief chat with the doorman.

She'd been right to follow the woman, right to trust her instincts and keep Ivan on the idiot's brother.

It wouldn't be a coincidence the brunette and the brother came out of the police station together, had a long talk together, not when the woman lived, so it seemed, in the same rich American complex as the idiot and his whore.

The police had a witness—this was her information. This woman must be the witness.

But what had she seen?

Her information also indicated the police were investigating a murder-suicide. But she had little hope, even with her disregard for police, that would hold up long, witness or no. She'd had to cobble that ploy together quickly due to Ivan's overenthusiasm with the whore.

Her employer was not happy the idiot had been disposed of before he'd given a location. When her employer was unhappy, very bad things happened. Jai usually made those very bad things happen, and didn't want to be on the receiving end.

So the problem must be resolved. A puzzle, she decided, and she enjoyed puzzles. The idiot, the whore, the skinny woman and the brother.

How did they fit, and how would she use them to reach the prize for her employer?

She would consider, study, resolve.

She strolled as she considered. She liked the wet heat, the crowded city. Men glanced at her, and those glances would linger. She agreed with them—she deserved much more than a second look. And still, in the hot, crowded city, even she would not make a lasting impression. In affectionate moments, her employer called her his Asian dumpling, but her employer was . . . an unusual man.

He thought of her as a tool, occasionally as a pet or a pampered child. She was grateful he didn't think of her as a lover, as she'd have been obliged to sleep with him.

The thought offended even her limited sensibilities.

She stopped to admire a pair of shoes in a display window—high, glittering gold heels, thin leopard-spot straps. There had been a time when she was lucky to have a single pair of shoes. Now she could have as many as she liked. The memory of hot, blistered feet, of hunger so deep and sharp it felt like death, crossed the years.

If she had business in China now, she stayed in the finest hotels—and still memories of dirt and hunger, of terrible cold or terrible heat, could haunt her.

But money, blood, power and pretty shoes chased ghosts away again.

She wanted the shoes, wanted them now. So she walked into the shop.

Within ten minutes she was walking out wearing them, enjoying the way they showed off the knife edges of her calf muscles. She swung the shopping bag carelessly, a striking Asian woman in black—short, tight cropped pants, snug shirt—and the exotic shoes. Her long tail of ebony hair swung down her back, and pulled high and tight, left her face with its deceptively soft curves, full red lips, large almond eyes of coal-black unframed.

Yes, men looked, and women, too. Men wished to fuck her, women wished to be her—and some wished to fuck her as well.

But they would never know her. She was a bullet in the dark, a knife slicing silently across the throat.

She killed not only because she could, not only because it paid very, very well, but because she loved it. Even more than the lovely new shoes, more than sex, more than food and drink and breath.

She wondered if she would kill the skinny brunette and the idiot's brother. It depended on how they fit into the puzzle, but she thought it might be both necessary and enjoyable.

Her phone pinged, and taking it out of her bag, she nodded in satisfaction. The photo she'd taken of the woman now had a name, an address.

Lila Emerson, but not the address of the building she'd entered.

Odd, Jai thought, but still it would not be a coincidence she'd gone into that building. But since she was there, she was not at the address displayed on the phone.

Perhaps she would find something interesting and useful at the address of this Lila Emerson.

Julie unlocked the door of her apartment just after nine P.M. and immediately pulled off the shoes she'd been in far too long. She should never have let her coworkers talk her into going to that salsa club. Fun, yes, but oh God, her feet had been wailing like colicky babies for over an hour.

She wanted to soak them in warm, scented water, drink a few gallons of water to filter out the far too many margaritas she'd downed, then go to bed.

Was she getting old? she wondered as she secured the door. Stale? Boring?

Of course not. She was just tired—worried a little about Lila, still raw from the breakup with David, and tired after about fourteen straight hours of work and play.

The fact that she was thirty-two, single, childless and would sleep alone had nothing to do with it.

She had an amazing career, she assured herself as she went straight into the kitchen to grab a giant bottle of Fiji water.

She loved her work, the people she worked with, the people she met. The artists, the art lovers, the showings, the occasional travel.

So she had a divorce under her belt. All right, two divorces, but she'd been insane and eighteen the first time, and it hadn't lasted a year. It really didn't count.

But she stood, drinking straight from the bottle in the gleaming, state-of-the-art kitchen used primarily to store water, wine and a few basics, and wondered why the hell she felt so unsettled.

Loved her work, had a great circle of friends, an apartment that reflected her taste—**just** her taste, thank you—a most excellent wardrobe. She even liked her looks most of the time, especially since she'd hired the Marquis de Sade as a personal trainer the year before.

She was a buff, attractive, interesting, independent woman. And she couldn't maintain a relationship for more than three months, not happily, she amended. Not happily for her.

Maybe she wasn't meant to. She shrugged it off, took the water with her across the living area with its warm, neutral colors and electric splashes of modern art, into the bedroom.

Maybe she should get a cat. Cats were interesting and independent, and if she could find one as sweet as Thomas, she'd . . .

She stopped short, a hand on the light switch. She caught the fading scent of perfume. **Her** perfume. Not her signature daytime scent, the Ricci Ricci, that stood as her go-to for work, but the heavier, sexier Boudoir she used only on dates, and then only when the mood struck.

In any case, thanks to salsa, what she wore now was a light hint of sweat, but she knew that scent.

It shouldn't have been there.

But the pretty gold-topped pink bottle should have been, and it wasn't.

Baffled, she crossed over to her dresser. The antique trinket box sat in its usual spot, as did her workday perfume, the tall, slim silver vase with its single red lily.

But the bottle of Boudoir was gone.

Had she moved it somewhere without thinking? But no, why would she? Yes, she'd been a bit hungover that morning, a little slow and blurry, but she **remembered** seeing it there. She'd dropped the back of her earring. Even now she could visualize herself trying to fumble it on, cursing when it dropped onto the top of the dresser—right beside the pink bottle.

Muttering to herself, she moved off into the bathroom to check. Looked in the train case she used for makeup. Not there, she mused. And, what the hell, neither was the YSL Red Taboo lipstick, or the Bobbi Brown liquid eyeliner. She'd just put them in there last week after a trip to Sephora.

She marched back to the bedroom, checked her evening bags—just in case, the travel makeup bag she kept at the ready and had used for the Hamptons Wedding Week From Hell.

She stood in her closet, hands on her hips. Then gaped when she saw—or rather didn't see—her brand-new, yet-to-be-worn Manolo Blahniks—five-inch platform sandals, diamond pattern in coral.

Frustration turned on a dime as her heart began to pound. She made a wild run back to the kitchen and her bag, dragged her phone out and called the police.

Just after midnight, Lila opened the door.

"I'm sorry," Julie said immediately. "Just what you don't need after last night."

"Don't be silly. Are you okay?"

"I don't know what I am. The cops think I'm crazy. Maybe I am."

"No, you're not. Here, let's take this into the bedroom."

She took the handle of Julie's overnight herself, wheeled it into the guest room.

"No, I'm not. I'm not crazy. Things were gone, Lila. Strange things, I'll give you that. Who breaks in, takes makeup and perfume, a pair of shoes and a leopard-skin tote, apparently to carry it all in? Who takes that and leaves art, jewelry, a really nice Baume & Mercier watch and my grandmother's pearls?"

"A teenage girl maybe."

"I didn't misplace them. I know that's what the cops think, but I didn't misplace those things."

"Julie, you never misplace anything. What about your cleaning service?"

Julie dropped down on the side of the bed. "The cops asked about that. I've been using the same service for six years. And the same two women come in every other week. They wouldn't risk their jobs for makeup. You're the only other one who has the key and the code."

Lila X'd her heart with her finger. "Innocent."

"You don't wear my shoe size or red lipstick—though you should think about the lipstick. You're in the clear. Thanks for letting me stay over. I just couldn't stay there alone tonight. I'm having the locks changed tomorrow, and I already changed the alarm code. A teenage girl," she considered. "There has to be some in the building. Maybe that's it, just a silly stunt. A kind of shoplifting."

"Silly, maybe, but still really wrong. Poking around in your things, taking stuff. I hope the police find her."

"Be on the lookout for a teenage girl in Manolos wearing Red Taboo lipstick and smelling of Boudoir?" Julie snorted. "Fat chance."

"It could happen." Bending over, she wrapped Julie in a hug. "We'll go out first chance, replace everything. Do you want anything now?"

"Just a good night's sleep. I can bunk on the couch."

"It's a big bed, plenty of room for you, me and Thomas."

"Thanks. Okay if I grab a quick shower? After-work salsa dancing."

"Fun. Sure, go ahead. I'll leave the light on on your side of the bed."

"Oh, I nearly forgot," Julie said as she rose to take her nightclothes out of the overnight. "Ash passed the screening. I talked to several people—discreetly. Upshot is, he can get pretty absorbed in his work, has a bit of a temper when buttons are pushed at the wrong time, doesn't socialize as much as his agent—and some of the ladies—might like, but that's it. No trouble, no reports of violent behavior, except for punching some drunk guy at a showing."

"He punched a drunk?"

"Apparently. The story I heard is, the drunk got touchy-feely with one of the models for one of the paintings when she didn't want to be touched or felt. My source said it was well earned, and took place in a London gallery. So, seal of approval if you decide to let him come look out the window."

"I guess I probably will, then."

She settled back into bed, thought about

stealing lipstick and designer shoes, about murder and suicide and hot-looking artists who punch drunks.

It all played through her head, mixed into odd little dreams. She never heard Julie slide into bed or Thomas's mew of delight when he curled between them.

She woke to the scent of coffee—always a plus—and wandered out to find Julie toasting bagels and Thomas chowing down on his breakfast.

"You fed the cat, you made coffee. Will you marry me?"

"I was thinking about getting a cat, but maybe I'll marry you instead."

"You could do both."

"In the queue for consideration." Julie took out two pretty glass bowls of berries.

"Aw, you made berries."

"You had the berries, the place had these really pretty berry bowls. There's some lovely things in here. I don't know how you resist poking around in drawers and closets. And I say that as someone who just had some evil teenage girl poking in mine."

With a vindictive gleam in her eye, Julie

tossed her flaming hair. "I hope she has zits."

"Macey?"

"Who— Oh no, the teenage girl."

"Right. Coffee not yet to brain. Zits, braces and an obsessive crush on the star quarterback who doesn't know she exists."

"I especially like the crush," Julie decided. "Let's have this out on the terrace, like I imagine the very tasteful couple who live here must do. Then I have to get dressed and go back to reality."

"You have a great apartment."

"You could fit two of my apartments in here, and the terrace is a big plus. Then there's the pool and gym right on-site. I've changed my mind," Julie said, as she loaded a tray. "I'm dumping you for the next rich guy I can get my hooks into. I'll marry him and move in here."

"Gold digger."

"My next ambition. No zit-faced teenage girl could get through the security in this place."

"Probably not." As she stepped outside, Lila looked over at the boarded-up window. "It wouldn't be a snap, would it, to get past security. But . . . if they let someone in, had someone over, or another tenant, or a really experienced burglar planned it. Except the police didn't say anything about burglary."

"He pushed her out the window, then shot himself. I'm sorry for Ashton, Lila, but that's what happened over there."

"He's so sure it couldn't have been that way. Not thinking about it," she said, and wiped her hands in the air. "I'm going to have breakfast with you, even though you've dumped me for some rich bastard."

"He'll be handsome, too. And probably Latin."

"Funny, I was seeing portly and bald." She popped some berries into her mouth. "Goes to show. Anyway, I'm not thinking about any of it right now. I have to work today. I'll put in a solid writing day, then I'll call the rich and handsome Ashton Archer. If he wants to look, he can look. Then, well, there's nothing else I can do, right?"

"There's nothing you can do. The police will do what they do, and Ashton will have to accept what happened. It's hard. I lost a friend—well, more a periphery friend—in college to suicide."

"You never told me that."

"We weren't tight, but we were friendly. Liked each other, but not tight enough for me to know how troubled she was, I guess. Her boyfriend dumped her—that couldn't have been all of it, but I guess it was the trigger. She took sleeping pills. She was only nineteen."

"Awful." For a moment Lila felt it, that terrible despair. "I don't want Zit-face to have the crush anymore. Just the zits."

"Yeah. Love, even when it's not real, can be deadly. We'll leave that part out. Do you want me to come back, be here when Ashton comes?"

"No, you don't have to do that. But if you're not ready to go home, you can stay as long as you need."

"I'm okay with it now. I can handle some teenager. And my guess is she got what she wanted, and will go play cat burglar somewhere else." But she sighed heavily. "I really liked those shoes, damn it. I hope she trips in them and breaks her ankle."

"Harsh."

"So's stealing another woman's Manolos."

She couldn't argue with that, so Lila drank her coffee.

Four

She felt settled again once she got back to work, back into her story. Werewolf wars and cheerleader politics both took some careful navigation. They kept her busy and involved into mid-afternoon, when Thomas demanded some playtime.

She broke off with Kaylee's beloved cousin hanging on the thin line between life and death after an ambush. A good place to stop, she decided, and getting back to see what happened would motivate her on the next round.

She played ball-on-a-string with the cat until she could distract him with one of his motion-activated toys, then tended the little terrace garden, harvested some tomatoes, cut herself a little bouquet of zinnias.

And she'd put it off long enough, she told herself. She picked up her phone, scrolled to Ash's contact number. It made it all real again. The beautiful blonde begging for mercy. The way her legs kicked the air on the horrible fall, the sudden, brutal impact of flesh and bones on the concrete below.

It was real, Lila thought. It would always be real. Tucking it away didn't change that, so she might as well face it head-on.

Ash worked with the music banging. He'd started off with Tchaikovsky, certain it would fit the mood, but the soaring notes only bogged him down. He switched to a mix of hard, head-banging rock. That worked— the energy of it pumped into him. And changed the tone of the painting.

He'd initially envisioned the mermaid lounging on a ledge of rock on the verge of a stormy sea as sexual, but now the sexuality took on a predatory edge.

Now there came a question. Would she

save the seamen who fell into that stormy sea when their ship crashed into the rocks, or would she drag them under?

The moonlight, not romantic now, no, not romantic, but another threat as it illuminated the teeth of the rocks, the speculative gleam in her sea-mist eyes.

He hadn't expected the violence when he'd done the initial sketches, hadn't expected the question of brutality when he'd used the model with her tumble of ink-black hair for the early stages.

But now, alone with the pounding music, the vicious storm at sea and the violence of his own thoughts, the painting evolved into something just a little sinister.

She Waits, he thought.

When his phone rang his instinct was annoyance. He always turned off his phone when he worked. With a family the size of his, he'd be deluged with calls, texts, e-mails all day and half the night if he didn't put up some boundaries.

But he had felt obliged to leave it on today. Even now he ignored the first two rings before he remembered why he'd left it on.

He set down his brush, took the second brush he had clamped between his teeth and tossed it aside, reaching for the phone.

"Archer."

"Oh, ah, it's Lila. Lila Emerson. I was— are you at a party?"

"No. Why?"

"It's loud. The music's loud."

He looked for the remote, shoved at some jars, punched the music off. "Sorry."

"No, it's fine. If you don't play Iron Maiden loud, there's no point. And since you're probably working, my apologies. I just wanted to call to let you know if you still want to come here, look at the . . . well, look from where I was that night, it's fine."

His first surprise was that she'd recognized the ancient "Aces High" as Iron Maiden, and the next that she'd correctly assumed he'd had it to ear-splitting while he worked.

But he'd think about that later.

"Is now good?"

"Oh . . ."

Don't push, he warned himself. Poor tactics. "Tell me when," he said. "Whenever it works for you."

"Now's good. I just didn't expect you to say it. Now's fine. Let me give you the address."

He grabbed a sketching pencil to scribble it down. "Got it. Give me about a half hour. I appreciate it."

"It's . . ." She caught herself before she said "fine" again. "I'd want to do the same in your place. I'll see you in about thirty."

Done it now, she thought. "So, what's the etiquette for this situation, Thomas? Do I put out a nice little plate of Gouda and sesame crackers? No, you're right. That's just silly. Makeup? Again you're wise beyond your years, my young student. That's a definite yes. No point looking like a refugee."

She decided to change out of her going-nowhere shorts, thin-with-age bubble-gum-pink T-shirt with its retro Wonder Twins silkscreen.

It might also help to look like an adult.

She wished she'd made some sun tea, which also struck her as adult and responsible, but since she'd left it too late for that, decided coffee would do if he wanted anything.

She hadn't quite finished dithering when she heard the bell.

Awkward, she thought. The whole thing was so damn awkward. She glanced through the peep—blue T-shirt today, and the stubble just a little heavier. Hair thick, dark, tousled—eyes smart-cat green and just a little impatient.

She wondered if it would be slightly less awkward if he was pudgy and bald or twenty years older. Or anything that didn't hit every single one of her yum buttons.

A woman shouldn't think yum in this situation, she reminded herself, and opened the door.

"Hi. Come on in." She thought about shaking hands, but the gesture seemed stiff and formal. So she just lifted them, let them fall. "I don't know how to do this. It all feels so weird and strange."

"You called. I'm here. That's a start."

As he didn't understand awkward, Thomas padded right over to greet Ash. "Your cat or theirs?"

"Oh, theirs. Thomas is great company though. I'll miss him when the job's finished."

Ash gave the cat one long stroke, head

to tail, as she often did herself. "Do you ever get confused when you wake up in the morning? Like, where am I exactly?"

"No, not in a long time. Crossing time zones can throw me off, but mostly I work in and around New York."

"This is a nice space," he said, when he straightened. "Good light."

"It really is. And you're making small talk so I won't feel so weird. Why don't I show you where I was when it happened? That's the hard part, and that'll be done."

"Okay."

"I'm staying in the guest room." She gestured. "It has a window facing west. That night I was unwinding after Julie left. Oh, she knows you. Julie Bryant. She manages Chelsea Arts."

Tall, glamorous redhead, he thought, with an excellent eye and a great what-the-hell laugh. "You know Julie?"

"We've been friends for years. She was here until a little before midnight that night. There was a lot of wine, then cupcakes involved, so I was restless. I picked these up."

She offered him the binoculars.

"I make up stories, it's what I do. I had a

few going on in some of the windows over there, so I was checking them out for the next scene. That sounds ridiculous."

"No, it doesn't. I make up images—that's just another kind of story."

"Well, good. I mean good it doesn't sound ridiculous. Anyway, I saw her. Sage Kendall."

"At the window that's boarded up now."

"Yeah. The one to the left with the little balcony is the bedroom."

"These take you right there, don't they?" He spoke softly as he looked through the glasses.

"It's always been a game for me—since I was a kid. Like television or a movie or book. I stopped a burglary once—in Paris a couple years ago. I saw someone break into the flat across from where I was staying one night when the tenants were out."

"Travel and adventure, and crime-solving. The life of a house-sitter."

"Mostly not the crime-solving, but . . ."

"You didn't see Oliver. My brother."

"No, just her. The bedroom light was off, and whatever light was on in the living area was on low. She was in front of the window. Like this."

She stepped up, angling herself. "Talking to someone who must have been standing just off to her left, in the wall space between windows. I saw him hit her. It was so fast, but I must have seen his hand. What I remember is the way her head snapped back, the way she put her own hand up to her face, like this."

Lila demonstrated, cradling her cheek and jaw in her hand.

"He hit her again. Fist, dark sleeve. That's all I saw, so fast I barely saw it. My phone was there, on the table by the bed. I grabbed it, then I looked back out. Then she was against the glass. I could only see her back, her hair coming down out of her updo."

"Show me. Would you mind?"

"Like . . ." She turned her back to the window, adjusted for the sill as she leaned back on the glass.

"And you only saw her. You're sure of it?"

"Yes. I'm sure."

"She was tall. Five-ten. I looked it up." He set the binoculars down. "Oliver was my height, six-one. That's three inches taller, and he was holding her back against the window . . ."

Ash stepped over. "I'm not going to hurt

you. I just want to show you." He laid his hands on her shoulders, carefully, eased her back, his hands warm through her shirt as if they were skin-to-skin. "If he held her this way, she'd be tipped back some, like you are."

Her heart kicked a little. He wasn't going to shove her out the window—she wasn't afraid of that, or him. But she wondered why such an awful thing—mimicking murder—seemed so strangely intimate.

"Why didn't you see him?" Ash demanded. "If someone looked in here now, they'd see me over your head."

"I'm only five-five. She had five inches on me."

"Even with that, his head would have been above hers. You should've seen some of his face."

"I didn't, but she could've been wearing heels. She had some great shoes, and . . . but she wasn't," Lila remembered. "She wasn't. She didn't have shoes on."

Her feet kicking as she fell. Bare feet.

"She wasn't wearing heels. She wasn't wearing shoes at all."

"Then you should've seen his face. At least some of his face."

"I didn't."

"Maybe because whoever pushed her was shorter than Oliver. Shorter than she was."

He picked up the glasses again, looked out. "You said a fist, a black sleeve."

"Yeah, I'm pretty sure. It's what pops into my head when I try to see it again."

"Someone closer to her height, wearing a black shirt. I need to ask the police what Oliver was wearing."

"Oh. But it might've been navy or dark gray. The light wasn't very good."

"A dark shirt, then."

"I'd talked myself out of thinking there'd been someone else. You talked me into it," she said when he looked at her again. "Then I talked myself out of it. Now you're talking me into it again. I don't know which is worse."

"There's no worse." He lowered the glasses again, his eyes sharp with an anger she could feel shimmering off his skin. "But there's the truth."

"I hope you find it. You can see the building from another angle from the terrace, if you want. I could use the air."

She went out without waiting for a

response. He hesitated a moment, then taking the binoculars, followed her.

"I want some water. Do you want some water?"

"That'd be good." And would give him a bit more time. He followed her through, past a dining area. "Workstation?"

"Laptop goes anywhere. I try not to spread out too much. You can forget things, and that's annoying for the client."

"So you write here, about teenage were-wolves."

"Yeah—how did you know?" She held up a hand. "Google. You can't escape it. And since I did the same with you, I can't whine about it."

"You're a military brat."

"You actually read the bio. Was. Seven different schools by the time I graduated from high school, so I sympathize with Kaylee—my central character—for want-ing to stay put through high school."

"I know the feeling. Divorce can uproot the same as military orders."

"I guess it can. How old were you when your parents divorced?"

"Six when they split—officially." He stepped outside with her, into the heat and the appealing scent of sun-warmed tomatoes and some spicy flower.

"So young, but I guess any age is hard. Just you?"

"A sister, Chloe, two years younger. Then we inherited Cora and Portia when our father remarried. They had Oliver, but split when he was a baby. Our mother remarried, and there was Valentina—step, then Esteban, and so on, down to Rylee, she's fifteen and might've read your book, and the youngest, Madison. She's four."

"You have a four-year-old sister?"

"My father's current wife is younger than I am. Some people collect stamps," he said with a shrug.

"How do you keep them all straight?"

"I have a spreadsheet." He smiled when she laughed—and again had the image of her in a red dress whirling in front of a campfire. "No, seriously. When you get an invitation to a college graduation or somebody's wedding, it's good to know if you're related to them. Who's the gardener?"

"The amazing Macey. I call her that because she's pretty close to perfect. I'd like to be her. She has one of your paintings."

"The people who live here?"

"No, sorry. My thoughts are like buckshot sometimes. Sage Kendall. Julie told me, realized she knew her—a little—as a client, and that she bought one of your pieces. A woman playing the violin in a meadow. I know the piece because I'd told Julie if I had a wall, I'd have bought it. I probably couldn't have afforded it, but if I'd had a wall and could've afforded it, I'd have bought it. It's wonderful. Now it's sad, because she must've thought it was wonderful, too. Screw water." She set the bottle aside. "Do you want a glass of wine?"

"Yeah, I do."

"Good." She rose, went inside.

Ash lifted the glasses again. Oliver might have nudged his latest girlfriend to buy the painting. Bragging rights again. Or she might have bought it thinking it would please Oliver. Who knew?

"Did you ever see anyone else in there? A visitor, a repairman, anyone?" Ash asked when she came back with two glasses of red.

"No, and I remember wondering about that. Everyone else I watched had someone. A little party, or friends over, a delivery. Something at some point. But not them. They went out a lot, nearly every night. And they both went out most days, not usually together. I figured they were going to work. Then again, they might have had someone over when I wasn't looking. I know it seems like I just sat here trained on the building, but honestly I might take a look in the morning, then in the evening. Or if I was restless, late at night."

"A place like that, you entertain. Oliver liked having parties, having people over, and he'd have wanted that in that kind of space. So why didn't they?"

"A lot of people get out of the city in the summer, which is why I'm usually really busy in the summer."

"Yeah, and why didn't they?"

"Didn't he work?"

"He worked for an uncle on his mother's side. Antiquities—acquisitions and sales. If he was still doing that. Mostly he lived on his trust fund when he could get away with it. But I think he'd been working for Vinnie—the uncle—for nearly a year now. I think it was working out, at least that's the family buzz. Oliver finally found his place. And now . . . I'll have to talk to Vinnie."

"It's hard. Especially with such a big family. So many people to tell or talk to about it. But it has to be a comfort, too. I always wanted a brother or sister."

She paused a moment because he was staring at the boarded-up window again.

"Did you talk to your father?"

"Yeah." Because that depressed him, Ash sat, studied his wine. "They're in Scotland for a few weeks. They'll come back to Connecticut when I let them know the arrangements."

"You're making them?"

"Looks like it. His mother lives in London now. This flattened her. Losing a child has to flatten you, but . . . She loves her daughters, but Oliver was the center for her."

"Is someone with her?"

"Portia lives in London, and Olympia's married again. Rick—no, that was her first husband, before my father." He rubbed a space between his eyebrows. "Nigel. Decent guy, from what I can tell. He's with her, but she's shattered so it ended up I should do what needs to be done for a private service, probably on the compound."

"You have a compound."

"My father does. The press is already getting ugly, so it's just as well they all stay away until it's time."

While you're in the middle of it, she thought. "Are reporters after you?"

He drank some wine, deliberately relaxed his shoulders. "Half brother, one of several halfs and steps. It hasn't been that bad, especially since I keep a fairly low profile otherwise."

"Not so low when you were dating the dancer." She smiled a little, hoping to lighten what must be a terrible weight. "Google and Julie."

"Well, that was mostly about her."

"Do you think so?" She sat back. "Successful artist with deep, deep family pockets and a swashbuckling air."

"Swashbuckling?"

Now she shrugged, pleased she'd amused him. "That's how it strikes me. I think it was just as much about you, and I hope the press leaves you alone. Do you have anyone to help you?"

"Help me what?"

"Make the arrangements? With a family that big, that spread out, it's a lot. Not even considering the circumstances, and with both his parents out of the country. I know it's not my place, but I could help if you need it. I'm good at making calls, following instructions."

He looked back at her, into those big dark eyes, saw only compassion. "Why would you offer that?"

"I'm sorry, it really isn't my place."

"That's not what I meant, at all. It's kind, very kind of you."

"Maybe it's the window watching, or the writing, but I have a habit of putting myself in someone else's place. Or maybe the habit is why I do the other. Either way, in your place I'd be overwhelmed. So if there's something, just let me know."

Before he could speak, before he could think what to say, his phone rang. "Sorry." He lifted a hip to pull it out of his back pocket. "It's the police. No, stay," he said when she started to stand up. "Please."

"Detective Fine." He listened a moment. "No, actually I'm not home, but I can come to you or . . . Hold on a minute. They have something," he told Lila. "The cops want to talk to me again. I can go there, or I can have them come here. They went by my place looking for me."

She'd offered to help, hadn't she? Lila reminded herself. She'd meant it, so here was something she could do. "You can tell them to come here. It's okay."

He kept his eyes on hers as he lifted the phone again. "I'm with Lila Emerson, where she's staying. You have the address. Yeah, I can explain that when you get here."

He slid the phone back into his pocket. "They didn't like me being here, connecting with you. I could hear that loud and clear."

Lila took a contemplative sip of wine. "They're going to wonder if we knew each other before, and if we somehow cooked all this up, and you killed your brother, I covered for you. Then they'll realize that doesn't work on many levels."

"It doesn't?"

"No, because you wouldn't have invited them here, with me, so they'd have this to wonder about. But more, I called nine-one-one seconds after she fell. How is that covering for anyone? Why call at all? Why not let some bystander call? And why not say I saw your brother push her when I called? Clean and simple. So they'll chew on it, then just want to know how we ended up sitting out on the Kilderbrands' terrace having a glass of wine. And that's a reasonable question with a reasonable answer."

"That's logical and straightforward."

"When you write you have to figure out what makes sense."

Compassion, he thought, married to logic and flavored with what he believed to be a well-honed imagination.

"High school werewolves make sense?"

"It doesn't have to be possible so much as plausible, within the world you create. In my world, my werewolves make perfect sense. Which doesn't explain why I'm so damn nervous. Too many police." She rose, grabbed the watering can though she'd already watered. "I've gone my entire life without any real contact with the police, and now it's all over. I'm talking to them, you're talking to them, and I'm talking to you, which is one degree of separation. Julie's talking to them, so—"

"Because she brokered the painting?"

"What? No. Her apartment was broken into last night. Just some kids—it had to be, because all they took were a pair of Manolos, a bottle of perfume, a lipstick—that sort of thing. But it's still a break-in, still a police report. And now here they come again. Now I'm overwatering the plants."

"It's hot. They'll be fine." But he stepped over to take the can from her, set it down again. "I can meet them downstairs."

"No, I didn't mean that. Besides, I want to talk to them now since you've talked me back into believing your brother didn't push her. Should I make coffee? I have a stash of goldfish—the little crackers. I could set them out. I never know what to do. Why didn't I make sun tea?"

"It's that buckshot again," he decided. "I think you should relax." He picked up the wine she'd set aside, handed it to her. "And we'll go inside and talk to the police."

"Right. I'm glad you're here," she said as they went inside. "Although if you weren't here they wouldn't be coming here. But I'm glad you're here. And here they are," she said when the bell rang.

Stop thinking about it, she told herself, and walked straight to the door.

"Detectives." She stepped back to let them in.

"We didn't realize the two of you knew each other," Fine began.

"We didn't—before."

"I overheard enough at the precinct yesterday to realize Lila was the nine-one-one caller." Ash took a seat in the living room, waiting for the others to do the same. "I caught up with her on her way out, asked if she'd talk to me."

Fine gave Lila a long, speculative look. "You asked him to come here?"

"No. We talked in the coffee shop across from the police station. Ash asked if he could see the perspective where I saw what happened. What I saw of what happened. I didn't see the harm, especially since Julie knows him."

Waterstone cocked his eyebrows. "Julie?"

"My friend Julie Bryant. She manages Chelsea Arts, and they carry some of Ash's work. I told you about Julie," she remembered. "I use her address."

"Small world."

"It seems that way."

"Small enough," Fine picked up. "The victim has one of your paintings in her apartment, Mr. Archer—purchased through Chelsea Arts."

"So I'm told. I didn't know her. It's more unusual for me to meet or know someone who buys my work than not. I'm not pushing myself into your investigation. He was my brother. I want answers. I want to know what happened. Tell me what he was wearing," Ash insisted. "What was he wearing when you found him?"

"Mr. Archer, we have questions."

"You told them what you saw?" he asked Lila.

"Yes, of course. You mean the fist, the dark sleeve? Yes." She paused a moment. "Oliver wasn't wearing a dark shirt, was he?"

"You saw a flash of movement," Waterstone reminded her. "In a dimly lit room, and through binoculars."

"That's true, but in that flash I saw a dark sleeve, and if Oliver wasn't wearing a dark shirt, he didn't push her. I should've seen his face. Ash said Oliver was six-one. Why didn't I see some of his face over her head when he had her against the window?"

"If you remember your statement," Fine said patiently, "you said it happened very fast, that you were more focused on her."

"That's all true, too, but I should've seen some of his face. I shouldn't have seen a dark sleeve—not if Oliver Archer pushed her."

"But you also didn't see anyone else in the apartment."

"No, I didn't."

Fine shifted to Ash. "Was your brother in any trouble? Do you know of anyone who'd want to hurt him?"

"No, not that I know of. Trouble didn't stick to him."

"And you never met Sage Kendall, whom he was involved with, living with, who purchased one of your paintings for a five-figure price tag? Upper five-figure."

"I knew I couldn't afford it," Lila muttered.

"I never met her, and he only recently told me about her—as I told you in my statement yesterday. He didn't push her. He didn't kill himself. I know why I'm sure of that, but why are you thinking it?"

"You had some problems with your brother," Waterstone pointed out. "Your half brother."

"He was a frustrating pain in the ass."

"You've got a temper, been known to throw a punch."

"Yeah, can't deny it. I never threw one at Oliver—it would've felt like punching a puppy. And I've never hit a woman, never will. Check on it, dig into it, look all you want, but tell me why you're not sure this is what it was made to look like."

"I can go outside or into the other room if you don't want to talk about it in front of me."

Fine just looked at Lila, then shifted back to Ash. "And whatever we discuss, you'll pass right on to her."

"She's done the right thing all the way down the line. And she showed a complete stranger genuine compassion when she could've just told me to leave her alone, she'd already done enough. Why wouldn't I tell her? And she doesn't leave the room for anyone."

Lila could only blink at that. She couldn't think of the last time someone had stood up for her—or had to.

"Your brother had a mix of alcohol and barbiturates in his system," Fine said.

"I told you, he'd never have mixed pills with alcohol."

"He had enough of both that the ME believes he would have OD'd if he didn't receive medical attention. The ME's findings are that your brother was unconscious at his time of death."

The hard look on Ash's face never changed. Lila knew, as she was watching him.

"Oliver was murdered."

"We are now pursuing this as a double homicide."

"Someone killed him."

"I'm so sorry." Going with instinct, Lila leaned over, laid a hand on his. "I know it's what you believed all along, but it's . . . I'm so sorry, Ashton."

"Wrong place, wrong time?" he said slowly. "Is that what it was? They put him out, but they smack her around, scare her, hurt her, push her. They finish him off so it looks like he killed himself in regret or despair. But she was the one they hurt, so she was the one."

"You state you didn't know her, so we'll stick with your brother for now. Did he owe anyone money?"

"He always paid back his debts. He'd tap the trust, or our father, his mother, me—but he always paid back his debts."

"Where did he get his drugs?"

"I have no idea."

"He traveled to Italy last month, went through London for several days, then into Paris before coming back to New York. Do you know anything about that travel?"

"No. For work, maybe? His mother lives in London. He would've gone to see her. I think our half sister Giselle's in Paris."

"You have their contact information?"

"Yes. I'll get it to you. He was unconscious?"

For a moment Fine softened. "Yes. The medical examiner's findings state he was unconscious when he died. Just a few more questions."

Lila kept her silence while they asked questions, while Ash struggled to answer. She walked them out when they were done—for now, she supposed. Then she went back, sat.

"Do you want another glass of wine, or some water? Maybe that coffee?"

"No, thanks, no. I . . . No, I need to go. I need to make some calls. And . . . thank you." He got to his feet. "I'm sorry this . . . landed on you. Thank you."

She shook her head, then went with her gut again and moved in, wrapping her arms around him for a hug. She felt his hands come lightly, carefully, to her back before she stepped away. "If there's something I can do, call. I mean it."

"Yeah, I can see you do." He took her hand a moment, held it a moment, then released it and walked to the door.

She stood alone, grieving for him, and certain she'd never see him again.

Five

Ash stood in front of the apartment building with his hands in his pockets. Until that moment he hadn't realized just how much he didn't want to go in. Some part of him had known it, he decided—and that part had called a friend.

Beside him, Luke Talbot mimicked his pose.

"You could wait for his mother to get in."

"I don't want her to have to deal with it. She's a fucking wreck. Let's just get it done. Cops are waiting."

"A sentence nobody likes to hear."

Ash approached the doorman, stated

his business, showed his ID to keep it smooth and simple.

"Very sorry about your brother, sir."

"Appreciate that." And was already weary of hearing it. For the past two days he'd made countless calls to countless people, heard every possible variation of condolence.

"We'll go have a beer when this is done," Luke suggested as they rode up to the fourteenth floor.

"I hear that. Look, I know Olympia's going to want to go through all of his things. I figured maybe I'd cull it all down some. She wouldn't know the difference, and it might not be as hard on her."

"Let her decide, Ash. You're taking on enough—and how the hell would you know if you cull out the sweater she gave him for Christmas?"

"Yeah, yeah, you're right."

"That's why I'm here." Luke stepped off the elevator with Ash, a man with broad shoulders, strong arms, big hands. He stretched to six feet, four inches, had a curling mass of brown hair streaked from the sun and falling over the collar of a plain white T-shirt. He hooked his sunglasses in the waistband of his jeans, took a quick scan of the hallway with eyes of arctic blue.

"Quiet," he commented.

"Yeah, I bet they have a noise ordinance in this place. They probably have an ordinance for everything."

"Rules and more. Not everybody can afford to buy a whole damn building so he doesn't have rules or neighbors."

"It's a small building." Ash hesitated at the door, one still marked with police tape, though he could see where it had been cut for entry. He thought, Shit, and pressed the buzzer.

It threw him off stride when Detective Waterstone opened the door.

"I figured you'd have a regular cop sitting on the place."

"Just doing some follow-up."

"Luke Talbot." Luke held out a hand.

"Okay. You don't look like a lawyer," Waterstone commented.

"Because I'm not."

"Luke's going to help me pack up what I can. Other than Oliver's clothes, I'm not sure what . . ." He trailed off as he glanced over, around, and saw the pale gray sofa with its ugly splash of dried blood, the deeper gray wall behind it with its horrible pattern of blood and gore.

"Jesus, you couldn't have covered that up?" Luke demanded.

"Sorry, no. You might want to talk to Kendall's next of kin, work out the cleanup. We can give you the name of a couple of companies that specialize."

Fine walked in from another area. "Mr. Archer. You're prompt." Her eyes narrowed on Luke a moment, then she pointed at him. "Baker's Dozen—the bakery on West Sixteenth."

"That's right, that's my place."

"I've seen you in there. I owe you an extra five hours a week in the gym."

"Thanks."

"It's the chunky brownies. They're deadly. Friend of yours?" she said to Ash.

"Yeah. He's going to give me a hand. Oliver's mother gave me a list—a few things. Heirlooms she'd passed to him. I don't know if he still has them, if they're here."

"You can give it to me. I can check."

"It's on my phone." He pulled it out, brought it up.

"I've seen these cuff links, the pocket watch. They're in the bedroom. Antique silver cigarette case, no, haven't seen that or any mantel clock. No, just the cuff links and watch are here. I don't think we'd have missed these other things."

"He probably sold them."

"You might ask his boss—his uncle at the antique place."

"Yeah." Ash took the phone back, looked around again. And saw his painting on the wall across from the ruined sofa.

"Nice painting," Fine commented.

"It makes sense." Waterstone shrugged at Ash's blank look. "A lot of them don't."

The model's name was Leona, he remembered. She'd been soft and curvaceous with a dreamy, barefoot look about her. So he'd seen her in a meadow, flowing hair and skirts with the violin poised to play.

And painted that way, she'd watched his brother die.

No, it really didn't make sense at all.

"I'd like to get this done. I was told we still can't claim his body."

"It shouldn't be much longer. I'll check on it myself and get back to you."

"All right. I'll get his clothes, and what's here on the list. That's what matters to his mother. I don't know about the rest."

"If you see something you recognize, just check with us."

"He must have had some files, paperwork, a computer."

"We have his laptop. We're still processing that. There's a box of documents. Insurance papers, trust documents, legal correspondence. It's been processed, and it's in the bedroom. You can take it. There's some photographs, too. Would you know if he kept a safe-deposit box?"

"Not that I know of."

"There was six thousand, four hundred and fifty dollars, cash, in his dresser. You can take that. When you're done, we'll need you to sign off. We'll also have a list of anything that was removed from the premises for evidence or forensics. You'll need to check on when any of it's cleared for pickup."

He only shook his head, walked back the way she'd come, and into the bedroom.

The deep, dark plum of the walls against stark white trim gave the room a stylish, faintly regal feel that worked well with the glossy wood of the massive four-poster.

The cops, he assumed, had stripped the bed down to the mattress. Forensics, he supposed. The painted chest at the foot had been left open, its contents jumbled. Everything seemed to hold a fine layer of dust.

The art was good, probably the woman's choices of the misty forest scene, the rolling, star-struck hills. They suited the baronial feel of the space—and gave him a little insight into his brother's doomed lover.

She'd been a romantic under the gloss.

"He'd have slid right into this," Ash commented. "This place, just lofty enough, stylish but with an edge of old class. That's what he'd have wanted. He got what he wanted."

Luke put together the first of the banker's boxes they'd brought. "You said he sounded happy when you talked to him last. Happy, excited."

"Yeah, happy, excited. Buzzed." Ash rubbed his hands over his face. "That's why I put him off. I could hear some scheme or deal or big idea in his voice. I just didn't want to deal with it, or him."

Luke glanced over, and because he knew his friend, kept his voice easy. "If you're going to beat yourself up, again, at least let me hold your coat."

"No, pretty much done with that."

But he walked to the window, looked out. Picked out Lila's windows immediately, imagined her standing there that night, entertaining herself with glimpses of other lives.

If she'd looked out ten minutes sooner, ten minutes later, she wouldn't have seen the fall.

Would their paths have crossed?

When he caught himself wondering what she might be doing as he looked out at her window, he turned away. He walked over to the chest of drawers, opened a drawer, looked down at the jumble of socks.

The cops, he thought. Oliver would have arranged them—folded, never rolled—in tidy rows. Seeing the disorder added another thin layer of grief, like the dust over the wood.

"I was with him once, can't remember why, and it took him twenty minutes to buy a pair of goddamn socks—ones that coordinated to his specifications with his tie. Who does that?"

"Not us."

"Some homeless guy's going to be

wearing cashmere socks." So saying, Ash took out the entire drawer, dumped the contents into a box.

At the end of two hours, he had forty-two suits, three leather jackets, twenty-eight pairs of shoes, countless shirts, ties, a box of designer sportswear, ski gear, golf gear, a Rolex and a Cartier tank watch, which made three including the watch Oliver had been wearing.

"And I said you wouldn't need so many boxes." Luke studied the stack on the floor. "You're going to need a couple more."

"The rest can wait, or just fuck it. I got what he had left that his mother wanted."

"Fine with me. Even with this, we're going to need a couple cabs." Luke frowned at the boxes again. "Or a moving van."

"No. I'm going to have it all picked up, sent back to my place." He pulled out his phone to make arrangements. "And we're going to go have that beer."

"Even finer with me."

Ash managed to shake off most of the mood just by leaving the building. The busy, noisy bar took care of the rest. All the dark wood, the yeasty smells, the clatter of glasses and voices.

Just what he needed to erase the terrible quiet of that empty apartment.

He lifted his beer, studied the umber tones under the lights. "Who drinks some fussy craft beer called Bessie's Wild Hog?"

"Looks like you are."

"Only because I want to know." He took a sip. "It's not bad. You ought to serve beer at your place."

"It's a bakery, Ash."

"What's your point?"

With a laugh, Luke sampled his own beer—something called Hops On Down. "I could rename it Brioche and Brew."

"Never an empty table. I appreciate today, Luke. I know you're busy frosting those cupcakes."

"Need a day away from the ovens now and again. I'm thinking about opening a second place."

"Glutton for punishment."

"Maybe, but we've been kicking ass the last eighteen months, solid, so I'm looking around some, mostly in SoHo."

"If you need any backing—"

"Not this time. And I couldn't say that, or

think about expanding, if you hadn't backed me the first time. So if I start up a second place and work myself to an early grave, it's on you."

"We'll serve your cherry pie at your funeral." Because that made him think of Oliver, he drank more beer. "His mom wants bagpipes."

"Oh, man."

"I don't know where she gets that, but she wants them. I'm setting it up because I figure if she gets them she won't think about a twenty-one gun salute or a funeral pyre. And she could, because she's all over the map."

"You'll make it work."

And that was practically the family motto, Ash thought. Ash will make it work.

"Everything's in limbo until they release the body. Even then, even when the funeral's done and over, it's not over. Not until we find out who killed him, and why."

"The cops might have a good line on that. They wouldn't tell you if they did."

"I don't think so. Waterstone's wondering, at least in some little corner, if I did it. He doesn't like the serendipity of me and Lila connecting."

"Only because he doesn't know you well enough to understand you need the answers—because everyone else asks you the questions. I've got one. What's she like, the Peeping Tammy?"

"She doesn't think about it that way, and you get it when she talks. She likes people."

"Imagine that."

"It takes all kinds. She likes watching them and talking to them and being with them, which is odd because she's a writer and that has to mean a lot of solo hours. But it goes with the house-sitting thing. Spending her time being in someone else's space, taking care of that space. She's a tender."

"A tender what?"

"No, she tends. Tends to people's things, their place, their pets. Hell, she tended to me and she doesn't even know me. She's . . . open. Anyone that open has to have gotten screwed over a few times."

"You've got a little thing," Luke observed, circling a finger in the air. "She must be a looker."

"I don't have a thing. She's interesting, and she's been more than decent. I want to paint her."

"Uh-huh. A thing."

"I don't have a thing for every woman I paint. I'd never be without a thing."

"You have to have some thing for every woman you paint or you wouldn't paint them. And like I said, she must be a looker."

"Not especially. She's got a good face, sexy mouth, about a mile of hair the color of the dark chocolate mochas you serve in the bakery. But . . . it's her eyes. She's got gypsy eyes, and they pull you in, they contrast with this fresh, open sense."

"How do you see her?" Luke asked, knowing just how Ash worked.

"Red dress, full skirt, mid-spin, gypsy camp, with moonlight coming through a thick green forest."

Idly Ash took the stub of a pencil he always carried out of his pocket, did a quick sketch of her face on a cocktail napkin.

"Rough, but close."

"And she's a looker—just not obvious about it. Are you going to ask her?"

"It doesn't seem appropriate." He shrugged when Luke simply raised his eyebrows. "And yeah, appropriate's not much of a concern to me when it comes to the work, but this situation's . . . awkward.

That's what she called it. Awkward. Me, I call it fucked to hell and back."

"Semantics."

That brought out a grin. "Yeah, words are words. Anyway, she's probably had enough of me, and the cops. I'd say she'll be glad to move on to the next job, the next place, so she doesn't have to remember what she saw every time she looks out the window. Added to it, apparently her friend had a break-in the night after this happened. Or thinks she did."

"It's pretty clear when you've had a break-in."

"You'd think, and I actually know the friend, which adds to the fucked up. She manages one of the galleries I work with. Lila says somebody broke in and took makeup and shoes."

"Come on." On a snort, Luke lifted his beer, gestured. "Shoes in the back of the closet, makeup in some purse she's forgotten she has. Case closed."

"I'd say just that if I didn't know the woman. She's pretty damn steady. Either way, more cops, more upset, more . . ." He straightened from broody slouch to furiously rigid. "Son of a bitch."

"What?"

"She uses that address—that's Lila's listed address. Maybe somebody did break in, but not to rob the place. Looking for her. If I found out she was a witness, someone else could."

"You're looking for trouble, Ash."

"No, if I was looking for trouble I'd've thought of this before. I've just been looking to get through. But when you step back, someone killed Oliver and his woman, tried to make it look like murder/suicide. She's the one who reported it, who actually saw an altercation and the fall. And the day after it happens, someone just happens to prowl around in the apartment she's listed as her official address?"

Concern moved over Luke's face. "When you put it that way. Still, it's a stretch. What kind of murderer takes makeup and shoes?"

"A woman. Maybe. Hell, a cross-dresser, a guy who has a woman he wants to impress. The point is it's awful damn close. I'm going to check on her," he decided. "And see if Julie's had any trouble."

"Julie?" Luke set his beer down. "I thought you said her name was Lila."

"Julie's the friend—mutual friend."

Very slowly, Luke set his beer down again. "Julie. Art gallery. Since this is fucked up to hell and back, tell me what this Julie looks like."

"After a date? She's a jackpot, not really your type though."

Ash turned the napkin over, thought for a moment, then did a sketch of Julie's face.

Luke picked up the napkin, studied it carefully, his face blank. "Tall," he said after a moment. "Built. Texas-bluebonnet eyes. Redhead."

"That's Julie. You know her?"

"I did." Luke took a long drink of beer. "I was married to her. For about five minutes. In another life."

"You're shitting me." He knew about the impulsive marriage, the quick divorce—all when Luke had barely been old enough to buy a legal beer. "Julie Bryant's the one that got away?"

"That would be her. You've never mentioned her before."

"She manages a gallery. We're professional friends. We don't hang out—never dated, in case that's an issue here. And she's not your type. You usually go for the bouncing balls of energy, not smoking-hot class with a side of arty."

"Because I still have the scars." He poked a finger on his own heart. "Julie Bryant. Son of a bitch. Now **this** is awkward, and I need another beer."

"Later. I need to talk to Lila, get more details on this break-in. I wasn't paying attention before. You should come with me."

"I should?"

"A murderer might be wearing your ex-wife's shoes."

"That's ridiculous, and it was a dozen years ago."

"You know you want to check it out." Ash tossed some bills on the two-top, then shoved the napkin toward Luke. "Beer and pencil portrait on me. Let's go."

Lila considered grabbing a shower. Since she'd dived straight into the book that morning, and had broken to entertain Thomas by trying out one of the amazing Macey's many workout DVDs, she probably needed one.

Plus, she and Julie hadn't decided if

they'd stay in and order in, or go out. Either way, since it was nearly six-thirty and Julie would be here before much longer, she really ought to clean up.

"I have book brain," she told Thomas. "And the perky blonde on the DVD was a sadist."

Maybe she had time for a hot—but reasonably quick—soak in the wonder tub. If she—

"Okay, no tub," she muttered when she heard the bell. "She'll just have to hang out while I grab that shower."

She went to the door, pulled it open without thinking to check. "You're early. I haven't— Oh."

She looked into Ash's eyes, and her thoughts went into a chaotic avalanche. She hadn't washed her hair in three days, she wore no make-up, and the yoga pants and sports top—both sweaty—she'd been meaning to replace for months.

She smelled like Pilates and the handful of Doritos she'd shoved in her mouth as a reward for the Pilates.

She managed another, "Oh," when he smiled at her.

"I should've called. We were just a couple of blocks away, and I wanted to talk to you about something. This is Luke."

Someone was with him. Of course someone was with him, she could see that perfectly well. She just hadn't really registered the cute guy with the killer shoulders.

"Oh," she said yet again. "I was working, then I decided to try this exercise DVD designed to make you cry like a baby, so I'm . . . Oh well," she said as she stepped back to let them in.

It didn't matter what she looked like, she told herself. It wasn't as if they were dating. More important, he looked less strained than he had the last time she'd seen him.

"It's nice to meet you. And you, too." Luke bent down to scratch Thomas, who sniffed busily at his pant legs.

"Are you with the police?"

"No, not a cop. I'm a baker."

"A professional baker?"

"Yeah. I've got a place a few blocks from here. Baker's Dozen."

"Mini cupcakes!"

Amused by the outburst, Luke straightened. "We've got them."

"No, I mean, I've had them. The red velvet brought tears to my eyes. I went back for more just the other day, and the sourdough bread. And a caramel latte. It's such a happy place. How long have you been there?"

"About three years now."

"I always wondered what it was like to work in a bakery. Do you ever stop noticing how wonderful it smells or how pretty all the tarts look, that kind of thing? Did you always want to be a baker? And I'm sorry."

She shoved at her hair. "I ask too many questions, and I haven't even asked you to sit down. Do you want a drink? I have wine, or the sun tea I finally got around to making," she added with a quick smile for Ash.

"We're fine. We just had a beer, and something occurred to me."

Luke leaned over again to pet the delighted cat, and his sunglasses fell to the floor. "That damn screw," he said as he picked them up, then retrieved the tiny screw that had popped out.

"Oh, I can fix that. Just a minute—go on and sit down."

"She can fix that?" Luke repeated when she walked out.

"Don't ask me."

She came back with what looked to Ash like the nuclear version of a Swiss Army knife. "Let's sit down," she said, and took the glasses and tiny screw from Luke.

"I want to ask if there's anything new." She sat, and the minute Ash took a chair, Thomas jumped in his lap as if they were old friends.

"They're not telling me much. They let me get his things from the apartment."

"That was hard. You had someone with you," she said with a glance at Luke before she opened the tool, selected a tiny screwdriver. "It's better to have someone with you when it's hard."

"They didn't find any signs of forced entry, so they're assuming they let whoever killed them in. Probably knew them. If they know more, they aren't saying."

"They'll find who did it. I can't be the only one who saw something."

Maybe not, he thought, but she might be the only one willing to get involved.

"There." She tested the glasses, winging the earpiece back and forth. "Good as new."

"Thanks. I've never seen one just like that." Luke nodded toward her Leatherman.

"Three hundred essential tools all in one handy package. I don't know how anyone lives without one." She folded it, set it aside.

"I'm a big fan of duct tape."

She smiled at Luke. "Its infinite uses have yet to be fully discovered." She looked back at Ash. "It's good to have a friend."

"Yeah. And speaking of that. The last time I was here, you mentioned Julie'd had a break-in. Anything new there?"

"No. The police think she just lost or misplaced what's missing. That's what she thinks they think anyway. She changed the locks, put in a second dead bolt, so she's okay about it, though she may never get over losing the Manolos."

"You have her place listed as your address."

"You need one for all sorts of things, and since I stay there now and again between jobs, even store some seasonal things there, it made the most sense."

"It's your address of record," Ash said, "and someone broke in the day after my brother was murdered. The day you called the police, gave a statement, talked to me."

"I know. It seems like everything rolled into one big ball of . . ."

He saw the thought strike home, watched her face fall into thoughtful lines, not fearful ones.

"You think it's connected. I didn't think of that. I should've thought of that. If someone wanted to find me who didn't know me, that would be the first logical point. I didn't see anyone, couldn't identify anyone, but they wouldn't know that. Or not that quickly. They could've broken into Julie's looking for me."

"You're pretty calm about the idea," Luke observed.

"Because she wasn't home, wasn't hurt. And because they probably know by now I'm not a threat. I wish I was. I wish I could give the police a description. Since I can't, there's no reason to bother with me. There's certainly no reason to break into Julie's again, or worry her."

"Maybe whoever killed Oliver and his girlfriend isn't as logical as you," Ash suggested. "You need to be careful."

"Who'd look for me here? And in another few days I'll be somewhere else. Nobody knows where I am."

"I know," he pointed out. "Luke knows, Julie, your clients, probably their friends, their family. The doorman," he continued. "You go out, walk around, shop, eat. They'd know you were in this area—had to be—that night. Why wouldn't they look here?"

"It's a big here." Irritation trickled in, as it always did when someone assumed she couldn't take care of herself. "And anyone who lives and works in New York knows how to be reasonably careful."

"You answered the door for us without knowing who it was."

"I don't usually, but I was expecting . . . that," she finished as the bell rang. "Excuse me."

"Hit a nerve," Luke said quietly.

"I'll hit as many as it takes to convince her to take precautions."

"You could use the 'I'm worried about you' card instead of the 'Don't be an idiot' card."

"I never said she was an idiot."

"Implied. If you really think—"

Everything in Luke's brain simply dropped away. A dozen years had changed her, of course they had, but every change hit the bell.

"Julie, you know Ashton."

"Of course. I'm so sorry, Ash."

"I got your note. I appreciate it."

"And Ash's friend Luke. Remember those amazing cupcakes? His bakery."

"Really? They were—" Her face filled with shock, maybe just a little awe. And years tumbled away and back again. "Luke."

"Julie. It's amazing to see you."

"But . . . I don't understand. What are you doing here?"

"I live here. In New York," he qualified. "About eight years now."

"You know each other. They know each other?" Lila asked Ash when neither spoke.

"They used to be married. To each other."

"They— He's the— This just gets more . . ."

"Awkward?"

She just shot him a look. "I think we should have that wine now," she said brightly. "Julie, give me a hand, will you?"

She took her friend's arm, pulled her firmly away and into the kitchen.

"Are you okay?"

"I don't know. It's Luke."

She looked like the lone survivor of an earthquake, Lila decided. Shaken, dazed and just a little grateful.

"I'll make them leave. Do you want them to go?"

"No. No, it's not like that. We were . . . It was years ago. It's just such a shock to walk in and see him. How do I look?"

"Considering how I look, that's a mean question. You look fantastic. Tell me what you want me to do, and it's done."

"The wine's a good idea. We'll be civilized and sophisticated."

"If that's on the order, I really need a shower, but we'll start with wine." Lila got down glasses. "He's awfully cute."

"He is, isn't he?" Julie smiled. "He always was."

"Since you're okay with it, we'll get this out there, then you have to entertain them while I pull myself together. I just need fifteen minutes."

"I hate you because I know you can do it in fifteen. Okay. Civilized and sophisticated. Let's do this."

Six

It wasn't so bad. Lila didn't know about sophisticated—she'd never been very good at that—but it was all pretty civilized.

At least until Ash pushed his break-in theory, and to Lila's surprise, Julie bought it wholesale.

"Why didn't I think of that!" Julie swung her attention to Lila. "That makes sense, that fits."

"You said the teenager fit," Lila reminded her.

"Because I was grasping. But what silly teenage girl can get through the locks without leaving a sign? The cops did check the locks."

"And a murderer takes away your Manolos and lipstick? Wouldn't somebody who'd committed double murder have, I don't know, different priorities?"

"They're great shoes, the lipstick is the perfect red—and that perfume isn't easy to come by. Plus, who says a murderer can't have sticky-finger impulses? If you can kill two people, stealing is pretty tame. Lila, you need to be careful."

"I didn't see anything that helps the police, and a well-heeled, sweet-smelling killer with perfect red lips would've figured that out by now."

"It's not a joke."

"I'm sorry." Lila turned to Ash immediately. "It's your brother, and I know it's not a joke. But you don't have to worry about me. Nobody has to worry about me."

"If she ever gets a tattoo," Julie commented, "it's going to say exactly that."

"Because it's true. And even if all this is also true, which is a long, long taffy stretch for me, in a few days I'll be in a swank apartment on the Upper East

Side, with a teacup poodle named Earl Grey."

"How do you get the jobs?" Luke wondered. "How do people find you?"

"A lot of word of mouth, client recommendations. And the gods of the Internet."

"You've got a website."

"I suspect even Earl Grey has a website. But no," she continued, following the line, "you can't access my location through it. There's a calendar showing when I'm already booked, but not where. And I never list clients' names."

"Your blog," Julie pointed out.

"I don't give specific locations, just areas. I never post clients' names, anywhere. Even the client comments I list only have initials. Listen, here's what I'd do if I were a murderer wondering if the annoying woman in the complex saw my face, saw enough to identify me. I'd walk up to her on the street one day and ask directions. If she gave them to me without a blink, I'd move along on my murderous ways. If she gasped out, 'It's you!' I'd stab her in the thigh—in the femoral artery with my stiletto—then move along while she bled out. Problem solved either way.

"Is anybody thinking dinner?" she said in a firm change of subject. "I'm thinking dinner. We can order in."

"We'll take you out." Luke's response flowed smoothly. "There's an Italian place just a couple blocks from here. Great food, stupendous gelato."

"Echo Echo."

He smiled at Julie. "That's it. I know the owner. I'll call over, make sure we can get a table. That work for you?" he asked Lila.

"Sure, why not?" It wasn't like a date, she reasoned. Not like some weird double date with her and the brother of the dead guy and her best friend and her best friend's ex-husband who didn't really count. It was just eating.

And eating really well, she discovered over fried calamari and bruschetta brought out as table appetizers. She found it simple enough to keep conversation moving, always a priority for her, by peppering Luke with questions about his bakery.

"Where did you learn to bake? There's so much to bake."

"My grandmother initially. Then I picked things up along the way."

"What happened to law school?" Julie wondered.

"I hated it."

"Told you."

"Yeah, you did. I gave it a shot. My parents really wanted either a doctor or a lawyer, and since medical school was worse than law school, I gave it a shot. Worked in an off-campus bakery to help pay the way for the two years I gave it, and liked that a hell of a lot more."

"How are your parents?"

"They're good. Yours?"

"The same. I remember the chocolate chip cookies—your grandmother's recipe—and the really fabulous cake you made me for my eighteenth birthday."

"And your mother said, 'Luke, you could make a living.'"

Julie laughed. "She did! But I never imagined you would."

"Neither did I. Actually, Ash pushed the idea. He's good at pushing because you usually don't know he's pushed you where he thinks you should be until you're there."

"I just said, Why are you working for someone else when you could have people working for you?"

"Or words to that effect," Luke finished. "And you, an art gallery. You always loved art, talked about studying art history, that sort of thing."

"And I did. I went back to school, moved to New York, wheedled my way into the gallery. I got married, met Lila, got divorced and moved up to manager."

"I had nothing to do with any of it," Lila claimed.

"Oh, please."

"Not on purpose."

"We met at yoga class," Julie began. "Lila and I, not me and Maxim—my ex. We hit it off during up dogs and down dogs, started hitting the juice bar together after. One thing led to another."

Lila sighed. "I was seeing someone, and it looked like it might get fairly serious. So, being females, we talked about the men in our lives. I told her about mine. He was great-looking, successful. He traveled a lot, but was very attentive when we were together. And Julie told me about her husband."

"Also great-looking and successful. Working longer hours than he once did, and not as attentive as he'd once been. In fact, things were a little rocky, but we were working on smoothing them out."

"So with a few yoga sessions, a few smoothies, some sharing of details, it turned out the guy I was seeing was married, to Julie. I was sleeping with her husband, and instead of drowning me in my own smoothie, she dealt."

"We dealt."

"We did." Lila tapped her glass to Julie's. "And our friendship is written in his blood. Not literally," she added quickly.

"No violence necessary when you take your husband's slut—"

"Ouch."

"When you take his slut home for drinks and introduce her to him as your new best friend. He packed up what he could in the twenty minutes I gave him and moved out. Lila and I ate the best part of a half gallon of ice cream."

"Ben & Jerry's Coffee Heath Bar Crunch," Lila remembered, with a smile that had the little dimple flickering. "Still a favorite. You were so amazing. I just wanted to crawl into the deep dark hole of shame, but not Julie. 'Let's get the bastard,' that was her reaction. So we did."

"I ditched the bastard, kept the slut."

"I ditched the bastard," Lila corrected, "and kept the pathetic and clueless wife. Someone had to."

"I want to paint you."

Lila glanced at Ash. Blinked. "I'm sorry, what?"

"I'll need you at the loft for some preliminary sketches. A couple of hours would do it to start. What size are you?"

"What?"

"She's a two," Julie said, "as so many sluts are." She angled her head. "What are you looking for?"

"Earthy, sexy gypsy, full skirt, flame red, bold colors in the underskirts."

"Really?" Fascinated, Julie turned to Lila, gaze sharp and assessing. "Really."

"Stop it. No. Thanks. I'm . . . The knee-jerk is flattered, but I'm more baffled. I'm not a model. I don't know how to model."

"I know what I want, so you don't have to." He glanced at the waiter, ordered the pasta special. "Day after tomorrow would work. About ten."

"I don't— What he said's fine," she told the waiter. "Thanks. Listen, I don't—"

"I can pay you by the hour or a flat fee.

We'll work that out. Do you know how to play up your eyes?"

"What?"

"Of course she does," Julie put in. "A full-length portrait? She's got long and excellent legs."

"I noticed."

"Really, stop."

"Lila doesn't like being spotlighted. Toughen up, Lila-Lou. You've just been tapped to model for a highly respected contemporary artist whose fanciful, sometimes disturbing, sometimes whimsical, always sensual paintings are acclaimed. She'll be there. I'll get her there."

"Might as well give it up," Luke told her. "You're going to end up standing where he wants you anyway."

"I'll paint you anyway." Ash shrugged. "But the work will resonate more, have more depth if you're involved. Lila-Lou?"

"Lila Louise, middle name after my father, Lieutenant Colonel Louis Emerson. And you can't paint me if I say no."

"Your face, your body?" He jerked a shoulder. "They're right out there."

"She'll be there," Julie repeated. "Come on, time for a little sortie to the ladies'.

Excuse us." To ward off protests, Julie simply rose, took Lila's hand and hauled her to her feet.

"He can't make me model," Lila hissed as Julie towed her along. "And neither can you."

"I bet you're wrong."

"Plus, I'm not an earthy, sexy gypsy type."

"There, you're definitely wrong." She led Lila down the narrow flight of steps to the restrooms. "You have the coloring, and you have the lifestyle."

"One fling with a married man I didn't know was married, and I have an earthy lifestyle?"

"A gypsy lifestyle." Julie drew her into the little bathroom. "It's a fabulous opportunity—and a chance for an interesting experience, and you'll be immortalized."

"I'll feel flustered and shy." Might as well pee since I'm here, Lila thought, and went into a stall. "I hate feeling shy."

"He'll find a way around that." Following the lead, Julie used the second stall. "And I'm going to lobby to be allowed to sit in on a session or two. I'd love to watch him work, and be able to talk about his process with clients."

"You sit for him. You be the sexy, earthy gypsy."

"He wants you. He has a vision and he wants you." At the sink Julie tried the pink-grapefruit-scented soap, approved. "Plus, doing this, giving him a new inspiration, a new project, will help him through the grieving process."

In the mirror, Lila narrowed her eyes at Julie's smug face. "Oh, that's dirty fighting."

"It really is." Julie refreshed her lip gloss. "Also true. Give it a chance. You're no coward."

"More dirty fighting."

"I know."

Laughing, Julie patted Lila's shoulder, then started out. Halfway up the steps she let out a muffled shriek.

"What? Mouse? What?"

"My shoes!"

Julie charged up the steps, skirted around the hostess station, had to dodge and weave around the group of people who'd just come in, then finally shoved her way out the door. Head swiveling left and right, she rushed up the two short steps to the sidewalk.

"Damn it!"

"Julie, what the hell?"

"The shoes, **my** shoes. The shoes, really great legs, some sort of ankle tat. Short red dress. I couldn't see much more."

"Julie, Manolo made more than one pair of those shoes."

"They were mine. Think about it." She whirled around, six feet of flaming female fury. "You see the murder, somebody breaks into my place, takes my shoes. Now I see a woman wearing them leaving a restaurant where we came for dinner—a restaurant just a couple blocks from the murder?"

Frowning, Lila rubbed at suddenly chilly arms in the evening heat. "Now you're creeping me out."

"Ash could be right. Whoever killed his brother's keeping tabs on you. You need to talk to the police again."

"Now you're seriously creeping me out. I'll tell them, fine, I will. I promise. But they're going to think I'm crazy."

"Just tell them. And put a chair under the doorknob tonight."

"They broke into your place, not where I'm staying."

"I'll put a chair under the doorknob, too."

Jai slid into the car about the time Julie hit the top of the stairs. She didn't like this connection between the brother of the idiot and this nosy woman who'd been watching the apartment.

She hadn't seen enough, so it seemed, to cause any problem. But no, Jai didn't like this connection.

Her employer wouldn't care for all these dangling ends.

They wouldn't be dangling if Ivan hadn't pushed the stupid whore out the window, and if the idiot hadn't passed out after a few drinks. She hadn't put that many pills in the bourbon.

So she could only deduce he'd already taken some before her arrival.

Bad luck, she thought. She didn't care for bad luck either, and this job brought a streak of it.

Maybe the brother knew something after all, had something.

He had his loft secured like a fortress,

but it was time to get around that. She had a couple hours, she imagined, as he was having dinner with the nosy one.

"The brother's place," she told Ivan. "Take me there, then go back, sit on the brother and the others. Contact me when they leave."

"We're wasting time. The bitch didn't know anything, and they didn't have anything. If they ever did, they sold it."

Why did she have to work with morons? "You're paid to do what I tell you. Do what I tell you."

And then, she thought, she'd deal with at least one of those dangling ends.

Lila didn't argue when Ash insisted on walking her home—because Luke insisted on doing the same with Julie, in the opposite direction.

"It's interesting you knowing both Julie and Luke, considering the history."

"Life's full of the strange."

"It is. And it was strange seeing all that sparkage between them."

"Sparkage?"

"Old flame, low smolder, a few fresh sparks." She made a **pow** sound as she flicked her hands in the air.

"Old flame, short, crappy marriage. Doused."

"Bet."

"Bet?"

"You're not paying a lot of attention because you keep repeating what I say, and I say I bet—let's say ten bucks—there's a **pow** and not a fizzle."

"I'll take that bet. He's already half seeing somebody."

"Half seeing's just sex, and the somebody isn't Julie. They look great together. All handsome and healthy and built."

"Come by my place."

"Wait. What?" She felt a quick buzz—fresh sparks—and thought it wise to avoid the singe. "I knew you weren't paying attention."

"It's just a few blocks that way. It's not late. You can see the work space, relax in it. I'm not going to hit on you."

"Now my evening's ruined. Sarcasm," she said quickly when she saw the change in his eyes. "Julie's going to hound me until I agree to let you at least do some sketches, and once I do, you'll see you're wrong about the whole thing."

"Come see the space. You like seeing new spaces, and it should help adjust your really crappy attitude."

"That's so sweet. But I do like seeing new spaces, and it's not very late. And since I know you're not interested in hitting on me, I'm safe so why not?"

He turned at the corner, toward his building, away from hers. "I didn't say I wasn't interested in hitting on you. I said I wouldn't. How'd you meet the cheating bastard? The one you shared with Julie."

She was still working on not not interested. "It sounds inappropriately sexy when you say it that way. We shared a cab, in a rainstorm. It was romantic, just one of those New York things. He wasn't wearing a ring, and definitely indicated he wasn't married or involved. I ended up having a drink with him, then we went out to dinner a few days later, then, then, then. What could've been a really horrible thing turned around and gave me my best friend, so the bastard was good for something."

She turned topics on a dime—a particular skill. "When did you know you had talent?"

"Don't like talking about yourself, do you?"

"There's not that much to talk about, and other people are more interesting. Did you do fabulous and insightful finger paintings in kindergarten which your mother has framed?"

"My mother's not that sentimental. My father's second wife framed a pencil sketch I did of her dog when I was about thirteen. Nice dog. It's this place."

He walked up to a three-story building, old brick, big windows. One of the old warehouses, she thought, converted to lofts. She loved spaces like this.

"I bet you have the third floor, for the light."

"Yeah, I've got the third floor." He unlocked the big steel door, stepped in, dealt with the alarm code while she walked in behind him.

Dazzled, she turned a circle. She'd expected some small common space, one of the old freight elevators, maybe, walls and doors of first-level apartments.

Instead she walked through a huge open space made fluid with arches of old brick. Wide-plank floors, scarred but gleaming, spread over a living area, rich colors against neutral walls, jewel-toned chairs arranged for conversation, the charm of a double-sided fireplace built into the leg of an arch.

The ceiling soared, opening the space for the second floor and its sleek rails and turned pickets of copper gone to verdigris.

"This is amazing." Since he didn't stop her, she wandered, studying the long stretch of kitchen, all black-and-white tiles, polished concrete counters and a dining area with a generously sized black table, a half dozen high-backed chairs.

The neutral walls throughout served as the backdrop for art. Paintings, sketches, charcoals, watercolors. A collection, she thought, any gallery would swoon for.

"This is yours. All yours."

She stepped into another area, a sort of den/library/sitting room with its own little fireplace. A cozier spot, she decided, despite the open floor plan.

"It's all yours," she repeated. "It's big enough for a family of ten, easy."

"Sometimes I am."

"You— Oh." She laughed, shook her head. "I guess that's true. Your spreadsheet family visits a lot."

"Now and then, off and on."

"And you kept the old elevator." She walked over to the wide, grated lift.

"It comes in handy. But we can use the stairs if you'd rather."

"I'd rather because then I get to be nosy about the second floor. It's a wonderful use of space—color, texture, everything." Because she was serious about the nosy, she walked to the angled stairs with their old copper rail. "I spend time in some spaces, and wonder what people were thinking. Why they put this here instead of there, or why they took out that wall—or didn't take it out. Not here. Anytime you need a house-sitter, you've got my number."

"Yeah, I think I've got it."

She glanced up at him, a quick, easy smile. "You've got my phone number, the rest could still surprise you. How many bedrooms?"

"Four on this level."

"Four, on this level. How rich are you—

and that's not because I plan to marry you for your money. It's the nosy again."

"Now you've ruined my night."

She laughed again, started toward what looked like a pretty guest room with an open canopy bed, and more compelling, a large painting of a field of sunflowers simply saturated with color.

Then she stopped, eyebrows drawn together. "Wait," she said, and followed her nose.

She walked quickly, heading away from the stairs, stopping again at what she assumed was the master bedroom with its big iron bed of steel gray and rumpled navy duvet.

"I wasn't thinking company when I—"

"No." She held up a hand, walked straight into the room. "Boudoir."

"Guys don't have boudoirs, Lila-Lou. They have bedrooms."

"No, no, the perfume. Julie's perfume. Don't you smell it?"

It took him a minute, and made her realize his senses had been caught up in her scent—something fresh and flirty. But he caught it, the deeper, more sensual tones lingering in the air.

"Now I do."

"This is crazy, God, it's crazy, but you were right." Heart thumping, she gripped his arm. "You were right about the break-in at Julie's, because whoever broke in there, they've been here. Maybe they still are."

"Stay right here," he ordered, but she not only tightened her grip, she grabbed his arm with both hands.

"Absolutely not, because the big brave man who says to stay right here is the one who gets cut to ribbons by the crazy slasher who's hiding in the closet."

He went straight to the closet with her still latched on, flung it open. "No crazy slasher."

"Not in this closet. I bet there are twenty closets in this place."

Rather than argue, he took her with him as he systematically searched the second floor.

"We should have a weapon."

"My AK-47's in for repair. There's no one up here, and no one on the first floor, since you went pretty much everywhere down there. Plus the scent's strongest in my bedroom."

"Wouldn't that mean she was in there last? Or longest? She, because I can't see a killer-slash-burglar-slash-potential-slasher who wears stolen Boudoir perfume being a man."

"Maybe. I need to check my studio. Look, lock yourself in the bathroom if you're worried."

"I will not lock myself in the bathroom. Did you read **The Shining**?"

"For Christ's sake." Resigned, he went back to the stairs, started up with her gripping his belt.

Ordinarily, the big, cluttered and colorful work space would have fascinated her. Now she looked for movement, braced for attack. But she saw only tables, easels, canvases, jars, bottles, rags, tarps. One wall held a massive corkboard crowded with photographs, sketches, the odd scribbled note.

She smelled paint, what she thought was turpentine, chalk.

"A lot of scents here," she commented. "I don't know if I'd find the perfume through it."

She looked up to the big dome of the

skylight, over to a cobbled-together sitting area with a long leather couch, a couple of tables, a lamp, a chest.

She relaxed enough to let go of his belt, stepped away enough to get a better sense of the room.

He'd stacked canvases against the walls, dozens of them. She wanted to ask him what inspired him to paint them, then stack them up that way. What he did with them all, if anything. But it didn't seem like the right time for questions.

Then she saw the mermaid.

"Oh God, she's beautiful. And terrifying. Terrifying in the way real beauty can be. She won't save them, will she? She's no Ariel looking for love, wishing for legs. The sea's the only lover she needs or wants. She'll watch them drown. If one makes it to her rock, it might be worse for him than drowning. And still the last thing he'll see is beauty."

She wanted to touch that sinuous, iridescent tail, had to put her hand behind her back to stop herself.

"What do you call it?"

"She Waits."

"It's perfect. Just perfect. Who'll buy

this, I wonder? And will they see what you painted, or just see the beautiful mermaid on the rocks over a stormy sea?"

"It depends on what they want to see."

"Then they're not really looking. And that distracted me. No one's here anymore. She came, she's gone." Lila turned back to see Ash watching her. "We should call the police."

"And tell them what, exactly? That we smelled perfume, which will have faded before they get here anyway? Nothing's out of place, not that I can tell."

"She took things from Julie's. She probably took something. Just little things. Souvenirs, the prizes in the box, however she thinks of it. But that's not as important, is it?"

"No. She wasn't looking for you here, but she was looking for something. What did Oliver have that she wants? She wouldn't have found it here."

"Which means she'll keep looking. I'm not the one who needs to be careful, Ash. You are."

Seven

Maybe she had a point, but he still walked her back to the apartment, went through the apartment room by room before he left her alone.

Then he walked home half hoping someone would try something. He was in the mood to give a hell of a something back—even if it was a woman, as Julie claimed, wearing designer shoes and sporting an ankle tat.

Whoever had killed his brother—or had, at least, been an accessory to the murders—had come into his home, past his pretty damn good security, walked through it much, he imagined, as Lila had.

Free, clear.

And didn't that mean someone was watching him? Didn't the woman have to know her way was free and clear? And more, hadn't she known to get out again? She'd been there literally minutes before he'd come in with Lila. The perfume would have faded, wouldn't it, with a little more time?

The tally to date? Two murders, two break-ins, and certainly some sort of surveillance.

What the hell had Oliver gotten himself into?

Not gambling this time, not drugs. Neither fit. What once-in-a-lifetime deal, what big score had Oliver wrangled?

Whatever it was, it had died with him. This woman, whoever she worked with or for, could watch him all she wanted, could search all she wanted. She'd find nothing because he had nothing.

Nothing but a dead brother, a grieving family and a world of guilt and fury.

He let himself back into his loft. He'd change the security code—whatever good that would do. And he supposed he'd have the company come back in, beef it up.

But for now, he should spend some time trying to figure out if his unwelcome visitor had taken any souvenirs.

He stood a moment, dragged both hands through his hair. A big space, he thought. He liked having a big space, plenty of room to spread out, to designate purposes. And to accommodate various members of his family.

Now he had to go through it, knowing someone had slipped through the locks.

It took him more than an hour to come up with a short, strange list of missing items.

The bath salts his mother particularly liked, the earrings his sister (half sister, mother's second marriage) left behind when she and their mother had stayed for a night a few weeks earlier, the little stained-glass sun catcher his sister (stepsister, father's fourth marriage) made for him one Christmas, and a pair of hammered silver cuff links, still in their little blue box from Tiffany.

She hadn't bothered with the cash, which he imagined she found in his desk drawer. Just a few hundred, but why wouldn't she take cash? Bath salts, but not cash.

Too impersonal? he considered. Not as appealing?

Who the fuck knew?

Restless, unsettled, he went up to his studio. He couldn't work on the mermaid—his mood was all wrong—but he studied it, thinking how Lila had expressed his thoughts, his feelings about the painting almost exactly. He hadn't expected she'd see what he did, much less understand it.

He hadn't expected to be fascinated by her. A woman with gypsy eyes who pulled out a hefty multi-tool like another might a tube of lipstick—and who used it just as casually. One who shared his own vision of an unfinished painting and offered comfort to a stranger.

A woman who wrote about teenage werewolves and had no place of her own—by choice.

Maybe she was right, maybe he didn't quite have her number.

But he would, once he painted her.

Thinking of that, of her, he set up another easel and began to prep a canvas.

❧❧❧

Lila stood outside Ash's loft, studying it in the bright light of day. It looked ordinary, she thought. Just an old brick building a few steps above street level. Anyone passing it might think, as she had, that it held maybe a half dozen apartments.

Nice ones, you might think, snapped up by young professionals after the downtown flavor.

In reality, it was nothing of the kind. In reality, he'd created a home that reflected exactly who and what he was. An artist, a family man. One who combined those two parts, and could create the room to seamlessly accommodate both exactly as he wished.

That, to her mind, took a clear eye and considerable self-awareness. Ashton Archer, she thought, knew exactly who he was and what he wanted.

And for reasons that made no sense whatsoever, he wanted to paint her.

She walked up, pressed the buzzer.

He was probably home. Didn't he have to work? She should be working, but she just couldn't focus. Now she was very likely interrupting his work, and really, she could've just sent him a text to—

"What?"

She literally jumped at the terse syllable— a very clear accusation—snapping through the speaker.

"Sorry. It's Lila. I just wanted to—"

"I'm in the studio."

"Oh, well, I—"

Something buzzed, something clicked. Carefully, she tried the tongue knob on the big door. When it opened, she assumed it equaled invitation.

Carefully she stepped in, closed the door behind her. Something clicked again, definitely. She started toward the stairs, turned and walked to the big grate of the elevator.

Who wouldn't want to ride in it? she asked herself. Stepping in, she dragged the gate closed, then punched three, and grinned as it groaned and creaked its way up.

She could see him through the grating when the elevator clunked to a stop. At an easel, sketching on a canvas.

No, not a canvas, she saw as she muscled the grate open. A really big sketch pad.

"I had to go out. I've got errands to run. I brought coffee. And a muffin."

"Good." He didn't spare her a glance. "Put it down, stand over there. Right there."

"I went to the police. I wanted to tell you."

"Stand over there and tell me. No, put this down."

He came over, snatched the takeout bag out of her hand, set it on a crowded worktable, then just pulled her over in front of the wide ribbon of windows. "Angle this way, but look at me."

"I didn't come to pose—and besides, you said tomorrow for that."

"Today's good. Just look at me."

"I didn't say I'd pose for you. In fact, I'm not really comfortable—"

He made a shushing sound—as terse as his greeting through the intercom. "Be quiet a minute. It's not right," he said, long before the minute was up.

Relief sighed through her. She'd felt, even for that half minute, like a pinned butterfly. "I told you I wouldn't be any good at it."

"No, you're fine. It's the mood." He tossed down his pencil, narrowed his eyes at her. Her heart beat a little faster; her throat went dry.

Then he shoved his hands at his hair. "What kind of muffin?"

"Oh, ah, it's French apple. It sounded fabulous. I went by Luke's bakery on the way back from the police. Then I thought I should just come by here and tell you."

"Fine. Tell me." He rooted through the bag, came out with two coffees and the oversized muffin.

When he bit into the muffin, she frowned.

"It's a really big muffin. I thought we'd share."

He took another bite. "I don't think so. Police?"

"I went there, and I caught Fine and Waterstone just as they were leaving. But they held up so I could tell them about your theory, then about the perfume here."

Watching her—too much, as he had been with the pencil in his hand—he gulped down coffee.

"And they said they'd look into it in a way that made it pretty clear they thought you were wasting their time."

"They were polite about it. It ticked me off. Why doesn't it tick you off?"

"Because I see their point. Even if they believed it, which is low on the scale, what does it give them to go on? Nothing. I've got nothing, you've got nothing. Whoever broke in here, and into Julie's, has probably figured that out by now. Whatever Oliver and his girlfriend were involved in, we're not. I'm going to ask the relatives, see if he told anybody what he was up to. But that's unlikely, not if it was illegal or sketchy, and it was probably both."

"I'm sorry."

"Nothing to be sorry about. Maybe he bragged about whatever it was—bits and pieces to this sib or that sib. I might be able to piece something together."

He broke what was left of the muffin in half, offered it.

"Gee, thanks."

"It's good. You should've gotten two." He grabbed the coffee before he crossed the studio, then yanked open double doors.

"Oh, my God! It's the costume department!" Delighted, Lila hurried over. "Look at all this. Dresses, scarves, baubles. And really, really skimpy lingerie. I did theater in high school—well, briefly because my father got transferred, but the costumes were the most fun."

"None of these are right, but this is close

enough for now." He pulled out a soft blue sundress. "Wrong color, wrong length but the shape's close from the waist up. Put it on, take off your shoes."

"I'm not putting it on." But she touched the skirt—the soft, fluid skirt. "It's really pretty."

"Wear it for an hour, give me an hour, and it's yours."

"You can't bribe me with a . . . it's Prada."

"It's yours for one hour."

"I have errands, and Thomas—"

"I'll help you with the damn errands. I have to pick up my mail anyway. I haven't picked it up in days. And Thomas is a cat. He'll be fine."

"He's a cat who likes a pal around."

Prada, she thought, touching the skirt again. She'd bought a pair of black Prada pumps, convincing herself they were serviceable. And on sale. In fact she'd fought a vicious war at Saks's annual shoe sale on the eighth floor to win them.

Labels don't matter, she reminded herself, while a sly little voice whispered, Prada.

"And why do you have to pick up your mail?" She asked as much to distract herself from Prada as innate curiosity. "Don't they just bring it?"

"No. I keep a box. One hour, and I'll run the stupid errands for you."

"Great." She beamed out a smile, tiny dimple winking. "I need several items in the personal female hygiene department. I'll give you the list."

He simply aimed an amused look out of those sharp green eyes. "I have sisters, a mother, a small bevy of stepmothers along with countless aunts and female cousins. Do you think that bothers me?"

"An hour," she said, defeated. "And I keep the dress."

"Deal. You can change in there. And take your hair out of that thing. I want it down."

Following his direction, she went into a roomy bathroom, white and black like his kitchen, but with a triple mirror. The sort that made her want to shed a few tears in every department store dressing room.

She changed into the soft blue dress. Reveled for just a moment in not only wearing it—she'd tried designer labels on before, for fun—but in knowing it could be hers.

A little big in the bust, she thought—big

surprise—but not a bad fit. And she could have it altered. As she wanted the damn dress, she slipped out of her sandals, pulled the band out of her hair.

When she stepped out again, he stood at the window, looking out.

"I don't have any makeup with me," she began.

"You don't need it for this. Just some preliminary work."

He turned, studied her. "The color's not bad on you, but you're better in bolder. Over here."

"You're bossy when you put the artist on." She walked by the easel, stopped. There was her face, over and over from different angles, with different expressions.

"It's all me. It's odd." And made her feel exposed again. "Why don't you use the mermaid girl for this? She's so beautiful."

"There are all sorts of beauty. I want your hair . . ." He simply pushed her over from the waist, scrubbed his hands through it, then pulled her back up. "Toss it," he ordered.

And when she did, her eyes flashed—not anger, but pure female amusement.

"That." He took her chin, angled her

head up. "Just exactly that. You know so much more than I do, than any man can. I can watch you in the moonlight, in the starlight, in the firelight, but I'll never know what you know, what you think. They think they can have you, the men who watch the dance. But they can't, not until or unless you choose. You belong to no one until you choose. That's your power."

He stepped back to the easel. "Chin up, head back. Eyes on me."

There went her heart again, and her throat. And this time she actually felt her legs go a little weak.

How did he do it?

"Do all the women you paint fall in love with you?"

"Some fall into hate. Or at least intense dislike." He tossed aside the page of sketches, began a new one.

"And that doesn't really matter to you, because you get what you're after, and it's not really them."

"Of course it's them, some part of them. Look at me. Why young adult novels?"

"Because it's fun. There's so much drama during the teenage years. All the longing, the discovery, the terrible need to belong to something, the terrible fear of not being like everyone else. Add werewolves, and it's an allegory, and more fun."

"Werewolves always bring the fun. My sister Rylee really liked your first book."

"She did?"

"Kaylee rules and Aiden's hot, but she's especially fond of Mel."

"Aw, that's nice. Mel's the best pal of the central character and a very awkward nerd."

"Makes sense, as she's a nerd herself, and always roots for the underdog. I promised her I'd get the second book for her, have you sign it."

Pleasure bloomed inside her. "I have some advance copies coming in about a month. I'll sign one for her, get it to you."

"Great. I'll be her favorite brother."

"I bet you are anyway. You listen, and even when things are bad, you give her something happy."

"Twirl around."

"What?"

He circled a finger in the air while he sketched. "No, no, twirl around." This time he whipped his finger.

She felt silly, but did a quick spin.

"Again, arms up, have some fun with it." Next time he'd put music on to distract her, keep her relaxed. "Better, hold it there, keep your arms up. Was your father stationed overseas?"

"A couple of times. Germany, but I was just a baby and don't remember. Italy, and that was nice."

"Iraq?"

"Yeah, and that wasn't nice. He was deployed out of Fort Lee in Virginia, so we stayed there."

"Tough."

"The army life's not for weenies."

"And now?"

"I try not to be a weenie. But you meant what's he doing now. He retired, and they moved to Alaska. They love it. They bought a little general store, and eat moose burgers."

"Okay, relax. Toss your hair one more time. Do you get up there?"

"To Juneau? A couple of times. I wrangled a job in Vancouver, then went to Juneau after, then got one in Missoula, did the same. Have you been there?"

"Yeah, it's staggering."

"It is." She brought it into her mind. "Like

another world, literally. Like a new planet. Not the ice planet Hoth, but close."

"The what?"

"Hoth, the ice planet. Star Wars—**The Empire Strikes Back**."

"Okay. Right."

Obviously a casual Star Wars fan at best, Lila decided, so shifted the topic back. "What did you paint in Alaska?"

"Some landscapes because you'd be crazy not to. One of an Inuit woman as an ice queen—probably ruling the ice planet Hoth," he added, and had her grin flashing.

"Why women, especially? You paint other things, but it's mostly women, and fanciful, whether benign like the violin-playing witch in the moonlit meadow, or the man-eating mermaid."

His eyes changed—from intense, looking straight into her, to calmer, more curious. "Why do you assume the woman in the meadow is a witch?"

"Because power, and her pleasure in it as much as the music, is right there. Or it's just how I saw it—and why, I guess, I wanted it."

"You're right. She's caught in a moment of embrace—her music, her magic. If I still had it, I'd make you a deal because you understood that. But then, where would you put it?"

"There is that little hitch," she agreed. "But again, why women most often?"

"Because they're powerful. Life comes from them, and that's its own magic. That's good for now." As his gaze hung on her, he tossed his pencil aside. "I need to find the right dress, something with movement."

Because she wasn't sure he'd say yes, she didn't ask if she could see what he'd done, but just walked over and looked.

So many angles, she thought, of her face, and of her body now.

"Problem?" he asked.

"It's like the triple mirrors in dressing rooms." She wiggled her shoulders. "You see too much."

He'd see more when he talked her into a nude, but one step at a time.

"So." He picked up the coffee again. "Errands."

"You don't have to help me run errands. I got a new dress."

"I have to get my mail anyway." He glanced around the studio. "And I need to get out of here. You probably need your shoes."

"Yes, I do. Give me a minute."

Alone, he pulled out his phone, turned it back on. Seeing over a dozen v-mails, e-mails and texts gave him an instant headache.

Yeah, he needed to get out.

Still he took the time to answer a few, in order of priority, stopped, stuck the phone away again when she came back out, wearing the cropped pants and top she'd worn in. "I just folded the dress up in my bag, in case you decided I couldn't keep it after all."

"It's not my dress."

"It's definitely too short for you, but—Oh." Instant distress. "It belongs to someone. Let me put it back."

"No, I said keep it. Chloe left it here—or maybe it was Cora—months ago. She, whichever one it was, knows the rules."

"There are rules?"

"Leave stuff here," he began as he herded Lila to the elevator, "for more than two months, it goes into wardrobe or the trash. Otherwise, I'd have their stuff scattered everywhere."

"Strict but fair. Cora. Sister? Model? Girlfriend?"

"Half sister, father's side." And since one of the messages had been from Cora, his thoughts circled back to Oliver yet again.

"They're releasing the body tomorrow."

She touched his hand as he pulled the grate open on the main level. "That's a good thing. It means you can have the memorial soon, say goodbye."

"It means an emotional circus, but you can't get out the push brooms until the elephants dance."

"I think I understand that," she said after a moment, "and it wasn't flattering to your family."

"I'm a little tired of my family right now." He grabbed keys, sunglasses, a small cloth bag. "Put this in your purse, will you? For the mail."

She couldn't imagine needing a bag for mail, but obliged.

He stuck the keys in his pocket, shoved the sunglasses on.

"It's a tiring time," she commented.

"You have no idea." He led her outside. "You should. You should come to the funeral."

"Oh, I don't think—"

"Definitely. You'll be a distraction, plus you keep your head in a crisis. There'll be several crises. I'll send a driver for you. Ten o'clock should work."

"I didn't know him."

"You're connected, and you know me. Luke will ride up with you. Sunday. Is Sunday a problem?"

Lie, she ordered herself, but knew she wouldn't. "Actually it's my interim day—between the Kilderbrands and the Lowensteins, but—"

"Then it works." He took her arm, steered her east instead of south.

"I was going down a block."

"One stop first. There." He gestured to a funky women's boutique.

Waiting for the walk signal, the rumbling mass of a huge delivery truck, the gaggle of what she knew to be tourists given the tone of their chatter, gave her a minute to catch her breath.

"Ashton, won't your family consider the nosy temporary neighbor an intrusion at your brother's funeral?"

"Lila, I have twelve siblings, many of whom have spouses, and ex-spouses, kids, stepchildren. I have assorted aunts, uncles and grandparents. Nothing's an intrusion."

He towed her across the street, around a woman with a wailing infant in a stroller, and into the shop, one with color and style. And, she imagined, really big price tags.

"Jess."

"Ash." The willowy blonde in a black-and-white mini and towering red sandals scooted around a counter to offer her cheek to Ash. "It's good to see you."

"I've got a few stops to make, thought I'd check to see if you found anything."

"I went to work as soon as you called. I've got a couple things that might work. Is this your model? I'm Jess."

"Lila."

"You're right about the red," she said to Ash. "And I think I know which is going to work. Come on back."

She led the way into a breathlessly cramped storeroom, then took two full-skirted red dresses off a wheeled rack.

"Not that. That."

"Exactly."

Before Lila had a chance to really see

both, Jess stuffed one back on the rack, held out the other.

Ash spread the flounced skirt out wide, nodded. "It should work, but I need the color under it."

"Got that covered. I came across this at a consignment shop weeks ago and picked it up thinking you might find it useful at some point. It's perfect for this, I think. Rather than the bulk of several slips or underskirts, this has the multicolor flounces on the bottom. And if it's not right, you could get a seamstress to make one."

"Yeah, let's see." He took both, pushed them at Lila. "Try them on."

"I'm the one with errands," she reminded him.

"We'll get to them."

"Let me show you a dressing room. Would you like something?" Jess said smoothly, as she nudged Lila out of the storeroom, around and into a dressing room with the damn triple mirror. "Some sparkling water?"

"Why not? Thanks."

Once again, she changed. The slip bagged at the waist so she dug a paper clip out of her purse to tighten it.

And the dress fit like a dream.

Not her style, of course. Too red, too in-your-face with the low scoop of bodice. But the dropped waist made her look taller, and she wouldn't argue with that.

"Are you in that thing?"

"Yes. I just . . . Well, come right in," she said when Ash did just that.

"Yeah, that's it." He circled his finger again. She rolled her eyes, but did the twirl. "Close. We'll need to . . ." He reached down, hiked a section of the skirt up.

"Hey."

"Relax. Ride this up here, show more leg, more color."

"The slip's too big in the waist. I clipped it."

"Jess."

"No problem, and she's going to want a better bra. Ummm, 32-A?"

Mortifyingly accurate, Lila thought. "Yes."

"Hold on." She scooted out.

Struggling to find her balance again, Lila sipped sparkling water while Ash studied her.

"Go away."

"In a minute. Gold hoop earrings, a lot of—" He ran his fingers up and down her wrist.

"Bangles?"

"Yeah."

"Excuse us a minute." Jess came back in with a flame-red bra, nudging Ash out. "He'd stay right there otherwise," she said with a smile. "If you'd try this on, I can measure the slip."

With a sigh, Lila set down the water and tried not to think she was stripping to the waist in front of a stranger.

Fifteen minutes later, they walked out with the dress, the bra—and the matching panties she'd agreed to in a moment of weakness.

"How did this happen? All I did was look out the window."

"Physics?" he suggested.

"Action and reaction?" She blew out a breath. "I guess I can blame it on science, then."

"What are the errands?"

"I'm not sure I remember."

"Think about it. We'll hit the post office while you do."

"Post office." She shook her head. "You bought me underwear."

"It's wardrobe."

"It's underwear. It's red underwear. I

didn't even know you, what, just over a week ago, and now you've bought me red underwear. Did you even **look** at the price tags?"

"You said you weren't marrying me for my money."

That made her laugh, and she remembered. "A cat toy. I want a toy for Thomas."

"I thought he had toys."

A man in an ankle-length trench coat stomped by, muttering obscenities. He left an amazing stream of body odor in his wake.

"I love New York," she said, watching pedestrians dodge and evade his angry path. "I really do."

"He lives around here somewhere," Ash told her. "I see him—or at least smell him—a couple times a week. He never takes off that coat."

"Hence the smell. It's forecast to hit ninety-three today, and I'd say we're already there. And yes, Thomas has toys, but this is a present for when I leave. And I need to pick up a bottle of wine for the Kilderbrands. I'll get flowers on Saturday."

"You're leaving them a bottle of wine and flowers?"

"Yes, it's polite. One of your many mothers should have taught you that." She breathed in the scent of sidewalk cart hot dogs—much more pleasant than Trench Coat Man. "Why am I going to the post office with you?"

"Because it's right here." Taking her hand, he drew her inside, then over to the wall of boxes. He dug out his key, opened one, said, "Shit."

"It's pretty full," she observed.

"It's been a few days. Maybe a week. Mostly junk. Why do people kill trees for junk mail?"

"At last, a point of absolute agreement."

He riffled through, tossed a couple of things in the cloth bag Lila handed him, dug out a padded envelope.

And stopped everything.

"What is it?"

"It's from Oliver."

"Oh." She stared at it, at the big looping scrawl, as Ash did. "It's postmarked . . ."

"The day he was murdered." Ash dumped the contents of the box in the mail bag, then ripped open the envelope.

He drew out a key and a handwritten note on a monogrammed card.

Hey, Ash.

I'll be in touch in a day or two to pick this up. Just sending it to you for safekeeping while I put the rest of a deal together. The client's a little touchy, so if I have to leave town for a couple days, I'll let you know. You could pick up the merchandise, bring it to me at the compound. I went with the Wells Fargo near my place. And since I forged your signature on the card—just like the old days!—you won't have a problem getting into the box. Appreciate it, bro.

Talk soon. Oliver.

"Son of a bitch."

"What merchandise? What client?"

"I guess I'm going to find out."

"We," she corrected. "I'm in this far," she added when he lifted his gaze to meet hers.

"All right." He slid the note into the bag, slipped the key into his pocket. "Let's go to the bank."

"This could be the why." She trotted to keep up with his long strides. "Shouldn't you take the key to the police?"

"He sent it to me."

She grabbed his hand to slow him down. "What did he mean, forging your signature like the old days?"

"Kid stuff mostly. School papers, that sort of thing. Mostly."

"But you weren't his legal guardian, were you?"

"No. Not exactly. It's complicated."

Not his guardian, Lila deduced. But the one he counted on.

"He knew he was in trouble," Ash continued, "but then he was in trouble half the time. Touchy client, which means pissed-off client. Whatever he had he didn't want it on him or in his apartment. So he put it in a vault, sent me the key."

"Because he knew you'd keep it for him."

"I'd've tossed the envelope in a drawer, and I'd've been annoyed enough to toss it at him when he came for it and tell him I didn't want to hear about it. He'd know that, so that's just why he did it. Because he not only wouldn't have to explain to me, I wouldn't let him explain."

"That doesn't make it your fault."

"No, it doesn't. Where the hell's the bank?"

"We turn left at the next corner. They won't let me go with you to open the box. You have to be authorized."

"Right." Thinking it through, he slowed for a moment. "I'll get whatever it is, I guess we'll take it over to your place. For now. I'm going into the bank, get this done. You go into one of the shops, buy something. Look at me."

He stopped her, turned her, moved in just a little. "It's possible somebody's keeping tabs on us—or one of us. So let's make this casual. Running errands."

"That was the plan of the day."

"Stick with the plan. Buy something, and when I finish in the bank, we'll walk to the apartment. A nice easy stroll."

"You really think someone's watching us?"

"It's a possibility. So." He leaned farther in, brushed his lips lightly over hers. "Because I bought you red underwear," he reminded her. "Go buy something."

"I . . . I'm going to the little market, just there."

"Poke around until I come for you."

"Okay."

It was all like some strange little dream

anyway, she told herself as she walked toward the market. Posing for a painting, red underwear, notes from dead brothers, being kissed on the sidewalk because someone might be watching.

So she might as well buy the wine, and see where the strange little dream took her next.

Eight

It didn't take long. Ash often thought Oliver could have made a living as a forger. The signatures matched—as would Oliver's version of their father's signature or countless others. The key worked, and once the bank official used her own, removed the box, stepped out, Ash stood alone in the private room staring at the box.

Whatever was in it had cost Oliver and the woman he might have loved, at least in his way, their lives. Whatever was in it had brought a killer into his home, and into the home of a friend.

Ash was sure of it.

He opened the box.

He glanced at the stacks of banded hundreds, crisp as new lettuce, at the thick manila envelope. And the box within the box carefully snuggled between. The deeply embossed rich brown leather case with gold hinges.

He opened it.

And stared at the glitter and shine, the opulence tucked perfectly into the thickly padded interior.

For this? he thought. To die for this?

Ash took out the envelope, slipped the documents out, read what he could. He thought again, For this? Pushing back the anger, he closed and fastened the box again. He took the tissue-wrapped purchases out of the shopping bag, laid the box inside, tucked the excess tissue over it, wedged the dress in the mail bag. He shoved the envelope, the money, in the shopping bag, making sure the tissue covered it. Hefting both bags, he left the empty safe-deposit box on the table.

He needed a computer.

❦

Lila poked around as long as seemed reasonable. She bought wine, two large and lovely peaches, a little wedge of Port Salut cheese. To string it out, she debated over olives as though they were her most important purchase of the day. Perhaps the year.

In the end, she filled her little basket with odds and ends. At the counter, she winced at what the poking cost her, made sure to smile at the counterman, then kept the smile going as she turned, glanced at the striking Asian woman in emerald-green sandals with high, glittery wedges.

"I love your shoes." She said it casually as she lifted her shopping bag, exactly as she might have under any circumstances.

"Thank you." The woman skimmed her exotic gaze down to Lila's pretty multicolored but seen-many-miles flat sandals. "Yours are very nice."

"For walking, but not for styling." Pleased with herself, Lila wandered out, strolled back toward the bank.

Boring shoes, Jai decided, for a boring life. But just what was the brother doing in the bank for so long? It might pay to watch a bit longer, and since the pay was good and New York appealed to her, she'd watch.

Ash came out of the bank just as Lila debated with herself whether to go in or just wait.

"I couldn't shop anymore," she began.

"It's fine. Let's just go."

"What was in the box?"

"We'll talk about it when we're inside."

"Give me a hint," she insisted, again lengthening her strides to keep up. "Blood diamonds, dinosaur bones, gold doubloons, a map with the location of Atlantis—because it's down there somewhere."

"No."

"It is too," she insisted. "Oceans cover most of the planet, so—"

"I mean none of those were in the bank box. I need to check some things on your computer."

"Nuclear launch codes, the secret to immortality, the cure for male pattern baldness."

That distracted him enough to have him look down at her. "Really?"

"I'm grabbing out of the ether. Wait, he

worked in antiquities. Michelangelo's favorite chisel, Excalibur, Marie Antoinette's tiara."

"You're getting closer."

"I am? Which? Hi, Ethan, how are you today?"

It took Ash a beat to realize she was speaking to the doorman.

"Oh, getting there, Ms. Emerson. Did some shopping?"

"New dress." She beamed at him.

"You enjoy it. We're going to miss you around here."

Ethan opened the door, exchanged nods with Ash.

"He's worked here eleven years," Lila told Ash as they walked to the elevator. "And knows everything about everyone. But he's very discreet. How would anyone know it was Michelangelo's favorite chisel?"

"I have no idea. I'm having a hard enough time following the maze of your brain."

"You're upset." She rubbed a hand up and down his arm. "I can see it. Is it bad? What you found?"

"He died for it. That's bad enough."

No more trying to lighten the mood, she ordered herself, even if it helped calm her own nerves. She took out her keys as the elevator opened, said nothing more as they walked to the apartment door.

She took a moment for Thomas, who rushed over to greet her as if she'd been gone for weeks. "I know, I know, I was longer than I thought. But I'm back now. They should get a kitten for him," she said as she carried her bag to the kitchen. "He hates being alone."

To make it up to Thomas, she dug out the cat treats, cooed to him as she offered them. "Can you tell me now?"

"I'll show you."

In the dining room, he set the bag on the table, took out the tissue, set it aside. Then took out the leather box.

"It's beautiful," she murmured. "Special. That means what's inside is beautiful and special."

She held her breath while Ash lifted the lid. "Oh! It is beautiful. Old—anything that ornate must be. Is that gold—real gold, I mean? All that gold. And are those real diamonds? A sapphire?"

"We'll find out. I need your computer."

"Go ahead." She waved a hand toward it. "Can I take it out?"

"Yeah, take it out." While she did, Ash keyed **angel chariot egg** into a search.

"The workmanship's incredible." She lifted it out, held it up as she might a small bomb—with intense care. "It's so ornate, even a little gaudy to my eye, but beautiful— exquisite when you look at the craftsman- ship. The gold angel pulls the gold wagon, and the wagon holds the egg. And the egg—God, look at the sparkle. Those have to be real jewels, don't they? If they are . . ."

It struck her all at once. "Is it Fabergé? Didn't he—they—I don't know much about it—they're the Russian egg designers. I never realized they were so elaborate—so much more than a fancy egg."

"Fabergé's he **and** they," Ash said ab- sently, as he braced his hands on the table on either side of the laptop and read.

"People collect them, right? Or they're in museums. The old ones, anyway. This must be worth thousands—hundreds of thousands, I guess."

"More."

"A million?"

He shook his head, continued to read.

"Come on, who'd pay over a million for

an egg—even one like this? It's— Oh, it opens, there's a . . . Ash, look!"

Her how-things-work sensibility simply danced in delight. "There's a little clock inside the egg. An angel clock! It's fabulous. Now, **that's** fabulous. Okay, I'll go for a million considering the clock."

"A surprise. They call what's inside the egg the surprise."

"It's a really great one. I just want to play with it." Her fingers actually tingled at the thought of figuring out how it had been made. "Which I'm not, considering if it's real it could be worth a million."

"Probably twenty times that."

"What?" Instantly, she whipped her hands behind her back.

"Easily. Gold egg with clock," he read, "decorated with brilliants and a sapphire, in a gold two-wheeled wagon pulled by a gold cherub. It was made under the supervision of Peter Carl Fabergé for Tsar Alexander the Third in 1888. One of the Imperial eggs. One of the eight lost Imperial eggs."

"Lost?"

"According to what I'm reading, there were approximately fifty Imperial eggs, made by Fabergé for the tsars—Alexander and Nicholas. Forty-two are known to be in museums or held in private collections. Eight are missing. The Cherub with Chariot is one of the eight."

"If this is authentic . . ."

"That's the first thing we have to verify." He tapped the manila envelope. "There are documents in there—some in what must be Russian. But again, what I read verifies this as one of the Imperial eggs. Unless both it and the documents are forgeries."

"It's too exquisite to be a forgery. If anyone had this talent, could take all this time, why forge? And people do just that," she said before Ash could. "I just don't understand it."

She sat, leaned down until she was eye level with the egg. "If it's a forgery, whoever agreed to buy it would have it tested. I know it's possible for a really exceptional forgery to pass those tests, but it's just unlikely. If it's real . . . Did you really mean twenty million dollars?"

"Probably more, from what I'm reading. It's easy enough to find out."

"How?"

"Oliver's uncle—his boss. Owner and proprietor of Old World Antiques. If Vinnie doesn't know, he'd know people who do."

It sat sparkling, reflecting an era of opulence. Not just great art, Lila thought, but history. "Ash, you need to take it to a museum."

"What, walk into the Met, say, 'Hey, look what I found'?"

"The police."

"Not yet. I want some answers, and they're not going to give them to me. Oliver had this—I need to know how he got it. Was it a deal? Did he steal it or acquire it?"

"You think he might've stolen it?"

"Not breaking-into-a-house stealing." He raked his fingers through his hair. "But cheat someone out of it? Lie? Manipulate? He'd do all of that. He said he had a client. Did he get this from the client, or was he to deliver it to the client?"

"Did you read all the documents in here? Maybe there's a bill of sale, some sort of receipt."

"Nothing like that—but I haven't gone through all his papers from the apartment. He had about six hundred thousand, in cash, in the box."

"**Hundred** thousand?"

"Give or take," Ash said so absently Lila just goggled.

"For Oliver to hold on to that much means he didn't have it very long, and had plans. He probably meant he didn't want to, or couldn't, report the money. Maybe he was paid to acquire this, then figured it wasn't enough and tried to squeeze the client for a bigger fee."

"If it's worth as much as you think, why not pay more? Why kill two people?"

He didn't bother to point out people killed for pocket change. Or simply because they wanted to kill.

"Maybe they planned to kill him all along, or maybe he just pissed off the wrong client. What I know is I need to have this authenticated. I need to find out where Oliver got it, and who wanted it."

"And then?"

Those green eyes went sharp as a blade. "Then they pay for killing my brother and pushing a woman out the window."

"Because when you find out what you need to find out, you'll go to the police."

He hesitated a beat because fury made him imagine, and revel in that image, exacting payment himself. But he looked into Lila's eyes, knew he couldn't—and she'd think less of him if he could.

It surprised him how much that mattered.

"Yeah, I'll go to the cops."

"Okay. I'm going to fix some lunch."

"You're going to fix lunch?"

"Because we need to think, and we need to eat." She lifted the egg, set it carefully in its padded form. "You're doing this because you loved him. He was a pain in your ass, sometimes an embarrassment, often a disappointment, but you loved him, so you're going to do what you can to find out why this happened."

She looked over at him now. "You're grieving, and there's a violence in the grief. It's not wrong to feel that." To reach that grief, she laid a hand over his. "It's natural to feel that, even to want to punish whoever did this yourself. But you won't. You have too much honor for that. So I'm going to help you, starting with lunch."

She walked into the kitchen, dug into the groceries she'd yet to put away.

"Why aren't you telling me to get out, get away, stay away?"

"Why would I do that?"

"Because I brought into your house—"

"Not mine."

"Into your work," he corrected, "an object potentially worth millions which was certainly obtained by unethical means, if not illegal ones. Whatever my brother was involved with prompted someone to break into your friend's apartment—looking for you or information about you, and it's likely that as long as you associate with me that person, probably a murderer, is keeping tabs on you."

"You forgot the tragic loss of my friend's shoes."

"Lila—"

"They shouldn't be discounted," she said as she put a small pot on to boil pasta. A quick pasta salad seemed like just the thing. "And the answer to all that is, you're not your brother."

"That's the answer."

"The first part," she qualified. "Maybe I'd have liked him. I think maybe I would have. I think, too, he'd have frustrated me because it seems like he wasted so much potential, so many opportunities. You don't, and that's another part of the answer. You

don't waste anything, and that's important to me—not wasting things, or time, or
people, or opportunity. You're going to stand
up for him, even though you believe he
did something not just stupid, not just dangerous, but wrong. But you'll stand up for
him anyway. Loyalty. Love, respect, trust?
All essential, but none of them hold strong
without loyalty—and that's the rest of it."

She looked at him, dark eyes open, so
full of feeling. "Why would I tell you to go?"

"Because you didn't know him, and all
this complicates your life."

"I know you, and complications **are** life.
Besides, if I kick you out, you won't paint
me."

"You don't want me to paint you."

"I didn't. I'm still not sure I do, but now
I'm curious."

"I already have a second painting in
mind."

"See, nothing wasted. What's this one?"

"You, lying in a bower, lush, green, at
sunset. Just waking up, your hair spilling
everywhere."

"I wake up at sunset?"

"Like a faerie might, before the night's
work."

"I'd be a faerie." Her face lit up at the thought. "I like it. What's the wardrobe?"

"Emeralds."

She stopped stirring the pasta she'd just added to the boiling water to stare at him. "Emeralds?"

"Emeralds, like drops of a magic sea, looped between your breasts, dripping from your ears. I was going to wait awhile before telling you about that one, but now I figure it's cards on the table while you still have time to change your mind."

"I can change my mind anytime."

He smiled, stepped closer. "I don't think so. Now's the time to cut and run."

"I'm not running. I'm making lunch."

He took the pasta fork from her, gave the pot a quick stir. "Now or never."

She took a step back. "I need the colander."

He closed a hand around her arm, pulled her back. "Now."

It wasn't like on the sidewalk—that light and casual brush of lips. It was a long, luscious, lingering possession with electric jolts of demand, shocking the system even as it seduced.

Had her legs gone weak in his studio

when he'd looked at her? Now they simply dissolved, left her uprooted, untethered.

It was hold on or fall away.

She held on.

He'd seen it in her, the first time he'd looked in her eyes. Even through his shock, even through the layers of raw grief, he'd seen this. Her power to give. That glow inside her she could offer or withhold. He took it now, that dark, dreamy center inside the light, and let it cloak over him like life.

"You'll look like this," he murmured, watching her eyes again. "When you wake in the bower. Because you know what you can do in the dark."

"Is that why you kissed me? For the painting?"

"Is this—knowing this was here—the reason you didn't tell me to go?"

"Maybe it's one of them. Not the main one, but one of them."

He brushed her hair back behind her shoulders. "Exactly."

"I need to . . ." She eased away, stepped back to take the pot off the heat before it boiled over. "Do you sleep with all the women you paint?"

"No. There's intimacy in the work, and

usually sexuality in the work. But it's work. I wanted to paint you when you sat across from me at that coffee shop. I wanted to sleep with you . . . You hugged me. The first time I came here, you hugged me before I left. It wasn't the physical contact—I'm not that easy."

He caught the quick smile as she dumped the pasta in the colander.

"It was the generosity of it, the simplicity. I wanted that, and wanted you. Maybe that was for comfort. This isn't."

No, not comfort, she thought. For either of them. "I've always been attracted to strong men. To complicated men. And it's always ended badly."

"Why?"

"Why badly?" She lifted a shoulder as she turned the pasta in a bowl. "They'd get tired of me." She tossed in the pretty little tomatoes, some glossy black olives, chopped a couple of leaves of fresh basil, added some rosemary, pepper. "I'm not exciting, not especially willing to stay home and, well, cook and keep the home fires burning or go out and party every night. A little of both is just fine, but it always seemed not enough of one or too much of the other.

"It's lunch. I'm going to cheat and use bottled dressing."

"Why is that cheating?"

"Forget I mentioned it."

"I'm not looking for a cook or a fire tender, or nightly parties. And right at the moment? You're the most exciting woman I know."

Exciting? No one, herself included, had ever considered her exciting. "It's the situation. Intense situations breed excitement—anxiety, too. Probably ulcers, though they pooh-pooh that now. Still, it would be a shame to waste the excitement and intensity."

After tossing the salad, she opened the bread drawer. "I've got one left." She held up a sourdough roll. "We share."

"Deal."

"I'm going to ask you for another deal. A little breathing space to think this through before the plunge. Because I'm usually a plunger, and usually end up going in too deep. Add the situation, because we have one. Your brother, that spectacular egg and what to do about both. So, I'd like to try inching instead of plunging."

"How far in are you now?"

"I was already past my knees when you started sketching me. About hip-deep now."

"Okay." Her response—fresh, simple, straightforward—struck him as sexier than black silk. He needed to touch, settled for toying with the ends of her hair, pleased she'd left it down. "Do you want to eat this on the terrace? Leave the situation inside for a little?"

"That's an excellent idea. Let's do just that."

They couldn't leave it for long, she thought, because the situation had weight. But she appreciated the sun, the easy food and the puzzle of the man who wanted her.

Other men had, for short sprints, even for a lap or two. But she'd never experienced a marathon. Then again, her life was a series of short spurts. Any sort of permanence had eluded her for so long she'd decided the desire for it was self-defeating.

She believed she'd crafted her life

around the temporary in a very productive, interesting way.

She could do exactly the same in a relationship with Ash.

"If we'd met through Julie—maybe at a show of your work—all of this wouldn't be so strange. Then again, if we'd met that way, you might not be interested."

"You're wrong."

"That's nice to hear. Anyway, we didn't." She looked across to the window, still boarded up. "You've got a lot going on, Ash."

"More all the time. You didn't push me out when you had the chance, so you've got the same."

"I'm the queen of multitasking. In a couple of days, I'll have a view of the river, a little dog, orchids to tend and a personal gym that'll either intimidate me or inspire me to exercise. I'll still have a book to write, a blog, a present to buy for my mother's birthday—which I think is going to be one of those little lemon trees because how cool would it be to grow your own lemons inside in Alaska? And I'll still have what may be a stolen Imperial egg worth more than I can fathom to figure out, the low-grade anxiety that I may have a killer watching me and the puzzle of potentially really good sex with a man I met because he lost his brother.

"That takes some juggling," she decided. "So I'll try to be nimble."

"You forgot the painting."

"Because it intimidates me more than the personal gym or the sex."

"Sex doesn't intimidate you?"

"I'm a girl, Ashton. Getting naked in front of a guy for the first time is monumentally intimidating."

"I'll keep you distracted."

"That could be a plus." She drew a tiny heart in the condensation on her glass of lemon water. "What are we going to do about the egg?"

And so, he thought, the situation was back. "I'm going to show it to Oliver's uncle— the one he worked for. If Vinnie can't identify and verify, he'll know someone who can."

"That's a really good idea. Once he does . . . Because either way it's valuable. Either reasonably valuable given the craftsmanship or scary valuable. So once he does, what are you going to do with it?"

"I'm going to take it with me tomorrow,

to the compound. The security there rivals the U.S. Mint. It'll be safe while I deal with the rest."

"Deal with how?"

"I'm working that out. Vinnie's bound to know collectors—big collectors. Or again, know someone who does."

She had an excellent imagination, and put it to work trying to imagine someone with countless millions to indulge a hobby. She house-sat annually for a gay couple who collected antique doorknobs. And had house-sat over the winter for a twice-widowed woman who had a fascinating collection of erotic netsukes.

But multiple millions? She'd have to work harder to imagine that. She needed a picture, she decided, a face, a background, even a name to give her a boost.

"There has to be something about this client in his files, in his correspondence, somewhere."

"I'll go through it."

"I can help with that. I can," she said when he didn't respond. "Sometimes clients pay me an additional fee to organize their home offices or paperwork while they're away. In any case, she had to know.

Oliver's girlfriend, Sage, had to know about this. All those intense conversations," Lila continued, staring at the boarded-up window, remembering. "All the arguments, the excitement, anxiety. I took them as personal relationship stuff, but now . . . It had to be about the egg, the client, what he, or they, were trying to pull off."

"She knew some," Ash agreed, "but not enough. You said she was crying, pleading, terrified. I think if she'd known where Oliver stashed the egg, she'd have given it up."

"You're probably right. She knew what it was, what he planned, but maybe not where he kept it. So she couldn't tell, and he was out of it, so he couldn't. Whoever killed them made a mistake, drugging him that way, assuming the woman would be the easier mark, would tell once she was scared or hurt enough."

She rose, picked up dishes. "You've got things to do, people to see."

He stood with her, took the dishes out of her hands, set them down again. Then closed his hands around her arms. "He'd have told her it was to protect her. 'Listen, beautiful, what you don't know can't hurt you. I'm just looking out for you.' Part of him would've believed it."

"Then it was partly true."

"He didn't tell her because he didn't trust her, and because he didn't want her to have as much control as he did. His deal, his way. And she died for it."

"So did he, Ashton. Tell me this." She closed her hands around his arms in turn—contact for contact. "If he could have, would he have told, would he have given it to this client to save her?"

"Yes."

"Then let that be enough." She rose to her toes, pressed her lips to his. Then found herself caught against him, sinking again, heart quivering as he took her under.

"I could distract you now."

"No question about it. But."

He skimmed his hands down her arms. "But."

They went back in. She watched him set the leather box in the shopping bag, lay the tissue over it and the envelope, the money. "I need to leave tomorrow. There are some arrangements I have to finalize in person. Since I'm cornering you into the funeral, why don't you see if Julie will come on Sunday, if you'd be more comfortable."

"It might be awkward for her and Luke."

"They're grown-ups."

"A lot you know."

"Ask her. And text me the address where you're staying next so I'll have it. You said Upper East?"

"That's right. Tudor City."

He frowned. "That's a haul from my loft. I'll get a car service for you when we schedule sittings."

"Subways—you might have heard of them—run right through the city. So do cabs and buses. It's a miracle of mass transit."

"I'll get the car service. Do me a favor. Don't go out again."

"I wasn't planning on it, but—"

"Good." He picked up the bags, started for the door.

"You should take a cab or a car rather than walk with that thing in that stupid bag. You should take an armored car."

"My armored car's in the shop. I'll see you in a couple days. Call Julie. Stay in."

Pretty free with the orders, she thought as he left. And he had a smooth and clever way of making them seem like favors or just good sense.

"I ought to go run around the block a few times just for spite," she told Thomas. "But it's not worth it. Dishes, then book. And what the hell, I'll call Julie."

Nine

Ash chilled a tall glass. A brutally cold gin and tonic was Vinnie's favorite summer drink, and since he was about to impose in a big way, the least he could provide was the man's drink of choice.

Vinnie hadn't asked questions when Ash called. He'd just agreed to swing by after he closed the shop. Ash heard the sorrow in his voice, and the willingness to help, and knew he'd need to use both when he pulled Vinnie into the . . . situation.

He was a good man, Ash thought as he surfed the Internet for more information on the egg. Happily married for nearly forty years, a canny businessman with an unerring eye for value, father of three, besotted grandfather of six. Or it might be seven by now.

Have to check the spreadsheet.

He'd taken Oliver on, knowing full well he was taking on the unreliable and capricious in his sister's only son. But it had seemed to work. Everyone got along with Vinnie, that was true enough, but he expected—and received—good value from his employees.

Whenever Ash had asked, Vinnie always said Oliver was doing well, was coming into his own, had a knack for the business and a way with the clients.

His way with them, Ash thought now, might be the root of the problem.

He sat back a moment, studied the egg. Where had it been, he wondered, this exquisite and whimsical gift created for Russian royalty? Who'd gazed upon it, run their fingers over its details?

And who wanted it enough to kill for it?

He pushed away from the computer at the sound of the buzzer.

"Archer," he said into the intercom.

"Hey, Ash, it's Vinnie."

"Come on in." He released the locks, walked out of the sitting area and started down.

Vinnie stood, leather briefcase in hand, his exceptional suit a subtle gray chalk-striped paired with a crisp white shirt—despite the heat and the workday—and a precisely knotted Hermès tie in bold paisley.

His shoes carried a high gloss shine; his hair swept back in white wings from a tanned face set off with a neat, natty goatee.

He looked, Ash always thought, more like one of his well-heeled clients than the man who bargained with them.

He looked up as Ash came down. "Ash." His voice still carried the Jersey of his boyhood. "A terrible time." Setting his briefcase down, he embraced Ash in a hard bear hug. "How are you holding up?"

"There's a lot to do. It helps."

"Busy always does. What can I do? Olympia's coming in tonight, but she's going straight to the compound. She told me not to come until Sunday morning, but I think Angie and the kids will go up tomorrow."

"She and Angie have always been close."

"Like sisters," Vinnie agreed. "She'd rather have Angie than me—than Nigel, when it comes to it. There must be something we can do for you, once we get there."

"Can you talk her out of the bagpipes?"

He barked a short laugh. "Not in a hundred years. She's convinced Oliver would want them. Do the police know any more?"

"Not that they're telling me."

"Who would do such a thing? Sage—they seemed to suit each other. I think they might have been happy together. I can only think it had to be a jealous ex. That's what I told the police when they came to talk to me."

"Did she have one?"

"A woman like that, with her looks, her lifestyle? She must have. Oliver never mentioned anyone, but she must have. But he was happy, that's something we have to remember. The last few weeks, he was so energized. He talked about taking her on a trip. I think he planned to propose. He had that excited, anxious air about him a man gets when he's about to take a major step."

"I think he planned a major step. I have something I want you to look at. Upstairs."

"Of course."

Ash led the way to the elevator. "Did he say anything to you about a deal he was making, a special client?"

"Nothing out of the ordinary. He did some very good work the last few months. Very good work. He handled two estates, acquired some excellent pieces, some with specific clients in mind. He had a knack, the boy had a real knack for the business."

"So you've said. Let me fix you a drink."

"I wouldn't turn one down. It's been a hard few days. The shop . . . we're all shaken. Everyone enjoyed Oliver, and bless him, he enjoyed everyone. Even when he infuriated you, you had to love him. You know how he was."

"I do." Ash led Vinnie into the compact studio kitchen, took the chilled glass out of the cooler under the wet bar. "G and T, right?"

"You know it. You've got a wonderful place here, Ash. You know, when you bought it, I thought, For God's sake, why doesn't the boy convert it into apartments and make some money off that real estate? I can't help myself."

"Me, either." Ash mixed the drink, added

a twist of lime, then got himself a beer. "Live in a crowded, busy city—have plenty of quiet personal space. Best of both."

"You've got just that." Vinnie tapped his glass to the bottle. "I'm proud of you. Did you know Sage bought one of your paintings? Oliver mentioned it."

"I saw it when I got his things. Most of his things. Come in here, will you, and tell me what you think of this."

He turned away from the studio, went across a hallway and into what he'd outfitted as his office.

The egg stood on his desk.

Vinnie had an exceptional poker face. As he'd lost to him more than once, Ash had a reason to know. But now, Vinnie's face filled with the stunned delight of a rookie drawing four aces.

"My God. My God." Vinnie rushed toward it, dropped to his knees like a man paying homage.

But Ash saw after a moment's shock, Vinnie had simply gone down to eye level.

"Where did you get this? Ashton? Where did you get this?"

"What have I got?"

"You don't know?" Vinnie pushed himself

up, circled the egg, leaned down to study it so closely his nose all but brushed the gold. "This is either Fabergé's Cherub with Chariot egg or the most magnificent reproduction I've ever seen."

"Can you tell which?"

"Where did you get it?"

"From a safe-deposit box, Oliver's box. He sent me the key, and a note asking me to hold on to the key until he got in touch. He said he had a testy client to deal with, and a big deal in the works. I think he was in trouble, Vinnie. I think the trouble is sitting on my desk. I think what got him killed is sitting on my desk. Can you tell if it's real?"

Vinnie dropped into a chair, rubbed his hands over his face. "I should have known. I should have known. His energy, his excitement, the mix of anxiety. Not about the woman, but this. About this. I left my briefcase downstairs. I could use it."

"I'll get it. I'm sorry."

"For what?"

"For bringing you into this."

"He was mine, too, Ash. My sister's boy—her only boy. I taught him about things like this. About antiques, collections, their value. How to buy and sell them. Of course you called me."

"I'll get your briefcase."

He'd known he'd add to the grief, Ash thought. A price paid. But family called to family first. He didn't know another way.

When he came back with the briefcase, Vinnie was standing over the egg, hunched over it, his glasses perched on the edge of his nose.

"I'm always losing these things." He took the glasses off, set them aside. "I can't seem to keep a pair more than a month, if that. But I've had my jeweler's loupe for twenty years." He opened the briefcase.

He took out thin white cotton gloves, pulled them on. He switched on the desk lamp, examined the egg through the loupe, inch by inch. He handled it with the care of a surgeon, peering at tiny mechanisms, brilliant stones.

"I've acquired two eggs—not the Imperials, of course, but two lovely pieces circa 1900. I've been fortunate to see, even be permitted to examine, an Imperial egg owned by a private collector. This doesn't make me a leading expert."

"You're mine."

Vinnie smiled a little. "In my opinion—and that's opinion—this is Fabergé's Cherub with Chariot, one of the eight missing Imperial eggs. There's only one photograph of this egg, and that is a poor one, and there are some slightly conflicting descriptions. But the workmanship, the quality of material, the design . . . and it bears Perchin's mark—Fabergé's leading workmaster of that period. It's unmistakable to me, but you'll want a true expert opinion."

"He had documents. Most of them are in Russian." Ash took them out of the envelope, handed them to Vinnie.

"I couldn't begin to translate these," he said, once he'd glanced through them. "This certainly looks like a bill of sale, dated 1938, October fifteenth. And signatures. The price is in rubles. It looks like three thousand rubles. I'm not sure of the exchange rate in 1938, but I'd say someone got a serious bargain."

He sat again. "I know someone who can translate the paperwork."

"I'd appreciate it. Oliver knew what it was, what it's worth. Otherwise, he'd have come to you."

"I think yes, he'd have known, or known enough to find out on his own."

"Do you have a client with a particular interest in something like this?"

"Not specifically, but anyone with a true interest in antiquities, with collecting, would be thrilled to acquire this. Had they the thirty million or more it's worth. It could, potentially, go for much more at auction or be sold to a collector with that particular interest. And Oliver would certainly have known that."

"You said he handled two estates in the last couple months."

"Yes. Let me think." Vinnie rubbed at his temple. "He accessed and organized the Swanson estate, Long Island, and the Hill-Clayborne estate in Park Slope."

"Swanson."

"Yes. Neither listed anything like this."

"Who did the listing?"

"In these cases, Oliver, working with the clients. He couldn't have afforded to acquire this separately—and I would certainly have noticed an acquisition for millions."

"He could have afforded it if, one, he

had a client in mind, or two, the seller didn't know the value."

"It's possible. Some people have a vastly inflated idea of the value of their grandmother's Wedgwood. Others see a Daum crane vase as clutter."

"There's a bill of sale in his personal papers. For an antique angel figure with wagon. Sold to him by Miranda Swanson for twenty-five thousand."

"Dear God. Miranda Swanson—that was the client. Her father's estate. She wanted to sell all or nearly all the contents of his home, and Oliver handled it. He never said . . ."

Vinnie looked back at the egg.

"Would he have known what it was?"

"Even if he wasn't certain, he should have wondered, checked. Perhaps he did. Twenty-five thousand for this?"

"Hell of a deal," Ash commented.

"It . . . If he knew, it was unethical. We don't do business that way. You don't keep clients that way. But . . . for finding it, recognizing it, I would've been proud of him. He could've brought it to me. I would've been proud of him."

"He didn't tell you because you wouldn't have allowed it. It's not stealing, not outright.

Some wouldn't even consider it cheating. You would have. He couldn't tell you."

Ash paced away when Vinnie said nothing. "He told his girlfriend, and very likely got the money to buy it from her. He hooked into a collector, either through her or from people he knew through your shop. Tried to cash in. Big payday. He'd know what you'd think, what you'd want, but he'd just seen the shine."

"And he paid a very high price for questionable ethics. You won't tell his mother."

"No. I'm not telling anyone in the family except you."

"That's for the best. I would've been proud of him," Vinnie murmured again, then shook it off. He straightened, looked back at Ash. "He left you with a mess, didn't he? A habit of his, I'm sorry to say. Make copies of the paperwork. I don't want to take the originals. I'll see about getting them translated, and I'll make some careful inquiries if you want a true expert to examine it."

"We'll hold that for now."

"I don't know nearly enough about the history. I know there were fifty Imperial eggs commissioned, and that Lenin ordered the ransacking of the palaces, had the treasures moved during the Bolshevik Revolution. Stalin sold several of the eggs in the thirties, I believe, to raise money, foreign money. This one's complete, with the surprise—and that adds value. Many of the ones currently in collections are missing the surprise, or elements of it. The eight were lost after the revolution. Stolen, sold, hidden or put in very, very private collections."

"I've been boning up. One of the descriptions of this one's from the 1917 inventory of seized treasure. Seems like it didn't actually make it to Lenin's coffers—or somebody plucked it out later."

Ash took the papers to the copier.

"Where are you going to keep it while you do this research?"

"I'm taking it to the compound."

"That's good. Even better than my vault. But if you put it in the main safe, even telling your father it's private, and to leave it alone, he won't."

"I have a couple of places I can put it, safely." He found another envelope, put the copies inside. "Let me get you another drink."

"Better not. Angie will know if I've had two. She's got radar. One's acceptable between work and home. Two is the doghouse." His voice was light, brisk, but Ash heard the grief, and worse now, the disappointment. "I'll get going anyway. I'll make a call when I get home about the translation. I might be able to have it for you when I get to the compound. You're going up tomorrow?"

"Yeah."

"The offer's still there. Anything we can do." Vinnie got to his feet, closed the documents in his briefcase. "This is an important find. Oliver did something important, something that matters in the world. He just didn't do it right."

"I know."

"Don't come all the way down," Vinnie said, giving Ash another hug. "Put the egg away, safely. Take care of it, and yourself. I'll be in touch before I leave if I have any information."

"Thanks, Vinnie."

"As it wasn't stolen, doesn't have to be returned to a rightful owner, it belongs in a museum."

"I'll see to it."

"I know you will."

With the sorrow back in his eyes, Vinnie gave Ash a pat on the back, then made his way out.

He'd put it safely away, Ash thought, but first he'd leave it where it was while he did more digging.

Miranda Swanson, he thought. Time to find out more.

He sat down again, the egg glittering, and keyed in the name.

Jai considered taking another pass through the brother's loft. The stop at the bank intrigued her. But the visit by the uncle, that intrigued her much more.

A visit there might be more productive.

"We should take the brother. Squeeze him some, and he'll tell us what he knows."

Jai settled on a pair of jade and pearl earrings. Very classy, very traditional, to accent her short, blunt-cut wig. She shifted her gaze to Ivan.

"The way the whore told us before you threw her out the window?"

"I didn't throw her. That got out of hand,

that's all. We take the brother, bring him here. Quiet, private. Wouldn't take long."

Ivan affected a Russian accent. Jai knew—always made it her business to know work associates—he was born in Queens, the son of a second-rate Russian mafia enforcer and a stripper whose love affair with heroin had put her in the ground.

"The idiot Oliver hadn't been in contact with his brother for weeks. Didn't I check his phone, his computer? No calls, no e-mails. But the uncle he worked for."

Though she disliked having Ivan in the room while she prepared, Jai selected the Red Taboo lipstick, carefully painted it on her lips.

He'd tried to touch her once, but the knife she'd held to his balls had discouraged that behavior.

He gave her no further trouble in that area.

"The uncle is in the business of antiques, and successfully," she continued. "It was the uncle's business that led the idiot to the egg."

"And the uncle knew dick about it."

"Then," Jai agreed. "Perhaps now he

knows more. The brother visited this bank, then the uncle visits the brother. I think the brother who's fucking the skinny bitch who saw the whore fall is learning more. Maybe Oliver wasn't as much of an idiot as we believed, and put the egg in the bank."

"You said the brother didn't come out with the egg."

"That I could see. If it was in the bank, he may have left it in there. Or he brought out information on the egg and its location. This would be good information. He consults Oliver's uncle, Oliver's boss. Why is this?"

She took a wedding ring set out of a box. She thought it a shame the diamond—square cut, five carats—was fake, but it was a very good fake. She slipped it on.

"The uncle has more knowledge of Fabergé. The uncle is older and not so fit as the brother. The uncle had much contact with the idiot. So I'll visit the uncle."

"Waste of time."

"Our employer has put me in charge," she said coldly. "The decision is mine. I'll contact you if and when I need you."

She took a long, careful study of herself in the mirror. The cheerful summer print of the dress with its conservative lines, the candy-pink heels, buff-colored bag, understated jewelry revealed nothing of the woman within.

It all said just as she wished. Wealthy, traditional Asian woman—married woman.

She checked the contents of the bag one last time. Wallet, card case, cosmetic bag, mobile phone, her compact combat knife, two pairs of restraints and her 9mm Sig.

She left without a backward glance. Ivan would do what she told him to do, or she'd kill him—and they both knew it.

What he didn't know was she fully intended to kill him anyway. Being obedient only prolonged the inevitable.

For Vinnie, concentrating on work, the clients, the staff helped get him through. His heart and his mind were torn between grief over a sincerely loved nephew and excitement over the lost egg.

He'd sent his copies of the documents to an old friend who could translate them. He considered texting Ash, but decided against it. They'd see each other the next day at the funeral. Best to keep as much of their communication regarding the egg verbal and private.

He hated not sharing it all with his wife. Once they knew more, he would, but again, for now, it seemed best not to speculate. Not to blur things. Oliver, whatever he'd done, deserved a memorial where those who loved him could grieve without the added weight.

Vinnie carried the weight. He'd barely slept the last two nights, and all that wakeful time, the pacing time, had added more.

He had loved his sister's boy, had seen the potential in that boy. But he wasn't blind to the flaws, and now he believed Oliver's tendency to look for the quick score, the shortcut, the big and shiny had lured him to his death.

For what? he thought. For what?

Discovering the lost egg would have boosted his reputation, would have brought him accolades and money. Vinnie feared his nephew had wanted more, just more. And so had gotten nothing.

"Mr. V, I wish you'd go on home."

Vinnie looked over at Janis, gave her a

little head shake. She'd worked for him for fifteen years, always called him Mr. V.

"It helps keep my mind busy," he told her. "And the fact is, Janis, my sister would rather have Angie than me right now. So I'll go up tomorrow, give her time with Angie. I'd just rattle around the place at home."

"If you change your mind, you know Lou and I will close up. You could go on up tonight, just be with your family."

"I'll think about that. I will. But for now . . . I'll take this pretty young lady," he said as Jai strolled into the shop. "She's sure to keep my mind off my troubles."

"Oh you!" She gave him a giggle because he wanted one, but she watched him cross the shop with worry in her eye. The man was grieving, she thought, and should give himself the time for it.

"Good afternoon. What can I show you today?"

"So many lovely things." Jai released the accent she'd so carefully bound, added the polish of education. "I see this piece as I walk. But now, so much more."

"This piece caught your eye?"

"Caught my eye." She laughed, touched a finger to the corner of her eye. "Yes."

"You have an excellent eye. This is a Louis the Fourteenth bureau. The marquetry is very, very fine."

"May I touch?"

"Of course."

"Ah." She ran her fingertips over the top. "It is very lovely. Old, yes?"

"Late seventeenth century."

"My husband, he wants the old for the apartment in New York. I am to find what I like, but what he likes. You understand? Please excuse my English, it is not well."

"Your English is very good, and very charming."

Jai did a little eyelash flutter. "You are so kind. This, I think he will like very much. I would— Oh, and this?"

"This is also Louis the Fourteenth. A brass-and-tortoiseshell Boulle marquetry commode. It's beautifully preserved, as you see."

"Yes, it looks new, but old. This is what my husband wishes. But I must not pick all the same? Do you understand? They must be . . ."

"You want complementary pieces."

"Yes, I think. These are complementary?"

Vinnie looked at the bureau that had

"caught her eye," and smiled. "Very complementary."

"And this! We have a small library in the apartment, and see how this pretty table has what looks like books, but is a drawer. I like this very much!"

"This is tulipwood," Vinnie began.

"Tulipwood. How pretty. This I like so much. And this lamp. This lamp to see on the . . . commode, you said."

"You have exceptional taste, Mrs. . . ."

"Mrs. Castle. I am Mrs. Castle, and very pleased to meet you."

"Vincent Tartelli."

"Mr. Tartelli." She bowed, then offered a hand. "You will help me, please. To select the pieces for our apartment. So many lovely things," she said again, with a dreamy look around. "My husband will come. I cannot buy without his approval, but I know he will want much of this. This." She turned back to the first piece. "He will like this very, very much. This is possible?"

"Of course."

"Then I will select, and I will call him. He will be so pleased."

He was easy to engage in conversation as they went through the shop, as he showed her pieces, as she exclaimed or fumbled a bit with her English.

She found and noted all the security cameras as they made the rounds—thoroughly—of the two-level shop. Gradually she steered him from furnishings to collectibles, and objets d'art.

"I would like to buy a gift for my mother. From myself. She enjoys pretty things. You have in this case? This is jade?"

"It is. A very exquisite jade bonbonniere. The carving is Chinese influence."

"She would enjoy," Jai said as Vinnie unlocked the display, then set the box on a pad of velvet. "It is old?"

"Late nineteenth century. Fabergé."

"This is French?"

"No, Russian."

"Yes, yes, yes. I know this. Russian, not French. He makes the famous eggs." She let her smile fade as she looked into Vinnie's eyes. "I have said something wrong?"

"No, no. Not at all. Yes, Fabergé created the eggs, originally for the tsar to give as Easter gifts to his wife, his mother."

"This is so charming. An egg for Easter. Do you have the eggs?"

"I . . . We have some reproductions, and one egg created in the early twentieth century. But most of the Imperial eggs, and those from that era, are in private collections or museums."

"I see. Perhaps my husband will want one and find it one day, but this box—this bonboon?"

"Bonbonniere."

"Bonbonniere," she repeated carefully. "I think it would please my mother. You can keep it for me? With the other selections? But this is for me to buy, for my mother, you understand?"

"Perfectly."

As do I, she thought. He knows of the egg. He knows where it is.

"I have taken so much of your time already," she began.

"Not at all."

"I would like to call my husband, ask him to come, to see the selections. He may see other things, you understand, or find something I selected not right? But I believe I have done very well with your valued assistance. I will tell you, I hope it does not insult, that he will wish to negotiate. He is a businessman."

"Naturally. I'll be happy to discuss prices with him."

"You are very good. I will call him now."

"Let me give you some privacy."

As he stepped aside, Janis finished with a customer. "Do you think she's serious?" Janis murmured.

"I do. We'll have to see if the husband is, but she's got a canny eye. And she may play subservient, but she knows who's in charge."

"Well, she sort of reeks—in a quiet way—of money and class. Add indulgence. And she's gorgeous. I bet you're right and she talks him into most of it, and wow, that's a sale, Mr. V."

"Not a bad Saturday afternoon."

"We close in thirty."

"You go on. You and Lou. It'll take more than thirty to settle this one."

"I can stay. It's not a problem."

"No, you go on. I'll close up. If this turns out like I feel it will, I might just drive up to Connecticut tonight after all. It'll give me a nice boost. I'll be back in New York Tuesday. You call if you need anything on Monday."

"You take care, Mr. V." She hugged

him, one good, strong squeeze. "You take care."

"I will. I'll see you Tuesday morning."

Jai moved toward them as she tucked her phone back in her bag. "Excuse me. My husband is happy to come, but he is not close. It will take perhaps twenty minutes? But you are to close?"

"Our regular hours, but I'll stay and work with your husband."

"A private negotiation? But this for you is much trouble."

"A pleasure, I promise you. Why don't I make us some tea while we wait? Or pour us a glass of wine."

"A glass of wine?" She sent him a sparkling smile. "A small celebration?"

"I'll just be a moment."

"Your employer," Jai said to Janis, taking care to note where Vinnie went, how he got there. "He is so knowledgeable, and so patient."

"He's the best there is."

"It must be happy for you, to work every day with such beauty and strong art."

"I love my job, and my boss."

"If it is not too ahead. No, not ahead . . . forward, may I ask? Up the stairs I found a bonbonniere for my mother—a gift. This is Fabergé?"

"The jade, yes. It's wonderful."

"I think it is wonderful, and my mother will enjoy it. But I asked about this Fabergé, and if Mr. Tartelli had any of the famous eggs. He seemed sad when I asked this. Do you know if I said something to upset him?"

"I'm sure you didn't. He might have been sad to disappoint you as we don't have any of the important Fabergé eggs."

"Ah." Jai nodded. She knows nothing of it, Jai concluded, this hovering clerk. So she smiled. "If that is all, that is no thing. I am not disappointed."

Vinnie came out with a tray holding wine, cheese and little crackers. "Here we are. A little celebration."

"Thank you. How very kind. I feel friends here."

"We think of our clients as our friends. Please, sit and enjoy. Janis, you go home now. You and Lou."

"On our way. It was a pleasure to meet you, Mrs. Castle. I hope you come see us again."

"You must have a good weekend." Jai

sat in a pretty little chair, lifted a glass of ruby-red wine. "I am glad to be in New York. I enjoy New York very much. I am glad to make your acquaintance, Mr. Tartelli."

"And I yours, Mrs. Castle." He tapped his glass to hers. "How long have you been in New York?"

"Oh, only days, but not the first time. My husband has much business here now, so we will come and live here, and we will travel back to London, where he also has much business. And to Hong Kong. There is my family so it is good to go back, but it is good to be here."

"What business is your husband's?"

"He does many things with finance and with property. It is more than I understand. When we have guests we must have the unique as you have here. Unique is important. And he must have what makes him happy so he is happy in his home and his work."

"I think he's a very fortunate man."

"I hope he feels the same. He is here!"

She jumped up, hurried over as Ivan came in. Her hand slipped into her bag in case Ivan didn't pull off the initial meeting. "My husband, this is the very kind Mr. Tartelli."

"Mr. Castle." Vinnie extended a hand. "It's a pleasure. I've enjoyed assisting your wife with her selections for your New York home. Mrs. Castle has an exceptional eye."

"You could say that."

"We are to have a private meeting," Jai told him. "Mr. Tartelli is so kind to stay after his closing to work with us."

"I'll just lock up so we're not disturbed."

"There is wine." When Vinnie's back was turned Jai motioned toward the back.

She moved with him, out of sight of the windows, while Vinnie locked them in.

"We have several pieces for your approval," Vinnie began as he walked to them.

Jai sidestepped, pressed her gun to Vinnie's back. "We're going to take this into that back room." Gone was the light accent and all the charm. "For our private negotiation."

"There's no need for this." Cold sweat slicked over him, a second skin. "You can take what you want."

"We intend to." Jai gave him a hard shove. "Into the back. Cooperate, this will be fast, smooth and easy on all of us. Otherwise, my associate will hurt you. He enjoys it."

She forced Vinnie back, through the door. She'd only caught glimpses, but saw it was as she'd assumed. A storeroom that doubled as an office.

Quickly, efficiently, she used one of the ties in her bag to restrain his arms behind his back, then pushed him into a chair.

"One question, one answer, and we walk away. No harm. Where is the egg?"

He stared at her. "Egg? I don't know what you mean."

She sighed. "One question. Wrong answer."

She gestured to Ivan.

The first blow had blood exploding from Vinnie's nose and sent the chair flying back. Jai held up a finger before Ivan could strike again. "Same question. Where is the egg?"

"I don't know what you mean."

Jai sat on the edge of the desk, crossed her legs. "Stop when I tell you to stop," she told Ivan.

Ivan rolled his shoulders once, hauled up the chair and began the work he most enjoyed.

Ten

As she watched Ivan do his work, Jai felt a
rise of admiration and respect. Not for
Ivan—the man was nothing more than an
ugly pair of fists with a shaved head. But
the uncle, she thought, he was a gentleman and a gentleman with **ethics**. She
admired ethics in the same way she might
admire a clever juggling act. As an interesting skill she had no particular need for.

Because she felt this admiration, she
would kill him quickly, and as painlessly as
possible, once he gave them the information she wanted.

Every few blows, she stepped forward

to stop Ivan, and to speak to Vinnie in a calm, quiet voice.

"The egg, Mr. Tartelli. It's a thing of beauty and great value, of course. But it isn't worth your pain, your life, your future. Only tell us where it is, and all this will stop."

He rolled his right eye toward her voice. The left was purpled, swollen closed, leaking both blood and tears. But the bloodied right could still open a slit.

"Did you kill Oliver?"

She leaned down so he could see her more clearly. "Oliver was a fool. You know this because you're not. He was greedy, and now he's dead. I don't think you're a greedy man, Mr. Tartelli. I think you want to live. Where is the egg?"

"Fabergé? Did Oliver have a Fabergé?"

"You know that he did. Don't try my patience." She leaned closer. "There are worse things even than death. We can give them to you."

"I don't have what you want." He choked, coughed out blood, which Jai nimbly evaded. "You can look. You can look, take whatever you want. I can't give what I don't have."

"What did the brother take from the bank if not the egg?"

"I don't have a brother."

She nodded to Ivan, stepped aside to avoid more sprays of blood.

"Oliver's brother. Ashton Archer. You went to see him."

"Ash."

Vinnie's head lolled. Ivan backhanded him to bring him around.

"Give him a moment," she snapped at Ivan. "Ashton Archer." She spoke gently, encouragingly. "The brother of Oliver. Why did you go to see him Thursday?"

"Ash. Funeral. Oliver. Help Ash."

"Yes, help Ash. You saw the egg? All the glittering gold. Where is it now? Tell me this one thing, Mr. Tartelli, and all the pain stops."

He looked at her again through the puffy slit of his right eye, spoke slowly through broken teeth. "I didn't have any eggs."

Ivan switched up, plowed a brutal fist into Vinnie's solar plexus. While Vinnie retched, Jai considered.

She'd seen something in that single bloodied eye. Fear, yes, but a steely determination with it. Not for himself, she realized.

For this brother? This part brother of a nephew? How odd, how interesting to find such loyalty. This was more than ethics, and perhaps it could be useful.

"I need to make a call. Give him a break," she ordered Ivan. "Do you understand me? I'll get him some water. Let him recover a bit."

She'd call her employer, she decided as she stepped out into the shop. While he gave her autonomy, she wouldn't risk his wrath by implementing a shift in strategy without his approval.

And this uncle, this ethical, loyal, determined uncle, might be of more use as a bargaining chip. Would the brother trade the egg for the uncle's life?

Perhaps.

Yes, the brother might also have ethics, and loyalty.

They would kill him. Even through his agony Vinnie understood that one unassailable fact. Whatever the woman said, they would never leave him alive.

He grieved for his wife, for his children, for the grandchildren he would never see grow. He would gladly trade the egg for his life, for more time with his family. But they would kill him either way. And if he told them Ash had the egg, they would kill Ash as well.

As they'd killed Oliver and the woman who might have loved him.

He had to be strong. Whatever they did to him, he had to be strong. He prayed for that strength, for acceptance, for the safety of his family.

"Shut the fuck up."

Vinnie kept his head down, continued to pray in garbled mutters.

"I said shut the fuck up." Ivan clamped a hand around Vinnie's throat, squeezed as he jerked Vinnie's head up. "You think this is bad? You think you're hurting now? Wait until I let loose on you. First I'll break all your fingers."

Ivan released Vinnie's throat, grabbing the left pinky finger while Vinnie choked and gasped for air. He yanked it back, snapping the bone, then clamped Vinnie's throat again to block the shocked, high-pitched scream.

Chink bitch would hear and come in, stop him. Chink bitch thought **she** was better than he was. He imagined ramming his fist into her face, raping her, killing her by inches.

And broke another of Vinnie's fingers because he could.

"Then I'll cut them off, one at a time."

The single eye bulged; Vinnie's body shook, convulsed.

"Tell us where the fucking egg is."

Infuriated, thrilled, Ivan closed his other hand around Vinnie's throat. Squeezed. Imagined Jai's face. "I'm not fucking around. Tell me or I'll cut you to pieces. Then I'll kill your wife, your kids. I'll kill your fucking dog."

But as Ivan raged, as he squeezed, as his breath came faster and faster with the thrill and the fury, the single eye only stared.

"Asshole." Ivan released Vinnie, stepped back. He smelled his own sweat, the asshole's urine. Pissed himself, Ivan thought. Asshole pussy pissed himself.

He'd talk. The bitch gave him a little more leeway, he'd make the asshole talk.

Jai stepped back in with a small bottle of water she'd found behind the counter. And she, too, smelled the sweat, the urine.

She smelled death, a particular scent

she knew well. Saying nothing, she walked over to Vinnie, lifted his head.

"He's dead."

"Bullshit. Just passed out."

"He's dead," she repeated in that same flat tone. "I told you to give him a break." Not, she thought, break his fingers.

"I gave him a fucking break. He must've had a heart attack or something."

"A heart attack." She breathed in and out once. "This is unfortunate."

"It's not my fault the asshole croaked."

"Of course not." She noted the raw bruising around Vinnie's throat. "But it's unfortunate."

"He didn't know shit. If he'd've known anything, he'd've spilled it once I gave him a few slaps. Waste of time. We go after the brother, like I said before."

"I'll need to make another call. We'll leave the body here. The shop is closed tomorrow, so this gives us a day."

"We make it look like a robbery. Grab some shit, mess shit up."

"We could. Or . ." She reached in her purse, but instead of taking out her phone, she drew out her gun. She shot Ivan neatly between the eyes before he had a chance to blink. "We could do that, which is a much better idea."

She regretted Vinnie. She'd found him to be an interesting man, and potentially very useful. Dead, he was of no use at all, so she ignored him as she emptied Ivan's pockets of wallet, phone, weapons. And found, as she suspected she might, the bottle of amphetamines.

It was good, she calculated. Her employer disapproved of drugs, and would tolerate if not fully approve of her actions when she told him about the drugs. She went out in the shop, retrieved a shopping bag, some bubble wrap. She went upstairs, took the bonbonniere.

Her employer would like it very much—like it more than he might dislike the killing of Ivan.

She wrapped it carefully, brought it downstairs. It pleased her to find a nice box, very classy thin gold ribbon. She boxed the gift, tied the ribbon.

She put Ivan's phone, wallet, knife and gun in the bag, padded it, added the box, then tissue paper.

After a moment's consideration, she unlocked a display, chose what had been designed as a woman's cigarette case. She liked the mother-of-pearl sheen and the pattern of tiny flowers that made her think of a peacock.

She could use it as a card case, she decided, and dropped it into her purse.

She considered taking the security tapes, destroying the system, but without some study couldn't be sure that wouldn't send an alarm. She'd rather have the head start. In any case the woman clerk, the male guard and several customers could certainly give a description of her. She didn't have the time or inclination to hunt them all down and kill them.

She would go back to the brownstone her employer provided as her base in New York. At least with Ivan dead, he wouldn't be there, lurking around, hoping to see her naked.

Best to walk several blocks before getting a cab. And the walk, the time to travel, would give her time to think how to outline her report for her employer.

Lila arranged the vase of sunflowers—a cheerful welcome home in her opinion—

then leaned the note she'd written against the base of the blue vase.

She'd done her room-by-room sweep—twice, as was her policy, consulting her checklist.

Fresh linens on the beds, fresh towels in the bath, fresh fruit in the bowl. A pitcher of lemonade in the fridge along with a chilled pasta salad.

Who wanted to think about cooking or ordering food when they'd just returned from vacation?

Food and water out for Thomas, plants watered, furniture dusted, floors vacuumed.

She said her goodbyes to the cat, giving him plenty of strokes and cuddles.

"They'll be home in a couple of hours," she promised him. "So happy to see you. Be a good boy. Maybe I'll come back and stay with you again."

With one last glance around, she shouldered her laptop case, her purse. She pulled up the handles of her suitcases and, with the skill of experience, maneuvered all out the door.

Her adventure at the Kilderbrands' was over. A new adventure would soon begin.

But first, she had to go to a funeral.

The doorman spotted her as soon as she rolled out of the elevator. He bustled in and over. "Now, Ms. Emerson, you should've called me to come give you a hand."

"I'm so used to doing it. I've got a system."

"I bet you do. Your car just pulled up. You must've already been heading down when they called up to tell you."

"Good timing."

"Go on and get in. We'll get this loaded up for you."

She felt a little odd when she spotted the limo. Not a flashy one, but still, long, dark and shiny.

"Thanks for everything, Ethan."

"Don't mention it. You come back and see us."

"I'll do that."

She slid inside, looked at Julie, at Luke, as the driver shut the door behind her.

"This is weird. I'm sorry, Luke, you knew him, but it's weird."

"I barely knew him. But . . ."

"We know Ash." Lila laid her purse on the bench seat beside her. "At least it's a nice day. I always think rain when I think of funerals."

"I bet you have an umbrella in your bag."
Lila shrugged at Julie. "Just in case."

"If you're ever on a desert island, in a war zone or an avalanche, you want Lila and her bag. If you sever a limb she's probably got something in there to reattach it. She once repaired my toaster with a screwdriver the length of my pinky and a pair of tweezers."

"No duct tape?"

"It's in here," Lila assured him. "A mini roll. So maybe you can give me—us—an overview of the playing field? Who'll be there?"

"They'll all be there."

"The entire spreadsheet?"

"You can count on all or most." Luke shifted, as if not quite at home in the dark suit and tie. "They come together for important events. Funerals, weddings, graduations, serious illness, childbirth. I wouldn't call the compound the demilitarized zone, but it's as close as they get to one."

"Is war common?"

"It happens. Something like this? Some small, petty battles maybe, but no major conflict. At a wedding, anything goes. The last one I went to, the mother of the bride and the father of the bride's current lady got into a hair-pulling, face-scratching, clothes-ripping free-for-all that ended with them duking it out in a koi pond."

Luke stretched out his legs. "We have the video."

"Won't this be fun?" Lila scooted forward, flipped open the lid on the built-in cooler, rooted around. "Anybody want a ginger ale?"

Ash sat under the pergola shaded by thick twists of wisteria. He needed to go back inside, deal with everything and everyone, but for now, for a few minutes, he just wanted some air, some quiet.

For all its size, the house felt close and crowded and too full of noise.

From where he sat he could see the trim lines of the guesthouse with its colorful cottage garden. Oliver's mother had yet to come out, instead closing herself in with her sister-in-law, her daughter and what his father called—not unkindly—her gaggle of women.

Just as well, he thought, and there was time enough for her to cling to those women and their comfort before the funeral.

He'd done his best to create her vision of that memorial. Only white flowers—and it seemed like acres of them. Dozens of white chairs arranged in rows on the long sweep of the north lawn, a white lectern for speakers. The photos she'd selected of Oliver framed in white. The string quartet (Christ!) instructed to dress in white as all the mourners had been instructed to wear black.

Only the piper would be allowed color.

He felt, and thankfully his father agreed, a mother should be given anything she wanted in the planning of a child's funeral.

Though he'd hoped for small and private, the event would host over three hundred. Most of the family and a few friends had arrived the day before, and were currently scattered all over the ten-bedroom house, the guesthouse, the pool house, the grounds.

They needed to talk, to ask questions he couldn't answer, to eat, to sleep, to laugh, to cry. They sucked up every drop of air.

After more than thirty-six hours of it, Ash could think of nothing he wanted more than his own studio, his own space. Still, he smiled when his half sister Giselle, the raven-haired beauty, stepped under the shading vines.

She sat beside him, tipped her head onto his shoulder. "I decided to take a walk before I drop-kicked Katrina off the Juliet balcony into the swimming pool. I'm not sure I could kick quite that far so a walk seemed smarter. And I found you."

"Better idea. What did she do?"

"Cry. Cry, cry, cry. She and Oliver barely spoke, and when they did it was to insult each other."

"Maybe that's why she's crying. Lost her insult buddy."

"I guess they did enjoy getting on each other's nerves."

"Hard on you." He put an arm around her.

"I loved him. He was a fuck-up, but I loved him. So did you."

"I'm pretty sure I used those exact words to describe him to someone. He loved you, especially."

Giselle turned her face, pressed it to Ash's shoulder for a moment. "Damn him. I'm so mad at him for being dead."

"I know. Me, too. Have you seen his mother?"

"I went over this morning. I talked to Olympia a little. She's leaning hard on Angie, and someone gave her a Valium. She'll get through it. So will we. I'm going to miss him, so much. He always made me laugh, always listened to me bitch, then made me laugh. And I liked Sage."

"You met her?"

"Hell, I introduced them." Giselle pulled Ash's pocket square out of his breast pocket, used it to dab at her eyes. "I met her last year in Paris, and we hit it off reasonably well. We had lunch when we were both back in New York. Well, I had lunch. She had a leaf and a berry. Half a berry."

Expertly, she refolded the pocket square, damp side in, tucked it back in the breast pocket. "She invited me to some party, and I decided to take Oliver—I thought they'd enjoy each other. They did.

"I wish I hadn't taken him." Giselle turned her face into Ash's shoulder again. "I know it's stupid, you don't have to tell me, but I wish I hadn't taken him. Would they both be alive if I hadn't introduced them?"

Gently, he brushed his lips over her hair.

"You said I didn't have to tell you that's stupid, but I'm compelled to."

"He was into something bad, Ash. He had to be. Someone killed him, so he had to be into something bad."

"Did he say anything to you? Anything about a deal? A client?"

"No. The last time I talked to him—just a few days before . . . before he died, he called me. He said everything was great, tremendous, and he was going to come see me. I could help him look for a place in Paris. He might buy a flat in Paris. I thought, That's never going to happen, but wouldn't it be fun if it did?"

She straightened up, blinked away threatening tears. "You know more than you're saying. I'm not going to ask—I'm not sure I'm ready to know, but you know more than you're telling the rest of us. I'll help if I can."

"I know you will." He kissed her cheek. "I'll let you know. I've got to go check on flowers and bagpipes."

"I'll look in on Olympia. Guests will be arriving soon." She rose with him. "Get Bob to help you. Bob's a rock."

True enough, Ash thought, as they parted ways. And he'd already tapped Bob—

stepbrother, mother's side—to monitor the alcohol intake on a select few.

He didn't want anyone ending up in the koi pond.

Lila decided "compound" was far too military and restrictive a word for the Archer estate. Yes, the walls stood high and thick—but the stone glinted with regal dignity. Yes, the gates loomed—sturdy and locked—but with gorgeous ironwork surrounding the stylized **A**. Bold orange tiger lilies speared up around the base of a charming gatehouse.

Two black-suited security guards checked credentials before passing the limo through. And maybe that part seemed to fit "compound." But that was all.

Tall, graceful trees rose over velvet lawns. Lush shrubberies, artistic plantings mixed among the green along the arrow-straight drive, and all led to the massive house.

It should've been almost too much, she thought, but the creamy yellow stone added a friendly vibe and its subtle U shape softened all. Pretty balconies, the hipped roofs on each wing, lent it a welcoming charm.

She spotted a little topiary—a dragon, a unicorn, a winged horse.

"Current wife," Luke said. "She goes for the whimsical."

"I love it."

The driver stopped in front of the covered portico. Thick vines covered with purple blooms big as saucers twined up columns, tangled over the balconies. Touches like that, she thought, turned the house from intimidating into approachable.

Still, if she'd had a do-over, she'd have bought a new dress. Her all-purpose black— now in its fourth season—didn't seem quite good enough.

She hoped the hair helped, maybe added a faint air of dignity since she'd fussed it into a loose chignon at the base of her neck.

Once the driver helped her out, Lila simply stood, admiring the house. Moments later a blonde streaked out of the massive front door, paused for a beat at the base of the trio of portico steps. Then launched herself at Luke.

"Luke." She sobbed it. "Oh, Luke."

Behind her back Lila exchanged lifted-eyebrow glances with Julie.

"Oliver! Oh, Luke!"

"I'm so sorry, Rina." He rubbed his hand over the back of her black dress with its flirty lace bodice and abbreviated hemline.

"We'll never see him again. I'm so glad you're here."

Very glad, Lila assumed, by the way the woman clung several seconds after Luke tried to untangle himself.

About twenty-two, Lila gauged, with a long, straight spill of blond hair, long, tanned legs and flawless skin where perfect crystal tears slid as if they'd been choreographed.

Unkind, she told herself. All true, but unkind.

The blonde wrapped her arms around Luke's waist, molded herself to his side, gave both Lila and Julie a long, assessing look.

"Who are you?"

"Katrina Cartwright, this is Julie Bryant and Lila Emerson. They're friends of Ash's."

"Oh. He was on the north side, doing things. I'll show you around. Guests are arriving. All these people," she said with a faraway look as another limo cruised toward the house, "to honor Oliver."

"How is his mother?" Luke asked.

"I haven't seen her today. She's cloistered in the guesthouse. Devastated. We're all devastated." She kept a proprietary grip on Luke as she led the way along a paved path. "I don't know how we'll go on. How any of us will go on.

"We've opened a bar on the patio." She gestured carelessly to the white-skirted table manned by a white-jacketed woman.

Beyond the generous patio the lawn stretched. Rows of white chairs faced an arbor dripping with roses. Under its arch sat a high table holding an urn.

All bride white, Lila thought, including the easels that held enlarged framed photos of Oliver Archer.

A quartet sat beneath a second arbor playing the quiet and classical. People dressed in funeral black mixed and mingled. Some had already hit the bar, she noted, and carried cocktails or wine. Others sat, talking in muted voices.

One woman wore a hat with a brim as round and wide as the moon. She dabbed at her eyes with a snow-white hankie.

Through a pretty stand of trees she saw what must have been a tennis court, and to the south the tropical blue waters of a swimming pool glinted in the sun. A little stone house nestled near it.

Someone laughed too loud. Someone else spoke in Italian. A woman in a white uniform moved silent as a ghost to take up empty glasses. Another brought the hat woman a flute of champagne.

And to think she hadn't wanted to come, Lila thought. It was all marvelous, like theater, like something out of a play.

She wanted to write about it—surely she could work some of it into a book—and began to commit faces, landscape, little details to memory.

Then she saw Ash. His face was so tired, so sad.

Not a play, she thought. Not theater.

Death.

Thinking only of him now, she walked to him.

He took her hand. For a moment he just stood, holding her hand. "I'm glad you came."

"So am I. It's . . . all sort of eerily beautiful. All the white and black. Dramatic. From what you've told me, he'd have liked it."

"Yeah, he would. Olympia—his mother—was right. Hell, Rina's got Luke. I need to get her off. She's had a crush on him since she was a teenager."

"I think he can handle it. Is there anything I can do?"

"It's done. Or will be. Let me get all of you a seat."

"We'll find seats. You have things to do."

"I need to get Olympia, or send someone to get her. I'll be back."

"Don't worry about us."

"I'm glad you came," he said again. "I mean it."

He had to make his way through guests, those who wanted to offer condolences, those who just wanted a word. He started toward the house—he'd cut through, he decided, go out the side—then stopped when he saw Angie.

She looked exhausted, he realized. Weighed down carrying her own grief and trying to shoulder some of her sister-in-law's.

"She wants Vinnie." Angie pushed a hand at her curly cap of hair. "Have you seen him?"

"No. I've been handling some things so I must've missed him."

"I'll try his cell again. He should've been here an hour ago. Two." She sighed a little. "He drives like an old lady, and won't use the hands-free. So if he's still en route, he won't answer."

"I'll look around for him."

"No, do what you have to do to get this started. She's got her guts up now, but it won't last long. If he's late, he's late. You should have the funeral director get people seated. Your father?"

"I'll get him. Is ten minutes enough time?"

"Ten minutes. We'll have her here." She took her phone out of the little purse she carried. "Damn it, Vinnie," she muttered as she strode away.

Vinnie could be inside, Ash speculated. He'd look around, tell his father it was time.

He gave the funeral director the signal, escorted Oliver's maternal grandmother to a chair himself before heading toward the house.

He caught sight of Lila sitting on Luke's left, Julie on the right. And to Lila's left sat Katrina, her hands gripping Lila's as his sister poured out some story.

Full of exclamation marks, he imagined.

But the image of them lightened him a little.

Yeah, he was glad she came, he thought one last time, then hurried inside to get his father so they could say their final good-byes.

PART TWO

Fate chooses our relatives,
we choose our friends.

JACQUES DELILLE

Eleven

Lila had never experienced anything like it. Despite the oddity of an open bar and a landscape of white, the grief was real and deep. She saw it in the pale and stricken face of Oliver's mother, heard it in the unsteady voices of those who stood at the white lectern to speak. She felt it weighing down the air while the sun beamed, while the scents of lilies and roses wafted along the fluttering breeze.

And still, it **was** a kind of theater, staged, costumed and choreographed, performed by people of striking good looks on an elaborate stage.

When Ash stepped up to the lectern she thought he could be an actor—the tall, dark and handsome sort. Smooth today, she noted, clean-shaven, perfect black suit. Maybe she preferred the scruff, the carelessly, casually arty of his every day, but he wore the gloss well.

"I asked Giselle to deliver the eulogy for Oliver. Of all the siblings, she and Oliver shared the closest bond. While we all loved him, will all miss him, Giselle understood him best, and appreciated his eternal optimism. On behalf of his mother and our father, thank you all for coming today to help us say goodbye to our son, our brother, our friend."

Was the entire Archer clan gorgeous? Lila wondered as she watched a stunning woman stand. She exchanged a hard hug with Ash, then faced the crowd.

Her voice didn't tremble, but remained strong and clear.

"I tried to think of my first memory of Oliver, but I couldn't pin it. He was always part of my life, no matter how much time passed without seeing him. He was, in so many ways, the laughter, the fun, the foolishness every life needs.

"Optimist." Now she smiled a little, looked over at Ash. "Leave it to you, Ash. Some of us are realists, some are cynics, some are, let's face it, just assholes. Most of us have a little of all of that mixed inside us. But for Oliver, Ash is right. Optimism ruled. He could be careless, but he was never cruel. And really, how many people can we say that about with honesty? He was impulsive, and unfailingly generous. He was a social creature to whom solitude was a kind of punishment. Because he was so charming, so bright, so beautiful, he was rarely alone."

A bird swooped behind Giselle, a bright blue streak that flashed over the white mounds of flowers and was gone.

"He loved you, Olympia, deeply and sincerely. And you, Dad." For a moment her eyes shimmered, then like the flash of blue, the shimmer was gone. "He so wanted you to be proud of him, maybe he wanted it too much. He wanted to be and accomplish the spectacular. There was no average or mediocre for Oliver. He made mistakes, and some of them were spectacular. But he was never hard, never cruel. And yes, always optimistic. If any of us had asked him for anything, he would have given it. It wasn't in his nature to say no. Maybe leaving us, so terribly, while he was still young and bright and beautiful was inevitable. So I won't search for that first memory of Oliver, or linger on the last. I'll just be grateful he was always part of my life, that he gave me the laughter and the fun and the foolishness. Now we'll have a party, because there was nothing Oliver enjoyed more."

As she stepped back from the lectern, the piper played. On cue, as the grieving notes of "Amazing Grace" carried down from a small knoll, hundreds of white butterflies rose with beating wings behind the arbor.

Fascinated, Lila watched Giselle glance back at the white cloud, look over at Ash. And laugh.

Because it seemed like the thing to do, Lila sipped some wine. Servers passed food and invited guests to long white tables where more substantial choices were offered. People gathered or wandered, around the grounds, into the house. Though she was curious, she didn't feel strolling into the house would be correct.

Gauging her timing, she made her way over to Oliver's mother to pay her respects.

"I don't want to intrude. I'm a friend of Ashton's. I'm so sorry for your loss."

"Ashton's friend." The woman was sheet-pale, glassy-eyed, but she extended a hand. "Ashton took care of all the details."

"It was a very beautiful service."

"Oliver always gave me white flowers on Mother's Day. Didn't he, Angie?"

"He never forgot."

"They're beautiful. Can I get you some water?"

"Water? No, I . . ."

"Why don't we go inside now? It's cooler inside. Thank you," Angie said to Lila, then with her arm firmly around Olympia's waist, took her away.

"A friend of Ashton's?"

Lila recognized the woman who'd given the eulogy. "Yes, from New York. Your eulogy was wonderful. Touching."

"Touching?"

"Because you meant it."

Giselle studied Lila and sipped champagne from a flute as if she'd been born with one in her hand. "I did. Did you know Oliver?"

"No, I'm sorry I didn't."

"But Ash asked you to come. That's interesting." She took Lila's hand, steered her toward a small group. "Monica? Excuse us a minute," Giselle said to the others, and drew the redhead who epitomized glamour in full bloom off to the side. "This is a friend of Ash's. He asked her to come today."

"Did he? How nice to meet you, even under the circumstances." Eyes, sharp and green, assessed. "I'm Ashton's mother."

"Oh. Mrs. . . ."

"It's Crompton at the moment. It can be confusing. How do you know Ash?"

"I . . . ah."

"A story," Monica stated. "We love a good story, don't we, Giselle?"

"Oh yes, we do."

"Let's find a cozy spot and hear all about it."

Trapped, Lila glanced around. Where the hell was Julie? "I was just—"

But there seemed little point in arguing when she was being steamrolled, with class and style, toward the big, imposing house.

"Ash hasn't told me he has a new lady in his life." Monica opened a door into what Lila assumed was a music room, given the grand piano, and the cello, the violin.

"I wouldn't say I was—"

"But then, Ash doesn't tell me nearly enough."

More than dazzled, Lila found herself steered out of the room, past some sort of dark-paneled game room where two men played pool and a woman sat at a bar watching, beyond some sort of parlor where someone wept, into a spectacular entrance area with lofted ceilings, actual columns, a dual sweep of graceful stairs, dripping chandeliers and beyond a two-level library where someone spoke in quiet tones.

"This will do," Monica announced when they arrived in the botanical wonder of a solarium with glass walls opening to all the staggering gardens.

"You could put in your three miles of cardio a day just walking from one end of this house to the other."

"It seems like it, doesn't it?" Monica sat on a buff-colored sofa, patted the cushion beside her. "Sit, and tell me everything."

"There isn't really everything."

"Has he painted you yet?"

"No."

Fiery eyebrows rose, lips in a perfect shade of sheer pink curved. "Now you surprise me."

"He did some sketches, but—"

"And how does he see you?"

"As a gypsy. I don't know why."

"It's the eyes."

"That's what he says. You must be so proud of him. His work is wonderful."

"Little did I know what was to come when I handed him his first box of Crayolas. So how did you meet?"

"Mrs. Crompton—"

"Monica. Whatever happens, I'm always Monica."

"Monica. Giselle." Lila blew out a breath, ordered herself to say it fast. "I met Ash at the police station. I saw Sage Kendall fall."

"You're the nine-one-one caller," Giselle said, linking fingers with the hand Monica laid over hers.

"Yes. I'm sorry. This has to be uncomfortable for both of you."

"I'm not uncomfortable. Are you uncomfortable, Giselle?"

"No. I'm grateful. I'm grateful you called the police. I'm more grateful you talked to Ash, because most people would've walked the other way."

"He just needed to understand what I'd seen. I don't think most people would walk away from that."

Giselle, her hand still linked with Monica's, exchanged an arch look with the older woman. "You forget what I said in the eulogy about assholes."

"Then I'm happy not to be one in this case, but—"

"They've kept your name out of the media," Giselle interrupted.

"There's not much reason for it to be in there. I didn't see anything that helps."

"You helped Ashton." Monica reached out with her free hand, took Lila's for a moment and linked the three of them together. "He has a need to find the answers, the solution, and you helped him."

"You need wine," Giselle decided. "I'll get you some wine."

"Please, don't bother. I—"

"Get us some champagne, sweetie." Monica kept her hand firmly on Lila's to keep her in place when Giselle hurried out. "Ash loved Oliver—all of us did as much as he infuriated. He tends to be responsible—Ash, that is. To feel responsible. If he's doing sketches, asking you here today, you've helped him over the first hump."

"Sometimes it's easier to talk to someone you don't really know. And it turns out we have a mutual friend, so that adds to it."

"So do your eyes—and the rest of you." Monica angled her head, assessing again. "Not his usual type—not that he has a type, per se. But the dancer. You may know about the dancer he was involved with. Beautiful young woman, tremendous talent—with an ego and temper to match. Ash has a temper when the button's pushed. I think he enjoyed the passion—and I don't mean sex, but passion. All the drama. But for the short term. Overall, and at the core, he likes his quiet, his solitude. You seem like a less volatile sort."

"I can be a bitch—when the button's pushed."

Monica flashed a grin, and Lila saw her son. "I hope so. I can't abide weak women. Worse than weak men. What do you do, Lila? Do you work?"

"I do. I write and I house-sit."

"A house-sitter. I swear I'd do the same at your age. Travel, see how other people live, enjoy the new places, new views. It's an adventure."

"It really is."

"But to make a living at it, to gain clients, you'd have to be responsible, reliable. Trustworthy."

"You're tending people's homes—their things, their plants, their pets. If they can't trust you, the adventure ends."

"Nothing lasts without trust. And what do you write?"

"I write a young adult series. Novels. High school drama, politics, romance, with warring werewolves."

"Not **Moon Rise**?" Delighted surprise popped into her voice. "You're not L. L. Emerson?"

"Yeah. You actually know . . . Rylee,"

she remembered. "Ash told me his sister Rylee liked the book."

"Liked? Devoured it. I have to introduce you. She'll be thrilled out of her mind."

She glanced over, inclined her head. "Spence."

Ash's—and Oliver's—father, Lila thought. Heartthrob handsome, tanned and fit, his thick dark hair perfectly touched with gray at the temples, his eyes a cool and canny blue.

"Lila, this is Spence Archer. Spence, Lila Emerson."

"Yes, I know. Ms. Emerson, we're very grateful."

"I'm so sorry, Mr. Archer."

"Thank you. Let me pour you some champagne," he said as a white-coated member of the staff brought in a silver bucket. "Then I'm going to steal her away from you for a bit, Monica."

"It wouldn't be the first time you went off with a pretty young thing." She held up her hands, shook her head. "I apologize. Habit. Not today, Spence." She rose, stepped over and kissed his cheek. "I'll get out of your way. I'll see you again, Lila. Be prepared for our Rylee to worship at your feet." She gave Spence's arm a squeeze, then left them.

"It was kind of you to come today," Spence began, and handed Lila the glass of champagne.

"It was important to Ashton."

"Yes, so I understand." He sat across from her.

She thought he looked tired and grim, understandably—and honestly wished herself anywhere else. What could she say to the father of a dead son she hadn't known, and the father of a son she shared a strange and dangerous secret with?

"It was a beautiful service in a beautiful setting. I know Ashton wanted to make everything as . . . comforting for you and Oliver's mother as possible."

"Ash always comes through. How long did you know Oliver?"

"I didn't. I'm sorry, it must seem strange for me to be here when I didn't know him. I was just . . . that night I was just looking out the window."

"Through binoculars."

"Yes." She felt the heat rise to her face.

"Just coincidence? It's more plausible to me you were spying on Oliver's apartment because you were one of his women. Or more troubling, you have a connection to the person who killed him."

The words, the matter-of-fact delivery, were so unexpected, so stunning, it took a moment to register.

"Mr. Archer, you're grieving for your son. You're angry, and you want answers. I don't have answers to give you. I didn't know Oliver, and I don't know who killed him."

She set down the champagne she hadn't touched. "I should go."

"You persuaded Ash to ask you here to-day, into our home. I'm told you've spent considerable time with him since your **chance** meeting at the police station the day after Oliver's death. That Ashton has already begun painting you. That's quick work, Ms. Emerson."

She got slowly to her feet, as did he. "I don't know you," she said carefully. "I don't know if it's your nature to be insulting. Since I don't, I'm going to chalk it up to shock and grief. I know what death can do to the people left behind."

"I know you're a woman of no fixed ad-dress who spends her time living in other people's homes while she writes fantasy stories for impressionable teenagers. A connection to Ashton Archer, with his name, his resources, would be quite a step up for you."

Every ounce of sympathy died. "I make my own way, take my own steps. Status and money don't drive everyone's train. If you'll excuse me."

"Trust me," he said as she started out of the room, "whatever game you're playing, you won't win."

She stopped for one last look at him, so handsome and polished, so broken and hard. "I'm sorry for you," she murmured, and walked out.

Blind with anger, she made a wrong turn but quickly corrected. She needed to get out, get away. She hated that Spence Archer had managed to make her feel both guilt and fury but knew she needed to chew on both—somewhere else.

Anywhere out of this huge and amazing space, full of people with their strange and convoluted relationships.

Screw his enormous and gorgeous home, his expansive lawns and pools and fricking tennis court. And screw him for trying to make her into a gold-digging social climber.

She made her way outside, remembered Luke had the driver's information, and the driver had her damn luggage in the trunk. She didn't want to talk to Luke or Julie or any damn body. She found one of the parking attendants, asked him for the number of a cab company, one that would take her into New York.

She'd leave her luggage—it would just go with Julie anyway. At some point she'd text Julie, let her know, ask her to haul her things up to her apartment for the night.

But she wouldn't stay here feeling humiliated, attacked and guilty one minute more than absolutely necessary.

She spotted the cab cruising down the long drive, squared her shoulders. She made her own way, she reminded herself, paid her own way. Lived her own way.

"Lila!"

She turned at the open door of the cab to see Giselle hurrying toward her.

"You're leaving?"

"Yes, I have to go."

"But Ash was just looking for you."

"I have to go."

"The cab can wait." Giselle took Lila's arm, firmly. "Let's just go back and—"

"I really can't." Just as firmly, Lila took Giselle's restraining hand, gave it a squeeze. "I'm very sorry about your brother." She got into the cab, closed the door. And sat back once she told the driver to go, trying not to think just how big a dent the cab fare back to the city would make in her budget.

Giselle retraced her steps, double-time, and found Ashton just outside the guest-house talking with a visibly upset Angie.

"You know it's not like him, Ash. He doesn't answer the phone—at home or his cell or the shop. I'm afraid he had an accident."

"I'm going to head back soon, but in the meantime let's have someone check the house."

"I could call Janis, ask her to get the spare set of keys from Vinnie's office at the shop. I talked to her already today. She hasn't seen him since she left work yesterday."

"Let's do that first. And I'll drive you back."

"I hate to leave Olympia, but I'm really worried. I'll call now, and tell Olympia I have to go."

"You're not the only one leaving," Giselle said when Angie went into the guesthouse. "Your friend Lila just left in a cab."

"What? Why?"

"I don't know for certain, but I do know Dad went in to talk to her, and the next thing I saw, she was piling into a cab. She looked pissed. Holding on to it, but seriously pissed."

"Goddamn it. Stay with Angie, will you? I need a few minutes to take care of this."

He pulled out his phone as he took the long way around to the main house in order to avoid the bulk of the guests. The call went straight to Lila's voice mail.

"Lila, tell the cab to turn around and come back. If you want to go, I'll drive you back. I'll handle it."

He shoved the phone into his pocket as he went in through the morning room, and spotted his mother.

"Have you seen Dad?"

"I think I saw him going upstairs a minute ago, maybe to his office. Ash—"

"Not now. Sorry, not now."

He went up the stairs, turned to the west wing, passed bedrooms, sitting rooms and finally, beyond the master suite, came to his father's private office.

Years of training had him knocking first, even if it was perfunctory, before he opened the door.

Spence held up a hand as he sat behind his massive oak desk, one that had been Ash's great-grandfather's.

"I'll call you back," Spence said into his phone, set it down. "I have a few things to deal with, then I'll be down."

"I take it one of the things you felt you needed to deal with was Lila. What did you say to upset her?"

Spence leaned back, laid his hands on the padded leather arms of his chair. "I simply asked her a few pertinent questions. I think we've had enough drama for the day, Ash."

"More than. What pertinent questions?"

"It's questionable, don't you think, that this woman—one who just happens to be connected to the manager of the gallery that displays your work—should be the one witness to whatever happened in that apartment the night Oliver was murdered?"

"No."

"And this connection of hers was once married to a man you're particular friends with."

Ash saw, clearly, where this rocky path would lead. He didn't want to make the trip, today of all days. "Connections happen. This family is living proof of it."

"Are you aware Lila Emerson was once the mistress of Julie Bryant's husband?"

Temper he'd hoped to avoid began to bubble in the blood. "You misuse the term 'mistress' in this case, but I'm perfectly aware Lila was once involved with Julie's ex. And since you are, I'm now also aware you hired investigators to dig into Lila."

"Of course I did." Spence opened a drawer, took out a file and a CD. "A copy of the report. You'll want to read it for yourself."

"Why did you do this?" Struggling to keep his temper on the leash, he stared at his father—recognized the impenetrable wall he faced. "She called the police. She talked to me, answered questions for me when she didn't have to, when a lot of people wouldn't have."

As if that proved his point, Spence

jabbed a finger on the desk. "And now you're buying her clothes, spending time in her company, preparing to paint her, bringing her here, today of all days."

Impenetrable, Ash thought again, but grieving, too.

"I don't owe you an explanation, but considering today of all days, I'll say this. I bought a costume selected for the painting, as I often do. I spent time in her company because she helped me, and because I enjoy her. I asked her to come here for my own reasons. I approached her—at the police station and thereafter. I asked her to pose for me, and pushed through her reluctance. I pressured her to come today because I wanted her here."

"Sit down, Ashton."

"I don't have time to sit. There are things that need to be done, and standing here trying to reason with you isn't getting them done."

"Have it your way."

Spence rose, walked to a carved sideboard, poured himself two fingers of whiskey from a decanter.

"But you will listen. Women of a certain

ilk have a way of making a man feel he's making the choices and decisions when in fact they're leading him. Can you really be sure, first and foremost, she had nothing to do with what happened to Oliver?"

He lifted his eyebrows, and the glass, as if in toast before sipping the whiskey.

"She who happened to witness this model falling because she was spying on their apartment through binoculars?"

"You can say that when you paid investigators to spy on her?"

Spence walked back to the desk, sat. "I protect what's mine."

"No, in this case you're using what's yours to attack a woman who's done nothing but try to help. She came here because I asked her to, and left because, it's becoming clear, you insulted her."

"She wanders around like a gypsy, barely makes a living. She had an affair—that we know of so far—with a married man considerably more well-off financially than herself."

More exhausted than angry now, Ash slid his hands into his pockets. "Do you really want to moralize about sleeping around? From where you sit?"

Temper snapped into Spence's eyes. "I'm still your father."

"You are, but that doesn't give you the right to insult a woman I care about."

Spence leaned back in the chair, swiveling it slightly side to side as he studied his son. "Just how involved are you?"

"My business."

"Ashton, you're simply not factoring in the reality. There are women who target a man for his status, his portfolio."

"And how many times have you been married—so far? How many **mistresses** have you paid off?"

"You'll show respect." Spence surged to his feet.

"But you don't." Fury battled back so fast and hard he had to clamp it down. Not here, he ordered himself. Not today.

"It's clear now this was never about Oliver. The police report and that report on your desk would have satisfied you Lila had nothing to do with Oliver or what happened to him. It's about me and my relationship with Lila."

"The gist remains the same," Spence pointed out. "And you're in a vulnerable position."

"It may be you figure having multiple wives, mistresses, affairs, canceled engagements and flings makes you an expert. I don't see it that way."

"It's a parent's job to steer their children away from mistakes they made themselves. This woman has nothing to offer, and she's used a tragedy to gain your trust and affection."

"You're wrong, on all counts. You should remember it was Oliver who needed your approval and your pride. I appreciate it when I get it, but I don't live for it the way he did. You crossed a line."

"We haven't finished here," Spence said when Ash turned to go.

"Wrong again."

He let raw temper carry him out, down the stairs and nearly out of the house before his mother caught up with him.

"Ash, for God's sake, what's going on?"

"Other than Dad hiring investigators to pry into Lila's life, then taking swipes at her so she called a cab and left, Oliver's all-white memorial and Vinnie among the missing, it's just your typical Archer get-together."

"Spence—God, I should've known. I left

that poor girl alone with him." She shot one fulminating glare toward the staircase. "You'll fix it with her—I like her, if that matters."

"It does."

"What's this about Vinnie?"

"I don't know yet. I have to get back to Angie. She's worried."

"I'm sure she is. It's not like Vinnie. I'd go over to the guesthouse, but Krystal just headed that way," she said, referring to her ex-husband's current wife. "She's being very decent to Olympia, so I'll keep my distance and avoid raising her hackles."

"For the best."

"I could speak with Spence."

"Don't—"

"Probably for the best, too." She hooked an arm through his, slowing him to a walk and—he knew—deliberately cooling his temper. "Do you want Marshall and me to take Angie back to the city?"

"I'll do it. Thanks, but I need to get back anyway."

"When you see Lila, tell her I'd love to have lunch sometime."

"Sure." He paused when Luke and Julie crossed his path.

"We heard Lila left," Julie began.

"Yeah, a little dust-up, we'll call it. If you see her before I do, tell her . . . Tell her I'll tell her myself."

"I should go." Julie looked at Luke. "She's staying with me tonight, so I should go."

"Then we'll go. Want a lift back?" Luke asked Ash.

"No, I have something to do. I'll be in touch."

Smoothly, Monica transferred to Luke and Julie. "I'll walk you out."

Nobody did it better than his mother, Ash thought, and slipped away under the pergola, then back into the sun. He relished the quiet, just for a moment, considered trying Lila's phone again. But his own signaled.

Hoping she'd returned his call, he checked the display, frowned at the name. "Janis?"

"Ash, God, Ash. I couldn't . . . couldn't call Angie."

"What is it? What's wrong?"

"Mr. V, Mr. V . . . The police . . . I called the police. They're coming."

"Take a breath. Tell me where you are."

"I'm at the shop. I came to get the

keys for Mr. V's apartment. In his office. Ash . . ."

"Take a breath," he repeated when she broke down in sobs. "You have to tell me what's happened." But the squeezing fists in his belly already had. "Just say it."

"He's dead. Mr. V. In the office. Somebody hurt him. And there's a man there—"

"A man?"

"He's dead, too. He's lying on the floor, and the blood. I think somebody shot him. Mr. V, he's tied to his chair, and his face is all . . . I don't know what to do."

Emotion had to wait. Now the unthinkable had to be handled, and quickly. "You called the police?"

"They're coming. But I couldn't call Angie. I couldn't, so I called you."

"Wait outside for the police. Go outside and wait for the police. I'm on my way."

"Hurry. Can you hurry? Can you tell her? I can't. I can't."

"I'll tell her. Wait for the police, Janis— outside. We're on our way."

He ended the call, simply stared down at the phone.

Had he done this? Had he caused this by asking for Vinnie's help?

Lila.

He called her number. "Answer the damn phone," he snapped at her voice mail. "Listen to me. Vinnie's been killed. I don't know what happened yet, but I'm on my way back to New York. Go to a hotel. Lock the door and don't open it for anyone. And the next time I call, pick the fuck up."

He shoved the phone in his pocket, pressed his fingers to his eyes. And asked himself how to tell Angie her husband was dead.

Twelve

She didn't want to talk to anyone—and her phone kept burping out the opening stomp-stomp-clap of "We Will Rock You."

She was changing that damn ringtone first chance.

It was bad enough to be stuck in a cab after being bitch-slapped by the über-rich father of the man she'd recently decided to sleep with without being constantly bombarded by Queen.

And she loved Queen.

Her temper had cooled about twenty miles out, so now she took the rest of the drive in a sticky pool of self-pity.

She'd rather be mad.

She ignored Queen, the African tribal music beating out of the driver's radio and the "Highway to Hell" guitar riff that was her text signal.

Calmer, clearer—if sulky—she relented a little when they drove into the city. Enough to take out her phone and look at her incomings.

Three calls from Ash, two from Julie. And one text from each. She blew out a breath, decided Ash won on a number of counts.

She listened to his first voice mail, rolled her eyes.

He'd handle it.

Men.

She handled herself and what came her way. That was Lila Emerson rule number one.

She pulled up Julie's first call next.

"Lila, I just bumped into Giselle Archer. She said you'd left. What's going on? What happened? Are you okay? Call me."

"Okay, okay. Later."

She listened to Ash's second message. Sneered at his demand that she answer the phone. Then everything froze. Her finger trembled as she played the message back a second time.

"No, no, no," she murmured, and immediately brought up his text.

Answer, damn it. On my way in via chopper. Need the name of your hotel. Lock the door. Stay.

Going on instinct, Lila leaned forward. "Change of plans. I need you to take me to . . ." What was the damn address? She dug into her memory, pulled out the name of the shop Ash had mentioned, keyed it into a search on her phone.

She rattled it off to the cabbie.

"Cost you more," he told her.

"Just take me there."

Ash stood in the doorway of Vinnie's office beside a uniformed cop. His rage, his guilt, his grief smothered under a thick layer of numb. The short and hellish flight from the compound, all the confusion, the panic faded away as he looked at the man he'd known and loved.

Vinnie's habitually dapper suit was stained with blood and urine. His face, always so smooth and handsome, showed the raw bruising, the engorged swelling of a vicious beating. The single eye stared out, filmed with death.

"Yes, that's Vincent Tartelli. In the chair," Ash added carefully.

"And the other guy?"

Ash took a deep breath. His aunt's sobs carried down the stairs, terrible sounds he thought might echo in his head forever. A female officer had taken her upstairs, away from this. Taken her and Janis, Ash corrected. Thank God they'd taken her upstairs.

Ash made himself look at the body sprawled on the floor.

Burly, broad-shouldered, big hands showing bruising and scraping along the knuckles. A shaved head, a square, bull-dog face.

And a tidy blackened hole dead center between his eyebrows.

"I don't know him. I don't think I've ever seen him before. His hands—he's the one who beat Vinnie. Just look at his hands."

"We'll take you up with Mrs. Tartelli. The detectives will talk to you."

Fine and Waterstone, he thought. He'd

called from the chopper himself, asked for Fine and Waterstone.

"She can't see this. Angie—Mrs. Tartelli. She can't see Vinnie like this."

"We'll take care of it." He drew Ash away, into the main shop. "You can wait upstairs until . . ." He broke off when another cop signaled him from the main door. "Stay here."

Where would he go? Ash wondered as the cop walked to the door. He looked around the shop Vinnie had such pride in—gleaming wood, sparkling glass, the glamour of gilt.

Old things, precious things. And nothing touched, nothing broken or disturbed that he could see.

Not just a robbery, not just some murderous fuck looking for money or something to pawn.

It all went back to Oliver. It went back to the egg.

"There's a woman outside looking for you. Lila Emerson."

"She's a . . ." What was she exactly? He couldn't quite pin it down. "She's a friend. We were at my brother's funeral this afternoon."

"Bad day for you. We're not going to let her in, but you can step outside to talk to her."

"All right."

She shouldn't be here. Then again, Angie shouldn't be weeping up the stairs. Nothing was as it should be, so he could only deal with what was.

She paced the sidewalk, stopped when she saw him step out the door. She gripped his hands, and like the first time he'd met her, compassion radiated from those big dark eyes.

"Ash." She squeezed his hands. "What happened?"

"What are you doing here? I told you to go to a hotel."

"I got your message. Your uncle was killed—Oliver's uncle."

"They beat him." He thought of the ugly bruising on Vinnie's neck. "I think he was strangled."

"Oh, Ash." Though he felt her hands tremble, they stayed strong on his. "I'm so sorry. His wife. I met his wife for a minute."

"She's inside. Upstairs. They have her upstairs. You shouldn't be here."

"Why should you have to deal with this

alone? Give me something to do, some way to help."

"There's nothing here."

Her fingers tightened on his. "You're here."

Before he could respond, before he could think of a response, he saw the detectives.

"I asked for Waterstone and Fine. They're here. You need to go to a hotel. No, go to my place." He started to dig for his keys. "I'll be there as soon as I can."

"I'm staying, for now. They see me standing here," she said quietly. "I can hardly run off—and I'm not leaving you to deal with all this on your own."

Instead she turned to stand side by side with Ash.

"Mr. Archer." Fine met his eyes, looked deep. "Once again, we're sorry for your loss. Let's talk inside. You, too, Ms. Emerson."

They stepped in, out of the summer heat and fuming traffic into the cool and the weeping.

"His wife," Ash began. "I know you have to talk to her, ask her questions. Could you do that quickly? She needs to go home, get away from this."

"We'll expedite that. Officer, find Ms. Emerson a quiet place to wait. Mr. Archer, you can go upstairs, wait with Mrs. Tartelli. We'll be up to talk to you as soon as possible."

Separating them, Ash thought, as Lila gave his hand a squeeze before releasing it to go with the officer.

It was standard procedure, he assumed, but still made him feel heavy with guilt and rawly frustrated.

He went upstairs, sat with Angie, held her while she trembled. Held Janis's hand while she fought not to cry.

And thought about what needed to be done.

They sent for Janis, who shot him a grief-stricken look out of red-rimmed eyes before she went down.

"Janis said he had a late customer."

"What?"

Angie hadn't spoken coherently until now. She'd wept, rocked, trembled. But leaning against him, she began to speak in a voice scraped raw from tears.

"When Janis left for the day yesterday, he had a customer. A woman who said she was furnishing a new apartment. She picked out a lot of things, good pieces. Her husband was going to come in and approve, Janis said. So he was here late. Someone came in before he'd locked everything up, or caught him before he'd finished. He was here alone, Ash. All the time I thought he was running late, or dallying, he was here alone. I didn't even call him last night. I was so tired after dealing with Olympia, I didn't even call him."

"It's all right," he said uselessly.

"When he left for work yesterday, I nagged him not to lose track of time. He can do that. You know how he can do that. He was so sad about Oliver. He wanted a little time by himself, but I nagged at him when he left for work not to lose track of time.

"He'd have given them whatever they wanted." Tears rolled like rain as she kept her eyes locked on Ash. "We talked about that all the time. If someone came in to rob him, he'd give them whatever they wanted. He always told the staff the same. Nothing here's worth your life or your family's grief. They didn't have to hurt him. They didn't have to do this."

"I know." So he held her until she wept

herself dry, and the detectives came up the stairs.

"Mrs. Tartelli, I'm Detective Fine, and this is Detective Waterstone. We're very sorry for your loss."

"Can I see him now? They wouldn't let me see him."

"We're going to arrange that in a little while. I know this is hard, but we need to ask you some questions."

Fine sat in a rosewood chair with cabbage roses covering the seat. She kept her tone soft, as she had, Ash remembered, when they'd come to tell him about Oliver.

"Do you know of anyone who'd wish your husband harm?"

"People like Vinnie. You can ask anyone who knows him. No one who knew him would hurt him."

"When did you last see or speak with him?"

Ash held her hand as Angie told them essentially what she'd told him, expanding when asked why he'd stayed behind another day.

"Olympia wanted me—Oliver's mother. She's Vinnie's sister, but we're close. We're like sisters. She needed me." Her lips trembled. "I went up with our kids, and their kids. Vinnie was supposed to come up last night or this morning, depending on how he felt. I could've made him go. He'd have come with us if I'd pushed. I didn't, and now—"

"Don't do that, Angie," Ash murmured. "Don't do that."

"He'd have given them whatever they wanted. Why did they have to hurt him like that?"

"It's our job to find that out," Fine told her. "There are a lot of valuable things in here. Is there a vault?"

"Yes. In the third-floor storage room. That's mainly for pieces on hold for a client, or in for appraisal."

"Who has access?"

"Vinnie, Janis. I would."

"We'll need to take a look. Would you know if anything was missing?"

"No, but Vinnie would have the records in his office, on his computer. And Janis would know."

"All right. We're going to have you taken home now. Is there someone we can call for you?"

"Ash called . . . my kids. Our kids."

"They're already at the house," he told her. "They'll be there for you."

"But Vinnie won't." Her eyes filled again. "Can I see Vinnie?"

"We have some details to go over, but we'll notify you when you can see him. An officer's going to take you home. We're going to do everything we can, Mrs. Tartelli."

"Ash—"

He drew her to her feet. "Go on home, Angie. I'll take care of things here, I promise. Anything you need, anything I can do, just ask."

"I'll walk you down, Mrs. Tartelli." Waterstone took her arm.

"These are your half brother's relatives," Fine said when Angie was downstairs. "You seem close, given that connection."

"In a family like mine you're all relatives." He pressed the heels of his hands to his eyes. "They've been married longer than I've been alive. What'll she do now?" He dropped his hands. "There'll be surveillance. I know he had good security here."

"We have the CDs."

"Then you've seen who did this. There had to be at least two of them."

"Why do you say that?"

"Because Vinnie didn't shoot the man dead in his office. The man who, from the look of his hands, beat Vinnie. You don't have to be a detective to figure that much out," Ash added. "You just have to use basic logic."

"When did you last see the deceased?"

"I saw Vinnie Thursday evening. He came to my loft. Let me see the CDs."

"Being logical doesn't make you a detective."

"You suspect Vinnie's murder is connected to Oliver's. So do I. I've never seen the man in his office, but maybe I've seen the other one, or the others. Detective, do you think Angie would lean on me this way if Vinnie and I had any friction? She's right in what she said before. Everyone liked him. He was a good man, a good friend, and it might not fit your definition, but he was family."

"Why did he come to your loft Thursday evening?"

"I'd lost a brother, he'd lost a nephew. If you want more, let me see the tapes."

"Are you bargaining with me, Mr. Archer?"

"I'm not bargaining, I'm asking. Two members of my family have been murdered. My brother worked for Vinnie, here in this shop. If there's any chance I can do something to help you find who did this, I'm going to do it."

"Was Vinnie keeping something for your brother?"

"No, but someone may have thought he was. Vinnie was absolutely honest—you don't have to take my word, and you won't. You'll check into it, and you'll see."

"And Oliver?"

The pounding in his head kicked up enough it nearly drowned out her voice. "Oliver could bend the line to suit the circumstances, and never understand—genuinely not understand—he'd crossed it. Detective, my family is shattered."

He thought of his father—inflexible, unreachable in his anger and grief.

"Finding who did this is a start to putting it back together."

"And family is the thing?"

"Yeah, it has to be. Even when it's fucked up." Again, he pressed the heels of his hands to his eyes. "Maybe especially when it's fucked up."

She got to her feet. "It won't hurt to show you. Why was Ms. Emerson here?"

"She was at the funeral, and left before
I did."

"She came to your brother's funeral?"

"I asked her to. I wanted her there. When
Janis called, after finding Vinnie, I contacted her. If this is connected to Oliver, it
could put her in the middle."

"What's your relationship?"

"Evolving," he said simply.

"We'll have her look at the recording.
Problem with that?"

"No." He shook his head as they walked
downstairs. "It's probably better if she does."

"A screwed-up family can bog down an
evolving relationship."

Oh boy, couldn't it just. "I guess we'll
find out."

More cops now, Ash noted. And techs—
crime scene techs, he assumed. Going
about the business of blood and death.
Fine signaled for Ash to wait, then walked
over to speak with one of the officers. As
he waited, Ash stepped over, looked into
the office.

Sometime during the endless interlude
of wait, comfort, wait, they'd taken Vinnie
and the other body away.

"She'll have to see him the way I saw

Oliver," he said when Fine came back. "On a slab, covered by a sheet. Through the glass. She'll never erase that memory, no matter how many others they made over the years. She'll never erase that single one."

"Come with me." She carried a laptop and a sealed evidence bag holding a CD. "Does Mrs. Tartelli have a minister, a priest, a rabbi?"

"They weren't especially religious."

"I can give you the names of a couple of grief counselors."

"Yes." He latched onto that. "Yes, thank you."

They made their way back, through chairs, tables, displays and shelves.

Lila sat with Waterstone at a pedestal dining table with Lila listening intently as Waterstone talked.

Waterstone glanced up, and a faint flush rose up his neck. Clearing his throat, he sat back.

"I'm going to have them look at the surveillance footage," Fine announced.

Waterstone's eyebrows drew together. Ash thought he started to speak, likely to object or question, then perhaps reading some silent signal from his partner, he shrugged.

"I'm going to start it when Mr. Tartelli was alone in the shop with an as-yet-unidentified female."

"A woman?" Lila watched Fine open the laptop, turn it on. "A woman did this? That's a stupid thing to be surprised about," she said immediately. "Women do terrible things just as men do." She reached over, touched Ash's hand when he stepped beside her chair. "Angie."

"They let her go home. Her family's there."

Fine inserted the CD, cued it.

Ash watched Vinnie offer wine to a woman in a floaty summer dress and heels. Short, dark hair, sleekly muscled arms, great legs. She turned, and he caught the full profile. Asian, he noted. Full, sculpted lips, angular cheek, almond eyes, a thick fringe of bangs.

"You'll see she doesn't worry about the cameras—and she knows they're there. Earlier footage shows her going through the shop, floor by floor, with the victim. She touches a number of things, so she's not concerned with prints either."

"I can't really see her face," Lila said.

"You will."

But Ash could. His artist's eye only needed that profile to put the rest together. Exotic, stunning, with features beautifully chiseled and balanced.

He'd have painted her as a Siren, one who called men to their deaths.

On the laptop screen, she smiled, turned.

"Wait. Can you— Wait. Can you stop it, just go back a few seconds and stop it?" Lips pressed together, Lila leaned closer. "I've seen her. I've seen her somewhere, but . . . The market! The market between the bank and the apartment I was sitting. But her hair was long. She was in the market. I spoke to her."

"You spoke to her?" Fine demanded.

"Yes. I was leaving, with my bags, and she was standing there. I told her I liked her shoes. They were great shoes. She said she liked mine, but she didn't. They were just my walking sandals."

"Are you sure it's the same woman?" Waterstone asked her.

"Look at that face. It's amazing. How many women have a face that fabulous?"

"Did she have an accent?" Fine asked.

"No, not at all. She was wearing a dress—shorter than the one there, and sexier. More skin, and these high wedge sandals. She looked a little surprised when I spoke to her, but people often do when you just blurt something out to a stranger. But she was polite. She had gorgeous skin, like gold dust over porcelain."

"Where's the market?"

Waterstone noted it down when Lila told him.

"And you? Do you recognize her?"

"No." Ash shook his head. "I'd remember that face. She's tall. Vinnie's about six feet, and in the heels they're eye level. She's got about an inch on him. So she's about five-nine. Slim, but ripped. I'd know her if I saw her again. She's playing client with a rich husband, major sale coming up."

"How do you know that?"

"Janis told Angie, Angie told me. Vinnie stayed after closing to wait for the husband."

Saying nothing, Fine continued the feed.

Vinnie shared wine with his killer, Ash thought, then walked to the door to let the accomplice in.

Then everything changed. Fear came

into Vinnie's eyes. He held up his hands, a gesture of surrender, of cooperation, before he was forced at gunpoint into the office. And the screen showed only the empty shop.

"Did you recognize the man?" Fine asked Lila.

"No. No, I don't think I've ever seen him. He didn't look familiar at all. Just her."

Fine ejected the CD, resealed it, remarked it. "They came here for something. The way it looks, the unidentified male tried to beat the information out of the victim. Approximately thirty minutes after they went into the office, the female came out, made a phone call. She talked for several minutes, seemed satisfied, and reentered the office. About four minutes later, she exited alone. She did not look satisfied, but annoyed. She went upstairs, where those cameras show her taking a decorative box off a shelf, padding it with bubble wrap. She came back down, boxed it, even tied it with a ribbon. She took another item, a cigarette case, from a display behind the counter—like an afterthought. She put both in a shopping bag and exited by the front door."

"The clerk identified the case as some Austrian thing." Waterstone took over. "Turn of the twentieth century, value about three grand. The box was a Fabergé bonbonniere, a lot more valuable—she estimated about two hundred grand retail. What do you know about that box?"

"Nothing. I don't even know what it is."

"It's a box made to hold candy or sweets," Lila put in. "Antique bonbonnieres can be very valuable. I used one in a book," she explained. "I didn't sell the book, but I used a bonbonniere to deliver poisoned truffles. Fabergé," she repeated. "Ash."

He nodded. "I don't know anything about the box. Maybe she took the case as a souvenir—like she did Julie's shoes and perfume. The box must be a gift, or why tie it in a bow? But she took a Fabergé piece, and that's probably not an accident. They came here looking for a different Fabergé piece, one worth a hell of a lot more than that box. Worth millions. One of the lost Imperial eggs. The Cherub with Chariot."

"How do you know that?"

"Oliver. The best I can put together is he acquired it at an estate sale—a legitimate sale where he represented Vinnie's business. But he bought the egg under the table. He didn't tell Vinnie. Vinnie didn't know about it until I told him Thursday evening."

"You didn't bother to tell us," Waterstone snapped.

"I didn't know about it until the day before, when I checked my post office box. Oliver sent me a package. Covering his bases, or counting on me to cover them for him."

"He sent you a Fabergé egg worth millions through the mail?"

"No. He sent me a key—safe-deposit box—and a note asking me to hold it for him until he got in touch."

"I was with him." For better or worse, Lila thought, it was time for details. "That's when I saw the woman in the market. Ash went to the bank to see what Oliver had put away, and I went into the market."

"I contacted Vinnie when I realized what it was. I made copies of the documents with it—most in Russian—and a bill of sale between Oliver and a Miranda Swanson, Sutton Place, but for her father's estate in Long Island. Vinnie confirmed that was one of the estates Oliver handled. Just a few weeks ago. Vinnie had a contact who could translate the documents. I didn't ask him who."

"Where's the egg?" Fine demanded.

"Safe."

He didn't speak to Lila, didn't so much as glance at her, but she clearly got the message. This detail wouldn't be shared.

"It's where it's going to stay until you find this woman and lock her up," Ash added.

"It's evidence, Mr. Archer."

"As far as I'm concerned, however un-ethical the deal, it was my brother's. He had a bill of sale, signed, dated, witnessed. And if I turn it over to you, I lose any lever-age I have if this bitch comes after me or mine. So it stays safe."

He reached into his inside breast pocket, drew out a photo. "That's it. If you can use them, I'll make a copy of all the documents, but the egg stays just where it is. You can try to push it," he added, "and I'll call out the lawyers. I'd rather avoid that—and I think you'd rather avoid it even more."

Waterstone sat back, tapped his blunt fingertips on the exquisite table. "Let's go back over the details and the timing, right back to the night of your brother's murder. This time don't leave anything out."

"I never did," Ash reminded him. "You can't leave out what you don't know."

Thirteen

Lila answered questions, filled in with her perspective, and literally let out a whoosh of relief when the police told them they could go.

For now.

"I feel like I should friend them on Facebook."

Distracted, Ash glanced down at her as he grabbed her hand to pull her to the corner.

"Fine and Waterstone. I've been spending so much time with them, I feel like we should stay connected. Or not. Ash, I'm so sorry about Vinnie."

"So am I." He stepped to the curb, held up a hand to hail a cab.

"I can't even imagine all you have to deal with. I'm just going to take the subway to Julie's. I'm staying there tonight before I start the new job. If you need anything, just call me."

"What? No. Yes, I have a lot to deal with. You're part of it." He snagged a cab, all but bundled her inside it, then gave the driver his address. "We'll go to my place."

She considered the circumstances, swallowed down the instinct to object to being told rather than asked. "Okay, then. I should call Julie, let her know what's going on. She'll be expecting me."

"I texted Luke. He's with her. They know."

"Well, you've got it all lined up."

He either ignored or missed the sarcasm and only shrugged. "What were you and Waterstone talking about—when Fine brought me down?"

"Oh, his son. Brennon's sixteen and driving Waterstone crazy. He dyed his hair orange, like a carrot, decided he's a vegan—except for cheese pizza and milkshakes. He's playing bass in a garage band and says he wants to quit school and pursue his music career."

Ash said nothing for a moment. "He told you all that?"

"All that, and we were just getting to his daughter. Josie's thirteen and spends too much time texting the friends she just left in real life ten minutes before. It must be an experience, having two teenagers in the house."

"I thought he was interrogating you."

"He did—I mean he questioned me, but I didn't really have that much to say. I asked if he had a family. It has to be hard being a cop, especially in New York, and trying to balance a family life. And getting him to talk about his kids took my mind off where we were. Plus it was nice knowing he loves his kids, he's just currently baffled by them."

"Now why didn't I think to ask Fine if she had a family?"

"She's divorced, no kids." Absently, Lila shoved a loose pin back in her chignon—and realized she was way past ready to let it down again. "But she's seeing some-body pretty seriously right now. Water-stone told me."

"I'm taking you to every cocktail party, and police interrogation, I have to deal with for the rest of my life."

"Let's try to cut back on the police interrogations." She wanted to ask what he intended to do about the egg, but didn't think the back of a cab was the right place.

"Did you really take a helicopter from Connecticut?"

"It was the quickest way to get Angie back, and there's a pad behind the tennis courts."

"Of course there is."

"I need to call her," he added, pulling out his wallet when the driver swung to the curb in front of his loft. "And my mother. I'll only have to explain things once to my mother, and she'll tell everyone else who needs to know."

"Are you going to tell her about . . . everything?"

"No." He paid the driver, held the door open for Lila. "Not yet."

"Why?"

"I told Vinnie, and now he's dead."

"That's not your fault. It's not," she insisted. "Oliver acquired the egg, Oliver worked for Vinnie. Oliver acquired the egg

while working for Vinnie. Do you really believe this woman wouldn't have . . . done what she did whether or not you told Vinnie? She had no way of knowing what you told him, but I bet she knew Oliver worked for him."

"Maybe."

"Not maybe, fact. It's just logical. If you take away the emotion, which is hard to do, you get to the logical."

"You want a beer?" he asked when they went inside.

"Sure, a beer, why not?" She trailed after him into the kitchen. "Ash, here's the logic, and I probably got there first because I didn't know Oliver or Vinnie." She paused as he took two bottles of Corona out of the fridge. "Do you want to hear my theory?"

"Sure, a theory, why not?"

"You get a pass for smart-ass, considering. All right, logic says this woman knew Oliver—he or Sage probably let them into the apartment that night. The police said there was no forced entry. He wrote you he had a client—she's the client. Maybe he met her through Sage, because it seems like Sage was the main target. The dead thug had to be the one I saw hitting her.

But she couldn't tell him where the egg was, because Oliver didn't tell her. How's that so far?"

He handed her the opened beer. "Logical."

"It is. The thug went too far, and Sage went out the window. Now they've got a mess on their hands, have to act fast. Oliver was half out of it anyway because they drugged him—which also points to them thinking Sage had the information, plus she'd be easier to get the information from. They have to get out, can't take Oliver with them, so they fake his suicide. I'm sorry."

"It's done. Keep going."

"I think they stayed fairly close, watched. Maybe they checked Oliver's phone, saw he'd called you a few days before. Aha, they think, maybe the brother knows something."

Despite a dragging fatigue, he smiled a little. "Aha?"

"Or words to that effect. They follow you to the police station, see you with me, see us talking. I'm the witness, what did I see—or could I be more involved? Anyway, they—probably just she—goes to Julie's, where she thinks I live, but there's nothing there. She takes her souvenirs, and thinks about it. Then I come here to see you, and the logic from her side is something's going on. She follows us—then me into the market, where I comment on her shoes. She had to see us go into the Kilderbrands' building."

"And figuring that gave her time, doubled back here, broke in, looked around."

"But you didn't have the egg, or anything about it, here. She may wonder why you went into the bank, but from all appearances you came out with what you went in with. Very likely she still thinks you—or we—are involved, but the next stop is Vinnie."

"And if she saw him come here, that cemented it."

"All right, yes, but she'd have gotten to him either way. The Fabergé piece she took makes me think she may have asked him about Fabergé eggs, just testing the waters. Don't you think she would?"

"If I were pretending to be a rich customer, yeah, I'd have asked about Fabergé."

"Logical," Lila confirmed. "She brings in the thug, who again takes things too far, but this time she gets rid of him."

He took a slug of beer, watched—interested and stirred—as Lila pulled pins from her hair. "Temper or cool blood?"

"It can be both. He was a thug, but she's a predator."

Intrigued, as he'd had the same image, he took another, slower sip of his beer. "Why do you say that?"

"The way she played Vinnie, going all around the store, selecting pieces?" Since her dress had no pockets, she set the pins on the counter, rubbed her hands through her hair, circled her neck. "She knew what was going to happen to him—maybe not the way it happened, but, Ash, they would've killed him even if he'd had the egg and given it to them. She's a spider, and she enjoyed spinning that web around Vinnie. You could see it."

"Can't argue with that. You lay out a pretty good theory. One point of disagreement."

"Which point?"

"The beautiful spider isn't the client."

"Look, it just makes perfect sense she's—"

"Then who did she call?"

"Sorry, what?"

"Who did she call when she left the murderous thug alone with Vinnie? She took the time, had a conversation. Who would she call in the middle of trying to beat information out of a defenseless man?"

"Oh. I forgot that part."

She lifted her hair off her neck, her shoulders, as she considered. Not a deliberate move, he thought—he recognized deliberate moves. But lifted it, let it fall again because she'd freed it from the knot she'd twisted it into, and it just felt good.

Lack of purpose aside, the gesture winged straight to his loins.

"She'd call . . . her boyfriend," Lila suggested. "Her mother, the woman who feeds her cat while she's out of town. No, shit! Her boss."

"There you go."

"She's not the client." Illuminated by the idea, she gestured with the beer she'd barely touched. "She works for the client. Somebody who could afford to buy that egg—even if she intended to steal it from Oliver—had to have some serious backing to convince him she was viable. If you can afford that, you don't go hiking around New York, breaking into apartments, beating people up. You hire someone to do it. Damn, I missed that. But together we have a very good theory."

"It's pretty clear the boss doesn't mind paying for murder. You could be right about Sage being the link between this client—or his spider—and Oliver. The thing to figure out is how and who."

"Ash." She set the beer down—he calculated she'd taken three girlie sips.

"Do you want something besides beer? You want some wine?"

"No, it's fine. Ash, three people—that we know of—are dead because of that egg. You have the egg."

"That's right."

"You could give it to the police, or the FBI—whatever. Make it known. Do interviews, make a splash. You turned this rare and almost priceless treasure over to the authorities for safekeeping."

"Why would I do that?"

"Because then they'd have no reason to try to kill you, and I really don't want them to try to kill you."

"They didn't have any reason to kill Vinnie."

"He'd seen them."

"Lila, bring back the logic. They—or at least she—knew their faces were on the shop security. She didn't care. They killed Sage, Oliver and Vinnie because it's what they do. Once I don't have the egg, I'm expendable. With it, or if they're not sure I have it or not, I might be useful."

She took another girlie sip of beer. "I hate that I think you're right. Why didn't you say that to the police?"

"Because they'd be pretty lousy detectives if they hadn't figured that out before I did. No point in telling lousy detectives anything."

"I don't think they're lousy."

"So, no point in telling good detectives either." He opened a wine cooler, selected a bottle of Shiraz.

"Don't open that for just me."

"I need you to sit for me for about an hour. You'll be more relaxed with a glass of wine in you. So it's for me, too."

"Ash, I don't think it's a really good time for that."

"You shouldn't have taken your hair down."

"What? Why?"

"Pay more attention to yourself the next time you do," he suggested. "And like you talking to Waterstone about his family"— Ash drew the cork from the bottle—"it'll take my mind off things. We'll let that breathe while you change," he said as he got down a glass. "The outfit's in the dressing room in my studio. I'm going to make those calls."

"I'm not sure, given everything, sitting for this painting's going to work. Plus I'm going to be staying on the other side of the city for the next several days, so—"

"You're not going to let my father intimidate you, are you?" He cocked his head when he saw he'd surprised her into silence. "We'll talk about that, but I need to make these calls. Go change."

She breathed in, breathed out. "Try this. 'I need to make these calls. Lila, would you change and sit for me for an hour? I'd really appreciate it.'"

"Okay, that." He smiled a little at her cool and steady stare, then tipped up her face with a hand under her chin. And kissed her, going slow, going deep—just deep enough to bring a purr of pleasure to her throat.

"I would really appreciate it."

"All right, and I'll take that wine after all, when you come up."

So he knew why she'd left the compound. Probably just as well, she thought as she took the stairs to the third-floor studio. And maybe she had decided not to sit for him after all—but not because she'd been intimidated.

Because she'd been pissed. And really, what was the point in getting tangled up sexually—because this was certainly going there—when his father pissed you off, and you pissed off his father?

"The sex," she muttered, answering her own question. The sex was the point—or part of it. The main part was Ashton himself. She liked him, liked talking to him, being with him, looking at him, liked thinking about sleeping with him. The situation very likely intensified all of that, and the ultimate resolution of the situation would very likely diffuse it.

But so what? she thought as she stepped into the dressing room. Nothing lasted forever. It made it all the more important to squeeze all the juice out of the right now.

She took the dress off the rack, studied it, and the colorful hem of the underskirt. They'd altered it lightning fast, but she supposed people did things lightning fast for Ash. Fortunately for him—or her—she was wearing the new bra.

She stripped down, hung up her all-purpose black dress, slipped out of her black shoes. And into the gypsy.

It fit now, dipping low where the new bra pushed her breasts high. An illusion, she thought, but a flattering one. And it skimmed down her torso to sweep out with that fiery skirt. One twirl and the boldly colored flounces of the underskirt flashed.

He knew just what he wanted, she mused. And got it.

She wished she had more than lip gloss and blotting papers in her purse—and the jewelry he'd envisioned.

She whirled around when the door opened.

"Here's your wine."

"You should knock."

"Why? The dress is right," he continued over her puff of breath. "Just right. I need more on your eyes—smoky, sultry—and darker lips."

"I don't have makeup with me."

"There's plenty over there." He gestured to a cabinet with a dozen drawers. "Didn't you look?"

"I don't open drawers that don't belong to me."

"You're probably one of five people in the world who can say that and mean it. Look now, use whatever you need."

She opened the first drawer, and her eyes popped. Eye shadows, eye pencils, liners—liquid, powder, cream, mascaras—with disposable wands for same. Everything arranged according to type, color palettes.

She opened the next—foundations, blushers, bronzers, brushes and more brushes.

"My God, Julie would weep with joy and rapture."

She opened more. Lipsticks, lip gloss, lip liners, lip dyes.

"I've had various sisters fill it out for me."

"You could open your own boutique."

She found jewelry in other drawers, earrings, pendants, chains, bracelets. "Shiny."

He moved beside her, pawed through. "Try this, and these, and, yeah—try that."

Like playing dress-up, she decided, and got into the swing.

Hell, maybe she could pull it off.

She selected bronzer, blush, considered her eye palette, then frowned at him. "Are you just going to stand there and watch?"

"For now."

With a shrug, she turned to the mirror, began to play.

"Should I apologize for my father?"

Her eyes met his in the glass. "No. He'll have to do that for himself. I won't hold my breath."

"I won't offer excuses for him either. He can be a hard man under the best of circumstances. These are far from the best. But he had no right, none, to treat you the way he did. You should've come out to find me."

"And what, tell you, boo-hoo, your daddy hurt my feelings? His house, and clearly he didn't want me there. What man would want a woman he sees as a scheming, gold-digging, opportunistic piranha around his son?"

"No excuses," Ash said again. "He was wrong in every possible way."

She blended shadows, studied the effect. "You fought with him."

"I wouldn't say we 'fought.' We laid out our opposing viewpoints, very clearly."

"I don't want to be a wedge between you and your father. Now especially, all of you need family."

"If you're a wedge, he put you there. He'll have to deal with that. You should've come and told me."

She swept color over her cheeks. "I fight my own battles."

"It wasn't just yours. Come out when you're done. I'm going to set up."

She stopped long enough to pick up the wine, take a sip because now she was just pissed off again, feeling what she'd felt when she walked out of that big, beautiful house in Connecticut.

Still, she could consider the whole matter tabled now. He knew, she knew, they knew, and that was that.

There were much more important things, much more immediate problems to deal with than the fact that his father held her in utter contempt.

"You're not going to sleep with his father," she muttered while she fussed with eyeliner. "You're not helping his father figure out what to do about a Fabergé egg and murder."

What happened was between her and Ashton—period.

She finished the makeup, decided she'd done a very decent job.

And for her own pleasure, did a spin.

The reflection made her laugh, so she picked up her wine, carried it out. When Ash turned from his easel, she lifted her skirts, gave them a flirty shake.

"Well?"

He stared, those eyes looking over, and in and through. "Almost perfect."

"Almost?"

"The necklace is wrong."

She pouted as she lifted the pendant. "I kind of like it."

"It's wrong, but it doesn't matter at this point. Over by the windows again. The light's gone, but I can make do for this."

He'd taken off his jacket, his tie, rolled up the sleeves of his shirt.

"You're not going to paint in that, are you? Shouldn't you have a smock or something?"

"Smocks are for little girls in meadows. I'm not painting today. Tonight," he corrected. "Finish the wine or put it down."

"You're very bossy in artist mode." But she set down the glass.

"Twirl. Arms up, eyes on me."

She obeyed. Actually, it was fun. The dress, the flounces, made her feel sexy, and powerful with it. She held, twirled again when he told her, and tried to imagine herself under a full white moon in front of the gold flames of a campfire.

"Again, keep your chin up. The men watch you, want you. Let them want. Make them want. On me. Eyes on me."

She spun until the room spun with her, held her arms up until they began to ache— and still his pencil worked, worked, worked.

"I've got maybe one more twirl in me before I fall on my face."

"It's all right. Take a break."

"Yay." She went straight to the wine, took a long sip this time. "And another yay."

She took it with her as she crossed to him. And all she managed was, "Oh."

She looked fresh and fiery and feminine all at once. He'd drawn her with her hair flying, the skirts swirling, her body turned at the hips, one leg flashing out of frothing flounces.

Her eyes looked straight out of the canvas, confident, amused and sultry.

"It's amazing," she murmured.

"Needs work." He tossed his pencil down. "But it's a good start." He looked at her again, that same intensity she felt straight through to her spine. "I'm starving. We'll order in."

"I could eat."

"You change, I'll order. What do you want?"

"Anything not involving mushrooms, anchovies or cucumbers. Otherwise, I'm not fussy."

"Okay. I'll be downstairs."

She went back, took off the dress—more reluctantly than she'd imagined. After hanging it up again, she brought the makeup down to almost normal, tied her hair back in a tail.

And in the mirror looked like Lila again.

"And that concludes our performance for the night."

She went down, found him in the living room, on the phone.

"I'll let you know when I find out. What-ever you can do. Yeah, me too. Talk later." He set the phone down. "My sister."

"Which one?"

"Giselle. She says hi."

"Oh, well, hi back. What are we eating?"

"I went Italian. My go-to place does a hell of a chicken parm. No mushrooms."

"Sounds just right."

"I'll get you another glass of wine."

"Ice water first. Twirling's thirsty work."

She walked over to the front window, watched the people stroll, strut and scramble. The streetlights laid pools, splashes of white, for them to slide into, slide out of.

Later than she realized, she thought. What a strange day—a long, strange, complicated day.

"You have a real show here," she said when she heard him come back. "No binoculars needed. So many people with so much to do. Thanks." She took the water he offered. "I love watching New York, more than any other city I've been in. There's always something to see, someone with somewhere to go. And a surprise around every corner."

She eased a hip down on the wide windowsill. "I didn't realize it was so late. I'm going to have to eat and run."

"You're staying."

She turned her face from the window to him. "Am I?"

"It's safe here—I beefed up the security. Luke's going to stay at Julie's—just a precaution."

"Is that what they call it in polite circles?"

"He did." Ash smiled a little. "He said he was taking your usual room."

"Which leaves me without a bed—or here with a bed, but not my luggage."

"I sent for it."

"You . . . sent for it."

"It doesn't have far to come. The delivery guy should have it here in a few minutes now."

"There you go, lining it all up again."

She pushed off the sill, started across the room.

"Where are you going?"

She waved a hand in the air, kept walking. "Wine. I'll get my own."

"Well, get me one while you're at it."

He smiled to himself. She just fascinated him, he had to admit. So much compassion, such an open mind, a keenly observant eye. And a spine that could stiffen like an iron rod.

He imagined that's how she'd walked away from his father. With fire in her eyes and steel in her back.

When she came back with two glasses, the fire had died to a smolder. "I think we need to get a few things—"

"That'll be either food or luggage," he said when his buzzer went off. "Hold that thought."

It turned out to be her luggage, wheeled right in. And the deliveryman strolled out again pocketing whatever denomination of bill Ash had handed him.

"I pay my own way, too."

"When you make the arrangements, you can pay. No problem."

He didn't mind the fire, or the smolder, but he was a little weary of confrontations, so tried a different method.

"It's been a hell of a day, Lila. I'll get through the rest of it better knowing you're here, you're safe. You could've opted for the hotel. You didn't."

"No, I didn't. But—"

"You came straight to me, because you

wanted to help. Let me help now. You stay here tonight, and I'll take you to your new job in the morning. Or afternoon. Whenever you go there."

He'd said goodbye to his brother, she thought—complete with white butterflies. He'd lost an uncle in a horrible way. And, with her shoved in the middle, argued with his father.

Add it all up, it equaled being cut a break.

"I appreciate the help. It's better to ask first."

"I heard that somewhere, once."

"It's generally true. I'm going to change out of this dress before the food gets here. I feel like I've worn it for a week."

"We'll get these upstairs, then." He wheeled the suitcases to the elevator. "You can have any room you want. Sleeping with me isn't a requirement."

"That's good. I wouldn't like the requirement." She waited for him to open the grate. "But if it was an option, that would be just fine."

He turned to her. "It's definitely an option." And pulled her against him.

She was caught in the kiss—a little fierce, a lot possessive this time—and halfway into the elevator with him when her ears began to buzz.

"Goddamn it. Chicken parm," he murmured against her mouth. "Fast delivery."

"Oh. I guess we need to get that."

"Give me a minute."

He went to the door, checked, then opened it to a short guy in a ball cap.

"Yo, Mr. Archer. How ya doing?"

"Good enough, Tony."

"Got yer two chicken parms, yer two side salads, yer specialty breadsticks. On yer tab, like you asked."

"Appreciate it."

Ash exchanged another bill for the large takeout bag.

"Thanks. You have a good one, Mr. Archer."

"I will." Ash closed the door, locked it with his eyes on Lila. "I definitely will."

Lila smiled. "I bet that parm will warm up just fine in the microwave. Later."

"We're going to find out." He set the bag down on a table and followed her crooked finger and smile into the elevator.

Fourteen

He yanked the grate closed, slapped a hand on the button to take them up. And as the elevator ground its way to the third floor, he pressed her back against the side wall. His hands swept up, from her hips, her waist, her ribs, the sides of her breasts, sparking quick little fires on the way until he caught her face between them.

Took her mouth with his.

He'd wanted her, maybe from the first, when he'd sat across from her in the little coffee shop. When he'd been so swamped with shock and grief, and she'd reached out to him.

He'd wanted her when she'd made him smile even through the morass of grief, and all the impossible questions. When she'd stood in his studio, in the light, posing for him, self-conscious and flustered.

She'd offered him comfort, given him answers and lit something in him along the way that helped burn away the raw edges of that grief.

But now, as the floor rose slowly beneath them, he realized he hadn't understood the depth of the want.

It spread through him, a living thing, tightening his loins, his belly, his throat as she rose on her toes, wrapped around him, fisted her hand in his hair.

So he didn't think; he acted.

His hands dropped from her face to her shoulders, gripped the straps of her dress to yank them down her arms. The move trapped her arms for just a beat, just long enough for him to close his hands over her breasts. Smooth skin, a frill of lace and the quick, quick pump of her heartbeat.

Then she wiggled, fast and agile, tugged the dress down over her hips. Rather than step out of it, she boosted up, rose up to hook bare legs around his waist, strong arms around his neck.

The elevator thudded to a stop.

"Hold on," he told her, letting go of her hips to drag the gate open.

"Don't worry about me." And with that little purr in her throat, scraped her teeth down the side of his neck. "Just don't trip."

He kept his feet, pulled the band out of her hair. He wanted it free. Winding it around his hand, he dragged her head back and found her mouth with his again.

In the dark, blued by the backwash of streetlights, he carried her into his bedroom, across the wide-planked floor, and fell with her onto the bed he hadn't bothered to make since he'd last slept in it.

Immediately she rolled, using the momentum of the drop to flip him onto his back. And straddled him. Her hair fell in twin curtains around his head as she leaned down, took a quick nip of his bottom lip. Her fingers were already busy on the buttons of his shirt.

"It's been a while." She tossed her hair back, and it fell silkily over one side of her face. "But I think I remember how this goes."

"If you forget a step . . ." He slid his hands up her thighs, down again. "I'll cue you."

Spreading his shirt open, she stroked the heels of her hands firmly up his chest. "Nice build, especially for a man who works out with paints and brushes."

"Don't forget the palette knife."

On a low laugh, she ran her hands over his shoulders. "Very nice." She lowered again, brushing her lips over his—touch, retreat, touch—then down his throat, over his shoulders.

"How'm I doing?"

"Haven't missed a step."

He turned his head until her lips came back to his. As she sank in, he rolled, reversed their positions—and added heat to lush.

She'd intended to set the pace this time, this first time, sort of ease herself into it. Keep it light, build up from there.

Now he undermined those intentions so they crumbled to dust.

How could she plan her moves, her rhythm, when his hands raced over her? He touched and took the way he sketched, with sure, strong strokes, with a skill that knew how to awaken the passion he wanted. As it rose in her, she reached for more, arching under him, offering, wrapping around him, taking.

Hard muscles, long lines, all hers to explore and possess in that soft wash of blue light.

They rolled together now, a little frantic, groping and grasping, pulses pounding as blood swam faster, faster under heated skin.

He flipped open the clasp of her bra, tossed it aside and, rearing up, took her breast with his mouth.

She arched, cat-like, purring with it, her fingers digging into his shoulders as she rode the wave of sensation. His tongue swept over her, his teeth tormented, all laser-focused on that single point of her body—until the whole of her rocked, trembled.

Open, so open to the pleasures, to the speed of them layered over each other, over her.

Skin slick now, his and hers as they tangled, as her fingers fought with the button of his pants. Then his mouth raced down her torso, down, down, down until her world exploded.

She cried out, embracing the glorious shock, riding it to its breathless peak, holding on, savoring the endless fall.

Now, oh God, now. Her mind all but wept the words, but she could barely moan his name as she all but clawed at him to come back, come back to her. To take her, finally, completely.

He watched her, watched those dark, gypsy eyes, black moons in the night. Then the graceful arch of her neck as he drove into her. His own body quaked as he struggled to hold on, just to hold on to the moment of discovery. Inside her, caught there, with her eyes on his, with her hair spread wild over the sheets.

She shuddered, then took his hands, gripped tight.

Joined, they broke the moment, surrendered to need, to speed, to the movement and the drenching, drowning heat.

She lay spent, hands sliding limply from his slick shoulders to drop onto the tangled sheets. She felt beautifully used, and wanted nothing more than to bask in that until she worked up the stamina to be used all over again.

She said, "Oh boy."

He made a sort of grunt she took as agreement. He sprawled over her, full weight, which she found absolutely fine and dandy. She liked feeling the gallop of his heart against her skin, the lines of his most excellent and sated body limp over hers.

"Do you usually cap off an art session this way?"

"Depends on the model."

She let out a snort, would have given him a light punch or pinch if she'd been able to lift her arms.

"Usually I have a beer. Sometimes I take a run or hit the treadmill."

"I don't get treadmills. You get all sweaty and go nowhere. Now, sex? You get all sweaty and go everywhere."

He lifted his head to look at her. "Now I'm going to think about sex whenever I'm on the treadmill."

"You're welcome."

He laughed, rolled off her and onto his back. "You're unique."

"A major goal achieved."

"Why a goal?" When she just shrugged, he hooked an arm around her, turned her onto her side so they lay face-to-face. "Why a goal?" he repeated.

"I don't know. Probably growing up in the military. Uniforms, regimentation. Maybe unique is my personal rebellion."

"It works for you."

"And shouldn't you be some big corporate honcho, taking the ambitious route—or the summering-in-Monte-Carlo private-jet-setter? Maybe you do summer in Monte Carlo."

"I prefer Lake Como. No, I'm not a summering type, or a honcho. I didn't have to go through the starving-artist stage, but I would have."

"Because it's not just what you do, it's who you had to be. It's good to have the talent and the love. Not everybody can or does."

"Is writing who you had to be?"

"It feels like it. I love it, and I think I'll get better. But I'd be a starving literary artist without the house-sitting. I like that, too, and I'm really good at it."

"You don't go through drawers that don't belong to you."

"Absolutely true."

"I would," he decided. "Most people would. Curiosity demands it."

"Give in to curiosity, draw unemployment. Plus, it's just rude."

"Rude gets a bad rap." Lightly, he touched his finger to the tiny dimple beside her mouth. "Let's nuke dinner."

"Now that you mention it, I'm officially starving. My dress is in the elevator."

He waited a beat. "The windows are covered with one-way film to frustrate people much like yourself."

"Regardless. Got a robe? Or a shirt? Or my luggage?"

"If you insist."

He rose, and she decided he must have eyes like a cat to move so easily through the dim light. He opened the closet, and since he stepped inside it, she judged it to be a pretty good size. And came back with a shirt he tossed at her. "It's too big for you."

"Which means it'll cover my ass. Asses must be covered at mealtime."

"That's strict."

"I don't have many rules," she said as

she put it on, "but those I do have are very firm."

It did cover her ass, and the tops of her thighs—and her hands. She buttoned it primly, rolled up the sleeves.

He'd paint her like this, too, he thought. Soft and mussed from sex, heavy-eyed, and wearing one of his shirts.

"There now." She smoothed down the hem. "Now you have something to take off me after dinner."

"When you put it that way, rules are rules."

He grabbed a pair of sweats, a T-shirt.

They took the stairs down.

"You took my mind off everything else for a while. You're good at that."

"Maybe letting it all go somewhere else—or everywhere else—will help us figure out what to do next." She poked her head in the delivery bag. "God. It still smells good."

He ran a hand down her hair. "If I could backtrack, I wouldn't have gotten you involved in this. I'd still want you here, but I wouldn't have gotten you involved."

"I am involved, and I'm here." Lifting the

bag, she held it out. "So let's eat. And maybe we can work out what to do next."

He had some thoughts on that, tried to line them up as they heated the food, settled down in the nook he used for most of his meals.

"You were right," she said after a bite. "It's good. So . . . what do you have in mind? You've got your thinking look on," she added. "Like when you're working out what to paint and how. Not the totally focused, wickedly intense look you have when you're drawing, but when you're preparing to."

"I have looks?"

"You do, and you'd see for yourself if you did a self-portrait. What are you thinking?"

"If the cops identify Hot Asian Girl, it may be moot."

"But you don't think so, and neither do I. HAG—an appropriate term for her—wasn't worried about the security cameras. So either she doesn't care if she's identified, or she's not in the system anywhere to be identified."

"Either way, she didn't appear particularly worried about police tracking her down on suspicion of multiple murders."

"She's probably done others, don't you think? God, this is weird, eating chicken parm and talking about multiple murders."

"We don't have to."

"No, we do." She focused on winding some pasta around her fork. "We do. Being weird doesn't make it less necessary. I thought I could think of it like the plot for a story, and a little removed. But that's not working for me. Reality is, and you have to deal with it. So. She's probably killed before."

The tidy black hole centered between the body's eyebrows came to Ash's mind. "Yeah, I don't think she's new at this. And if we're right, her boss has to have deep pockets. He wouldn't hire amateurs."

"If he hired her to get the egg from Oliver, she hasn't delivered."

"Exactly."

Lila wagged her fork at him. "You're thinking of a way to lure her out, with the egg. If she doesn't deliver, she could lose her job, or her fee—or maybe even worse since whoever's paying her doesn't worry about having people killed to get what he wants."

"If it's the egg she wants—and what else?—she's run out of options. I don't know what Vinnie might have told her under that kind of duress. I think, considering who he was, he didn't tell her anything. But if he did, he knew I'd taken it to the compound, to hide it for safekeeping, but not where in the compound."

"If she somehow figures out it's there somewhere, it still puts her in a bind. It's a big place. And even if she could get in—"

"Big **if** with my father's security. But if she was smart enough to, say, get hired as staff, or wheedle an invitation, she still wouldn't know where to start looking. I put it—"

"Don't tell me." Instinctively she covered her ears. "What if—"

"What if something goes very wrong and she gets to you? If it does, you're going to tell her the Cherub and Chariot is in the small safe in the office of the stables. We don't have horses currently, so it's not being used. It's a five-digit code. Three-one-eight-nine-zero. That's Oliver's birthday, month, day, year. If I'd told Vinnie, maybe he'd be alive."

"No." She reached out to touch his hand. "They meant to kill him all along. If they'd left him alive, he would have told you, told the police. I think, I honestly think, if he'd had the egg himself, given it to them, they still would've killed him."

"I know that." He tore a breadstick in two, more for the act of rending than out of a desire for it. Still, he offered her half. "And it's hard to accept it. But you need to know where it is."

"To use as a bargaining chip for myself, or to retrieve it if she gets to you."

"Hopefully neither one. Oliver had it. He must have reneged on the deal, or changed the terms of the deal looking for a bigger payoff. He'd never have considered they'd kill him for it, kill his lady—and he must have used her as the contact."

"The optimist," she said quietly. "The optimist always believes the best will happen, not the worst."

"He'd have believed it. Give them some grief, sure, so he covered his bases sending me the key. But he'd have figured he'd convince them to pay up—maybe dangled finding other items of particular interest to the client."

"That's a fool's game."

"He was." Ash looked down into his wineglass. "I could play a variation on it."

"What sort of variation?"

"Oliver had to have a way to contact this woman or her boss, or knew someone who had a way to contact them. I have to find that. Then I contact them and propose a new deal."

"What's to stop them, once they know you have it, from coming after you, the way they did Oliver and Vinnie? Ash." She laid a hand over his. "I really meant it when I said I didn't want them to try to kill you."

"I'll make it clear the egg is well secured. Let's say a location that requires my presence and that of an authorized representative to remove. If anything happens to me—I'm killed, have an accident, go missing—I've left instructions with another representative to transfer the box and its contents to the Metropolitan Museum of Art for immediate donation."

To her mind, he said it all—especially the words "I'm killed"—too casually. "Maybe it would work. I need to think about it."

"Since I have to figure out how to let her or her boss know I'm in the market, there's time to think."

"Or you could donate it now, make that previously suggested splash about it, and they'd have no reason to come after you."

"She'd disappear. Either to evade the authorities or to evade them and the man who hired her. Three people are dead, and two of them meant a lot to me. I can't just step aside."

She had to take a moment. She had feelings for him—she'd slept with him—she was **involved** with him on a number of levels now. And still she wasn't quite sure how to approach him on this.

Direct, she told herself, was always best.

"I think you're probably right about her disappearing. If that happened, the worry and risk would be over."

"Maybe, maybe not."

"Let's be optimistic ourselves on that, just for now. And still you'd never have justice or closure, or at least the possibility of justice and closure would be out of your hands. And that's really it, isn't it? You want them, at least a part of them, in your own hands. You need to deal with her the way you need to deal with an obnoxious drunk in a bar."

"I wouldn't punch her. She's a woman, and some rules are too ingrained."

She sat back, studied his face. He had a way of appearing calm and reasonable, but the underlayment was steely determination. He'd made up his mind, and he'd move forward with or without her help.

"Okay."

"Okay what?"

"I'm in. We'll need to refine things, work it all out step-by-step because I doubt running a con is in your repertoire."

"Maybe we should sleep on it."

She picked up her wine, smiled. "Maybe we should."

Julie couldn't sleep. Hardly a wonder given the circumstances. She'd started her day attending a funeral, where her closest friend had stormed off after being insulted by the departed's father, and ended it with her ex-husband sleeping in her guest room.

And in between there'd been another murder, which was horrible, especially since she'd met Vincent Tartelli and his wife at one of Ash's shows.

But knowing it all generated from the discovery of one of the lost Imperial eggs? That was fascinating.

She really wished she could see the egg, and knew she shouldn't be thinking about the thrill of seeing a lost treasure when people were dead.

But thinking about that was considerably less uncomfortable than thinking about Luke sleeping in the next room.

She rolled over—again—and finding herself staring at the ceiling, tried to use it as a backdrop, constructed her image of the Cherub with Chariot there.

But the compass of her thoughts veered right back to her true north, and Luke.

They'd had dinner together, just two civilized people discussing murder and priceless Russian treasures over Thai food. She hadn't argued about his staying over. She'd been unnerved, understandably, she told herself. It seemed perfectly clear now that whoever had killed Oliver, and now poor Mr. Tartelli, had broken into her apartment.

She wouldn't come back, of course she

wouldn't come back. But if she did . . . Julie could stand for women's rights and equality, and still feel safer having a man in the house, considering everything.

But when the man was Luke, it brought back all those memories—most of them good. A lot of them sexy. Good, sexy memories didn't encourage sleep.

Obviously she shouldn't have gone to bed so early, but it had seemed safer, smarter, to tuck herself into her own room with Luke tucked away elsewhere.

She could get her iPad, do some work, play some games. She could read. Any of that would serve as a productive distraction. So she'd just go quietly into the kitchen, get the tablet and make herself some of the herbal tea recommended by the nutritionist she'd fired for being completely unreasonable—her body **needed** regular infusions of caffeine and artificial sweetener. But the tea relaxed her.

She rose, took the precaution of putting a robe over her chemise. Easing her door open, careful as a thief, she tiptoed into the kitchen.

Using only the stove light, she put water

in the kettle, set it on to boil. Better, much better than tossing and turning and reliving old sexy memories, she decided as she opened a cupboard for the tin of tea. A nice, soothing drink, a little work, then maybe a very dull book.

She'd sleep like a baby.

Already more content, she got out her pretty little teapot because the soft green color and the lilac blooms made her happy. The process of heating the pot, measuring the tea, getting her strainer kept her focus on the homey task at hand.

"Can't you sleep?"

She let out a distinct and embarrassing squeal, dropped the tea tin—which fortunately she'd just closed—and stared at Luke.

He wore nothing but his suit pants—zipped but not buttoned—so it was hardly her fault her first thought was the boy she'd married had filled out really, really well.

The second was regret she'd taken off her makeup.

"Didn't mean to startle you." He came forward, picked up the tin.

"I didn't mean to wake you."

"You didn't. I heard you out here, but wanted to make sure it **was** you."

Civilized, she reminded herself. Mature. "I couldn't turn my brain off. And I don't know what to think or what to feel having murder so close to home. Then the egg. I can't get my mind off that either. It's a major find, a huge discovery in the art world, and my closest friend is involved in all of it."

Talking too fast, she told herself. Can't seem to slow down.

Why was her kitchen so small? They were all but on top of each other.

"Ash will take care of Lila."

"Nobody takes care of Lila, but yes, I know he'll try."

She pushed at her hair, imagined it a wild mess after the tossing and turning in bed.

Naked face, bad hair. Thank God she hadn't turned on the overhead light.

"Do you want some tea? It's an herbal mix with valerian, skullcap, chamomile and some lavender. Really good for insomnia."

"Have a lot of that?"

"Not really. More your basic stress and restlessness."

"You should try meditation."

She stared at him. "You meditate?"

"No. I can't turn my mind off."

It made her laugh as she reached for a second mug. "The couple times I've tried it, my **ohm** turns into: Oh, I should've bought that fabulous bag I saw at Barneys. Or should I be marketing this artist this way instead of that way? Or why did I eat that cupcake?"

"Me, it starts spinning around staff scheduling, health department inspections. And cupcakes."

She set the lid on the pot to let the tea steep. "Tonight, it was murder and Fabergé and . . ."

"And?"

"Oh, things."

"Funny, mine was murder and Fabergé and you."

She glanced toward him, then away when that single quick meeting of eyes made her stomach flutter. "Well, considering the circumstances . . ."

"There's always been a lot of you in my

head." He trailed a finger from her shoulder to her elbow—an old habit she remembered well. "A lot of wondering with you in the center. What if we'd done this instead of that? What if I'd said this and not that? Asked this instead of not asking?"

"It's natural to wonder."

"Have you?"

"Yes, of course. Do you want honey? I take it plain, but I have honey if—"

"Do you ever wonder why we couldn't make it work? Why both of us did stupid things instead of working toward figuring out how to fix it?"

"I wanted to be mad at you instead. It seemed easier to be mad at you instead of wishing I'd said this, or you'd done that. We were just kids, Luke."

He took her arm, turned her, took her other arm. Held her so they were face-to-face. "We're not kids anymore."

His hands so firm, warming her skin through the thin silk of her robe—and his eyes so fixed on hers. All the wondering, all the thoughts, all the memories simply cut through the line she'd told herself was common sense.

"No," she said, "we're not."

With nothing holding her back, she moved to him, moved into him, to take what she wanted.

And later, with the tea forgotten on the counter, with her body curled to his, she slept like a baby.

Fifteen

Knowing she needed to play catch-up, and having nowhere else practical to play it, Lila made coffee, then set up a temporary workstation in Ash's eating nook.

And there, pushed herself back into the story—one she knew hadn't gotten enough of her attention in the last few days.

Dressed in Ash's shirt, she blocked everything else out, and went back to high school and werewolf wars.

She put in a solid two hours before she heard Ash come in. She held up a finger to ask for quiet, then finished off the last thought.

Keying it to save, she looked up, smiled. "Good morning."

"Yeah. What are you doing?"

"Writing. I really needed to get back on schedule there, and you timed it perfectly. It's a good place to stop for now."

"Then why are you crying?"

"Oh." She brushed tears away. "I just killed off a sympathetic character. It had to be done, but I feel really bad about it. I'm going to miss him."

"Human or werewolf?"

She pulled a tissue from the mini pack always kept handy at her workstation. "Werewolves are human except for three nights—in my lore—a month. But werewolf. My main character's going to be shattered."

"Condolences. Do you want more coffee?"

"No, thanks. I've already had two. I thought setting up here would be the most out of your way," she continued as he tapped his machine for his own cup. "I can't go to my next job until this afternoon, and I don't feel like I can go to Julie's now. Not sure what's what there."

"You're fine."

"Is something wrong?"

"Everything's wrong before coffee." He took the first gulp of it black. "I could probably scramble some eggs if you want."

She looked at him, hair tousled, face scruffy again—and definitely cranky around the eyes. "Scrambled eggs is one of the few things I cook really well. I'll trade that for a place to hang out until two."

"Sold." He reached in the fridge, found a carton of eggs.

"Sit down and have your coffee, and I'll fulfill my part of the deal."

He didn't sit, but watched her go back to the fridge, root around until she found some cheese, the butter. Drinking his coffee, he just leaned against the counter as she poked through the cabinets for his skillet, a little bowl, a whisk—a tool he couldn't quite remember buying.

"You look good in the morning," he told her.

"Ah, coffee's doing its work." She glanced back with a smile as fresh and cheerful as a spring tulip. "I feel good in the morning, usually. Everything starts fresh in the morning."

"Some things hold over. Is there any

way you can cancel this job? Just stay here until the only egg we have to think about is scrambled?"

"I can't. There's not enough time to find a replacement, or to clear that with the clients. They're counting on me. Besides," she went on as she broke eggs into the bowl, "HAG can't know where I'll be."

"You have a website."

"That only lists when I'm booked, not where or any client information. She'd have no reason to look for me in Tudor City."

"Maybe not, but it's a good distance from here if anything happens."

She added cheese to the eggs, a touch of salt, a bit of pepper. "You're worried about looking out for me, but I have many skills for looking out for myself. You just haven't had occasion to see them in action." She poured the egg mix into the skillet, where she'd melted a pat of butter. "Want some toast with this? Got any bread?"

He got the bread, popped a couple slices in the toaster. He could work on her, and this part of the problem, later. "How much more time do you need with the werewolves?"

"If I can get this next scene drafted—where Kaylee finds Justin's mauled body—I'd feel very accomplished. I've got it in my head, so another couple of hours should do it."

"Then you'll have a couple hours after that and between your next job to pose for me again. That'll work."

He finished his coffee, immediately made a second before getting out two plates.

"Try this," she suggested. "Will that work for you, Lila?"

He snagged the toasted bread, dropped one on each plate. "Will that work for you, Lila?"

"I don't see why not." She divided up the eggs, skillet to plates, then handed him one. "Let's see how the writing goes."

"Fair enough."

A few blocks away, Julie woke. She felt amazing, wonderfully loose, blissfully rested, and let out a long, contented sigh as she stretched her arms high. Her mood bumped down a notch when she saw Luke wasn't beside her, but she shook that off.

He ran a bakery, she reminded herself. He'd told her he'd be up and gone before five A.M.

Gone were the days when she considered five A.M. a reasonable hour to fall into bed after a party, but she was a long way off from finding it a reasonable hour to get up and go.

She had to admire his work ethic, but a little lazy morning sex would've been so perfect. Especially followed up with breakfast where she could've shown off her own kitchen skills. Limited, yes, she thought, but she made killer French toast.

Catching herself dreaming of lazy mornings and long nights, she pulled herself up short. Those days were over, she reminded herself, just like all-night parties.

It had just been sex. Really great sex between two people with a history, but just sex.

No point in complicating it, she told herself as she climbed out of bed, found the robe where it had landed the night before—on top of her bedside lamp. They were both adults now, adults who could treat sex—whether a one-time thing or an affair—in a reasonable, responsible way.

She had no intention of thinking of it beyond just that.

Now, like a reasonable, responsible adult, she'd get her coffee, grab a bagel—or some yogurt because she hadn't remembered to buy bagels—then get ready for work.

She strolled into the kitchen, humming, then stopped dead.

There on her counter, sitting on one of her pretty china cake plates, was a big golden muffin, glistening with sugar. One of her glass bowls sat upside down over it like a dome.

Slowly, carefully, she lifted the bowl. Leaned down, took a little sniff.

Blueberry. He'd found the blueberries she'd bought the other day and used them in the muffin. Though given its perfect proportions it seemed almost sacrilegious, she broke off part of the top, sampled it.

It tasted every bit as perfect as it looked.

He'd baked her a muffin. From scratch.

What did that mean?

Did a muffin mean thanks for the really

good sex? Or did it mean relationship? Did it mean . . . ?

How the hell was she supposed to know what it meant? Nobody but her grandmother had ever baked her a muffin before. And he'd thrown her off with this before she'd even had a chance to clear her head with a cup of coffee.

She broke off another piece, ate it while she brooded over it.

In the basement below the bakery, Luke kneaded dough on the floured butcher-block worktable. He had a machine that efficiently cut this labor out of the process, but when he could, he preferred getting his hands in it.

It gave him time to think—or just not think at all, with the rhythm of his hands and arms, the texture of the dough. The first batches of the morning had already been mixed, finished their two risings, and were baking in the brick oven behind him.

Today he needed this second round of loaves for a specific customer request.

He and his main baker had done the

muffins, rolls, Danishes, donuts and bagels for the early-morning crowd in the main ovens during that first rising—and started the cookies, pies, scones and cupcakes during the second.

Once he had this dough rising, he'd head up, pitch in.

He glanced at the clock set prominently on the stainless steel shelves against the far wall. Nearly eight now, so he imagined Julie was up.

He wondered if she'd found the muffin he'd left her. She'd always had a fondness for blueberries.

And dark chocolate. He'd have to make her something special there.

God, he'd missed her. So much more than he'd let himself admit all these years. He'd missed the look of her, the sound of her, the feel of her.

He'd sworn off redheads after Julie. Tall redheads with great bodies and bold blue eyes. For months, maybe years, after they'd split he'd ached for her at odd moments— when he saw something he knew would make her laugh, while he struggled through the hell of law school. Even the day he opened Baker's Dozen he'd thought of her, wished he could show her he'd found his way, had made something of himself.

Every woman who'd passed through his life since Julie had done just that. Passed through. Distractions, diversions, all temporary no matter how much he'd wanted to make something solid and real. She'd always been there, in the back of his mind, in the center of his heart.

Now he just had to figure out how to reel her slowly back into his life, and keep her there.

"Nearly done here," he called when he heard someone coming down the stairs. "Five minutes."

"They said it was all right if I came down. Well, the girl with purple hair did," Julie added when he looked up.

"Sure. Come on down."

She lit him up, that flaming hair tamed back with silver combs, the amazing body poured into a dress the color of the blueberries he'd mixed in her muffin.

"I didn't expect to see you, but welcome to my cave. I'm nearly finished with this. iPod's on the shelf there, turn the music down."

She did so, muting Springsteen, and remembering he'd always been high on the

Boss. "I spend a lot of time down here, or in the main kitchen, in the back office. It must be why I never saw you come in. There's cold drinks in the cooler," he added, watching her while he kneaded the mass of dough. "Or I can get you a coffee from upstairs."

"I'm fine. Thanks, I'm fine. I need to know what it means."

"What? Like the meaning of life?" He shoved at the dough with the heels of his hands, gauged the texture. Just a couple more minutes. "I haven't come to any firm conclusions on that."

"The muffin, Luke."

"The meaning of the muffin?" God, she smelled good, and he realized the scent of her mixed with the yeasty smell of bread would fuse together in his head. "Its meaning, in fact entire purpose, is: Eat me. Did you?"

"I want to know why you baked me a muffin. It's a simple question."

"I'm a baker?"

"So you bake a muffin in the morning for every woman you sleep with."

He knew that clipped tone—it came back to him with perfect pitch. Nerves and annoyance, he thought. Over a muffin? "Some prefer a Danish—and no, I don't. But I didn't see baking one for you as a questionable move. It was a muffin."

She hitched her enormous work bag more securely on her shoulder. "We slept together."

"We certainly did." He continued to knead—kept his hands busy—but his pleasure in the work, in the morning, in her, caved in. "Is that the questionable move or is the muffin?"

"I think we need to be clear about all of it."

"Proceed to be clear."

"Don't take a tone. We had a difficult day yesterday, and we have friends involved in something scary and confusing. We have a history, and we . . . we couldn't sleep so we had sex. Good sex, as adults. Without any . . . complications. Then you baked me a muffin."

"I can't deny it. I baked the muffin."

"I just want to be clear we both know what it was—last night. That it doesn't need to be complicated, especially when, through Lila and Ash, we're in a very complicated situation."

"It's all simple, just like it was, I thought, a simple muffin."

"All right, then. Good. Thanks. I have to get to work."

She hesitated a moment, as if waiting for him to say something more. Then she walked upstairs. She walked away, with him left in silence, just as she had over a decade before.

When Ash insisted on taking Lila to her next job, she didn't argue. If seeing where she'd be, checking the security for himself, made him feel better, what was the harm?

"They're repeaters," she told him as the cab wound its way uptown. "I've worked for them twice, just not in this location because they only moved here a few months ago. And Earl Grey is a new addition, but he's really sweet."

"The new location might be better all around."

"It's a gorgeous space, wonderful views. A nice neighborhood to walk around in—with Earl Grey. And I got an e-mail from Macey this morning."

"Macey?"

"Kilderbrand—last client. They're very satisfied with my service—and she thinks Thomas misses me. As they're planning a skiing trip out West next January, they'd like to book me now. So, despite everything that happened, score one for me."

"But this is a shorter job."

"A quick one for the Lowensteins—eight days altogether, to visit some friends and check on some property in Saint Bart's."

When the driver pulled over in front of the East Forty-first Street entrance of the massive neo-Gothic complex, Lila swiped her credit card.

"I'll get it."

She shook her head, keyed in her tip. "My job, my business expense. I may have a rich lover, but I'm just using him for sex."

"He's a lucky guy."

"Oh," she said as she pocketed the receipt and slid out, "he is. Hi, Dwayne." She beamed at the doorman as he hustled over to the cab. "Lila Emerson. You may not remember, but—"

"I remember you, Ms. Emerson, from when you came to see the Lowensteins. I've got the keys for you. You're right on time."

"I try to be. Did the Lowensteins get off all right?"

"Saw them off myself not an hour ago. I'll get that." He hefted the second suitcase out of the cab's trunk before Ash could. "Can I help you up with these?"

"No thanks, we've got it. This is my friend Ashton Archer. He's going to help me settle in. Do you happen to know the last time they walked Earl Grey?"

"Mr. Lowenstein took EG out for a last round right before they left. He should be good awhile."

"Excellent. What a gorgeous building. I'm going to love staying here."

"You have any questions, where things are, need transportation, whatever, you just let me know."

"Thanks." She took the keys he handed her, and walked into the lobby and its cathedral light through the stained glass windows. "Tell me my job isn't awesome," she said to Ash as they took an elevator. "How else would I be able to spend a week in a penthouse apartment in Tudor City? Did you know they used to have a little golf course? And a tennis court. Famous people played tennis on it. I can't remember who because I don't really follow tennis."

"My father thought about buying it—with partners—when Helmsley sold it."

"Really? Wow."

"I don't remember the details, why or why not. Just vague talk."

"My parents bought a little campground in Alaska. There was a **lot** of talk, and considerable nail biting. I love working in buildings like this, the old ones," she said as they got off the elevator. "I'm fine with new ones, but buildings like this are something special."

She keyed open the locks, opened the door. "As in." She gave a sweep of her hand before turning to the alarm pad to key in the code.

The wall of floor-to-ceiling casement windows let New York in, with the glamour of the Chrysler Building front and center. Lofty ceilings, gleaming hardwood, the soft, rich glow of antiques served as the forefront for the spectacular view.

"Pretty great. I should've taken us to the second floor—it's a triplex—but I thought you'd appreciate the wow factor of the main level."

"It's got it."

"I need to check the kitchen. Earl Grey's either in there or hiding up in the master bedroom."

She walked through to a dining area with a long mahogany table, a little gas fireplace and a breakfront holding a clever mix of mismatched china. Into a kitchen that reflected the building's character with its brick accent wall, dark, deeply carved walnut cabinets and lots of copper accents.

There, on the slate-colored floor, was a little white dog bed. In it was the smallest dog—Ash didn't really consider it a dog—he'd ever seen.

White like the bed, it sported a traditional poodle cut, and in lieu of a collar, a miniature bow tie. Purple with white polka dots.

It trembled like a leaf in the wind.

"Hey, baby." Lila kept her voice cheerful, but very quiet. "Remember me?" She opened the lid of a bright red canister on the counter and took out a dog biscuit no longer than his thumb.

"Want a cookie?"

She crouched down.

The trembling stopped. The tail—what there was of it—wagged. The dog that wasn't a real dog hopped out of the tiny bed, rose on its hind feet and danced.

Ash grinned despite himself, and on a laugh, Lila offered the biscuit.

"You don't have to worry about a thing with a vicious fake dog like that around," Ash commented.

"I think the security system's good enough for me, and for Earl Grey." She scooped the dog up, nuzzled it. "Want to hold him?"

"I'll pass. He actually weirds me out a little. I'm not sure a dog should fit in your shirt pocket."

"He's small, but he has a big brain." She kissed the poodle on the nose, set him down. "Do you want a tour before I un-pack?"

"I wouldn't mind it."

"Mostly so you can scope the place out, get the lay of the land in case you have to rush in and rescue me."

"What do you care? We have to take your suitcases up anyway."

He imagined, even as she took him around the main floor, she'd set up her workstation in the dining room, and enjoy the view. Even as she started to take one of the suitcases, he lifted them both to take them upstairs.

"Is that a man thing or a manners thing?"

"I'm a man with manners."

"And this is a unit with an elevator. Small, but adequate."

"Now you tell me."

"Three bedrooms, all with baths, manly home office, and hers, more a sitting room where she keeps her orchids. They're fabulous. I'm using this room."

She walked into a compact guest room done in soft blues and greens, the furnishings in distressed white, and a painting of poppies on the wall to add an unexpected splash.

Lila gave herself a mental hug. This would be hers, just hers, for the next eight days.

"It's the smallest, but it's got a soothing, restful feel to it. You can just leave those over there, and we'll check out the third level to be thorough."

"Lead the way."

"Do you have your phone on you?"

"Yeah."

"Let's take the elevator, just to make sure it's all good. I know it has an emergency button, but it's always good to have a phone."

He'd have taken it for a closet, which showed a clever design.

"Not as much fun as yours," Lila commented as they rode up.

"A lot quieter."

"I can fix the clunking, I think."

"You repair elevators with that strange tool of yours?"

"It's a Leatherman, and brilliant. Yours would be my first, as far as elevators go, but I actually like the clunks and grinds. Lets me know it's working."

When it stopped, they stepped out into a media room larger, by his eye, than most studio apartments.

It boasted a projection screen, six roomy leather recliners, another half bath, a wet bar with built-in wine cooler.

"They have an outrageous DVD collection I'm cleared to take advantage of. But my favorite?"

She picked up a remote. The blackout

drapes opened to reveal wide glass doors, and the pretty bricked terrace beyond, complete with a central fountain—currently off.

"There's nothing like having outdoor space in New York."

She unlocked the door, pulled the doors open. "No tomatoes or herbs, but some nice patio pots of flowers—and that little shed there holds the garden tools, extra chairs."

Automatically, she checked the dirt in the pots with her thumb, pleased to find it lightly damp. "A nice spot for a pre- or post-dinner drink. Do you want to have dinner with me later?"

"I'm just using you for sex."

She laughed, turned to him. "Then we'll order in."

"I've got some things to do. I could come back around seven or seven-thirty, bring dinner."

"That sounds perfect. Surprise me."

He went to see Angie, getting out of the cab several blocks from the apartment to walk. He needed the walk, but more, if the woman was watching, she might tag the cab number, find a way to trace it back to where he now felt Lila was safe.

Paranoid, maybe, but why take chances?

He spent a hard, unhappy hour with Angie and her family. Then opted to walk from there.

How was his radar? he wondered. Would he feel it if she was watching him, following him? He'd recognize her, that he was sure of, if he spotted her, so he took his time half hoping—more than half—she'd make some move.

He saw Trench Coat Man marching and muttering, and a woman pushing an infant in a stroller. He remembered her walking the neighborhood weeks before, hugely pregnant. But he didn't see a tall, stunning Asian woman.

He took a detour into a bookstore, wandered the stacks, one eye on the door. He found and purchased a coffee table book on Fabergé eggs, and another on the history, then struck up a conversation with the clerk so he'd be remembered should anyone ask.

He considered it laying a trail.

And maybe he did feel a prickle at the back of his neck when he crossed the street only a block from his loft. He pulled his phone out of his pocket as if to answer it, fumbled a little with his shopping bag, shifted angles, glanced behind him.

But he didn't see the woman.

Before he shoved the phone back in his pocket, it rang in his hand. He didn't recognize the number on his display.

"Yeah, Archer."

"Mr. Archer. My name is Alexi Kerinov."

Ash slowed his steps. The accent was light, he thought, but definitely Eastern European. "Mr. Kerinov."

"I'm a friend of Vincent Tartelli's—Vinnie. I heard only a short time ago what happened, when I tried to reach him. I'm . . . This is devastating."

"How did you know Vinnie?"

"Both as a client and an occasional consultant. He recently asked me to translate some documents for him—from Russian to English—and he gave me your name and number."

Not the woman's boss, Ash thought. The translator.

"He told me he was giving them to you. Have you had a chance to look at them?"

"Yes, yes. I haven't finished completely, but I found . . . I wanted to speak to Vinnie right away, but when I finally tried his home, Angie said . . . This is a terrible shock."

"For all of us."

"He spoke fondly of you. He said you'd acquired the documents and needed to know what they said."

"Yes. He did me a favor." And that would weigh forever. "And took them to you."

"I need to discuss them with you. Can we meet to discuss this? I'm not in New York until tomorrow. I had a brief trip to D.C., and brought them with me. I come back tomorrow. Can we meet?"

When he reached his house, Ash took out his keys, went through the more laborious process of opening his own front door, keying in his new codes. "Yeah, no problem. Have you been to Vinnie's house?"

"Yes, many times."

"For dinner maybe?"

"Yes, why?"

"What's Angie's specialty?"

"Roast chicken with garlic and sage. Please, call Angie. You worry, I understand. She'll tell you who I am."

"You got the chicken, that's good enough. Why don't you tell me a little of what you found?"

Ash stepped inside, scanned the room, and the new monitor, satisfying himself before he locked the door behind him.

"Do you know anything about Fabergé?"

Ash dropped the book on a table. "As a matter of fact, yeah, some."

"Do you know of the Imperial eggs?"

"I do, and about the eight lost ones. Specifically the Cherub with Chariot."

"You already know? You understood one of the documents?"

"No, not those documents." How to play it? "There were also some in English."

"Then you know it's possible to trace the egg, through the documents. It's an enormous find. As is the other."

"What other?"

"The other lost egg. There are two documented in these papers. The Cherub with Chariot and the Nécessaire egg."

"Two of them," Ash murmured. "When do you get in tomorrow?"

"I arrive just after one in the afternoon."

"Don't tell anyone about this."

"Vinnie asked I only speak with him or

you, not even my wife or his. He was a friend, Mr. Archer. He was my good friend."

"Understood, and appreciated. I'm going to give you an address now, and I'll meet you there. Tomorrow as soon as you get in."

He gave Kerinov Lila's address at Tudor City. Safer, he thought. Away from his own place, and Vinnie's shop. "You have my number. If anything happens, if you feel uneasy about anything, contact me. Or the police."

"Is this responsible for what happened to Vinnie?"

"I think it is."

"I'll come straight to you tomorrow. Do you know the value if these could be found?"

"I've got a pretty good idea."

When he hung up, Ash grabbed both books, took them straight to his office. And dug into research on the second egg.

Sixteen

Lila unpacked, enjoying, as always, the feeling of the new. Her client had left some provisions for her, and she appreciated it, but she'd take Earl Grey for a walk later, pick up a few things. For a while she played with the dog, who—as advertised—enjoyed chasing a little red rubber ball rolled over the floor. So they played chase and fetch, then find-the-ball until Earl Grey retreated to one of his little beds to nap.

In the quiet, Lila set up her workstation, poured herself a tall glass of lemon water and updated her blog, answered e-mails, booked two jobs.

She considered dipping back into the book when her house phone rang.

"Lowenstein residence."

"Ms. Emerson, this is Dwayne on the door. There's a Julie Bryant in the lobby."

"She's a friend. You can send her right up. Thanks, Dwayne."

"No problem."

Lila checked the time, frowned. Much too late for Julie's lunch hour, and still a little too early for the usual end of her day. But the visit couldn't have been more welcome—she **had** to tell Julie about Ash, about her and Ash, about the night after the awful day.

She went to the door, opened it, waited. No point having Julie ring the bell and wake up the dog.

It wasn't until she heard the elevator ping, saw its doors begin to open, that the thought jumped into her head. What if it wasn't Julie, but HAG using Julie's name to gain access? On the heels of it, as she started to slam the door, Julie stepped out.

"It's you."

"Of course it's me. I said it was me."

"Mind tricks." Lila tapped her temple. "Did you get off early?"

"I took off early. I needed a little mental health time."

"You've come to the right place." She swept her arm. "Amazing view, huh?"

"It really is." Taking it in, Julie dumped her work bag in a tufted-back armchair. "I went to a party in this building last year, but the apartment wasn't nearly as wow as this—and it was pretty wow."

"You have to see the third-floor terrace. I could live out there all summer. You brought wine," she added when Julie pulled a bottle out of her bag as slickly as a rabbit from a magician's hat. "This is a wine visit."

"Definitely."

"Good, because I have to tell you something that goes with wine."

"Me, too—you," Julie said as she followed Lila to the wet bar. "Yesterday was crazy and awful, and then—"

"I know! That's just it." Lila used the fancy counter-mounted corkscrew. "It's all about the then and then."

She pulled the cork out.

"I slept with him," they said in unison.

They stared at each other. "You did?"

"You did?" Julie echoed, pointing.

"You mean Luke, because I slept with

Ash, so if you'd slept with him I'd have noticed. You slept with Luke. Slut."

"Slut? You're more qualified as slut here. I used to be married to Luke."

"My point exactly. Sleeping with the ex?" Amused, Lila clucked her tongue as she reached for glasses. "Definitely slut territory. How was it? I mean, was it like a stroll down memory lane?"

"No. Well, yes, in a way. Knowing him, being comfortable with him. But we've both grown up, so it wasn't like a rerun. I thought it was maybe, I don't know, a kind of closure we didn't really have. We were both just so sad and mad when we split. So young and stupid. Looking back, I understand we just saw it like playing house, didn't consider being mostly broke, scrambling to pay rent—and with his parents still nudging him toward law school. No direction for either of us," she added with a shrug. "Just run off, get married without a thought toward reality, then we were both like what do we do about all this **real**?"

"Real's hard."

"And has to be dealt with, but we couldn't seem to figure out how we could want each other and want other things, too. How we could have each other and have other things. I guess— No, I know I decided it was his fault, and it wasn't. He probably decided it was mine, but he never said it. Which was my other issue. He'd just say whatever you want, and it made me crazy. Say what you think, damn it."

"He wanted you to be happy."

"He did, and I wanted him to be happy— and we weren't, and it was mostly because we just kept fumbling the real. Little fights, piling up to one big one until I walked out. He didn't stop me."

"You wanted him to."

"God, I wanted him to. But I hurt him, so he let me go. And I've always . . ."

"Regretted it," Lila supplied. "The split, not Luke. You told me that once after two chocolate martinis."

"Chocolate martinis should be illegal, but yes, I guess I've always regretted how it ended, and maybe I've always wondered what if. And now . . ." She took the wine Lila offered. "Now it's all messed up and tangled up and confused again."

"Why? Don't answer yet. Let's go up. Bring the bottle and we'll sit outside."

"Sit outside, but leave the bottle," Julie

qualified. "I still have paperwork to do at home since I left early. One glass is all I get for skipping out early."

"Fair enough."

She let sleeping dogs lie and took Julie up to the terrace.

"You're right, you could live out here. I need to move," Julie decided. "I need to find an apartment with a terrace. I need a raise first. A really big one."

"Why?" Lila repeated, and sat, lifted her face to the sky. "On Luke, not the raise."

"He baked me a muffin."

Lila looked at Julie again, smiled and said, "Aw."

"I **know**. It means something. It's not just 'Here's a baked good.' He baked for me. At dawn. Before dawn, probably. It means something."

"It means he was thinking of you, before dawn, and wanted you to think of him when you woke up. It's so sweet."

"Then why didn't he say that when I asked him?"

"What did he say?"

"That it was just a muffin. I went to his bakery, and he's down in this"—she circled a hand in the air—"this baking cave working with this big mound of dough. Damn it, why is that sexy? Why is it sexy when he's up to his elbows in dough in this baking cave?"

"Because he's sexy anyway, and a man in any kind of cave adds another layer of sexy. Add working with his hands, and it's a triple threat."

"It's not right, that's all. Sex, then muffin, then sexy baking cave. I went there for a simple answer."

"Oh."

"What do you mean, 'Oh'? I know that 'Oh.'"

"Then I shouldn't have to elaborate, but okay. He baked you a muffin, which, I agree, has meaning. And you went to his work space and asked him what it meant."

"That's right. What's wrong with that?"

"Maybe you could've just eaten the muffin and thanked him later."

"I wanted to know." Julie dropped into the chair beside Lila.

"I get that. But from his perspective—do you want my take on his perspective?"

"I probably don't. No, I definitely don't. But I should, so go ahead."

"He did something nice, something

thoughtful—and given he's a baker, something that fits. He wanted to make you smile, and think of him because he thought of you—and I bet he smiled. Instead, it worried you."

"It did worry me—it does—even though there's a rational woman in my head shouting, 'Stop being stupid. Just stop, stop, stop.'" She tossed back some wine. "I wanted it to be a fling. Simple, easy, grown-up. And the minute I saw that damn muffin . . ."

"You're still in love with him."

"I'm still in love with him. It would never have worked with Maxim—I knew it, wouldn't accept it, when I married him. It wouldn't have worked even without you sleeping with him. Bimbo slut."

"Clueless wife."

"Luke would never cheat. It's not in him. And last night, it was like coming home, but everything fit better, made more sense."

"Then why aren't you happy?"

"Because I don't want to be here, Lila. I don't want to be this woman who can't let go of this"—the hand circled again—"this frothy illusion of the past. I could've handled the sex. I was handling the sex."

"And the muffin changed that."

"I know that sounds ridiculous."

"It doesn't." Lila laid a hand over hers. "It absolutely doesn't."

"I guess that's what I needed to hear. I should've accepted the thoughtful and sweet—because that's all it was—and left it alone instead of wondering if it meant more. Hell, wanting it to mean more even as meaning more scared me."

"Second chances are scarier than first chances, because the second time you know how much you're risking."

"Yes." Julie closed her eyes. "I knew you'd get it. I'll have to smooth it over with him, especially since he's close friends with Ash, I'm yours. And I'm a crappy friend today because I haven't asked anything about how you're feeling. About you and Ash."

"I feel great—but then I didn't get a muffin. I did scramble eggs for both of us."

"You look so good together. I didn't say so before, because you'd start putting up blocks."

"No, I wouldn't, and yes, I would," she corrected before Julie could. "Probably.

Look good together? You really think so? He's so gorgeous, both ways."

"Both ways?"

"The artist—jeans, T-shirt, a couple of paint smudges here and there, a couple days of scruff on his face. And the wealthy heir apparent, polished up in an Armani suit. Or it might've been Armani. What do I know?"

"Yesterday? Tom Ford. Definitely."

"You'd know better."

"I would. And yes, you look good together. You're both gorgeous."

"Only my best friend, and maybe my mother, would say so. But I can look pretty good when I put some time and effort into it."

"You have amazing hair—a yard of it, fabulous eyes, a very sexy mouth and perfect skin. So shut up."

"You're so good for my ego. Last night was good for my ego. I think he'd have made a move—you know how you can tell."

"For good or ill."

"But I made it first—or opened the door. He walked through and . . . it wasn't like coming home. It was like discovering a new continent. But—"

"Here come the blocks." Julie lifted her glass to the Chrysler Building.

"No, no blocks—I'm still exploring the new world. It's that he's carrying all this guilt, Julie. It's not right that he carry so much. But as I've gotten to know him—and especially after seeing the family dynamics for myself yesterday—he's really the head of the family. His father's the figurehead. Ash is the go-to."

"From what Luke told me, it's been that way for years. His father runs the businesses, but Ash tends the family. Luke says 'Ashton will handle it' should be the family motto."

Lila let out a breath, sipped some wine. "That's an issue—not a block," she insisted. "He takes over a little too much for me—it's his wiring. He decides I'm staying at his place because Luke was at yours—and that made sense. But 'discuss' is better than 'decide,' and he sent for my luggage before any of the discuss."

"His perspective?"

"Crap, reap what you sow." She stuck

out her chin, tapped a finger on it. "Okay, hit me."

"Dealing with the details, and yes, looking out for you. It's not a bad thing to have someone look out for you, as long as they're willing to learn where the lines are, and you're willing to let some of the lines flex."

"Maybe. I know he's painting me now when I didn't think I wanted him to, and now I do. So I ask myself, Do I want him to paint me or did I get roped into it? And I'm not sure. I am sure I want to be with him, and I'm sure I want to see this whole strange Fabergé thing through with him, and I want to sleep with him again. Those are definite check marks."

Putting her wine down, Julie leaned over, tapped her hands on Lila's cheeks. "Look at that face. You're happy."

"I am. It tells me something—not sure just what—that I can be happy even with all that's going on. Three people are dead, two who were important to Ash, and he's got a priceless Fabergé egg hidden away. And there's a ridiculously gorgeous Asian woman who killed or helped kill those three people who wants that egg. She knows who I am, she has your perfume."

"I think she's ruined that scent for me. I know you want to help Ash. We all do. But as much as I like him, you're my girl. You have to be careful."

"I am. I will. The woman may be looking for us, and the egg, but the cops have their eye on us. Plus, think about it. Killing Oliver and his girlfriend didn't get her what she wanted. Why would she make the same mistake twice?"

"I don't know, because she's a killer. Potentially a psycho. You can't depend on logic, Lila."

Considering, Lila nodded—Julie had a very big point. "Then I'll be smarter. I think I am—and don't give me that eye roll. I think I am. It wasn't smart to take things from your place. If she hadn't, we'd never have known she was there. It wasn't smart to wear your perfume when she broke into Ash's loft—though part of that, I accept, was luck that we came in soon enough after she'd been there for it to linger. It wasn't smart to leave that thug alone with Vinnie after he'd already demonstrated his lack of control with Oliver's girlfriend. All that's arrogance and impulse, Julie, not smart. I'll be smart."

"Just be safe. I'll settle for safe."

"I'm sitting on the roof of a very secure building where only a scant handful of people know I am. I'd say I'm safe."

"Stay that way. Now I should go, hit the paperwork."

"And figure out how to untangle things with Luke."

"And that."

"I'll walk out with you. I need to take the dog for a walk anyway, and pick up a few supplies."

"What dog? I didn't see a dog."

"He's easy to miss. You know you can bring your paperwork here if you don't want to be alone," she said as she led the way back to the little elevator. "It's a big place."

"I probably need a little brooding time, and I expect Ash is coming back tonight."

"He is, with dinner. But like I said, it's a big place. You're my girl, too."

Julie gave her a one-armed hug as they stepped out onto the main floor. "Work and brooding tonight. I may take you up on it later this week."

She set her empty glass on the wet bar, picked up her work bag as Lila came back from a detour into the kitchen with a little blue leash studded with rhinestones.

"Oh!" she said when Lila picked up the little white ball that was Earl Grey. "He's so tiny, he's so adorable."

"And very sweet. Here."

She passed him to Julie, who made kissy noises and coos while Lila got her own purse. "Oh, I want one! I wonder if I could take him to work. He'd completely disarm clients and they'd end up buying more."

"Always thinking."

"How else am I going to get that major raise, my terrace apartment and a tiny little dog I can carry in my purse? I'm glad I came by," she added as they walked out. "I came in feeling frustrated and stressed, and I'm leaving feeling like I just finished a good yoga class."

"Namaste."

They parted ways on the sidewalk, with Julie slipping into a cab hailed by the efficient doorman. She settled in for the ride downtown, checked her e-mail. Nothing from Luke—but why would he contact her?

She'd figure out how to approach him, but for now she had enough messages from work to keep her occupied.

She answered her assistant, contacted a client directly to discuss a painting, then, checking the time, decided she could reach out to the artist—currently in Rome. When a client wanted to negotiate, it was her job to broker the best deal for the gallery, the artist and the client.

She spent the ride soothing artistic moodiness, boosting pride, hammering a bit of practicality. Then advising her artist to go celebrate because she believed she could persuade the client to purchase the second piece he'd shown interest in if they made it seem like a deal.

"You have to buy paint," she muttered when she ended the call. "And food. I'm about to make you almost rich . . . Mr. Barnseller! It's Julie. I think I have a very good proposition for you."

She signaled the cabbie as she went into her pitch, pointed to the corner, fumbled out her wallet. "Yes, I've just spoken with Roderick personally. He has such an emotional attachment to **Counter Service**. I did tell you he worked in that diner to support himself through art school? Yes, yes, but I've explained your reaction to it—and to the companion piece, **Order Up**. They're wonderful individually, of course, but as a set, so charming and compelling."

She paid off the cabbie, wiggled her way out of the cab, balancing phone and bag. "As he's so reluctant to break the set, I've talked to him about pricing them as a set. Personally, I'd hate to see someone else snatch away **Order Up**, especially since I believe, strongly, Roderick's work is going to go up in value very quickly."

She let him wheedle, express reluctance, but she heard the closing deal in his voice. He wanted the paintings—she only had to make him feel he'd gotten a bargain.

"I'll be frank, Mr. Barnseller, Roderick's so reluctant to break the set he won't budge on the price for it alone. But I was able to convince him to agree to two hundred thousand for the set—and I know I can get him to agree to one-eighty-five—even if it means adjusting our commission to make both of you happy."

She paused a moment, did a little happy dance on the sidewalk even as she kept her voice cool and professional. "You have wonderful taste, an exceptional eye for art. I know you'll be pleased every time you look at the paintings. I'm going to contact the gallery, have them mark them as sold. We'll pack and ship them for you. Yes, of course you can settle that with my assistant over the phone, or come in and see me tomorrow. Congratulations, Mr. Barnseller. You're very welcome. There's nothing I love more than putting the right art with the right person."

She did a second dance, then contacted the artist. "Buy champagne, Roderick. You just sold two paintings. We got one-eighty-five. Yes, I know I told you I'd ask for one-seventy-five. I didn't have to go that low. He loves your work, and that's as much to celebrate as your forty percent. Go, tell Georgie, celebrate, and tomorrow start painting me something fabulous to replace the ones you sold. Yes, I love you, too. **Ciao.**"

Grinning, she texted her assistant with instructions, automatically veering around other pedestrians. Still looking at her phone, she turned at the short steps of her building. And nearly tripped over Luke.

He'd been sitting on her front steps for

nearly an hour, waiting. And he watched her progress down the sidewalk—the rapid-fire conversation, the pause to bounce from foot to foot, the big, happy grin.

And now her jolt of surprise.

"I went by your gallery. They said you'd left early, so I figured I'd wait."

"Oh. I went by to see Lila uptown."

"And got some good news in the last block home."

"A good sale. A good one for the gallery, for the artist, for the client. It's nice to be able to broker for all three parties." After a moment's hesitation, she sat on the steps beside him, and for another moment watched, as he did, New York rush by.

God, she thought, how could a twice-married, twice-divorced urbanite feel so much the way she had at eighteen, sitting on her parents' stoop in Bloomfield, New Jersey, with her high school sweetheart? Stupid in love.

"What are we doing here, Luke?"

"I figured out an answer to your question from this morning."

"Oh, that. I was going to get in touch. That was just silly. I don't know what got into me, and I'm—"

"I've loved you since the first day I saw you—first day of high school, first day of Mrs. Gottlieb's deadly U.S. history class."

It had been deadly, Julie thought, but pressed her lips together to hold in words, emotions, tears.

"It's about half my life. Maybe we were too young, maybe we screwed it up."

"We were." Tears blurred her vision; she let them come. "We did."

"But I never got over you. I'm never going to get over you. I did pretty well between then and now—damn well. But it's now, and it's still you. It's always going to be you. That's it." He looked at her. "That's what I've got."

A ball of emotion rolled up from her heart into her throat. The tears could come, but they were warm, and sweet. Her hands trembled a little as she lifted them to frame his face. "It was you, that first day. It's still you. It's always going to be you."

She laid her lips on his, warm and sweet, while New York rushed by, and thought of her mother's hydrangeas, big balls of blue, beside the stoop where they'd sat in summers so long ago.

Some things came back to bloom.

"Let's go inside."

He laid his forehead on hers, let out a long, long breath. "Yeah, let's go inside."

Lila planned candles and wine, pretty plates and glasses on the terrace. Whatever the takeout meal, it could be romantic and lovely with the right accessories. And she considered New York on a summer night the best of them.

Then it started to rain.

She reassessed. A cozy meal in the dining room in front of the rain-lashed windows. Still romantic, especially since thunder began to roll.

She took time to fuss with herself as well, brushing her hair smooth into a low, loose tail, makeup that didn't look like she fussed but took forever to perfect. Slim black pants and a sheer copper-colored top she liked to think brought out the gold in her eyes—over a lacy camisole.

It occurred to her if she and Ash continued to see each other, she'd have to reup her very tired wardrobe.

It also occurred to her he was late.

She lit candles, put on music, poured herself a glass of wine.

By eight, she was on the point of calling him when the house phone rang.

"Ms. Emerson, this is Dwayne on the door. You have a Mr. Archer in the lobby."

"Oh, you can . . . put him on, would you, Dwayne?"

"Lila."

"Just making sure. Give the phone to Dwayne, I'll have him send you up."

See, she thought after she'd cleared Ash, careful. Smart. Safe.

When she opened the door, Ash stood, hair dripping, holding a takeout bag.

"Your smile didn't work as your umbrella. Come in, I'll get you a towel."

"I got steak."

She poked her head out of the powder room. "Takeout steak?"

"I know a place, and I wanted a steak. I guessed on yours, went with medium. If you want rare, you can take mine."

"Medium's fine." She came back with a towel, exchanged it for the bag. "I have wine open, but I picked up beer if you'd rather."

"Beer would be perfect." Scrubbing his

hair with the towel, he followed her, and stopped at the dining room.

"You went to some trouble."

"Nice plates and candles are never trouble for a girl."

"You look great. I should've told you right off—and brought you flowers."

"You're telling me now, and you brought me steak."

When she held out the beer, he took it, set it aside. And took her.

There it was, she thought, that buzz, that frisson in the blood, all highlighted by a throaty boom of thunder.

With his hands on her arms, he eased her back. "There's a second egg."

"What?" Those gold-rimmed eyes went huge. "There are two?"

"The translator Vinnie contacted called me just as I got home. He says there are documents describing another egg, the Nécessaire, and he thinks it can be tracked." He pulled her back, kissed her again. "We just got more leverage. I've spent hours researching it. He's coming back to New York tomorrow, and I'm meeting him here. We're going to find the second egg."

"Wait a minute. I need to take this in."

She pressed her hands to the sides of her head. "Did Oliver know? Does HAG know?"

"I don't know, but I don't think so. Why wouldn't Oliver have used the second one? Have gone after it, or bargained with the documents? But I don't know."

Ash picked up the beer again. "I can only try to think the way Oliver would, and he'd have tried to find it. He couldn't have resisted. Hell, I can't resist, and I'm not anywhere near as impulsive. I should've asked about Kerinov coming here."

"Kerinov's the translator?"

"Yeah. I should've asked you. It seemed safer, and more efficient, for him to come straight here from the station."

"It does, it's fine. My head's spinning. A second egg—Imperial egg?"

"Yes. I want to talk to the woman he bought the first one from. He must've gotten the documents from her. She couldn't have known what she had, but she might be able to tell us something. She's out of town, according to her housekeeper, and I couldn't pull where out of her, but I left my name and number."

"One was beyond, but two?" Trying to take it in, she sat on the arm of the tufted chair. "What does it look like? The second egg."

"It was designed as an etui—a small, decorative case for women's toiletries. It's decorated with diamonds, rubies, sapphires, emeralds—at least according to my research. The surprise is probably a manicure set, but there aren't any known pictures of this one. I can follow it from the Gatchina Palace, to when it was seized in 1917, sent to the Kremlin, then in 1922 it was transferred to the Sovnarkom."

"What's that?"

"Lenin's council—Bolshevik-dominated power. And after that transfer, there's no record I could find."

"A manicure set," she murmured. "Worth millions. It would be millions again?"

"It would be."

"It doesn't seem real—any of it. Are you sure you trust this Kerinov?"

"Vinnie did."

"Okay." She nodded, rose. "We probably need to warm up the steaks."

"There are a couple of salted baked potatoes in there, and some asparagus."

"So we heat and eat—I can't think of the last time I had a steak—and we'll plot and we'll plan." She opened the bag. "I'm pretty good at the plotting part."

She glanced up when he ran a hand down her hair. "What?"

"It occurred to me that outside all of this, and all of this is quite a bit, I'm glad I'm here, having dinner with you. I'm glad that later I'll go upstairs with you, be with you. Touch you."

She turned, wrapped her arms around him. "Whatever happens."

"Whatever happens."

And that, she thought, holding on another moment, was all anyone could ask for.

Seventeen

Lila opened one eye when her phone on the nightstand sang to her.

Who the hell would text her this early? Her sleep-blurred mind couldn't come up with a single person she knew who'd be up and functioning before seven A.M.

She told herself to ignore it, to snuggle back to sleep. And gave up within thirty seconds.

She was a girl, she admitted. She knew no girl who could comfortably ignore her phone.

"Get it later," Ash mumbled, drawing her back as she levered up to reach the phone.

"I'm a slave to communication." With her head cuddled on his shoulder, she called up the text.

Luke was waiting for me when I got home and made me a turnover before he left this morning. He's my muffin.

"Aw." So saying, she texted back just that.

"What is it?"

"It's from Julie. She and Luke are together."

"Good. Better somebody stay with her until all this is done."

"No—I mean yes, but he's not there to look out for her." After setting the phone down, Lila curled back to Ash. "Of course he'll look out for her. I mean, they're together."

"You said that." His hand slid down her back, over her butt.

"Together-together."

"Hmm." The hand detoured up her side, skimmed her breast. Stopped. "What?"

"They're a couple—and don't say a couple of what. A couple-couple."

"They're having sex?"

"That's a definite yes, but that's not all. They still love each other, which Julie told me when she came by yesterday. But she didn't need to tell me because I already knew."

"You already knew."

"It's all over them. Anyone with eyes can see it."

"I have eyes."

"You just weren't looking. You've been distracted by this and that. And . . ." Her own hand got busy, trailed up between them and found him hard and ready. "This."

"This is distracting."

"I should hope so."

Her lips curved as he lowered his to them, then warmed, parted, welcomed.

She felt so soft—her skin, her hair, the curve of her cheek. Soft everywhere his lips and hands roamed. She'd left a chink in the curtains when she'd drawn them the night before, so sunlight beamed through in a narrow slant.

He touched her in the dreamy light, wakening her body as she wakened his and all the needs inside him. No rush in the light as they both seemed to feel in the dark. No need to hurry the climb. Instead, they savored the long, easy ride, wallowed in the sensations, skin against skin, the slide of tongues, the brush of fingers, until together they reached for more.

Just a little more.

And more still when he slipped inside her, with the rise and fall like a slow, sleepy dance. Her hands framed his face, fingers stroking as her eyes stayed on his. Watching him watching her as if there was nothing else.

Only this. Only her.

Only this, she thought, as she arched up to give him more.

Only him, as she drew his face to hers, poured that only into the kiss.

Gentle, tender, the quiet pleasure flowed like wine until, drunk with it, they spilled over the crest.

Later, she shuffled her sleepy, satisfied way downstairs to make coffee with Earl Grey on her heels. "Just let me get this down, okay? Even half of it. Then I'll take you for your walk."

She winced even as she said the word "walk." As she'd been warned, the dog let out piping yips, rose up on his hind legs to dance in joy and anticipation.

"Okay, okay, my mistake. One minute."

She opened the little utility closet for the

leash, the plastic baggies and the pair of flip-flops she'd stowed with them for just this purpose.

"What's all this?" Ash asked when he came in. "Is he having a seizure?"

"No, he's not having a seizure. He's happy. I erred in speaking the word W-A-L-K, and this is the result. I'm going to take him out before he dances himself into a heart attack." She grabbed a travel mug, filled it with black coffee. "It shouldn't take long."

"I'll take him out."

"My job," she reminded him, and pulled a hair clamp out of her pocket to bundle her hair up in a couple of expert wrist flicks. "But I made eggs yesterday." She eyed Ash as she clipped the leash onto the nearly hysterical dog. "Luke baked Julie a muffin— from scratch—yesterday. Today he made her a turnover."

"That bastard's just showing off. I can make breakfast. I'm excellent at pouring cereal. It's one of my major skills."

"Fortunately I stocked Cocoa Puffs—top cabinet, left of the fridge. We'll be back."

"Cocoa Puffs?"

"It's a weakness," she called back as

she grabbed her keys and let the little dog race her to the door.

"Cocoa Puffs," he repeated to the empty room. "I haven't had Cocoa Puffs since . . . I don't think I've ever had Cocoa Puffs."

He found them, opened them, studied them. With a what-the-hell shrug, reached in and sampled some.

And realized he'd been a cereal snob his entire life.

He had some coffee, poured two bowls. Then remembering she'd fussed the night before—and it seemed he was now in competition with Luke—put together a tray.

He found a notepad, a pencil, and wrote his version of a note before hauling everything up to the third-floor terrace.

Lila rushed in as she'd rushed out—but this time carrying Earl Grey. "This dog's a riot! He wanted to take on a Lhasa apso—to fight or have sex, I'm not sure. After that adventure we're both starved, so . . . and I'm talking to myself," she realized.

Frowning, she picked up the notepaper on the counter. And the frown turned to a brilliant smile.

He'd sketched them sitting at the table on the terrace, clinking coffee cups. He'd even added Earl Grey standing on his hind legs, front paws waving.

"That's a keeper," she murmured while her heart mimicked the sketch of the dog. "Who knew he could be adorable? Well, EG, it appears we're to breakfast on the terrace. I'll just get your kibble."

He stood at the high wall, looking west, but turned when she came out balancing the little dog and two small bowls.

"What a great idea." She set Earl Grey down in some shade, with his bowl of kibble, filled his tiny water bowl with the hose. "And look how pretty—you and your artist's eye."

He'd arranged the blue cereal bowls, another of strawberries, glasses of juice, a ribbed white pot of coffee with its matching cream and sugar bowl and blue-and-white-striped napkins. And added a spear of yellow snapdragon—one he'd obviously stolen from the garden pot—in a bud vase.

"It's no turnover, but . . ."

She walked to him, rose on her toes to kiss him. "I'm cuckoo for Cocoa Puffs."

"I wouldn't go that far, but they're not bad."

She tugged him to the table, sat. "I especially loved the sketch. Next time I'll remember to brush my hair before I take the dog out."

"I like it messy."

"Men do go for the mongrel look. Milk?"

He eyed the contents of his bowl dubiously. "What happens to this stuff when you add milk?"

"Magic," she promised, and poured for both of them. "God, it's a gorgeous day. The rain washed everything, including the humidity, away. What are you doing with your morning?"

"I thought about doing more research, but it feels like a waste of time. Might as well wait to see what Kerinov has to tell us. Maybe I'll work up here for a while, do some sketching. Bird's-eye of New York. And I have some calls to make.

"It's not bad," he repeated as he spooned up the cereal. "It looks bad, but if you don't look, it's okay."

"I'm going to try to work. And when this guy gets here, I guess we'll see. Shouldn't we consider they—whoever they are— might already have this other egg? The Nécessaire?"

"Possible." He hadn't thought of that. "But not from Oliver, and he had the documents. I spent a lot of time going through his paperwork. If they have it, they still want the one I have. But considering Oliver, I think he counted on cashing in big time on the one, using some of that to finance finding the other for an even bigger payoff. Big and bigger, that was Oliver's MO."

"Okay, so we go on that assumption. It's probably not still in Russia. It just seems like it wouldn't still be lost if it had stayed in Russia. It was probably smuggled out, or sold off the books, something. The odds of it being with the same person your brother dealt with are pretty slim. Just hard to believe one person had two, and he'd have asked, right—arranged to buy both? Big and bigger?"

She nibbled on a strawberry. "So that potentially eliminates Russia and one person in New York. Progress."

"We wait for Kerinov."

"We wait. I hate waiting." She propped

her chin in her hand. "I wish I read Russian."

"So do I."

"I can read French—a little. Very little. I only took French in high school because I imagined I'd move to Paris and live in a clever little flat."

He could see her there, he realized. He could see her anywhere. "What were you going to do in Paris?"

"Learn how to wear scarves a million ways, buy the perfect baguette and write a brilliant and tragic novel. I changed my mind when I realized I really just wanted to visit Paris, and why would I want to write a brilliant and tragic novel when I don't want to read one?"

"How old were you when you realized all this?"

"My second year in college, when a dried-up, narrow-minded snob of an English lit professor made us read brilliant and tragic novel after brilliant and tragic novel. Actually I didn't see what was so brilliant about some of them. The kicker was selling a short story to **Amazing Stories**—a kind of precursor, as it turned out to be the series I'm writing now. I was insanely excited about it."

"You'd've been what, nineteen or twenty?" He'd make a point of finding it, reading it—gaining some insight into who she'd been. "It's something to be insanely excited about."

"Exactly. Even my father got a kick out of it."

"Even?"

"I shouldn't say it like that." She shrugged it off, scooped up more cereal. "To his way of thinking, writing fiction's a fine hobby. But he assumed I'd knuckle down, be a college professor. Anyway, word got back to this college professor, who announced it to the class—and said it was poorly written popular dreck, and anyone who read or wrote popular dreck was wasting their time in her class, and in college altogether."

"Well, that's a bitch, and a jealous one."

"A bitch, no question, but she believed it. Anything written in the last hundred years was dreck to her. In any case, I took what she said to heart. Walked out of her class, walked out of college. Much to my parents' consternation. So . . ."

She started to shrug again, but he laid a hand over hers. "You showed them all."

"I don't know about that. How did you—"

"No, don't ask me how I spent my college years. What did you do when you walked out?"

"I took some courses in popular fiction and started blogging. Since my father started making noises about how the army would give me direction and discipline, I waited tables so I didn't have to feel guilty for taking his money when I absolutely wasn't going to take his advice. He's proud of me now. He keeps thinking I'll write something brilliant, if not tragic, but he's good with what I do. Mostly."

He tucked her father away for now. He knew all about fathers who weren't quite satisfied with their child's career direction.

"I bought your book."

"You did not." Flustered, delighted, she studied him. "Did you?"

"And read it. It's fun, and it's clever—and it's incredibly visual. You know how to paint a picture with words."

"A huge compliment from someone who actually paints pictures. On top of the compliment of actually reading a young adult novel."

"I'm not a teenager, but it hooked me in. I can see why Rylee's jonesing for the second book. And I didn't mention it before," he added, "because I thought you'd figure I was saying it so you'd sleep with me. Too late for that now."

"That's . . . nice. I probably would've thought that—you'd still have gotten points. But you get more this way. This is nice," she said, with a gesture that swept over the skyline. "Uptown, but normal. It makes Imperial eggs and ruthless collectors thereof seem like the fiction."

"Kaylee could find one."

Thinking of her fictional heroine, Lila shook her head. "No, not Fabergé, but some mystical egg of legend. A dragon's egg, or a magic crystal egg. Hmm. That could be interesting. And if I'm going to have her do anything, I better get back to her."

He rose with her. "I want to stay again tonight."

"Oh. Because you want to sleep with me or because you don't want me here alone?"

"Both."

"I like the first reason. But you can't set yourself up as my co-house-sitter, Ash."

He touched her arm as she began to load the tray. "Let's just leave it, for now, at tonight."

Short-term plans worked smoother, to her mind. "All right."

"And tomorrow you can give me a couple hours in the studio. You can bring the dog."

"Can I?"

"We can take a walk by Luke's bakery."

"Cupcake bribery. My favorite. All right. We'll see how it goes today. We've got Kerinov first on the list."

He liked lists, and long-term plans, and all the steps it took to get from here to there. He liked being here, with Lila. But he was starting to consider what it might be like—and what it might take—to get there.

Lila returned with Earl Grey from his afternoon walk to find the doorman speaking with a spindly little man with a soccer ball paunch and a long, graying braid. He wore faded jeans, a Grateful Dead T-shirt, and he carried a battered shoulder-strap satchel.

She took him for a messenger, would have walked by with a smile for the doorman, but heard him say, with the faintest of accents:

"Alexi Kerinov."

"Mr. Kerinov?" She'd expected someone older than what she gauged as midfifties—someone in a suit with white hair and maybe a natty little goatee.

He gave her a wary look from behind tinted glasses. "Yes."

"I'm Lila Emerson. I'm with Ashton Archer."

"Ah yes." He offered her a hand, soft as a baby's butt. "It's good to meet you."

"Would you mind showing me some ID?"

"No, of course." He pulled out a wallet, offered her his driver's license. Approved, she noted, for operating motorcycles.

No, she thought, he was nothing like she'd imagined.

"I'll take you up. Thanks, Dwayne."

"You got it, Ms. Emerson."

"Can I leave my case?" He gestured to the wheeled suitcase beside him.

"Sure," Dwayne told him. "I'll put it away for you."

"Thank you. I was in D.C.," he told Lila as he followed her to the elevator. "A quick business trip. A teacup poodle?" He held out the back of his hand for Earl Grey to sniff. "My mother-in-law has one she calls Kiwi."

"This is Earl Grey."

"Distinguished."

"So. Deadhead?" She nodded at his shirt, watched him grin.

"The first concert I went to after coming to America. I was transformed."

"How long have you lived here?"

"I was eight when we left what was the Soviet Union."

"Before the wall came down."

"Yes, before. My mother was a dancer for the Bolshoi, my father a teacher of history, and a very clever man who kept his political leanings so close, even his children weren't aware."

"How did you get out?"

"We were allowed, my sister and I, to attend a performance in London, of **Swan Lake**. My father had friends in London, contacts. He and my mother planned for months, not telling Tallia or me. One night after a performance, we got in a cab—a late supper, my sister and I thought, but it wasn't a cabdriver. This friend of my father's drove us—like a madman—through the streets of London and to the embassy, and we were given asylum. And from there, we went to New York. It was very exciting."

"I bet. As exciting for an eight-year-old boy as it must've been terrifying for your parents."

"I didn't understand the risk they took until it was all done. We had a good life in Moscow, you see, even a privileged one."

"But they wanted freedom."

"Yes. More for their children than themselves, and they gave us that gift."

"Where are they now?"

"They live in Brooklyn. My father is now retired, but my mother has a little school of dance."

"They left everything behind," she said as they stepped out of the elevator. "To give their children a life in America. They're heroes."

"Yes, you understand. I owe them . . .

Jerry Garcia, and everything else. Were you, too, a friend of Vinnie's?"

"No, not really. But you were." She unlocked the penthouse door. "I'm sorry."

"He was a good man. His funeral is tomorrow. I never thought . . . We talked only days ago. When I read the documents, I thought, Vinnie will go crazy. I couldn't wait to talk to him, to come back and meet with him and plan what to do. And now . . ."

"You have to bury your friend." She touched a hand to his arm, led him inside.

"This is wonderful. Such a view! This is George the Third." He moved straight in and to a gilded cabinet. "Beautiful, perfect. Circa 1790. I see you collect snuff bottles. This opal is particularly fine. And this . . . I'm sorry."

He turned back to her, shook his hands in the air. "I forgot myself in my interest."

"One you shared with Vinnie."

"Yes. We met competing at auction for a bergère chair—caned satinwood."

She heard it in his voice, the affection, the regret. "Who won?"

"He did. He was fierce. You have exquisite taste, Ms. Emerson, and a brilliant eye."

"It's Lila, and it's not actually—"

Ash stepped out of the elevator. With one quick glance at Kerinov, he moved quickly to Lila, angled her behind him.

"Ash, this is Alexi Kerinov. I met him in the lobby when I came back with Earl Grey."

"You're early."

"Yes, the train came early, and I was lucky with a cab. I came straight here, as you asked." Kerinov held his hands up, as if in surrender. "You're right to be cautious."

"He showed me his driver's license before we came up. You have a motorcycle."

"I do, a Harley, a V-Rod. My wife wishes otherwise." He smiled a little, but kept his gaze warily on Ash. "There's a picture of you," Kerinov told him, "with Oliver and your sister Giselle, among pictures of Vinnie's children, on the William and Mary marquetry table in the first-floor sitting room of his home. He thought of you as his."

"I felt the same. I appreciate you coming." Now Ash extended a hand.

"I'm nervous," he confessed. "I barely slept since we spoke. The information in the documents is important. There's often some talk, some buzzing in my world, about information on the lost Imperial eggs. In London, in Prague, in New York. But nothing that leads to any of them. But this? You have a kind of map here, an itinerary. I've never come across anything as definitive."

"We should sit," Lila said. "I can make tea? Coffee? Something cold?"

"Something cold would be welcome."

"We'll use the dining room," Ash decided. "It should be easier to see what you have."

"Can you tell me what the police know? About Vinnie. And Oliver. I should have said I'm sorry for your brother. I met him at Vinnie's shop. So young," he said with real regret. "He was very charming."

"Yes, he was."

"The documents were his? Oliver's?"

"He had them." Ash gestured Kerinov to a chair at the long table.

"And died for them, like Vinnie. Died for what they may lead to. These eggs are worth almost countless millions of dollars. Historically? Their recovery is priceless. For a collector, their worth is beyond the telling. There are some who would kill to get them, without question. Historically again, they already have the blood of the tsars on them."

Seated, Kerinov opened his satchel, took out a manila envelope. "These are the documents Vinnie gave to me. You should keep them safe."

"I will."

"And my translations." He took out two more envelopes. "One for each egg. These should also be kept safe. The documents were primarily in Russian, as Vinnie—and you, I think—believe. Some were Czech. It took longer to translate those portions. May I?" he asked before opening an envelope.

"You see here the description—this we already know from Fabergé's invoice, from the inventory documented of the seized Imperial treasures in 1917, the revolution."

Ash read the typed translation of the Cherub with Chariot.

"This egg was commissioned by Alexander the Third, for his wife Maria Feodorovna. Its cost at the time was twenty-three hundred rubles. A princely sum in those days, and some would say more than frivolous given the condition of the country, its people. Still, this is nothing compared to its value now.

"Thank you," he said when Lila came in,

set down a tray with a pitcher of lemonade and tall glasses of ice. "Lemonade is a favorite of mine."

"Mine, too."

He lifted the glass as soon as she poured, drank deep. "My throat's dry. This is both terrible and exciting."

"Like fleeing the USSR after the ballet."

"Yes." He took a slow breath. "Yes. Nicholas, who was tsar after his father, sent millions of peasants into the Great War. There was a terrible toll on the people, the country, and the revolution brewed. The workers united to overthrow the government. The provisional government—bankers and the like—was opposed by the Soviets. Lenin took power with a bloodbath in the fall of 1917, and confiscated the Imperial treasure, the property, and the royal family was slaughtered. Some of the treasure he sold—this is documented. He wanted foreign currency in his coffers, and wanted to end the war. This is history, I know, but the background is important."

"You learned to value history from your father." Lila glanced at Ash. "His father was a professor of history in the USSR before they escaped."

It didn't surprise Ash in the least she'd already learned Kerinov's family background.

"My father, yes. We learned the history of our country—others as well, but the country of our birth." Kerinov took another drink. "So the war continued, and the attempts by Lenin to negotiate a peace with Germany failed. He lost Kiev, and the enemy was only miles from Petrograd when the treaty was signed and the Eastern Front was no longer a war zone."

"A terrible time," Lila murmured. "Why don't we learn from it?"

"My father would say those in power too often crave more. Two wars, the civil and the world, cost Russia blood and treasure, and the peace had a price as well. Some of the treasure of the tsars was sold outright, some in a quieter fashion. And some remained in Russia. Of the fifty Imperial eggs, all but eight found their way into museums or private collections. That we know," he added.

He tapped a finger on the printout he'd made. "Here we see the Cherub with Chariot sold in 1924. This is after Lenin's death, and during the power struggle with the troika collective, just before Stalin gained power. War and politics. It would appear one of the troika gained access to some of the treasury, and perhaps simply for personal gain sold the egg to Vladimir Starski for two thousand rubles. Less than its worth, but a huge sum for a Soviet. This states that Starski transported the egg to his home in Czechoslovakia, as a gift for his wife."

"And this wasn't officially documented because, essentially, the egg was stolen?"

Kerinov nodded at Lila. "Yes. Under the rule of law and culture of that time, the treasure belonged to the Soviets. But the egg traveled to Prague, and resided there until it was again sold in 1938. In that year, the Nazis invaded Czechoslovakia, and Hitler's goal was to assimilate the country and its people, to rid it of its intellectual class. It was sold to an American, Jonas Martin, of New York, for the amount of five thousand U.S. dollars, by the son of Starski."

"This Starski may have been desperate," Lila considered. "To get himself and his family out of Czechoslovakia, away from the war, he might have sold as many of his valuables as he could. Travel light, but with deep pockets, and get the hell out of Hitler's way."

"This is what I think." Kerinov punctuated his agreement with a fist tapped on the table. "War again, more blood. A wealthy American banker, from what I can find on this Jonas Martin. And the money would be nothing to Martin. I think the egg would be a kind of trinket, an ornate souvenir. The son sells it, perhaps not knowing its full origin. It comes then to New York, to a fine house in Sutton Place."

"Where Oliver tracks it to the Martin heir, Miranda Swanson."

"The granddaughter of Jonas Martin. The record ends with the sale to Martin. But . . ."

Kerinov opened the second envelope. "The Nécessaire. The description as with the Cherub with Chariot. And its history much the same. War, revolution, a change of power. Confiscated, with its last official entry in 1922, and its transfer to the Sovnarkom. From there it traveled with the first egg—a pair, you could say—from Russia to Czechoslovakia, from there to New York. Alexander to Maria, to Lenin, to the troika thief, to Starski, his son, to Martin."

"Both in New York." Ash glanced at Lila. "We had that wrong."

"Both," Kerinov confirmed, "until the twelfth of June, 1946, when the Nécessaire took another journey. This . . . excuse me."

He opened the envelope holding the Russian documents. "Here, here." And tapped a section. "This is Russian again, but incorrect. Grammatically, and some of the spelling. This was written by some-one who isn't fluent, but has a working knowledge. It has the egg not by name but by description. It calls it an egg box with jewels. Lady's manicure set with thirteen pieces. Won by Antonio Bastone from Jonas Martin Junior in five-card draw."

"In a poker game," Lila murmured.

"It's my interpretation. As I said, it's not completely correct, but understandable. And Junior, you see."

"The son tosses what he thinks of as a fancy trinket into the pot, probably when he runs low on cash, and thinks he has a winning hand."

Kerinov nodded at Ash. "Surmising, yes. See here? Value agreed at eight thousand. 'Hard luck, Jonnie,' it says. I found the younger Martin in the **Who's Who** for that year. He was twenty, a student at Harvard

Law. I haven't yet found more than this name on Antonio Bastone."

"Almost like a joke," Lila put in. "Adding to the document in Russian. They never bothered to find out what they had. And this Jonnie certainly didn't care. Toss it into the pot, just some tchotchke around the house."

"It's something Oliver would've done," Ash said quietly. "Just as carelessly. It makes a kind of circle, doesn't it?"

Lila covered Ash's hand with hers, linked fingers. "Oliver didn't get the chance to learn from his mistakes. Now we have a chance to make it right."

"We can find them." Kerinov leaned forward, earnest, urgently. "I believe it absolutely. Their history has to be more thoroughly researched, the blanks filled in. Think of where they've been, where they've traveled. What they survived. They're not lost because they can be found. Vinnie—we would have poured vodka and toasted to the search."

"And what would you do if you found them?" Ash wondered.

"They belong in a museum. Here. In the greatest city in the world. The Russians would perhaps complain, but the documents. It's all here. Sold and sold. They're great art, historical pieces. They should belong to the world."

He picked up his glass again, then put it down abruptly. "You don't mean to keep them. To put them away in your own glass case? Mr. Archer, you're a wealthy man, you can afford to be generous. You're an artist, you must understand the value of accessible art."

"You don't have to convince me. I wanted to know where you stood on it. Lila?"

"Yes."

"Okay. Oliver acquired these documents and the Cherub with Chariot."

"I'm sorry, 'and'? You maybe mean 'for'?"

"And," Ash repeated. "He acquired the documents **and** the egg."

Kerinov all but collapsed back in his chair. His face went deathly pale, then filled with wild color. "My God. My God. He— You have it? You have one of the lost Imperial eggs. Here? Please, I have to—"

"Not here. It's safe. I think Oliver made a deal with someone, then played fast and loose, trying to up the ante. It got him and his girlfriend killed. And in trying to help me piece it together, Vinnie was killed. This is more than a treasure hunt."

"I understand. Please, a moment." He rose, walked to the window, back to the table, to the window again. "My heart is pounding. I think, what would my father say—a man who studies the past and has little use for rich men's toys. What would he say if I could tell him his son had some part in bringing this piece of history back to the world?"

He came back to the table, sat down as slowly, as carefully as an old man. "It's foolish perhaps to think of my father at such a time."

"No." Lila shook her head. "No. We want their pride."

"I owe him"—Kerinov tapped his T-shirt—"so much. For myself, one who perhaps looks at rich men's toys as art, this is a life's work all at once. Vinnie . . ."

He trailed off, pressed his fingers to his eyes. When he lowered them, he linked his hands on the table. "You've taken me into your trust. I'm grateful. I'm humbled."

"Vinnie trusted you."

"I'll do for you what I would have done for him. Anything I can. He thought of you as his," Kerinov said again. "So I'll do everything I can. You've actually seen it. Touched it."

Saying nothing, Ash took his phone out of his pocket, brought up the pictures he'd taken.

"God. My God. It's beyond exquisite. You have, as far as I know, the only clear photograph of this work of art. A museum, the Metropolitan. It must not be shut away again."

"When it's done, it won't be shut away. The people who want this killed two members of my family. It's not only a work of art, a piece of history, but it's my leverage. And now, there's another. I want to find it before they do. To do that, we need to find Antonio Bastone, or more likely his heirs. If he's still alive, he'd be easily in his nineties, so odds are slim on that."

"Odds aren't that slim he sold it again, or lost it in another poker game, or gave it to some woman." Lila lifted her hands. "But I don't think, even for rich men's sons—if he was one like Hard Luck Jonnie— winning a really shiny trinket in a poker game was an everyday thing. So maybe the story got passed down, and with that, what happened to the prize. It's a good springboard anyway."

"Harvard Law, 1946. They might've gone to school together. And maybe Miranda Swanson knows something about the story. I can push those buttons," Ash decided.

"I'll do more research. I have some work, but I can pass it on. I'll focus on this. I'm grateful to be a part of this, a part of history." After another long look, Kerinov handed Ash back his phone.

"Give me a minute." Lila rose, moved off.

"This has to be kept confidential," Ash began.

"Understood. You have my word."

"Even from your family."

"Even from them," Kerinov agreed. "I know some collectors, know of others who'd know more. With my contacts, I can find out who might have a particular interest in Fabergé, or in Russian antiquities."

"Ask carefully. They've killed three times. They won't hesitate to kill again."

"It's my business to ask questions, to gather information on collectors and collections. I won't ask anything that would arouse suspicion."

Lila came back with three shot glasses and a frosty bottle of Ketel One on a tray.

Kerinov looked at her with soft eyes. "You're very kind."

"I think the moment calls for it." She poured three shots of ice-cold vodka, lifted her own. "To Vinnie."

"To Vinnie," Kerinov murmured, and tossed back the shot.

"And one more." Lila poured again. "To the endurance of art. What's Russian for 'Cheers,' Alexi?"

"If I drink to your health, I say **Za vashe zdorovye.**"

"Okay. **Za vashe zdorovye.**"

"You have a good ear. To the endurance of art, to our health and to success."

They touched glasses, three bright notes blending to one.

And that, Lila thought as she knocked back the vodka, signaled the next step.

Eighteen

Lila put her work aside for the rest of the day and considered the advantages of technology. While Ash made his calls to Harvard contacts, she tried the social media.

Maybe a man—if he still lived—who'd nearly hit the century mark wouldn't have a Facebook page, but she figured the odds were good some of his descendants would.

A grandson maybe, named for his grand-father. A granddaughter—Antonia? She thought it worth a shot to dig into Google and Facebook, using the little they knew.

Add Jonas Martin, she considered, dig down further to see if she could find a connection of mutual friends linking each name.

She signaled Ash to come ahead when he hesitated at the wide archway of the dining room.

"I'm not writing. I'm doing my version of research. Did you have any luck?"

"A friend asking a friend for a favor, and a link to the Harvard Law yearbook. None published in 1943 to 1945, but there's one for 1946, no pictures. I'm going to get access to it, and given Martin's age, to the couple years after."

She sat back. "That's a good one."

"I could hire an investigator to do all this."

"And take away our fun and satisfaction? I'm trolling Facebook."

"Facebook?"

"You have a Facebook page," she pointed out. "I just put in a friend request, by the way. In fact it appears you have two, one personal, one professional. You haven't updated your professional page in over two months."

"You sound like my agent," he muttered. "I put new art up when I think about it. Why are you trolling Facebook?"

"Why do you have a personal page?"

"It helps, when I think of it again, to see what the family's up to."

"Exactly. I bet some in the Bastone and Martin families do the same. Bastone—Italian name. I bet you didn't know Italy is ninth in Facebook users worldwide."

"I can't say I did."

"There are also sixty-three Antonio Bastones on Facebook, and three Antonias. I'm playing with Tony and Toni with an **i** now. Then there's Anthony, if they went there. I'm going to go through them, see if I can access their friends list. If I find a Martin on it, or a Swanson, as that's the Martin heir's name, it could be pay dirt."

"Facebook," he said again, and made her laugh.

"You didn't think of it because you can't even keep your page up-to-date."

He sat across from her. "Lila."

She nudged her laptop aside, folded her hands on the table. "Ashton."

"What are you going to do with these sixty-six Facebook names?"

"I think we'll have more with the Tony/Toni deal. The friends list, as I said. With or without that connection, I'll start contacting, via Facebook, asking if they're a descendant of the Antonio Bastone who attended Harvard in the 1940s. We're not positive he did—hell, they could've met in a strip club for all we know, but it's using the springboard for a considered leap. I could get lucky, especially cross-referencing with Google."

"That's pretty creative."

"Creative is my god. Technology my cherished lover."

"You're enjoying this."

"I know. Part of me says I shouldn't be because if I did get lucky there's someone out there who'd kill me for it, given the chance. But I can't help it. It's all just fascinating."

He reached over for her hand. "I'm not going to let anything happen to you. And don't tell me you can take care of yourself. I'm telling you. You're with me now."

"Ash—"

He tightened his grip on her hand. "You're with me. We both may need time to get used to it, but that's the way it is. I talked to Bob."

Her mind tried to spin in the new direction. "Who?"

"My brother Bob."

Among the Giselles and Rylees and Estebans, there was a Bob? "I need a copy of your spreadsheet."

"He's at Angie's today. He and Frankie—that's Angie and Vinnie's oldest son—are pretty tight. I asked him to talk to Frankie about getting me the information Vinnie had on the Swanson estate, and the acquisitions Oliver brokered."

"So you can see if there's anything pertaining to the Nécessaire or to Bastone."

"Long shot, but why not bet? I've got another call in to the Swansons. Which led me to call my mother. She knows everyone, and is indeed mildly acquainted with Miranda Swanson, whom she describes as a fashionable dimwit. My mother's agreed to make some calls and find out where Miranda Swanson and her husband, Biff, are vacationing."

"He's not really Biff. No one's really a Biff."

"According to my mother, he is." He glanced at the phone he'd set on the table as it signaled. "Obviously, I should've thought of my mother before. Mom," he said when he answered. "You work fast."

She left him to his call, went upstairs for shoes, a ball cap and her sunglasses. She tucked her little zip wallet—keys, some money, ID, in her pocket. She started downstairs, meeting Ash on the way up.

"Where did you go?" he began. "Or rather, where are you going?"

"I went up for what I need to take Earl Grey for a . . . promenade. Or rather what I need for us to take him. You can use a walk in the park, too—and then you can tell me what your mother said."

"Fine." He studied her hat—and his eyes narrowed. "You're a Mets fan."

She merely put up her dukes. "Go on, start something."

He only shook his head. "This is a severe test of our relationship. I'll get the leash."

"And baggies," she called out.

Armed, and led by a thrilled Earl Grey, they went down, then took the staircase connecting Tudor City with the park.

"Is it a sign?" Lila wondered. "Walking down the Sharansky Steps—named for a Russian dissident."

"I think I'll have had my fill of all things Russian for a while once this is done. But you're right about the walk in the park. I can use it."

He let the air wash over him, and the hum of traffic from First Avenue as they strolled behind the tiny, prancing dog along the wide walkway, in and out of shade from locust trees.

From there they walked around one of the greens, into the quiet and calm of a shady urban oasis. Others walked there—pushing babies or toddlers in strollers, walking dogs, strutting along with Bluetooths at their ear or, in the case of the guy with skinny white legs clamped into black compression shorts, bopping to whatever played through his earbuds.

"So, your mother?" Lila asked while Earl Grey sniffed the grass with a full-body wag.

"Looked in her book—if you think my spreadsheet's something, you should see my mother's social book. You could plot a war. She contacted another acquaintance who's friendly with Miranda Swanson. They're in the Hamptons until after Labor Day, though they both make the occasional trip back to the city to meet friends or, in his case, tend to some business. She got an address, and Miranda Swanson's cell phone number."

"Call her." Lila grabbed his hand, led him toward a bench. "Call her now."

"Actually, I don't have to. My mother already did."

"She does work fast."

"Like lightning. My mother, who's also in the Hamptons, netted herself an invite for cocktails at the Swansons' tonight. The invitation includes me and my date. Want to have cocktails on the beach?"

"Tonight? I don't have cocktails-on-the-beach—at the Hamptons—wear."

"It's the beach. It'll be casual enough."

"Men," she muttered. "I need an outfit." Dating would break her bank yet, she thought. "Take Earl Grey back, okay?" She dug out her key, passed it to him, then the leash. "I have to shop."

She raced off, leaving him in her dust. "It's just the beach," he repeated.

She performed miracles by her standard. Cool, beachy pink with a low, low back crisscrossed by thin straps. Heeled gladiator sandals in turquoise, and a straw bag, striped with both colors and big enough to hold her main accessory.

A charming teacup poodle.

Her cell phone rang as she added one more coat of mascara.

"Ready?" Ash asked.

"Two minutes." She clicked off, annoyed he'd managed to go back to his loft, change and come back in less time than it had taken her to dress. She tucked the dog's provisions into her new bag, then tucked him in with them. She folded the scarf the clerk talked her into—turquoise with hot-pink waves—beside the dog, then dashed out to keep to the two minutes.

Outside, she found Ash leaning against what even she recognized as a vintage Corvette, and chatting with the doorman.

"Let me get that for you, Ms. Emerson." The doorman opened the car door. "You have a nice evening."

"Thanks." She sat a moment, studied the dash as Ash skirted the hood to slip into the driver's seat.

"You have a car."

"I do. I don't get it out much."

"You have a really hot car."

"If you're going to drive a hot woman to the beach, it should be in a hot car."

"Well played. I got nervous."

"About what?" He negotiated traffic as if he commuted daily—with ruthless determination.

"About everything. I imagined this Miranda saying, 'Oh, Antonio! Of course, what an old dear. We've got him propped up in the corner over there. Do go say hello.'"

"I don't see that happening."

"Of course not, but I started thinking it. Then we'd go over, and he'd say—or shout because I see him as stone deaf—'Poker? Hard Luck Jonnie! Those were the days.' Then he'd tell us he gave the egg to the girl he was sleeping with at the time. What was her name? He'd cackle out a laugh, then drop over dead."

"At least he died on a happy memory."

"In another version Hot Asian Girl bursts in—she's wearing Alexander McQueen, I'm pretty sure—holding everyone at gunpoint while the boss comes in behind her. He looks like Marlon Brando.

Not hot-and-sexy Brando in the old black-and-white movies, the really fat Brando. He's wearing a white suit and a panama hat."

"It is summer at the beach."

"Because this is my fantasy, I know kung fu, and HAG and I square off. I completely kick her ass, and you restrain the boss man."

Ash spared her a glance before he bulleted between two taxis. "You get the hot woman, I get fat Brando? It doesn't seem right."

"It's just the way it was. But when we thought everything was okay, the terrible happened. I couldn't find Earl Grey. I looked everywhere, but I couldn't find him. I'm still a little sick about it."

"Then it's a good thing it never happened—and it won't."

"I still wish I knew kung fu." She peeked into her bag, where Earl Grey curled and slept.

"What's in there? You didn't put the dog in there? You brought the dog?"

"I couldn't leave him. He's my responsibility. Besides, women have tiny dogs like this so they can carry them around in their fashionable bags." She gave him a smiling glance. "They'll just think I'm eccentric."

"Where would they get that idea?"

She loved new spaces, and though she wouldn't have chosen the Swansons' Hamptons house for herself, she could appreciate the theme. All white, acres of glass, slick and ultramodern, it offered white terraces adorned with white pots filled with red flowers.

Casual, she thought, it wasn't, but stood as a testament to money and determined contemporary style.

People already were mixing on the terraces—women in floaty dresses, men in soft-colored suits and sport coats. The light held bright, and the whoosh of the waves mingled with music streaming from the open windows.

She saw waitstaff passing trays of what she thought were Bellinis, of champagne, of pilsner glasses and finger food.

Inside, the sky and sea dominated through the walls of glass. But all the white hurt the eyes, chilled the skin.

Furnishings with silver or mirror finishes

paired with hard reds, blues, greens of chairs and sofas, the same colors echoed in the slashes and strokes of the art framed in silver on the white walls.

Not a soft edge anywhere, Lila thought.

"I couldn't work here," she murmured to Ash. "It would give me a constant head-ache."

A woman—again in white, short and snug—hurried toward them. She had a tumble of ice-blond hair and eyes so eerily green Lila credited tinted contacts.

"You must be Ashton!" She grabbed Ash's hand, then leaned in for the European double-cheek buss. "I'm so glad you could join us! I'm Miranda."

"It was nice of you to ask us. Miranda Swanson, Lila Emerson."

"Aren't you as fresh as a strawberry par-fait? Let me get you both a drink." She circled her finger in the air without looking around. "We're having Bellinis. Of course, we can get you anything else you like."

"I'd love one." Lila beamed at her, very deliberately. She felt a little pang of sym-pathy.

She judged the woman to be about the same age as Ash's mother, but Miranda had sculpted herself down to a sharpened stick, one that appeared to run on nervous energy and whatever frothy substance she had in her glass.

"You have to come meet everyone. We're all very casual here. I was delighted when your mother called, Ashton. I had no idea she was here, spending some of her summer."

Lila took a glass from the server's tray. "You have a gorgeous spot."

"We just love it. We completely redid the house when we bought it last year. It's lovely to get out of the city with all the heat, the crowds. I'm sure you know just what I mean. Let me introduce you to—"

Earl Grey took the opportunity to poke his head out of the corner of the straw bag.

Miranda's mouth dropped open, and Lila held her breath, half expecting a scream.

Instead, there came a squeal.

"Oh, it's a little puppy! She's like a little toy."

"He. This is Earl Grey. I hope you don't mind, but I didn't want to leave him home alone."

"Oh, oh, he's precious. Just precious."

"Would you like to hold him?"

"I'd love it." Miranda gathered the dog in her hands, immediately lapsed into lisping baby talk.

Lila just slanted a look toward Ash, and smiled. "Is there anywhere I could take him for a little walk outside?"

"Oh, of course! I'll show you. Want to go for a walkie?" Miranda cooed, rubbing noses with Earl Grey, then giggling when he lapped his tiny tongue on her face.

This time Lila just batted her eyes at Ash as she followed the besotted Miranda back out the front door.

Bellini in hand, Monica wandered over to her son. "That's a clever girl you have."

He leaned down to kiss his mother's cheek. "I don't know if I have her, but she's pretty damn clever."

"My son knows how to get what he wants, and always has." She kissed his cheek in turn. "We need to mingle a bit, but then we're going to find a nice quiet spot in this ridiculous house for you to tell me just why you wanted an intro to Miranda Swanson."

"Fair enough." But he glanced toward the door.

"I think Lila can handle her end of things."

"So she's always telling me."

"Quite a contrast for a man who's gotten used to handling too much for too many. Let's be social." She took his hand, strolled with him into the gathering in the main living area. "Toots, I don't think you've met my son."

Toots? Ash thought, then resigned himself to the social hour.

Outside, Lila walked a wide white path between sharp blades of ornamental grasses and thorny rosebushes. And waited for her opportunity.

"Biff and I travel so much I never thought about getting a dog. So much trouble. But now . . ." Miranda held the leash while Earl Grey sniffed the grasses. "I'd love to have the name of your breeder."

"I'll get that for you. I really appreciate you inviting us tonight, and being so understanding about Earl Grey. I didn't realize until Ash mentioned it, you knew his half brother Oliver."

"Who?"

"Oliver Archer, he handled the estate sale through Old World Antiques for you."

"Oh! I never put that together. He did mention he was Spence Archer's son. I'd forgotten. Such a bother, all that estate business, and he was so helpful."

"I'm sure he was."

"Biff and I just couldn't see the point in keeping that old house, and all the **things**. My grandmother collected everything." She rolled her eyes. "You'd think it was a museum, full of stuff, musty old place."

"Still, it must've been hard, selling off family things."

"I prefer living in the now. Antiques are just old things somebody else already used, aren't they?"

"Well . . ." In a nutshell, Lila supposed. "Yes, I guess they are."

"And so much of it's heavy and dark, or gaudy. Biff and I like clean and modern. Oliver—I remember him, of course—was a huge help. I should invite him out for a weekend this summer."

"I'm sorry, I thought you knew. Oliver was killed a couple weeks ago."

Instant shock and distress flew into her eyes. "That's terrible! Oh, he was so young and good-looking. That's tragic. How did it happen?"

"He was shot. It was all over the news."

"Oh, I try never to listen to the news. Always so depressing."

"There is that," Lila agreed.

"Shot." Miranda gave a shudder. "A mugging, a robbery, I guess."

"Something like that. You sold him an egg."

"There's a good boy, going pee-pee. A what?" She glanced back at Lila. "An egg? Why would I sell anyone an egg?"

"A decorative egg. An angel with a chariot."

"How odd. I don't remember— Oh, wait. Yes, I do. God, it was so **gaudy** and old-fashioned. It had all these papers with it written in some strange foreign language. But Oliver was taken with it, and asked if I'd consider selling it to him outright. I didn't see the harm."

"The papers were actually for two eggs."

"Really? Well, as I said, that old place was full of things. Biff and I are more minimalist."

"Ash learned about it—he's handling his brother's estate. You know what that's like."

Miranda rolled her eyes wearily. "An enormous eater of time and energy."

"Yes. And in going through all the papers, he learned Jonas Martin Junior lost the second egg in a poker game. To Antonio Bastone."

"Bastone?" Something bright came into her face. "Was that it? There's some family legend about that—some treasure wagered away. My grandfather—Jonas Martin—was the black sheep with a weakness for gambling and women."

"Do you know the Bastones?"

"I dated Giovanni one whirlwind summer when we were in Italy—I wasn't quite eighteen. I was wild for him, probably because my father didn't fully approve due to this poker business."

"Where in Italy, if you don't mind me asking?"

"Florence, at least we spent a lot of time in Florence. The Bastone villa is in Tuscany. Giovanni married some Italian model and had a herd of children. I haven't seen him for years now, but we still exchange cards at Christmas. A woman only has one first love."

"It's a lucky woman to have an Italian first love with a villa in Tuscany. Did you ever talk about the egg his grandfather won from yours?"

"We had much more important things to talk about—when we talked. I should get back—I could stay out here with this little sweetie all night." She gathered Earl Grey up in her hands. "Do you think he's finished?"

"Yeah, I'd say we're finished."

By the time they circled back to the house, Lila steered the conversation into empty small talk by dropping the name of clients who also had a house in East Hampton. They parted ways when Miranda introduced her—as Leela—to two couples on the east terrace.

She let it go, decided Leela was a trust fund baby who dabbled in fashion design. She entertained herself with that persona for a few minutes, then excused herself to hunt for Ash.

He scooped her up from behind, an arm firm around her waist. "There you are. You have to see the view from the second floor."

"I do?" she asked as he carted her briskly to the glossy white staircase.

"Yes, because my mother's there, and

I'm under orders to bring you up. I had to fill her in," he added quietly.

"Did you?"

"I mostly filled her in. You can keep her entertained while I hunt up Biff Swanson and see what I can find out about the egg."

"That's not going to be necessary. Mrs. Crompton. It's nice to see you again."

"Monica. Let me see your ploy."

"My ploy?"

"The famous Earl Grey."

At the sound of his name, the dog poked his head out of the bag, gave one cheerful yip.

"I'm more inclined toward big, sturdy dogs, but he's certainly cute. And he has a very happy face."

"That's his charm for me. Happy face."

"First"—she took Lila's arm, led her farther away from a small group of guests— "I'm going to apologize for Ashton's father."

"There's no need for that."

"I wouldn't have left you alone with him if I'd known where he'd gone in his head. And as I had two children with him, I should have known, or guessed. His current wife and I don't have much in common, or any particular liking for each other, but she would've been appalled if she'd known how he treated a guest in their home. As would Oliver's poor mother, and Isabella—Spence's third wife. So on behalf of all the formers and the current, I'm sorry you were treated so shabbily."

"Thank you. It was a difficult day for everyone."

"A horrible day that went from awful to even worse. Ash has told me what's going on, or as much of what's going on as he's decided to tell me. I'm going to say I was terribly fond of Vinnie. He and Angie, their family, are all part of mine, and a welcome part. I want to see the people responsible for taking his life, for breaking Angie's heart, caught and punished. But I don't want it at the risk of my son, or a young woman I'm already fond of."

"I understand. Basically we're just gathering information right now."

"I'm not Oliver, Mom," Ash put in.

"And thank God for it." The breeze caught at her hair, fluttered the golden-red waves. "Among countless other differences, you're not greedy, entitled or stupid. Oliver was, and often all at the same time. It's ridiculous to say not to speak ill of the dead. We're all going to be dead eventually. What would we talk about in the meantime?"

Lila let out a quick laugh before she could swallow it. "Ash says he's going to take care of me—and while he's trying to do that, I'll take care of him."

"Both of you make sure you do."

"And since you're filled in, I can tell you—both—my ploy hit the jackpot. Condensed version. Miranda didn't have a clue about the egg Oliver bought—she just saw it as old-fashioned and gaudy. To her, it was just more clutter in an old house she didn't want."

"The Martin estate is one of the most beautiful homes on Long Island," Monica told her. "It's been let go far too long, as Miranda's grandmother—her father died several years ago—has been ill for a long time. I've been to parties there, back in the day. I was pregnant with you, Ash, the first time I went there."

"It's a small, incestuous world. What about the Bastone connection?"

"In the vein of small, incestuous worlds, Miranda had her first love affair with Giovanni Bastone one long-ago summer in Tuscany. The Bastones have a villa there. It has to be near Florence, as she said she and Giovanni spent a lot of time there. And she vaguely recalls a family legend about Jonas Martin—the black sheep in his time—losing a family treasure in a wager with Antonio Bastone—one of the reasons her father wasn't happy about her dating the young Bastone. He—Giovanni—married a model, and they have several children."

Monica sent her a look of pleased approval. "You got all of that by walking the dog?"

"I did. I also got that she had no idea what happened to Oliver, and even knowing he was killed, hasn't connected it to the egg. She's a very nice woman. Kind of silly, but nice. I have to remember to get her the name of Earl Grey's breeder, because she wants her own. When I do, I think I could get Giovanni Bastone's contact information. But we should be able to find it ourselves."

Satisfied, Lila snagged another drink from a passing server. "Don't you just love cocktail parties?"

"I do." Monica tapped her glass to Lila's.

"Poor Ash tolerates them only when he can't find a way out. He's already thinking exit strategy here. Give it another thirty minutes," she advised. "See and be seen, then slip out. I'll cover for you. And you." Monica slipped an arm around Lila's waist, as her son often did. "We absolutely have to have a long, long lunch the next time I'm in New York."

Thirty minutes, Ash thought, and checked his watch before leading his women back downstairs.

Nineteen

When they got back to New York, Ash decreed—though he felt no man should walk a dog the size of a hamster—it was his turn to take Earl Grey out and about. Fine with that arrangement, Lila foraged through her kitchen supplies. A few samples of party finger food had only sharpened her appetite. By the time Ash returned, she had her comfort favorite—mac and cheese—ready to serve and was already busy checking Facebook for any responses.

"You made mac and cheese."

"From a box. Love it or leave it."

"The blue box, right?"

"Of course. I have my standards."

He got a beer from the fridge. Driving meant he'd had to get through the cocktail bullshit on a single beer. He'd more than earned his second of the night.

"That blue box was the only thing I could make when I got my first place. That and Eggos," he remembered, with some fondness. "I'd toss one or the other together if I worked late. Nothing tastes as good as mac and cheese at three in the morning."

"We could wait and see if that still holds true, but I'm hungry now. Oh, Jesus! Ashton, I got a hit."

"A hit on what?"

"My Facebook trolling. Antonia Bastone answered. In response to my query—are you related to the Antonio Bastone who played poker with Jonas Martin in the 1940s? She writes back: 'I am the great-granddaughter of Antonio Bastone who was a friend of the American Jonas Martin. Who are you?'"

He stuck a fork in the bowl of mac and cheese. "Antonia could be a forty-year-old man with a beer gut hoping to score with some naive girl playing on the Internet."

Her head still bent toward her laptop

screen, she merely lifted her eyes. "Who just happened to pick that name for a cover? Have a little faith—and get me a fork. If we're going to eat out of the serving bowl, I want my own fork."

"Picky." He ate another bite first. "God, this takes me back. I remember making this after a long night with . . . a fork," he said, and went into the kitchen.

"That memory involved mac and cheese and a naked woman."

"Maybe."

He brought back a fork and a couple of napkins.

"Just FYI, I have memories of naked men."

"Then it's all good." He sat. "Okay, the middle-aged beer gut's a stretch. She answers the American—possible she got that because she checked your page, then assumed. But yeah, it's likely you hit. You're handy, Lila. I wouldn't have gone with the dog or the social media. You scored on both."

"I'd say it's just luck, but false modesty's so irritating. How much should I tell her, Ash? I never thought I'd get anything this quickly, so I haven't thought of the next step, not clearly. I can't tell her I'm a friend of the half brother of the man who was killed because of the Fabergé egg her ancestor didn't win from Jonas Martin. But I need to tell her something, enough of something to continue a dialogue."

"You're a writer. You write good dialogue—your teenagers sound like teenagers."

"I know I'm a writer—and thanks—but I haven't plotted this part out."

"No, you tell her you're a writer, which is true. She can verify that. You're acquainted with Miranda Swanson, also true, who's the granddaughter of Jonas Martin—and remains friendly with Giovanni Bastone. All true. You're researching the family histories, particularly the Martin/Bastone connection and the wager, for a potential book. Not true, but plausible."

"That's pretty good plotting on the fly." She dipped into the serving bowl again. "Maybe I will write a book about all this, eventually, so I can go in that direction. I am researching. Okay, that's good. The truth, and the possible truth."

She typed in a response. "And ending it

with: 'Are you, or any member of your family, willing to talk to me?'" She hit send.

"So now . . ." She dug more enthusiastically into the mac and cheese. "We wait and see."

"We can do better than that. What's your schedule like?"

"My schedule? I'm here until Monday afternoon, then I have two days before I start a job in Brooklyn, then—"

"Two days might not do it. Can you get someone to cover you in Brooklyn?"

"I could, but—"

"Cover Brooklyn," he said. "Let's go to Tuscany."

She just stared at him. "You sure know how to class up the mac and cheese."

"We'll leave Monday, as soon as you're clear. That's enough time to pinpoint the Bastone villa—and with some luck get an invitation to visit. No luck, we'll figure something else out."

"Just . . ." She wagged her hands in the air. "Go to Tuscany?"

"You like to travel."

"I do, but—"

"I need to take the next step, and that's

verifying the Nécessaire. I can't go without you, Lila. I won't leave you on your own until this is over. You don't like those terms, but that's what they are. So consider it doing me a favor."

Now, brooding a little, she poked at the orange pasta. "You've got some moves, Ashton."

"Guilty, but you want to go. You want in. You don't want to be here while I'm tugging the Italian threads."

There was a cat, and a dog, and an aquarium of saltwater fish—and a garden—in Brooklyn. She'd been looking forward to her two-week stay.

But weighing it against Tuscany, another piece of the puzzle, and Ashton . . .

"I have to cover Brooklyn, to the satisfaction of my clients."

"Agreed."

"Let me see what I can do."

Lila checked on Earl Grey, who rode happily in her straw bag, before she walked into Julie's gallery. She spotted a couple of tourists—browsers, not buyers, by her gauge—and one of the staff talking earnestly to a sharp-faced couple over a sculpture of a woman weeping into her hands.

She wondered why anyone would want something that unhappy in their space, but art spoke to whom it spoke.

She found Julie—as discussed in morning texts—in the back room carefully preparing a painting for shipment.

"Another big score, one I promised I'd prep for shipping personally." Julie blew a stray curl out of her eyes. "Great bag. When did you get that?"

"Yesterday. Why are you barefoot?"

"Oh, I caught my heel in a grate walking to work—I know better. It cracked, so it's wobbly. I'll get it to the shoemaker this afternoon."

Lila just opened her bag, dug out her little pack of sandpaper and her superglue. "I'll fix it." She picked up the shoe—a very nice peep-toe Jimmy Choo—and got to work.

"The bag," she continued as she carefully sanded the two bases. "I went to the Hamptons, to a cocktail party, and needed something to carry Earl Grey."

"You took the dog to a cocktail party in the Hamptons?"

"Yes. This would be better with actual shoe glue, but . . ." Lila gave the newly glued heel a tug. "That should hold. So. Here's a quick update. I need advice."

She ran Julie through the progress of the day before edging out of the way while her friend unrolled reams of bubble wrap.

"Only you would've thought of Facebook to track down objets d'art, and murderers."

"She hasn't answered my last message, so all of that might be a bust. But whether she does or doesn't, Ash wants to go to Tuscany—next week. He wants me to go with him."

"He wants to take you to Italy?"

"It's not a romantic getaway, Julie, which I couldn't even consider when I have jobs booked."

"Excuse me, it may not be a getaway, but a trip to Italy—to Tuscany—is swarming with romance." Aiming a stern look, Julie fisted her hands on her hips. "Tell me you're going."

"That's the advice I'm after—and don't just jump on it. I can get someone to cover my next job. It'll take a bite out of my budget, but she's really good, and the clients will be fine with it. I want to go because . . . so many reasons. I have to tell him, one way or the other. I'm going over there next. I had to all but push him out the door this morning to Vinnie's funeral, and swear I'd take a cab over there this afternoon."

"That's a reasonable precaution."

"Which I'd catch no less than ten blocks away from where I'm working. I'm starting to feel like Jason Bourne."

She pushed at her hair. "Julie, what am I getting into?"

"I think you're safe with Ash, but it's dangerous. If you're at all nervous or unsure about—"

"Not that part. I can't walk away from that part." No, she thought, walking away from that wasn't an option. "I've been in it since I looked out the damn window that night. I mean with Ash. What am I getting into?"

"I think it's pretty clear. You're involved, romantically, and looking for problems."

"I'm not looking for them. Exactly. I like to anticipate, to be prepared. If you're not prepared for the variables, they can bite you in the ass."

"You know how to enjoy the moment better than anyone I know, until it's personal. You like being with him, you have feelings for him. It's clear it's the same on his end. Why anticipate trouble?"

"He hovers."

"The situation calls for hovering, if you're asking me."

"All right, that's fair. He's used to handling the details, and people, and situations. Add that to the way he feels because he didn't handle Oliver's situation. It's intense. He's got a way of making things happen, and . . ."

"And you like to take care of your own details, keep everything loose." Satisfied with the padding, Julie got out the strapping tape. "Sometimes tying yourself to someone else's life, managing those details together, is the answer. It's another kind of adventure."

"You've got stars in your eyes," Lila accused. "And the moon, too."

"I do. I've been in love with Luke since I was fifteen. I denied it for a long time, but it's always been Luke."

"That's romantic." Lila pressed a hand

to her heart. "That's Elizabeth and Darcy romantic."

"To me it just feels like reality."

"That only makes it more romantic."

"I guess it does." Smiling to herself, Julie secured the padding. "Still, I was doing just fine on my own. I can be happy—and so can you—on my own. I think that's what makes it all the more special, all the more strong, when we can take that step, when we can say okay, this is someone I can trust, and be with, and plan with."

"You're planning?"

"I was talking about you, but yes. We're taking it slow. Slower," she said with a smile when Lila narrowed her eyes. "But we tossed away the last twelve years. That's enough waste. You want my advice? Don't toss away something because you're projecting variables and escape hatches. Go to Tuscany, be safe, solve a mystery and be in love. Because you are."

"I don't know how to feel this way."

"You'd be the first to tell me, just feel."

"It changes everything."

Julie just waved a finger in the air. "And despite the fact that you live somewhere new a couple dozen times a year, change is your phobia. When you're not at the controls. Try something different. Take turns driving."

"Take turns, go to Tuscany, go sit for a painting I had no intention of doing and now can't wait to see finished. Be in love. Add all that together, baiting a killer with objets d'art seems like child's play."

"You forgot be safe. I mean it, Lila. And e-mail me every single day while you're gone. Twice a day. We'll go shopping before you leave."

"I can't afford to go shopping—I'm losing Brooklyn."

"You're going to Italy. You can't afford not to go shopping."

That settled that, Lila thought as she left the gallery. She'd just damn her summer budget to hell, go a little crazy. And really, it had been years since she'd gone a little crazy—the contents of her suitcases were beginning to show it.

Live a little, she decided, and opted to walk to Ash's loft, doing some window-shopping along the way. A couple new summer dresses, some cropped pants, some tanks and some flowy tops.

She could recycle some of her going-out-and-about wear to work wear, purge some of her work wear. As long as it fit into her suitcases, she was good to go.

A window display caught her eye—the white, faceless mannequin in the breezy dress with boldly colored swirls, and the strappy wedges in emerald green.

She shouldn't buy green sandals. She should buy a neutral color, something that would go with anything—just like what she had on.

Green could be neutral. Grass was green, and it went with everything when you thought about it.

As she debated with herself, she felt a presence behind her, and before she could step aside, a tiny prick in her side.

"You should be very still and very quiet, or the knife will go much deeper, and very quickly. Nod if you understand me."

In the window glass, Lila saw the reflection now, the stunning face, the black rain of hair. She nodded.

"Good. We should talk, you and I. My associate has a car, just around the corner."

"You killed your associate."

"There's always more of that kind. He

was . . . unsatisfactory. Knowing that, you should take care to be satisfactory. We'll walk to the car, just two friends enjoying a summer day."

"I don't have what you're looking for."

"We'll talk. I have a quiet place." The woman put an arm firmly around Lila's waist, as if they were the best of friends, or lovers. The knife pressed a deadly reminder into her side.

"I just looked out the window." Stay calm, Lila ordered herself. They were on the street in broad daylight. There had to be something she could do. "I didn't even know Oliver Archer."

"Yet you went to his funeral."

"For his brother."

"And the brother you know very well. It can all be a simple thing, an easy thing. The brother gives me what was promised, and all is satisfied."

Lila scanned faces as they walked. Look at me! her mind shouted. Call the police.

Everyone passed by, in a hurry to get somewhere else.

"Why do you do this? Why do you kill?"

"Why do you sit in other people's houses?" Jai glanced down, smiled. "It's what we do, our living. There are many commendations on your website. We're good at what we do."

"So it's just a job."

"There's an American expression. It's not a job, it's an adventure. My employer pays well, and expects superior work. I give him superior work. My associate must circle the block, I think. New York, so busy, so much movement. I like it. We have that in common, I think. And we travel for our work. Much in common. If we have a good talk, you can go back, buy that pretty dress in the shop window."

"If we don't?"

"Then I do my job. You understand responsibility to an employer."

"I wouldn't kill for one. The police have your face. You can't—"

The knife dug a little deeper, brought a sharp sting. "I don't see the police, do you?"

"I don't see your associate either."

Jai smiled. "Patience."

Lila spotted Trench Coat Man stomping in their direction. She could use him, she thought. Use that simmering rage, that fuck-you attitude. She'd just need to time it perfectly, then—

At that moment, Earl Grey popped his head out of the corner of Lila's bag, gave a happy here-I-am yip.

It was only a moment, the jolt of surprise, the slight loosening of the hold, but Lila seized it.

She shoved, putting her back into it so Jai skidded backward a step. And Lila plowed her balled fist into that stunning face. Off balance, Jai went down on her ass on the sidewalk.

Lila ran.

First it was blindly, full panic, ears ringing, heart thudding. She risked one quick glance back, saw the woman pushing aside a man who had stopped to help her up.

She's wearing heels, Lila thought, and felt a little spurt of hope through the panic. Vanity would cost her.

She sprinted, gripping her bag and the dog that had burrowed back inside tight. Too far to double back to Julie and the gallery, and she'd need to cross the street to get to Ash's loft.

But the bakery. Luke's bakery.

She ran another block, full out, dodging pedestrians, shoving through them and ignoring the curses when they didn't part way for her. With her breath heaving, her legs singing, she careened around the corner and burst through the door of Baker's Dozen.

People stopped, stared over their peach pie or kiwi tart, but she kept running, straight around the counter where one of the staff called after her, and back into a huge kitchen smelling of yeast and sugar.

A burly man with scruff covering most of his round face stopped in the act of piping rosettes on the edges of a three-layer cake. "Lady, you can't be back here."

"Luke." She managed to wheeze in a breath. "I need Luke."

"Another one." A woman with purple hair pulled a baking dish of brownies out of an oven. Chocolate dripped through the air.

But something in Lila's face got through. The woman set aside the tray, dragged over a stool.

"You better sit down. I'll get him."

Lila pulled in another breath, shot a hand in her purse for her phone, and felt a trembling Earl Grey. "Oh, baby, I'm sorry."

"You can't have that thing in here!" The cake artist dropped his piping tool as his voice rose two full octaves. "What is that thing? Get it out of the kitchen."

"I'm sorry. Emergency." Lila pressed the shaking dog against her breast, reached back in her purse for her phone.

Before she could dial 911, Luke barreled up the stairs.

"What happened? Where's Julie?"

"Gallery. She's fine. She had a knife."

"Julie?"

"No. The Asian woman. She had a knife. I had to run. I don't know if she saw me come in here. I didn't look back. Or there was a car. I don't know."

"Sit." Luke literally picked her up, put her on the stool. "Simon, get her some water."

"Boss, she's got an animal. We can't have animals in the kitchen."

"He's a teacup poodle." Lila only snuggled the dog tighter. "His name is Earl Grey, and he saved my life. He saved my life," she repeated, looking back at Luke. "We need to call the police. And Ashton."

"I'll take care of it. Drink this now."

"I'm okay. I just panicked a little. I haven't run that far that fast since track and field in high school." She gulped down water. "Can I get a bowl? I need to give Earl Grey some water. He's pretty shaken up, too."

"Get her a bowl," Luke ordered.

"Boss!"

"A bowl, goddamn it. I'm going to take you to Ash, and we'll call the cops. You can tell us what happened."

"Okay." She took the bowl Simon reluctantly offered.

"That ain't no dog," he muttered.

"He's my hero."

"Well, he ain't no—Lady, you're bleeding."

"I—" Panic reared back when she looked down, saw the blood on her shirt. She yanked up the hem, then shuddered in relief. "She just poked me with the knife a couple times. It's just a scratch."

"Hallie, the first-aid kit."

"It's nothing, really—except now I've got this little hole in my good white shirt, and the bloodstain."

"Here, lady, I'll water the dog."

"I scared him when I ran." Lila looked up into Simon's eyes, saw the softness come into them. "It's Lila. I mean, I'm Lila. This is Earl Grey." Carefully, she handed the dog and the bowl to Simon.

"I'm just going to clean this," Luke told her, his voice, his hands gentle as a mother's soothing a frightened child. "I'm just going to clean and bandage it."

"Okay, okay. I'm going to call Detective Fine. Ask if they can meet me at Ash's. He's expecting me. I'm late."

She felt drifty, she realized. Once the adrenaline leaked away, her body felt just a little too light. She appreciated Luke's arm around her shoulders on the short walk to Ash's loft. Without it anchoring her, she felt she might float up and away.

He'd been so calm and gentle in the bakery, and now felt as sturdy as a tree that would stand up to any storm.

Of course Julie loved him.

"You're her tree."

"I'm what?"

"You're Julie's tree. With good, deep roots."

"Okay." He kept that sturdy arm around her, and used a gentle hand, rubbing her arm to soothe and calm.

She saw Ash running toward them, bolting toward them, almost blurry with it.

She felt him gather her up, right off the sidewalk.

"I'm fine," she heard herself say.

"I need to go check on Julie," Luke said. "I need to make sure she's okay."

"Go. I've got her."

"I can walk. This is silly. I ran for three blocks. About. I can walk."

"Not right now. I should've waited for you. Or come for you."

"Stop it." But since she didn't have the energy to argue, she let her head rest on his shoulder while he carried her up and into his loft.

He carried her straight to a sofa. "Let me see where she hurt you."

"Luke already fussed with it. She grazed me, that's all. She just wanted to scare me, which she did. She really did. But that's all she did, and she didn't get what she wanted. Bitch ruined my shirt."

"Lila."

When he lowered his forehead to hers, she let out a long sigh, and felt the light-headed sensation pass.

Rooted again, she realized. She wouldn't float away because he held on to her.

"Earl Grey scores again."

"What?"

"He poked out of my bag, startled her. I was timing it to use Trench Coat Man, but Earl Grey was better. Who expects to see a dog poke out of a purse, especially when you're focused on abducting someone in broad daylight? He startled her, and I shoved her, then I punched her and knocked her on her ass. And I ran. She was wearing heels, which tells me she's vain and overconfident. She underestimated me, which makes her another kind of bitch. I have to get up."

She pushed off the couch, scooping the dog out of her purse, and paced up and down the floor with him as she might with a fretful baby.

The anger came now, such a relief. Anger and insult bubbled up and boiled the lingering fear away.

"She didn't think I'd give her any trouble. She figured I'd just go along with her, trembling and weak and **stupid**. She comes at me in the middle of the morning in the middle of Chelsea, and doesn't expect me to fight back?"

She spun on her heel, paced back. Eyes firing, her face no longer pale but flushed with righteous fury.

"For God's sake, I'm the daughter of a lieutenant colonel of the United States Army, retired. I may not know kung fu, but I know basic self-defense. I know how to handle a weapon. I know how to handle myself. She's the one who landed on her ass. Who's the bitch now?"

"She cut you."

"She **taunted** me." The panic, the mild shock, the shakes, all gathered together to re-form into that sheer, boiling rage. "'We're going to have a little talk,' she says in her snotty, superior voice. And if it's not satisfactory, well, she'll just have to do her job. Which is killing people. She wanted me shaking and crying and begging like Oliver's poor girlfriend. Well, she didn't get it, did she? She may have ruined my best white shirt, but she's going to think of **me** every time she looks in the mirror or sits down for the next couple days."

He crossed to her, then just stood with his hands in his pockets. "Finished yet?"

"Nearly. Where's Luke?"

"He went to check on Julie."

"That's good, except now she's going to be upset and worried." Glancing down, she saw Earl Grey was asleep with his head on her breast. "All this drama wiped him out."

She went to her purse, took out his little blanket to spread on a section of the couch, then tucked him in for a nap.

"I was going to do just what I did—shove her and run. But I would've needed a trip to the ER and stitches. She'd have given me more than a poke with the knife. But Earl Grey gave me just that instant, just enough, so I could do it, and not get hurt. I'm taking him to the pet store and getting him whatever he wants."

"How will you know what he wants?"

"We have a psychic bond now. It's almost a Jedi thing." More settled, she sat on the arm of the couch, watching over the dog as she looked at Ash.

"I'm pretty good at reading people. I observe—I always have. I've always been the outsider—the new kid in town always is. So you learn, or I did, to watch, to gauge, to get a read. And I'm pretty good at it. Whatever I had told her, if she'd gotten me to that private place she told me she had for our talk, she'd have killed me when she was done with me. She'd have enjoyed it. It's her skill and her vocation."

"I'll give her the Fabergé, and we'll be done with it."

"It won't be enough, not for her. That's what I'm telling you. It might be enough for her employer, and she does have one, she mentioned one. But it's not going to be enough for her, especially not now."

She rose, went to him, ready now, she realized, to be held, to hold. "She has flawless skin. Up close, her face is just breathtaking, and her skin's perfect, but there's something wrong with her eyes. **In** her eyes," Lila corrected. "I have this character in my books. She's feral, whether in human form or wolf. I imagined her eyes like this woman's."

"Sasha."

"Yes." She nearly laughed. "You really did read it. I knew what she was when I looked in her eyes today. She's a killer. It's not just what she does. It's what she is. Feral, and for her the moon's always full."

She let out a breath, coldly calm now. "Ash, we could give her the Fabergé tied up in a ribbon, and she'd still kill me, and you, and anyone who got in the way of that. She needs it, the way you need to paint and I need to write. Maybe more than that."

"I need you safe, more than that."

"Then we have to finish it, because until we do, until she's in prison, neither of us will be safe. Believe me, Ash. I saw it in her eyes."

"I believe you. Believe me when I say until she's in prison, you don't go out alone. Don't argue," he snapped before she could. "The next time she won't underestimate you."

It irritated, hampered, but it rang true. "You have a point there."

"What did you mean you can handle a weapon?"

"I'm an army brat," she reminded him. "My father taught me how to handle a gun, how to shoot. Maybe I haven't done either in five or six years, but I could if I needed to. And I can box a little—more, I know basic and effective self-defense. Some jerk tried to mug me about a month after I moved to New York. I kicked his balls into his throat. They've probably yet to fully descend."

"You always manage to surprise me."

He gathered her in again, held on to comfort her and himself. He thought she wouldn't need a gun if and when they came upon the woman again. He'd never struck a female in his life, had never considered doing so. But he'd make an exception for the one who'd spilled Lila's blood.

He took care of what was his.

He lifted her face, touched his lips to hers.

"I'll get it," he told her when his buzzer sounded. The police, he thought, or Luke. Either way, it was all about to move forward. He was more than ready for it.

Twenty

Julie rushed in, launched herself at Lila. "Are you all right? Oh, God, Lila."

"I'm all right. Luke told you I was all right?"

"Yes, but . . ." She released Lila just enough to look down into her face. "She attacked you."

"Not exactly."

"She had a knife. Oh God! She cut you! You're bleeding."

"No." Lila cupped Julie's face so their eyes met. "She scratched me, and Luke fixed it. And I knocked her on her ass."

"She must've followed you from the gallery."

"I don't know. I think she was probably trolling the neighborhood, hoping to get lucky. She did—up until I knocked her on her ass. Plus, for the cost of a nice white shirt, she gave me more than I gave her."

"People always do," Julie stated. "I think you should go stay with your parents for a few weeks. Alaska's too far away for her to follow."

"That's not going to happen. Ash and I can explain what is, after—"

She broke off at the buzzer.

"The cops," Ash announced with a glance at his monitor.

"We'll talk." Lila squeezed Julie's hand while Ash went to the door. "Trust me."

Fine and Waterstone came in, gave the group a short, impassive once-over. Then Fine zeroed in on the blood on Lila's shirt. "You were injured?"

"It's very minor. Should we make coffee or something? Something cold. I could use something cold."

"I'll take care of it." Luke stepped toward the kitchen. "I know my way around in here."

"Let's sit down." Careful to avoid the wound, Ash tucked his arm around Lila's waist. "Lila should sit down."

"I'm fine, but I could sit."

Since he kept his arm around her, she sat on the couch with him while the detectives sat opposite.

"Why don't you tell us what happened?" Fine began.

"I'd gone to see Julie at her gallery on my way here. Ash wanted to work on the painting this afternoon." She settled in, told them the rest in as much detail as she could manage.

When she produced Earl Grey, Fine looked mildly shocked. But Waterstone's lived-in face brightened up with a blasting grin.

"That's the damnedest thing I've ever seen."

"He's awfully sweet." She set him down so he could check out the area. "And my current hero. When he popped up out of my purse, it took her by surprise, gave me an opening. I knocked her down, and I ran."

"You never saw this associate she spoke of?" Fine gave the dog a wary look when he sniffed at the toes of her shoes.

"No. New York traffic is another hero today. She couldn't catch me on foot. She was wearing heels, and I got a good head start. When my brain clicked in, I headed for Luke's bakery."

She glanced up with a smile as he brought in tall glasses of iced tea. "I think I was a little hysterical."

"No." He passed out the glasses. "You handled it."

"Thanks. Then I called you, and here we are. She has long hair—shoulder-blade long. She's about five-eight without the heels, and she doesn't have an accent. Her cadence is a little off, but her English is good. She has green eyes, light green, and killing is what she does, for a living and for her own enjoyment.

"But you know all this," Lila concluded. "You know who she is."

"Her name is Jai Maddok. Her mother is a Chinese national, her father was British—now deceased." Fine paused, as if considering, then continued. "She's wanted for questioning in several countries. Assassinations and theft are her specialties. Three years ago she lured two members of MI6 who were tracking her into a trap, killed both of them. Since then, there have been a few sightings. Information on her is sketchy, but investigators who've been involved or studied her agree, she's ruthless, she's canny and she doesn't stop until she gets what she's after."

"I'd agree with all of that. But canny isn't always sensible." Again, Lila thought of those pale green eyes. "She's a sociopath and a narcissist."

"I didn't realize you had a degree in psychiatry."

Lila met Fine's eyes coolly. "I know what I was looking at today. I got away from her because I'm not stupid, and because she was overconfident."

"Anyone who can take out two trained agents might be entitled to some confidence."

"She had time to plan," Ash said before Lila could speak. "And that was a matter of her own survival. Add in going up against two people she probably respected, as far as skill went."

Lila's lips curved as she nodded. He understood, she thought. He understood exactly what she thought, what she felt.

"With Lila? She figured a slam dunk, and she got sloppy."

"Don't count on that happening again," Waterstone put in. "You got lucky today."

"I don't count on anyone making the same mistake twice. Even myself," Lila added.

"Then give us the Fabergé, let us make an announcement. It'll be out of your hands, and she won't have any reason to go after either of you."

"You know that's not true," Lila said to Fine. "We're loose ends she'd need to tie off. More, I insulted her today, and she won't let that slide. If we give you the egg, the only thing she'll need from us is the kill."

Waterstone edged forward on his seat, and his tone, his demeanor, took on the patience Lila imagined he tried holding on to with his two teenagers. "Lila, we can protect you. FBI, Interpol—this is now a multi-agency investigation task force."

"I think you could, and you would. For a while. But eventually the budget—money and man power—would kick in. She can afford to wait. How long has she been an assassin for hire?"

"Since she was seventeen, possibly sixteen."

"About half her life, then."

"Close enough."

"You have details about her, information," Ash began, "but you don't know who she's working for now."

"Not yet. We're working on it, we have good people working on that," Fine said briskly. "We'll get to whoever's paying her."

"Even if you did, even if you were able to get to him, it wouldn't stop her."

"All the more reason you need protection."

"Lila and I are going away for a few days. You should come," he said to Luke, to Julie. "We'll talk about it."

"Where?" Fine demanded.

"Italy. We'll get out of New York for a while. If you get her while we're gone, problem solved. I want Lila safe, Detectives. I want my life back, and I want the person responsible for Oliver and Vinnie caught and locked up. None of that happens until Jai Maddok is stopped."

"We need your contact information in Italy, when you're going, when you plan on coming back."

"I'll get you all of it," Ash agreed.

"We're not looking to make your job harder," Lila told them.

Fine leveled a look. "Maybe not, but you're not making it any easier."

Lila brooded about it after the detectives left.

"What are we supposed to do? Go off somewhere and hide until they find her and put her away—which nobody's had a lot of luck doing for over a decade? We didn't start this, or ask for it. I looked out the window. You opened a letter from your brother."

"If hiding would take care of it, I'd do everything I could to make you hide. But . . ." Ash came back from locking the door, sat beside her again. "You were right when you said she could—and likely would—just wait. If she goes under now, there's no telling when and where she'll come at you again."

"Or you."

"Or me. So, Italy."

"Italy," Lila agreed, then looked over at Julie and Luke. "Can you go?"

"I don't know. I haven't thought about taking any time off right now. I'd love to,"

Julie added. "But I don't know what we'd do."

"Cover more ground," Ash pointed out. "Four of us instead of two. And after today, I don't want Lila to go anywhere alone. Being able to handle yourself," he added to forestall her, "doesn't mean you always have to."

"Safety in numbers. I could probably work something out," Luke considered. Then he caught Ash's eye, read the message—Needsomehelphere—nodded slightly. "Yeah, I can work it out. Julie?"

"I could morph it into a business thing. Visit some galleries, scope out some of the sidewalk artists. I'll talk to the owners, play it that way, and since I'm coming off a couple of major sales, I think they'll go for it."

"Good. I'll take care of the rest."

Lila turned to Ash. "What do you mean you'll take care of the rest?"

"We have to get there, stay somewhere, get around once we're there. I'll take care of it."

"Why you?"

He put a hand over hers. "My brother."

Hard to argue with the simplicity and

sincerity of that, she decided, and turned her hand under his to twine fingers. "Okay, but I'm the one who contacted Antonia Bastone. I'll take care of that."

"Which means?"

"When we get there, stay somewhere, get around somehow, it would be helpful to have some entrée into the Bastone villa. I'll take care of that."

"I bet you can."

"Count on it."

"Looks like we're going along for the ride. I need to get back," Luke said, "unless you need me."

"I've got it from here." Ash skimmed a hand down Lila's hair as he rose. "Thanks. For all of it."

"I'd say anytime, but I hope I don't end up stanching your lady's wounds again anytime soon."

"You did it so well." Rising, Lila stepped over to hug him. "If I ever need wound stanching by a calm, efficient hand, I know just where to go."

"Stay away from crazy women with knives." He gave her a light kiss, exchanged another silent message with Ash over the top of her head. "I'll take you back," Luke told Julie. "And come get you when you're done for the day."

She stood, angled her head. "Are you my bodyguard?"

"Looks that way."

"I'm fine with that." She went over to Lila, hugged her again. "Be careful."

"I promise."

"And do something you excel at. Pack light. We'll shop in Italy." She turned to Ash, hugged him in turn. "You watch out for her, whether she wants you to or not."

"Already there."

She pointed at Lila as she and Luke walked to the door. "I'll call you later."

Lila waited for Ash to set the locks again. "I'm not reckless."

"No. Tendencies toward risk taking aren't necessarily reckless. And tendencies to take care of details aren't necessarily controlling."

"Hmm. It can seem that way to someone used to taking care of her own details."

"Probably, just the way for someone used to taking his own risks, having someone determined to take them with him might seem reckless."

"That's a little bit of a dilemma."

"It could be, but we have a bigger one." He crossed to her, laid a hand lightly on her injured side. "Right now, my priority is seeing this never happens again. The way to that is finding the way to put Jai Maddok behind bars."

"And the way to that may be in Italy."

"That's the plan. If I'd known this would happen, you'd be hurt, I'd never have approached you at the police station. But I'd have thought of you. Because even with everything that was going on, you got in my head. First look."

"And if I'd known this would happen, all of this, I'd have come after you."

"But you're not reckless."

"Some things are worth the risk. I don't know what's going to happen in the next chapter, Ash, so I want to keep going until I find out."

"So do I." But he was thinking of her. Just of her.

"I'll trade Brooklyn for Italy, let you handle the details and I'll get us the Bastone connection. And we'll take the rest as it comes."

"That works. Are you up for sitting for me?"

"That's why I'm here. The rest was a detour."

"Then let's get started."

She walked over, picked up the dog. "He goes where I go."

"After today, I wouldn't argue with that."

He blocked it out when he painted. She could see it, the way everything focused on the work. The sweep or swirl of his brush, the angle of his head, the firm stance of his legs. At one point he clamped one brush between his teeth, wielded another, mixing, blending paint on his palette.

She wanted to ask how he knew which brush to use, how he decided on that or the mix of colors. Was it a learned technique or did it all come from the belly? Just a knowing.

But she thought when a man looked that intense, when he could peer into her as if he could see every secret she had—had ever had, ever would have—silence served them both.

Besides, he rarely said a word while the music thumped, and his hand swept or arrowed into the canvas for some minute detail.

And for a time that green laser of a gaze focused solely on the canvas. She thought he'd forgotten she was there. Just an image to create, just colors, textures, shape.

Then his eyes locked on hers again, held, held until she swore the breath just left her body. One hot, vibrant moment before he trained his attention on the canvas again.

He was, she thought, an emotional roller coaster. She had to remind herself she liked fast, wild rides—but a man who could leave you breathless without a word, without a touch, held formidable power. Did he know what he did to her, the way her heart bounced around in her chest, the nerves he had racing over her skin?

They were lovers now, and she'd always been comfortable with the physical. But this emotional whirlwind was new, and heady, and just a little unnerving.

Just as her arms began to tremble, the dog woke, whined and pranced over to her.

"Don't," he snapped when she started to lower her arms.

"Ash, my arms weigh a ton each, and the dog wants to go out."

"Just hold it, another minute. A minute."

The dog whined; her arms trembled. His brush moved in long, slow strokes.

"Okay. All right." He stepped back, eyes narrowed, brows drawn to study the day's work. "Okay."

Lila scooped up the dog, rubbed aching shoulders. "Can I see?"

"It's you." With a shrug, he stepped to a worktable, began to clean his brushes.

He had her body, the long flow of the dress, the flirtation of the underskirts. She could see the outline where her arms would be, her face, but he'd yet to paint those in. Just the lines of her, the angles, one exposed leg with the foot lifted onto her toes.

"I could be anyone."

"But you're not."

"The Headless Gypsy."

"I'll get to it."

He'd done some of the background— the orange and gold of the campfire, the billow of smoke behind her, a section of star-slashed sky. He wouldn't need her for that, she realized.

"Why do you wait to paint the face?"

"Your face," he corrected. "Because it's the most important. The lines, the colors, the curve of your arms—they're important, they all say something. But your face will say it all."

"What will it say?"

"We'll find out. You can go ahead and change, and you can grab something from the dressing room if you want to replace your shirt. I'll take the dog out. I need to toss a few things together, then we can go back. I'll stay tonight."

"Just like that?"

The faintest flicker of annoyance ran over his face. "We've crossed that point, Lila. If you want to backtrack you can tell me to sleep in one of the other bedrooms. I won't, I'll seduce you, but you can tell me."

Since she couldn't decide if his matter-of-fact tone was irritating or exciting, she left it alone, walked back to the dressing room.

She considered her options, settled on a mint-green tank, studied her bandaged graze before she put it on. And then studied her face.

What would it say? she wondered. Did

he already know? Was he waiting? She wished he'd painted it so she could know what he saw when he looked at her.

How could she settle in, settle down without the answers? How could she until she knew how it all worked—how he really worked?

She took down the dramatic makeup wondering why she'd bothered with it since her canvas face remained a blank. He'd probably have some artistic reason she needed to be fully in this character he envisioned.

Seduction? she thought. No, she didn't want to be seduced. That implied an imbalance of power, a kind of involuntary yielding. But he was right, they'd crossed that line—and both knew she wanted him to stay with her, to be with her.

Posing for him had left her feeling edgy, she admitted. Better to put that aside, as God knew there were bigger things to feel edgy over.

The blood on her ruined shirt served as a stark reminder of that. Studying it, she took herself back through the attack. She could admit she should've been more aware, paid more attention. If she'd been more aware she might not have been taken by surprise—and might not have a ruined shirt and a bandaged side. She could and would correct that. Still, she felt she'd won that little battle.

Jai drew a little blood, but that's all she got.

She rolled up the shirt to stuff it in her bag. Better to toss it out in the trash at her client's than at Ash's. If he came across it, he'd only toughen his stance on protecting her.

She pulled her phone out, pushed the shirt in. And since the phone was in her hand, did a quick check.

Five minutes later, she rushed down the stairs just as Ash brought the dog back in.

"Antonia got back to me. I got the hook in, Ash. She spoke to her father—the one who dated Miranda Swanson. The name-dropping worked, plus she has a friend who read my book. It worked."

"What did her father say?"

"He wants to know more about what I'm doing, what I'm looking for. I told her I was traveling to Florence with some friends next week, asked if it would be possible to meet him—when and where at his choosing.

Then I dropped the Archer name because, well, money talks to money, right?"

"It might listen more willingly."

"Same thing." Pleased with herself, she dug into her purse for a little ball, rolled it so the dog could give chase. "I'm doing a research-slash-pleasure trip with you and two friends. I think the door just cracked open a little wider."

"Maybe. The Bastones have to know what they have. Miranda Swanson might be clueless, but I'm not buying that a man like Bastone doesn't know he has a rare objet d'art worth a fortune."

Since Earl Grey brought the ball back to him, dropped it hopefully at his foot, Ash gave it a boot.

"If he still has it at all," he added, while the dog ran joyfully after the rolling ball.

"If he— Crap, they might have sold it. I didn't think of that."

"Either way, the family businesses— vineyards, olive groves—generate millions a year, and he's their CEO. You don't hold and maintain that position being clueless. If he still has it, why would he tell us, show us?"

"You did some very pessimistic thinking while walking the dog."

He kicked the ball again. "I consider it more realistic thinking."

"We've got our toe in the crack of the door. We need to see what happens next."

"That's what we're going to do, but with realistic expectations. Let me toss some stuff into a bag, then we'll go back to your place." He crossed to her, then cupped her face in his hands. "With realistic expectations."

"Which are?"

He laid his lips on hers, easy, for a moment easy. Then he dived, fast and deep, dragging her with him, leaving her no choice. And for a moment, another moment, to wish for one.

"We have something." He kept her face in his hands. "Something I think we'd have whenever, however, we met. It needs attention."

"There's so much happening."

"And this is part of it. This door's open, Lila, and I'm going through it. I'm taking you with me."

"I don't want to be taken anywhere."

"Then you need to catch up. I won't be long."

As she watched him walk up the stairs, every inch of her body vibrated, from the kiss, from the words, from the steady, determined look in his eyes.

"What the hell have I gotten myself into?" she muttered to the dog. "And if I can't figure it out, you're sure no help."

She picked up his leash and, tucking it into her bag, noted her balled-up shirt. Time to pay more attention all around, she told herself.

Being taken by surprise could cause more than a little damage.

She didn't mind the circular route back. She considered it a kind of safari. Going out by Ash's service entrance, a subway to midtown, where he detoured into Saks to replace her shirt. Then the walk east to Park to catch a cab uptown.

"The replacement cost twice what I paid for the original," she said as she unlocked the apartment—where Earl Grey raced to his squeaky bone in wild joy. "Plus you can't keep buying me clothes."

"I haven't bought you any clothes."

"First the red dress—"

"Wardrobe, necessary for the painting. Do you want a beer?"

"No. And you just bought me a shirt."

"You were coming to me," he pointed out. "If I'd been coming to you, you'd be buying me a shirt. Are you going to work?"

"Maybe—yes," she corrected. "For a couple hours anyway."

"Then I'll take this upstairs, finish making the arrangements for the trip."

"I came to you because of the painting."

"That's right, and now I'm here so you can work." He ran his hand down her hair, gave the ends a little tug. "You're looking for trouble, Lila, where there isn't any."

"Then why do I feel like I'm in trouble?"

"Good question. I'll be on the third floor if you need me."

Maybe she wanted to use the third floor, she brooded. He didn't think of that. Sure, all her work was set up on the main floor, but what if she had a sudden creative whim to work on the terrace?

She didn't—but she could have.

There was almost more than a possibility

she was being a moron—worse, a bitchy moron—but she couldn't seem to stop.

He'd boxed her in so neatly, so skillfully, she hadn't seen the walls going up. Walls made her feel restricted, so she didn't own or rent any. That kept things simple, loose and ultimately practical, given her lifestyle.

He'd changed things, she realized, so she found herself standing in a brand-new floor plan. Instead of enjoying it, she kept checking to be sure the door was handy.

"A moron," she muttered.

She plucked her ruined shirt out of her bag, buried it in the kitchen trash she'd take out later. She made a pitcher of cold lemon water, settled down with it in her work space.

A big perk of writing was that when her own world got a little bit too complicated, she could dive right into another.

She stayed in it, hit the sweet spot where words and images began to flow. She lost track of time, moving from wrenching loss, to steely determination and a quest for revenge, and ended with her Kaylee preparing for the final battle of the book—and final exams.

Lila sat back, pressed her fingers to tired eyes, rolled tensed shoulders.

And noticed for the first time Ash sitting in the living room, angled toward her with his sketch pad, and the little dog curled on his foot.

"I didn't hear you come down."

"You weren't finished."

She shoved at the hair she'd bundled back and up. "Were you drawing me?"

"Still am," he said idly. "It's a different look for you when you're into the work. Intense. Almost weepy one minute, obviously pissed off the next. I could do an entire series on it."

He continued to sketch. "Now you're uncomfortable, and that's too bad. I can go back upstairs until you're finished."

"No, I'm done for the day. I have to let what's coming circle around a little."

She got up, walked to him. "Can I see?" Then took the sketch pad from him. Paging through, she saw herself, hunched over—very bad posture, she thought, instinctively straightening—her hair a wreck, and her face mirroring the mood she was writing.

"God." She reached up to pull the clamp from her hair, but he caught her hand.

"Don't. Why do you do that? It's you, working, you caught up in whatever you see in your head, then put on the page."

"I look a little crazy."

"No, involved." He tugged on her hand until she relented, sat on his lap with the pad.

"Maybe both." She let herself laugh now, coming to one of her with her head back, her eyes closed. "You could call this **Sleeping on the Job**."

"No. **Imagining.** What were you writing?"

"A lot today. It was one of those good, long stretches. Kaylee's grown up some— hard and fast. I'm a little sorry, but it had to happen. Losing someone that close to her, knowing one of her kind could do that, kill someone she loved—did do that to punish her—it . . . Oh! It's her."

She'd flipped to another page, and there was her Kaylee, in wolf form in deeply shadowed woods.

Wildly beautiful, her body the sleek and muscled wolf, and her eyes eerily human and full of sorrow. Above the denuded trees, a full moon soared.

"It's exactly how I see her. How could you know?"

"I told you I read the book."

"Yes, but . . . It's her. Young, sleek, sad, caught between dual natures. It's the first time I've **seen** her, except in my head."

"I'll frame it for you, then you can see her whenever you want."

She let her head rest on his shoulder. "You drew one of the most important people in my life as if you knew her. Is that a form of seduction?"

"No." He trailed his fingers up her side. "But I'll show you what is."

"Not before I walk the dog."

"Why don't we walk the dog, go out to dinner, then come back and I'll seduce you?"

New floor plans, Lila remembered, were meant to be explored, tried on. "All right. But since I now have a very clear idea how I look, I need ten minutes first."

"We'll wait."

He picked up his pad and pencil again as she dashed upstairs. And began to draw her from memory—naked, wrapped in tangled sheets, laughing.

Yes, he'd wait.

PART THREE

Wealth lost, something lost;
Honor lost, much lost;
Courage lost, all lost.

OLD GERMAN PROVERB

Twenty-one

Lila lived by lists. Words on paper, to her mind, became reality. If she wrote it down, she made it happen. A list simplified a quick trip to Italy, made for more efficient packing, and all the steps to be taken before boarding.

In anticipation, she created the packing list, then set about making piles on the bed in the guest room.

One pile to go with her, another to leave at Julie's and a third for potential donations. Lightening her load, and leaving room for the shopping Julie would talk her into.

Ash came in. "Kerinov just called me. He's coming over."

"Now?"

"Soon. He has some information to pass on. What are you doing? We don't leave for three days."

"This is planning. A pre-packing stage. Since I won't be setting up house, so to speak, there are things I don't need to take. Plus my wardrobe needs a little turnover. Plus to plus, I'll need room to pack things I can't carry on."

She lifted the trusty Leatherman tool she habitually carried in her purse. "Such as. And such as the travel candles I always take with me, my lighter, my box cutter, my—"

"I get it, but there's no restrictions on those things on private."

"Private what? Plane?" She dropped her Leatherman. "We're flying to Italy on a private plane?"

"There's no point in having one and not using it."

"You . . . you have a private plane?"

"The family has one. Two actually. We each get a certain amount of air time a year—as long as the time isn't already taken. I told you I'd take care of the details."

"Details." She decided she needed to sit down.

"Do you have a problem being able to take your intimidating multi-tool and box cutter on board?"

"No. And flying in a private jet is a thrill—will be a thrill. It all just makes me feel out of balance."

He sat beside her. "My great-grandfather started it. The son of a Welsh coal miner who wanted better for his children. His oldest son made good, came to New York, made better. Along the way some of us squandered it, some expanded it. And if you let anything my father said to you get a grip, it's going to piss me off."

"I'm used to paying my own way. I can't keep up with private planes."

"Do you want me to book commercial?"

"No." Now she smiled. "I'm not a complete neurotic. I'm just telling you I don't need private planes. I'll enjoy the experience, and I don't want you to think I take it for granted."

"It's hard to think that when you looked like I said we were going on a jump ship instead of a G4."

"You're wrong. I've been on a jump ship. I'd have looked vaguely green. Well." She picked up her Leatherman, turned it over in her hands. "I'll adjust my packing strategy. I could make dinner."

"That'd be nice."

"I meant for Kerinov."

"I don't think he plans to be here that long. He's coming by after a meeting and before meeting his wife for some family thing. You can fill him in on where we are with the Bastones."

"Then I'll make us dinner." She glanced at her ordered piles of clothes. "I need to reevaluate."

"You do that," he said, then pulled out his ringing phone. "My father. I'll take it downstairs.

"Dad," he said as he started out.

She stayed as she was. She hated feeling guilty, but that's exactly how Spence Archer made her feel.

Forget it, she ordered herself, and started a new list.

While Lila adjusted her travel strategy

Ash stared out at New York while he spoke with his brother Esteban on the phone. One of the upsides of having so many siblings was a connection to almost everything.

"I appreciate it. Yeah, I thought you might. I don't know how far Oliver went. Too far. No, you're right, I probably couldn't have stopped him. Yes, I'll be careful."

He glanced at the stairs, thought of Lila and knew he had plenty of reasons to be. "You did help. I'll let you know what comes of it. I'll be in touch," he added as the house phone rang. "Yes, I promise. Later."

He shoved one phone in his pocket, picked up the other to clear Kerinov upstairs.

Momentum, he thought. He could feel it building. Where it would take them, he couldn't be sure, but the wind was finally at his back.

He went to the door, opened it for Kerinov. "Alexi. It's good to see you."

"Ash, I just heard from—" Lila paused on her run down the stairs. "Alexi. Hello."

"I hope this is a good time."

"Anytime is good. I'll get you a drink."

"Please, don't trouble. I have to meet my family soon."

"Let's sit down," Ash suggested.

"We couldn't talk, not about this," Kerinov said to Ash as they sat in the living room, "at Vinnie's funeral."

"It was a hard day."

"Yes. So many of your family came." He looked down at his hands, spread them, linked them. "It's good to have family on the hard days."

After a quiet sigh, he uncoupled his hands. "I have some information." He dug into his satchel for a manila envelope. "I've written up some notes, but wanted to tell you I've spoken to several colleagues more knowing on Fabergé and the era of the tsars than I. There are rumors, always. Perhaps one of the lost eggs is in Germany. It's reasonable to believe an Imperial egg was confiscated by the Nazis with other treasures. Out of Poland, the Ukraine, Austria. But none can be substantiated. There's no map, such as we have for the two."

"One in New York," Lila said, "one in Italy—or hopefully in Italy."

"Yes, Ashton tells me you're going there, to try to track the Nécessaire. There are collections, public and private. Some of the private, as we discussed, are very private. But I have some names, in my notes. Possibilities. One to me stands out."

He leaned forward, dangling his hands between his knees.

"There was a man, Basil Vasin, who claimed to be the son of the Grand Duchess Anastasia, the daughter of Nicholas and Alexandra. This is long before it was proven Anastasia was executed along with the rest of the family. After the execution by the Bolsheviks and for decades after, there were rumors she survived, escaped."

"They did a movie," Lila recalled. "With . . . Oh, who was it? Ingrid Bergman."

"Anna Anderson," Kerinov confirmed, "was the most famous of those who claimed to be Anastasia, but she was not the only. Vasin made this claim, bilked many wishing to believe it. He was very handsome, very charming, and convincing enough to marry a wealthy heiress. Annamaria Huff, a distant cousin of the Queen of England. She began to collect Russian art for him, a tribute to his family, including Fabergé. It was her greatest wish to recover the lost Imperial eggs, but she was unable to do so—at least publicly."

"You think she might have acquired one?" Ash asked.

"I can't say. My research shows they lived lavishly, opulently, often trading off her royal blood, and his claim to his own."

"Then if they'd gotten one," Lila concluded, "they'd have beat the drum."

"Yes. I think, but who can say? They had a son, an only child who inherited their wealth and property—their collection. And from my research, their quest to acquire the lost eggs."

"He'd know his father's claims to the Romanovs were disproved. I've researched, too," Ash pointed out. "They found her body, they've done DNA."

"People believe what they want to believe," Lila murmured. "What son wants to believe his father was a liar and a cheat? There was a lot of confusion, right—also did my research—reasons why women could claim to be Anastasia with some level of credence, or descendants. The new Russian government was trying to negotiate a peace treaty with Germany, and claimed the girls had been taken to a safe location."

"Yes, yes." Kerinov nodded rapidly. "To cover up the brutal murder of unarmed women, children."

"Rumors started to hide the murders became rumors that she'd, at least, survived. But they found the graves," Ash added. "The science wouldn't matter to some." No, not to some—and he thought of Oliver.

"Yes, some people believe what they want to believe." Alexi smiled a little. "No matter the science or the history."

"When did they conclusively prove she'd been executed with her family?" Lila asked.

"In 2007. A second grave was found, and scientists proved the two remains were Anastasia and her young brother. Cruelty," Alexi added, "even after death, to separate them from the other family, to try to hide the murders."

"So, the son would have been a grown man. It would be humiliating or infuriating— probably both—to have your family history, your bloodline, proven a lie."

"He continues to claim it." Alexi tapped his index finger on the envelope. "As you will see. There are many who prefer to

believe the discoveries and documenta-
tion were falsified. The claim she survived
is more romantic."

"And their deaths were brutal," Lila
added. "You think he—this Vasin—is the
one Oliver acquired the egg for?"

"There are other possibilities—I have
their information in my notes. A French
woman who can indeed trace her bloodline back to the Romanovs, and an American rumored to be open to buying stolen
artworks. But this one—Nicholas Romanov
Vasin—my mind goes back to him. He
has many international interests, finance,
industry, but is largely a recluse. He has
homes in Luxembourg, France, Prague,
and in New York."

"New York?"

Kerinov nodded at Ash. "Long Island's
North Shore. He rarely entertains, does
most of his business by remote—phones,
e-mails, video conferences. It's rumored
he suffers from mysophobia—the fear of
germs."

"Doesn't like to get his hands dirty," Ash
murmured. "That fits. Hire someone else
to do the dirty work."

"I have these names for you, and what

information I could get, but there's not been so much as a whisper about the discovery or acquisition of the eggs. I wish I had more to give you."

"You've given us names, a direction to take. Names we can mention to Bastone when we meet with him."

"Which we will be," Lila said, "Thursday afternoon. Antonia contacted me before I came downstairs," she explained. "Her father's agreed to talk to us. He'll contact us with details, but we're invited to Villa Bastone next Thursday."

"At two o'clock," Ash finished. "My brother Esteban's in the same business. I had him give Bastone a nudge."

"Well. Good for us."

"The next point on the map," Kerinov said. "You'll keep me updated? I wish I could go with you, but family and business keep me in New York for the next few weeks. Speaking of family, I have to go to mine." He rose. "So I'll say **udachi**—good luck."

He shook hands with Ash, flushed a little when Lila hugged him after she walked him to the door. She turned back, rubbed her hands together.

"Let's Google this Nicholas Romanov Vasin. I know we have Alexi's notes, but let's do some digging."

"I've got a better source than Google. My father."

"Oh." Money talks to money, she thought. She'd said so herself. "Good idea. You do that, and I'll see about dinner, as promised. I guess we need to check out the other two possibilities. Maybe he knows them, too."

"Or of them. I haven't forgotten he owes you an apology, Lila."

"It's not on the top-ten list of things to worry about right now."

"It's on mine." He went into the kitchen ahead of her, poured two glasses of wine. "For the cook." He handed her one. "I'll stay out of your way."

Alone, she looked down at the wine, shrugged, took a sip. His father might be able to add more meat to the bone, and that's what counted. It couldn't matter, not now, that she'd made excuses about not attending Vinnie's funeral—and both of them knew they'd been excuses. It couldn't matter, not now, what his father thought of her.

Later . . . Who knew what could or would matter later?

Right now she had to figure out what to cook.

He gave her nearly an hour before he wandered back through. "Smells great. What is it?"

"I'm not sure. It's not scampi, it's not linguine, but has elements of both. We'll say it's scampine. My head's in Italy, I guess. Whatever it is, it's about ready."

She served it in wide, shallow bowls, with hunks of the rosemary bread Ash had picked up at Luke's bakery, and another well-earned glass of wine.

She sampled, nodded. Just enough garlic, she decided, and a good lemony flavor throughout. "Not bad."

"Better than that. It's great."

"Generally I have more successes than failures when I make something up, but my failures are really stupendous."

"You should write this one down."

"That eliminates the spontaneity." She stabbed a shrimp, rolled some noodles. "So, was your father any help?"

"He knows Vasin—in that he met him

once, nearly a decade ago. According to my father, Vasin wasn't particularly social, but not the recluse he's become in recent years. He never married, never was reported to be particularly attached to any woman, or man for that matter. Even back then he wouldn't shake hands—though they met at a very high-powered affair that included various heads of state. He brought along an assistant who served him his own specially bottled water throughout the evening. According to my father, Vasin was pompous, fussy, eccentric without the charm, and physically very attractive."

"Tall, dark and handsome. I did a quick Google, found some photos from the eighties and nineties. Movie-star glam."

"Which was one of his interests at one time. He financed a few films, and was on the point of financing a remake of **Anastasia**—the script was being written, casting nets were going out. Then with the DNA, the general consensus that Anastasia died along with the rest of her family, the project fell apart."

"A big disappointment, I imagine."

"He got out of the movie business about then, to the best of my father's recollection. And the event they both attended was one of the last times Vasin accepted an invitation to a major affair. He became more reclusive, gradually began doing all of his business as Kerinov said, by remote."

"To have that kind of wealth, and not use some of it to see the world, to go places, enjoy them, meet people." Absently she wound more pasta around her fork. "He must be a serious germaphobe."

"It doesn't, according to my father's gauge, make him any less of a ruthless businessman. He's been accused of corporate espionage, but his fleet of lawyers tamp that down, or pay it off—my father's not sure which. Hostile takeovers are a specialty."

"Sounds like a prince."

"He certainly thinks so."

"Ha." Amused, she stabbed another shrimp.

"He did once allow certain access to his art collection—for articles—but that's been shut down for a number of years, too."

"So he shutters himself off from society, hoards art, runs his empire of businesses through technology—all of which he can do as he's rich."

"So rich, no one's exactly sure just how rich. There's something else that makes me lean, along with Alexi, in Vasin's direction."

"Uh-oh."

"Twice that my father knew of, a business competitor met with a tragic accident."

"That's a big step up from ruthless," she commented.

"In addition, a reporter in the mid-nineties was reputedly working on a book on Vasin's father, who was still living. On assignment covering the Oklahoma City bombing, he went missing. He's never been heard from again, no body was ever found."

"You got that from your father?"

"He dug back, thinking about what happened to Oliver. He doesn't know what I'm after—"

"You haven't told him yet? About the egg? Ash—"

"No, I haven't told him. He's smart enough to realize my interest in Vasin connects to what happened to Oliver. And he's concerned enough as it is without me giving him all the details."

"Giving him the details would at least give him answers. And I can't lecture you on it"—she brushed her own words away—"since all I told my parents was I'm taking a little vacation."

"Probably best."

"That's what I told myself, but I still feel guilty. You don't."

"Not in the least," he said easily. "As to the other two names Alexi gave us, Dad doesn't know the woman, but he does know the American, and reasonably well. My take after his rundown on Jack Peterson is the man wouldn't quibble about buying stolen goods, cheating at cards or insider trading, he'd consider all that a game. Murder, especially of an acquaintance's son, wouldn't be on the table. My dad's summary was Peterson likes to play, likes to win, but he can also take losing with good grace."

"Not the type to hire an assassin."

"No, it didn't strike me he would be."

"Okay, so for now, the focus is on Nicholas Romanov Vasin. What do you think might happen if we drop that name on Bastone?"

"We'll find out. Did you sort out the packing?"

"Yes, all under control."

"Good. Why don't we clear this up? I guess we need to take the dog out. Then I want some more sketches of you."

To prolong the moment, and to postpone the dishes, the dog, she leaned back with her wine. "You've already started the painting."

"This is another project. I'm thinking of putting together some new pieces for a show, next winter." He rose, taking up both their bowls. "I want at least two more of you, and what I have in mind first is the faerie in the bower."

"Oh, right, you mentioned that before. Emeralds. Like glittery Tinker Bell."

"Definitely not like Tinker Bell. Think more Titania, waking up from a midsummer sleep. And naked."

"What? No." She laughed at the idea, then remembered she'd said no to the gypsy. "No," she repeated, and a third time, "No."

"We'll talk about it. Let's walk the dog. I'll buy you an ice cream cone."

"You can't bribe me out of my clothes with ice cream."

"I know how to get you out of your clothes." He grabbed her, pressed her back against the refrigerator. His mouth ruled hers, his hands roamed, took, teased.

"I'm not posing naked. I'm not hanging in Julie's gallery naked."

"It's art, Lila, not porn."

"I know the difference. It's still my naked . . . ness," she managed when his thumbs brushed over her nipples.

"You have the perfect body for it. Slender, almost delicate but not weak. I'll do a few sketches, some concepts. If you don't like them, I'll tear them up."

"You'll tear them up."

He lowered his lips to hers again, lingered. "I'll let you tear them up. But first I need to touch you, I need to make love with you. Then to sketch you when your eyes are still heavy, your lips soft. If you don't see how perfect you are, how powerful, how magical, you'll tear them up. Fair enough."

"I . . . yes, I—"

"Good." He kissed her again, took his time, then eased back. "I'll get the dog."

Half dreaming, Lila went to the closet for the leash. Stopped.

She'd gone from a firm no, she realized, to a qualified yes.

"That was very underhanded."

"You still have first refusal," he reminded her, and took the leash. "And an ice cream cone."

"For an artist, you're a hell of a negotiator."

"Archer blood." He clipped on the leash, set Earl Grey down. "Let's go for a walk," he said, and grinned as the little dog danced.

Since room wouldn't be an issue, Lila divided what she thought she needed to take between her suitcases. Room for new that way, she decided. Though she'd intended to send a bag of not-going-to-Italy items to Julie's, Ash took them to his place, and carted her bag of to-be-donated items with him.

He'd take care of it.

She had to admit it was easier, even more efficient—but she couldn't quite pinpoint when she'd started adjusting to "I'll take care of it."

Plus, she'd caved and posed nude. She'd felt awkward and self-conscious—until he'd showed her the first sketch.

God, she had looked beautiful, and magical. And though the faerie she'd become was obviously naked, the way he'd posed her, the addition of the wings he'd given her, had added just enough modesty to relax her.

The emeralds had become sparkles of dew in her hair, the shimmering leaves in her bower.

The nudity was implied, she thought—but she wasn't sure what the Lieutenant Colonel would have to say about that, if he ever saw the work.

She hadn't torn up the sketches. How could she?

"He knew that," she said to Earl Grey as she finished arranging the welcome-home flowers for her clients. "He knew he'd get just what he was after. I can't figure out how I feel about that. You have to admire it, though, don't you?"

She hunkered down where the dog sat, watching her with his paws protectively over the little toy kitten she'd gotten him as a parting gift.

"I'm really going to miss you—my teacup hero."

When the buzzer sounded, she went to

the door, used the peep, then opened it for Ash.

"You could've just called up."

"Maybe I wanted to say goodbye to Earl Grey. See you around, pal. Ready?"

Her two cases, her laptop and her purse sat by the door. "Stay and be good," she told the dog. "They'll be home soon." She took one last glance around—everything in place—then picked up her purse, took the handle of one of the suitcases.

"I picked Luke and Julie up on the way, so we can head straight to the airport. Got your passport? Sorry," he added when she flicked him a glance. "Habit. Ever travel to Europe with six siblings, three of whom are teenage girls?"

"I can't say I have."

"Trust me, this is going to be a lot easier, even considering the main purpose of the trip."

Then he ran a hand down her hair, leaned down, kissed her as the elevator started down.

He did things like that, she thought. Everything practical, organized, "taken care of," then he'd touch her or look at her, and nothing inside her stayed practical or organized.

She rose up to her toes, tugged his head back to hers. Kissed him back. "Thanks."

"For?"

"First, for stowing my excess at your place, and taking my cast-offs away. I didn't thank you."

"You were too busy telling me I didn't have to bother."

"I know. It's a little problem, but I'm thanking you now. Next, thanks for the trip—whatever the main purpose, I'm going to Italy, one of my favorite places. I'm going with my best friend and her guy, who I like a lot. And I'm going with you. So thanks."

"I'm going with my best friend, and his lady, and with you. Thanks back."

"One more thanks, this time in advance. Thanks for not thinking less of me when we get on the private jet and I can't hold back the squeal. Plus there are bound to be buttons and controls for various devices—I looked up the G4. I'm going to want to play with all of them. And talk to the pilots, talk them into letting me sit in the cockpit for a while. Some of this might embarrass you."

"Lila." He guided her off the elevator. "I've herded teenage girls around Europe. Nothing embarrasses me."

"It's a good thing. So, **buon viaggio** to us."

She took his hand, walked out with him.

Twenty-two

She didn't squeal, but she did play with everything. Before the wheels were up she'd progressed to first-name basis with the pilot, copilot and their flight attendant.

Minutes after they boarded, she followed the flight attendant into the galley for a tutorial.

"There's a convection oven," she announced. "Not just a microwave, but an actual oven."

"You cooking?" Ash wondered.

"I could, if it was like **2012**—the movie—and we had to fly to China. And we have

BBML. You didn't say anything about BBML."

"Possibly because I don't know what it is."

"Broad band multi-link. We can e-mail while we're flying over the Atlantic. I have to e-mail somebody. I love technology."

She did a little turn in the aisle. "And there's flowers in the bathroom. That's so nice."

She laughed at the pop of the champagne cork, said, "Hot damn!"

And drank deep.

She embraced, Ash thought. Maybe he'd seen that without recognizing it in that first meeting, even through the grief, the anger, the shock. Her openness to the new, interest in whatever came her way. And what seemed to be an absolute refusal to take anything for granted.

He could enjoy this, with her and friends, this in-between. New York and death behind, Italy with whatever they found ahead. But these hours spread into a welcome limbo.

Somewhere over the Atlantic, after a lovely little meal and wine, she made her way to the cockpit.

He had no doubt that before she was done she'd have the life stories of the pilots. It wouldn't surprise him if they let her take the controls for a stretch.

"She'll be flying us before she comes out," Julie said.

"I was just thinking that."

"You already know her well. She's getting used to you."

"Is she?"

"It's hard for her to accept things she didn't earn, to accept someone giving her a hand, and even more, to let herself rely on someone. But she's getting used to you. As someone who loves her a whole lot, it's good to see. I'm going to settle in with my book for a while."

She rose to move to the front of the cabin, kicked her seat back, snuggled in.

"I'm going to ask her to marry me. Again."

Ash blinked at Luke. "What?"

"We said we were going to take it slow." He looked forward, toward the bright fire of her hair. "If she says no, wants to wait, I'm okay with it. But she's going to marry me sooner or later. I'd rather sooner."

"A month ago you swore you'd never

get married again. You weren't even drunk."

"Because there's only one Julie, and I thought I'd blown it with her. Or we'd blown it with each other," Luke qualified. "I'm going to buy a ring in Florence, and ask her. I thought I should tell you as we have an agenda, and I'm in for whatever you need. I just need to fit that in."

He poured the last of the champagne into their glasses. "Wish me luck."

"I do. And I don't have to ask if you're sure. I can see that."

"Never been surer." He looked toward the front of the cabin. "Don't say anything to Lila. She'd try to keep it zipped, but girlfriends have a code. I think."

"It's in the vault. You're breaking Katrina's heart."

On a laugh, Luke shook his head. "Seriously?"

"Dead serious. Thanks for that. She'll stop texting me, trying to get me to bring you to a club, or go sailing, or whatever other ploy she thinks of."

"She does that? She's twelve."

"She's twenty, and yeah, she does

that. I've been your shield, man. You owe me."

"You can be my best man."

"I already am."

He thought about being sure and moving ahead, about accepting. He thought about his brother, who had always tried to grab too much and held on to nothing.

He slept lightly when Lila finally wound down and stretched out beside him. When he woke in the darkened cabin with her curled toward him, he knew what he wanted.

He'd always known what he wanted, found the way to get it.

But now it was someone he wanted, not something. To win Lila, he needed more than her acceptance, but he wasn't quite sure what the more was. How could he see clearly when so much blocked the way?

Death brought them together. They'd gone beyond that, but it remained the start. Death and what had followed, and now what they pursued together.

They needed resolution, both of them, to see the way clear.

He checked his watch, saw they'd land in just over an hour.

The in-between was almost done.

They walked off the plane into Italian sunshine and to a waiting car with a young, flirty driver named Lanzo. With cheerful and excellent English he welcomed them to Florence, vowed to be at their disposal anytime, night or day, during their visit.

"My cousin owns a trattoria very near your hotel. I have a card for you. You will have most wonderful service. My sister, she works at the Uffizi, and she can arrange for you a tour. A private one if you wish it."

"Do you have a big family?" Lila asked.

"Oh, **sì**. I have two brothers, two sisters and many, many cousins."

"All in Florence?"

"Most are here, some are not too far away. I have cousins who work for the Bastones. I drive you to the villa in two days' time. They are a most important family, and the villa is very beautiful."

"Have you been there?"

"**Sì, sì**. I have been, ah . . . a waiter there for important parties. My parents, they have flowers, a shop of flowers. I sometimes take flowers there."

"You're a jack-of-all-trades."

"**Scusi?**"

"You work many jobs. Have many skills."

He drove like a maniac, but then so did everyone else. Enjoying him, Lila engaged him in conversation all the way from the airport, through Florence and to the hotel.

She loved the city, where the light made her think of sunflowers, and the air seemed to breathe art. Florence spread under a bowl of summer blue, motorbikes zipping and weaving along narrow streets, between wonderful old buildings, around colorful piazzas.

And people, she thought, so many people of so many nationalities mixing, mingling at cafés and shops and wonderful old churches.

Red-tiled roofs simmered in the August heat with the curve of the Duomo rising above. Bold blooms in baskets, boxes and fat pots flashed against sun-baked walls.

She caught a glimpse of the lazy snake

of the River Arno, wondered if they'd have time to take a walk along its curves, climb up to the bridges—and just **be**.

"You have a most excellent hotel," Lanzo announced. "You will have such service here."

"And your cousins?"

"My uncle is bellman here. He will take good care of you." Lanzo gave her a wink as he pulled up to the hotel.

Tall, thick, dark wood-framed windows against whitewashed walls. The moment Lanzo stopped the car, a man in a perfect gray suit stepped out to greet them.

Lila let it all flow around her—the manager, shaking hands, the welcomes. She simply stood for the moment, basking in it—the pretty street with its shops and restaurants, the buzz of traffic, the feel of being somewhere new and different.

And where she wasn't, she had to accept, in charge. She wandered the lobby while Ash dealt with the details. Everything so quiet and cool, big leather chairs, pretty lamps, more flowers.

Julie joined her, held out a glass. "Sparkling pink grapefruit juice. It's wonderful. Everything okay? You got so quiet."

"Absorbing. It's all so beautiful, and just a little surreal. We're actually here, all four of us."

"We're here, and I'm dying for a shower. Once I clear the cobwebs, I'm going straight out to visit a couple of galleries so I feel like I'm earning my keep. Tomorrow, you and I are going to carve out some shopping time. We're both going to look like we visit the villa of an important Florentine family every day."

"You were listening."

"And so happy I could do that and not make conversation with our unquestionably charming driver—who probably has as many women pining over him as he does cousins."

"He looks straight into your eyes when he talks to you—which worried me a little since he was driving. But it's so **mmm**," she said for lack of a word.

Then realized Ash did exactly the same. When he spoke to her, when he painted her, he looked straight into her eyes.

They rode the tiny elevator up, with Lila content that their manager escort directed most of his conversation to Ash. And with a subtle flourish, he welcomed them into what turned out to be two combined suites.

Spacious, airy, it combined Old World and modern luxury in a perfect blend.

She imagined herself writing at the little desk angled toward the windows, where the city's rooftops jutted, or sharing breakfast on the sunny terrace, curled up with a book on the creamy white cushions of the couch.

Tangled and wrapped around Ash in the majestic bed under a gilded ceiling.

She plucked a perfect peach from a fruit bowl, sniffed it as she wandered into the bath with its generous glass shower, deep, deep jet tub and acres of black-veined white marble.

She made a date on the spot—candles, Florence glowing against the moonlit sky outside the window. With her and Ash together in hot, frothy water.

She needed to unpack, settle in, get her bearings. She had a steady routine for beginning in a new space. But she continued to wander, breathing in the peach, tossing windows open to the air, the light, the scents of Florence.

She circled back around to the living space just as Ash closed the main door.

"I've stayed in a lot of impressive spaces," she told him. "This one just leaped straight to number one. Where are Julie and Luke? We could lose each other in here."

"In their section. She wanted to unpack, get freshened up. She has a list of galleries to go to, make contact."

"Right."

"You didn't ask the manager his marital status, political affiliation and favorite pastimes."

She had to laugh. "I know, so rude. I was caught up in my own little world. It's wonderful to be in Florence again, and I've never seen it quite this way. But better than that? It's wonderful to be here with you— and even ahead of that? To be here with you when neither of us have to look over our shoulders. Everything's just a little brighter, just a little more beautiful."

"When we're done, we'll be done looking over our shoulders. We can come back here, or go wherever you like."

With a little hitch around her heart, she rolled the peach in her hands, studied him. "That's a big promise."

"I make them, I keep them."

"You would."

She set the peach aside—she'd savor it later—because now she had another indulgence in mind.

"I should be practical, unpack, get things in order, but I really want a long, long, hot shower in that amazing bathroom. So . . ." She turned, started back. Then glanced over her shoulder. "Interested?"

He arched an eyebrow. "I'd be a fool not to be."

"And you're no fool." She stepped out of her shoes, just kept going.

"You're pretty fresh for somebody just off a transatlantic flight."

"Ever travel coach?"

"Okay, got me."

Yes, she thought, she did. "Even in that mode of travel I'm like jersey." She pulled out the band she'd used to tie back her hair, tossed it on the long, smooth counter.

"You're like Jersey."

"The fabric, not the state. I'm easy care and travel well." Testing, she opened the shampoo in a basket on the counter, sniffed. Approved. With another glance at him, she smiled, peeled out of her shirt, her pants, the lacy tank she'd worn in lieu of a bra.

"And I can take a lot of handling before I show any wear."

She gathered the shampoo, the shower gel, strolled to the shower. "Silk's gorgeous, but jersey holds up better."

She turned on the shower, stepped inside. Left the door open. "I did mean long, and hot, by the way."

"Yeah, I'm getting that."

He watched her as he undressed, the way she lifted her face to the spray, let the water run down her hair until it was sleek as a seal.

When he stepped in behind her, she turned, linked her hands behind his neck. "This is the third place I've had sex with you here."

"Was I in a coma?"

"It was in my mind, but it was excellent."

"Where were the other two?"

"Trust me." She rose on her toes to meet his mouth. "You'll find out."

He caught the scent of peaches as she skimmed her hand over his cheek, as she pressed her body, already wet and warm, to his.

He thought of the gypsy, daring a man

to take her, and the faerie queen, lazily waking after taking one for herself.

He thought of her, so open, so fresh—with little secret pockets holding so much more than she revealed.

Steam rose; water pulsed. And her hands roamed over him in challenge and invitation.

The wanting of her was a constant hum in his blood. It built now with the feel of her against him, thickened like the steam with them alone in the wet and the heat.

He lifted her another inch, held her like a dancer **en pointe**, ravishing her mouth, her throat, until she fisted a hand in his hair for balance. She'd loosed something in him, she could feel it in the violent thud of his heart, in the rough race of his hands on her body.

Thrilled by it, she fell into the wild with him.

Taking, just taking, all greed and lust and insatiable hunger for flesh. The feel of it under groping hands, the taste of it along seeking tongues. With a breathless impatience, he gripped her hips, lifted her yet another inch.

And plunged into her, so fierce and desperate she cried out in shock as much as triumph.

To be wanted like this—unreasonably—and to want in return was more than she'd ever imagined knowing. She clung to him, her breath sobbing out against the sharp slap of flesh striking wet flesh.

She took him in, surrounded him, possessed as she allowed herself to be possessed.

And finally, when pleasure screamed through her, blood and bone, surrendered all.

She clung to him, would have slithered down in a liquid pool to the shower floor without his body bracing hers.

She'd lost her grip on where they were, could barely remember who they were, so just hung on with the mad gallop of her own heart thundering in her ears.

He'd have carried her into bed if he'd had the strength. Instead he held on as she did, drenched by the spray. Saturated with her.

When he had his breath back, he rested his cheek on the top of her head. "Hot enough?"

"Definitely."

"Not especially long."

"Sometimes you're just in a hurry."

"And sometimes you're not." He eased back, opened the shampoo.

He watched her face as he poured shampoo into his hand, as he slicked his hands over her hair, combed his fingers through it. Then he turned her, gathered her hair up, dug his fingers into her scalp.

A new thrill shivered along her skin. "God. You could make a living."

"Everyone needs a fallback."

This time, it was long.

He woke in the quiet dark, reached for her. A habit now, he realized, even as he did so. And rolled over, unsatisfied when he didn't find her.

He checked the time, saw it was well into the morning. He'd have been happy to stay just where he was—if she'd been there—slip into sleep, or that half-state with her.

But alone, he rose, opened the curtains and let the Italian sun beam over him.

He'd painted scenes much like this—the shapes, sunbaked colors, the textures.

Beautiful, but too typical for the canvas—
for his canvas.

But add a woman on a winged horse,
hair flying, sword raised, it changed things.
An army of women—leather and glinting
armor—flying above the ancient city. Where
did they go to wage the battle?

He might create it, and find out.

He walked out of the bedroom, found
the large parlor as empty as the bed. But
he caught the scent of coffee and, following it, found Lila in the smaller second
bedroom, sitting at her laptop at a small,
curved-leg desk.

"Working?"

She jumped like a rabbit, laughed. "God!
Make some noise next time, or call the
paramedics. Good morning."

"Okay. Is that coffee?"

"I ordered some up—I hope that's okay."

"It's more than okay."

"It's probably not really hot. I've been up
awhile."

"Why?"

"Body clock, I guess. Then I looked out
the window and I was done. Who can
sleep with all this? Well, apparently Luke

and Julie, as I haven't heard a peep out of them."

He drank some coffee—she was right, hot it wasn't. But for now it would do.

"It was nice going out last night," she said. "Walking around, eating pasta, having a last glass of wine together on the terrace. They're so great together."

He grunted—thought of what he had in the vault. "Are you interested in breakfast or do you need to work awhile? I'm going to order more coffee anyway."

"I could eat. I'm done working for now. I finished the book."

"What? Finished? That's great."

"I shouldn't say 'finished' because I still need to go through and polish, but essentially finished. I finished my book in Florence. I finished my first in Cincinnati. It doesn't have quite the same cachet."

"We should celebrate."

"I'm in Florence. That **is** a celebration."

But he ordered champagne, a pitcher of orange juice for mimosas. She couldn't argue with his choice—especially when Julie wandered out, sleepy-eyed, and said, "Mmmm."

It was good, Lila realized, sharing a little

celebratory breakfast with friends. She'd been alone in Cincinnati for the first, alone in London for the second.

"It's nice." She passed Luke a bakery basket. "I've never been to Italy with friends. It's very nice."

"This friend is dragging you out to the shops in . . . one hour," Julie decided. "Then I'm going to check out some of the street artists, see if there's anyone I can make rich and famous. We can meet you back here or wherever you like," she told Luke.

"We can keep it loose. I'm going to play tourist." He gave Ash a meaningful look. "I'm hiring Ash as my personal guide. Free day, right?"

"Yeah."

One day, Ash thought. They could all take one day. Tomorrow, there would be questions, digging, and a renewed focus. But they deserved one day of normal.

And if his friend wanted to spend it finding a ring so he could leap into marriage again, he'd be the springboard.

"Why don't we meet up again about four?" he suggested. "Have a drink, figure out what's next?"

"Where?"

"I know a place. I'll text you."

Three hours later, Lila sat glassy-eyed staring down at the impressive pile of what she now thought of as shoe candy. Heels, flats, sandals, in every color imaginable. The scent of leather seduced her senses.

"I can't. I have to stop."

"No, you don't." Julie spoke firmly as she studied the mile-high pumps in electric blue with glittery silver heels. "I can build an outfit around these. What do you think? They're like feet jewelry."

"I can't even see them. I've gone shoe blind."

"I'm having them, and the yellow sandals—like daffodils. And the flat sandals—these, with the pretty weaving. Now."

She sat again, picked up one of the red sandals Lila had tried on before going shoe blind. "You need these."

"I don't need them. I don't need all this. Julie, I have two bags of stuff! I bought a leather jacket. What was I thinking?"

"That you're in Florence—and where better to buy leather? That it looks amazing on you. And that you just finished your third book."

"Essentially finished."

"You're having these sandals." Julie waved one seductively in front of Lila's face. "If you don't buy them, I'm buying them for you."

"No, you're not."

"You can't stop me. Red shoes are classic, and they're fun, and as pretty as these are, they're going to wear like iron. You'll have them for years."

"That's true." Weakening, Lila thought, she was weakening. "I know better than to go shopping with you. Where am I going to keep all this stuff? I bought a white dress, and that little white jacket—nothing's less practical than white."

"Which both also look amazing on you, and the dress will be perfect for tomorrow. With these." She held up another shoe—strappy heeled sandals in spring-leaf green.

Lila covered her face with her hands, then peeked out between spread fingers. "They're so pretty."

"A woman who doesn't buy shoes on a trip to Florence isn't a real woman."

"Hey!"

"And you can leave anything you want at my place, you know that. Actually, I'm seriously thinking of looking for a bigger place."

"What? Why?"

"I really think we'll need more room after I ask Luke to marry me."

"Holy crap!" Stunned, Lila stood straight up, gaped, then dropped straight down again. "Are you serious?"

"I woke up this morning, looked over at him, and I knew this is what I want." Smile dreamy, Julie laid a hand on her heart. "He's what I've always wanted. I want him there, every morning—and I want to be there for him. So I'm going to ask him. I'm not even nervous, because if he says no I'll just push him into traffic."

"He won't say no. Julie." She reached over, grabbed Julie in a hard, swaying hug. "This is so great. You have to let me help plan the wedding. You know how good I am at planning."

"I do, and I will. I want a wedding this time—I might even wear white."

"You absolutely will wear white," Lila decreed. "You absolutely will."

"Then I absolutely will. It doesn't have to be a big and crazy wedding, but it has to be real."

"Flowers and music, and people dabbing their eyes."

"All of that this time. No running off to a justice of the peace. I'm going to stand up with him in front of family and friends—with my best friend as my maid of honor—and make promises with him. This time, we'll keep them."

"I'm so happy for you."

"I haven't asked him yet, but I guess it's like essentially finishing your book." Beaming, she leaned over, gave Lila a smacking kiss on the cheek. "We're buying the shoes."

"We're buying the shoes."

Now she had three bags, Lila thought as they left the shop. She'd sworn she'd only buy the practical essentials, good-value replacements for what she'd culled out.

Lied to myself, she admitted, but damn, she felt really good about it.

"How are you going to ask him?" she demanded. "When? Where? I need all the details before we meet them for drinks."

"Tonight. I don't want to wait."

"On the terrace, at sunset." Lila only had to close her eyes to see it. "Sunset in Florence. Trust me, I know how to set a scene."

"Sunset." Now Julie sighed. "It sounds pretty perfect."

"It will be. I'll make sure Ash and I are out of the way. You'll have some wine— wear something fabulous, then as the sun sinks down, the sky over the city goes red and gold and gorgeous, you'll ask him. Then you have to immediately come tell us so we can all toast you—then go out to Lanzo's cousin's trattoria and celebrate."

"It may not be immediate."

"The least you can do after browbeating me into three bags of clothes is hold off on the engagement sex until after we celebrate."

"You're right. I was being selfish. Why don't we—"

Lila grabbed her arm. "Julie, look!"

"What? Where?"

"There, up ahead. Just turning down that— Come on."

Snagging Julie's hand, Lila began to run.

"What? What? What?"

"It's the woman, the HAG—Jai Maddok. I think."

"Lila, it can't be. Slow down."

But Lila bolted across the cobblestones, turned the corner—caught just another glimpse. "It's her. Take these." She shoved the bags at Julie. "I'm going after her."

"No, you're not." Julie used superior size to block Lila's path. "First, it's not her because how could it be? And if it is her, you're not going after her alone."

"I'm just going to make sure—and see where she's going. I'm going." Smaller, but wilier, Lila feinted, ducked and skimmed by Julie's block.

"Oh, for God's sake." Hampered by a half dozen bags, Julie scrambled behind her—and dug out her phone on the run.

"Luke, I'm chasing Lila, and she thinks she's chasing the killer. The woman. She's too fast for me, I can't— I don't know where I am. Where am I? She's running into a piazza, a big one. I'm dodging tourists. It's . . . it's the one with the fountain—Neptune. Luke, I'm going to lose her in a minute, she's fast. Piazza della Signoria! I see Bandinelli's **Hercules and Cacus**. Hurry."

Julie did her best, racing by the fountain, but Lila had too great a lead.

Twenty-three

Lila slowed her pace, slipped behind a statue. The woman she was pursuing walked at a steady clip—with purpose. It was Jai Maddok, she was sure of it. The way the woman moved, her height, the hair, the body type. Lila came out of cover, put on her sunglasses, blended with a tour group, then broke free, closing a little more distance as her quarry moved through wide, columned arches, beyond what she knew from previous visits led to the street.

Lila knew exactly where she was.

She followed her onto the street, trying to keep what she estimated to be half a block between them. If the woman turned, looked, it would be either fight or flight. She'd decide if and when.

But Jai continued to stride, turned another corner, moved steadily down another street. And into an elegant old building.

Private residences—flats, Lila determined—and dug out her phone to key in the address. As she did, it rang.

"Where the hell are you?" Ash demanded.

"I'm standing on Via della Condotta near the Piazza della Signoria. I just saw Jai Maddok go inside a building. Apartments, I think."

"Start back to the piazza. Now. I'm coming your way."

"Sure. We can—" She winced as he cut her off. "Ouch," she murmured, and after a last glance at the building, started back to the square.

She saw him coming, decided "ouch" wasn't going to cover it. The raw, roiling fury on his face closed the distance and slapped her like a backhand.

"What the hell were you thinking?"

"I was thinking hey, there's the woman who wants what we have and doesn't mind killing for it."

He gripped her arm, began to quick-walk her back the way they'd come. "Ease off, Ashton."

"Don't even think about telling me to ease off. I leave you alone for one afternoon, and you go haring off after someone who tried to kill you? Or you think it's her."

"It **was** her. And the more important thing is, what's she doing here? How did she know we're here, because it's not a damn coincidence."

"No, the important thing is you taking an idiotic risk like this. What if she'd come after you again?"

"She'd have to catch me first, and I've already proven I'm faster. And this time, I'd take her by surprise, not the other way around. **And** she didn't see me. I wanted to see where she went, and I did. I have an address. You'd have done exactly the same thing."

"You can't run off on your own. She's already hurt you once. I have to be able to trust you, Lila."

Like he was speaking to a wayward child, Lila thought, and felt her hackles rise.

"It's not a matter of trust—don't put it like that. I saw her, saw an opportunity. I took it. And I have an address—did you hear me? I know where she is right now."

"Did you see her face?"

"Enough of it. I'm not stupid enough to confront her directly. I saw enough of her face. Add her height, her shape, the hair, the way she moves. She followed us. We should've been looking over our shoulder after all."

"Thank God!" Julie pushed from her perch at the Fountain of Neptune, rushed forward to throw her arms around Lila. Then she pulled back, gave Lila a shake. "Are you crazy?"

"No, and I'm sorry I ditched you, but I needed to keep up with her."

"You're not allowed to scare me like that. You're not allowed, Lila."

"I'm sorry. I'm fine." But she caught Luke's eye. "You're pissed at me, too," she realized, and let out a breath. "Okay, three against one, I have to bow to the majority. I'm sorry. I hate knowing I upset my three favorite people. You're mad and upset, but can't we put that to the side for just a minute, and call the police? I know the current whereabouts of a wanted criminal—internationally wanted."

Saying nothing, Ash pulled out his phone. Lila started to speak, but he just paced away.

"He was out of his mind," Luke told her. "You didn't answer your phone, we didn't know where you were or if you were all right."

"I didn't hear it. It was in my purse, and it's noisy. I took it out to key in the address, and I answered as soon as I heard it ring. I'm sorry."

Ash stepped back. "Give me the address."

The minute she relayed it, he walked away again.

"Does he stay this mad for long?" she asked Luke.

"It depends."

"I gave the information to Detective Fine," Ash said. "They'll get through the channels quicker than a foreign tourist. We should go back to the hotel, make sure it's secure."

Outnumbered again, Lila thought, and made no argument.

Ash stopped at the desk before leading the way to the elevator.

"No one's come by or called looking for us—any of us. The hotel staff won't forward any communications to the suite, or confirm we're registered. If she's here, and looking for us, it'll make it harder for her to find us."

"She's here. I'm not wrong."

He just ignored her. "I gave them her description. Hotel security will keep an eye out for her."

They walked out of the elevator, down to the suite.

"I need to make some calls," he announced, and went directly out onto the terrace.

"Cold shoulders are brutal."

"Try to imagine how he'd feel if anything had happened to you," Luke suggested. "The fact that it didn't doesn't change that ten minutes of fear that it could, or had."

But he relented, kissed the top of her head. "I think we could all use a drink."

Defeated, Lila sat while he opened a bottle of wine.

"You don't get to sulk." Julie pointed at her, then dropped into a chair.

"I'm not sulking. Yes, I am, and if every-one was mad at you, you'd sulk, too."

"I wouldn't have run like a crazed rabbit after a known killer."

"I pursued, in a quick-thinking and care-ful manner. And I said I was sorry. Nobody's saying good job on getting her location, Lila."

"Good job." Luke brought her a glass of wine. "Don't ever do it again."

"Don't be mad," she said to Julie. "I bought the shoes."

"There is that. I couldn't keep up. If you'd given me a chance I'd have gone with you. Then there would've been two of us if any-thing happened."

"You didn't believe I'd really seen her."

"Not at first, then I was terrified you had. But you did buy the shoes. Speaking of which," she added, and rose when Ash came in, "I should put my trophies away. Luke, you need to come see what I bought."

Escape or discretion? Lila wondered. Probably a little of both, she decided as Luke carried Julie's bags, going with her to their part of the suite.

"I apologized to them again," she began. "Do you need another, too?"

"I talked to the airport where we keep the family planes." His tone, cool and brisk, directly opposed the heat snapping in his eyes. "Someone using my father's personal assistant's name contacted them to confirm my flight information. It wasn't my father's assistant."

"So she tracked us."

"It's a good bet." He walked over, poured himself a glass of the wine. "I booked Lanzo and the hotel separately, on a recommendation my sister Valentina gave me more than a year ago. Harder for her to track all that, but if she digs around enough, she could."

"We should tell Lanzo."

"I already did."

"You can be angry about how I went about it, but isn't it better knowing? Any of us could have wandered off to get a gelato and run into her. Now we know."

"You're in this through me. There's no getting around that. Oliver's dead, through his own actions, but the fact is I didn't pay attention. I brought Vinnie into it, and never anticipated. That's not going to happen with you."

He turned back to her, that temper still

snapping. "It's not going to happen with you. You either give me your word you won't go off on your own no matter who or what you think you see, or I'm putting you on the plane back to New York."

"You can't put me anywhere. You can say get out, but that's as far as it goes."

"Do you want to put that to the test?"

She shoved out of the chair, walked around the room. "Why are you cornering me this way?"

"Because you matter too much for me to do anything else. You know you do."

"You'd have done exactly what I did."

"Then this would be a different conversation. I need your word."

"Should I have just said, 'Oh, gee, there's Jai Maddok, international assassin, who'd like us all dead,' then gone back to shopping with Julie?"

"You should have said, 'I think that's Jai Maddok,' taken out your phone, contacted me. Then if you'd followed her, I'd have already been on my way to you. You'd have been on the damn phone with me so I wouldn't think she might have turned on you, sliced you open with the knife this time while I'm buying you a fucking neck-lace."

"Don't swear at me, and you have a point. Okay, you have a point. I'm not used to checking in with anyone."

"Get used to it."

"I'm **trying**. You've got half a million sib-lings, this enormous family. You're used to checking with, in and on. I've been on my own for years, through my own choice. I never thought about scaring you, any of you. I . . . you matter, too. I can't stand thinking I spoiled things, with us—with everyone."

"I'm asking for your word. You can give it to me, or you can't."

Outnumbered, Lila thought again, strug-gling against her own temper. When three people who cared about her saw things the same way, she had to admit her vision needed the adjusting.

"I can give my word I'll try to remember I have someone to check with, that it's im-portant to him I do. I can do that."

"Okay."

She let out a breath she'd been holding, shakier than she realized. She didn't mind a fight, but she couldn't fight when she clearly saw where she'd gone wrong.

"I hate knowing I worried you so much, that I didn't hear the stupid phone when you tried to reach me. If the situation had been reversed, I'd have been scared, too, angry, too. I reacted the way I'm used to reacting and . . . You bought me a necklace?"

"It seemed like the thing to do at the time. Now I'm not so sure."

"You can't stay mad at me. I'm too charming."

"I'm pretty mad."

She shook her head, went to him, wrapped around him. "I'm very charming. And really sorry."

"She kills people, Lila. For money."

And fun, Lila thought. "I can tell you I was careful, but you weren't there and can't be sure. She had a big, stylish purse, no shopping bags and no heels this time. She never looked back. She moved like a woman who had somewhere to be. She's either staying in that building or she was meeting someone there. We could call in an anonymous tip to the local police."

"Fine and Waterstone are handling it."

"So we just wait?"

"That's right. And tomorrow we go see Bastone, as planned." He glanced over her head at the shopping bags. "Are those all yours?"

"It's Julie's fault. We should release her and Luke. I know she wanted to check out some of the artists."

"We'll all go. From this point, we all stick together."

"Okay." Adjust, she reminded herself. "We stick together."

They may need to look over their shoulders again, but Lila thought it did them all good to just go out, walk together, be together. They strolled along the bridge, with the river running below, so Julie could study and assess the paintings in progress, chat with artists.

Lila leaned against Luke. "I never know exactly what she's talking about when she gets into art mode," Lila commented. "And now, Ash either."

"I can't translate, but I like the painting they're looking at."

Lila studied the dreamy image of a

courtyard, flowers spilling from pots, climbing madly up a rough plaster wall. A little drama played out with a small child, bowing his head over a broken pot, and a woman standing just outside a doorway, hands on her hips.

"She has a little smile on her face—just a hint of one," Lila observed. "She loves him, her sad and sorry little boy. She'll make him clean it up, then they'll replant the flowers."

"I'd say you understand a lot more than I do. But I can see Julie likes it, enough to look at some of his other work."

"And we can't neglect your work. We have to visit a few bakeries before we go back to New York. What a hardship that'll be."

"I went to a couple this morning. I sampled a **cornetto al cioccolato** I think I can duplicate, and I got a line on a couple of secret bakeries."

"What's secret about them?"

"You have to hunt for them—off the beaten path. Industrial bakeries," he explained. "They start making pastries in the middle of the night for the cafés. They're not supposed to sell to individuals, but they do—on the side."

"A middle-of-the-night hunt for secret bakeries. I'm absolutely in. Julie said you're going to open a second location. Tell me about that."

She hooked her arm through his, wandered down the line of artists, canvases until, flushed with success, Julie joined them.

"I may have just changed a life. The boss gave me the go-ahead to sign him up—the kid-in-the-courtyard artist. It's him—in the painting. Painted from memory, of his home, his mother and a little accident with a soccer ball one summer afternoon."

"That's so sweet. I love it."

"His work has movement and tells a story. We're taking three of them. The first thing he did—after kissing me—was call his wife."

"Also sweet."

"Fabulous foot jewels and a new artist." With her easy laugh, Julie lifted her arms high. "My day is complete."

Luke grabbed her hand and gave her a

spin that made her laugh again. "Nothing's complete without gelato. You up for that?" he asked Ash.

"Sure."

"If gelato's on the agenda, I need more walking to earn it." Julie glanced back, then at Ash. "You liked his work."

"You could smell the flowers, the heat, feel the mother's amused exasperation and the boy's resignation to whatever was coming. He paints with heart, not just technique."

"I felt the same. He doesn't even have an agent. I hope he follows up on that."

"I gave him some names," Ash said. "Once he comes down, I think he'll make some contacts."

"Do you remember your first sale?" Lila wondered.

"Everyone remembers their first."

"Which was?"

"I called it **Sisters**. Three faeries concealed in the woods, all watching a horseman approach. I'd just finished it, working outside at the compound, when my father brought the woman he was seeing at the time over to meet me. She wanted it," he said as they walked. "He said she could have it."

"Just like that."

"He didn't get what I was doing, or trying to do, at that point. She did. She was an agent. I've always thought he brought her over so she'd tell me I should give it up. Instead, she gave me her card, offered to rep me and bought that piece outright. She's still my agent."

"I love happy endings—and gelato. I'm buying," Lila announced. "A tangible apology for before."

They walked to the park, wandered down the wide path of the Boboli Gardens. Ash steered her toward the pool where Andromeda rose and into the dusky green of plantings.

"Sit down there, cross-legged."

She obliged, thinking he wanted a photo, then waved her hands when he pulled out his sketch pad.

"A camera's faster."

"I have something in mind. Five minutes. Turn your head, just your head, toward the water. Good."

She resigned herself as Julie and Luke wandered off.

"He's going to be a while," Julie predicted.

"I know how it works." Luke swung her hand up, as he had when they'd been teenagers, and pressed his lips to her knuckles. "It's beautiful here. Let's sit down a minute, enjoy it."

"It's a gorgeous day. It's been a great day, even with the break for high drama. They look good together, don't they? I don't know Ash the way you do, but I've never seen him so focused on a woman the way he is with Lila. And I do know her. She's crazy about him, and that's a real first."

"Julie."

"Mmm." She tipped her head onto his shoulder, smiling as she watched Ash sketch.

"I love you."

"I know. I love you. It makes me so happy."

"I want to make you happy, Julie." He shifted, turned, turned her so they faced each other. "I want us to make each other happy, for a lifetime."

He took the ring box out of his pocket, flipped it open. "Marry me, and let's get started."

"Oh, God. Luke."

"Don't say no. Say 'Let's wait' if you have to, but don't say no."

"No? I'm not going to say no. I was going to ask you, tonight. At sunset. I had it planned."

"You were going to ask me to marry you?"

"I don't want to wait." She threw her arms around his neck. "I don't want to wait. I want to marry you, again. And like it was the first time, like this is the first time. You bought me a ring."

"I didn't want to go with a diamond. New start. So." He slipped the square-cut emerald on her finger. "For today, and all the tomorrows we can pack in."

"We found each other again." Her eyes filled as she framed his face in her hands, and the stone flashed in the white sun. "And it's perfect, Luke." She laid her lips on his. "We're perfect."

It was closer to twenty minutes than five, but Ash finally walked to her, crouched down. He turned his sketch pad around.

She scanned the various views of herself sitting among the shrubs with the water at her back, the god rising.

He'd had her lift her hand, palm up.

"What am I?"

"A latter-day goddess, drawing new power from the old. I might do it in charcoal, an absence of color, with a hint of a storm in the western sky." He rose, held out a hand to help her up.

"You got all that from the pool?"

"It's you," he said simply, then glanced around. "There they are." He took Lila's hand, walked to the bench. "Sorry. I got distracted."

"Me, too." Julie held out her hand.

"Oh, what a gorgeous ring. When did you— Oh my God!"

"We're getting married." Julie leaped up, hugged Lila, then Ash.

"What about sunset?"

"He beat me to it."

"Congratulations." Lila threw her arms around Luke in turn. "I'm so happy. We need to have a toast."

"I know a place," Ash said.

"So you said before. Lead us to it. We're going to drink to true love, lost then found."

"Sorry," he said when his phone signaled. "I should get this."

"Is it—"

He only held up a finger, moved off.

Focus on the moment, Lila ordered herself. "We have a wedding to plan."

"And fast. The end of September."

"That is fast, but I'm up to the job. We need the where. I'm going to make a list. And . . . What is it?" she asked when Ash came back.

"She wasn't there. Maddok."

"I'm telling you it was her. I watched her go in."

"You weren't wrong. It was her—she wasn't there. But an art dealer by the name of Frederick Capelli was. She'd slit his throat."

Jai texted her employer from her pretty suite of rooms in Florence. **Package dispatched.**

And simple enough, she thought as she set aside the phone, sat to thoroughly clean her knife. The little side job added to her account, and the efficiency would please her employer. She needed something on that side of the scale after the debacle in New York.

The skinny bitch should never have gotten away from her, she had to admit she'd been careless there. Who would've thought the bony bimbo had enough guts to run—or packed a real punch.

She wouldn't forget it.

She wasn't to blame for Oliver and his whore, or his ethical uncle. She'd been saddled with a fool in Ivan, a hotheaded one.

But she understood, very well, her employer didn't care for excuses.

She studied the knife, watched it glint clean and silver in the light spearing through the windows. The art dealer had been easy and quick—one easy slice.

Slitting his throat had brightened her day, even though it had been a pathetically pedestrian kill. She glanced over at what she thought of as her bonus.

His wallet—with some nice fresh euros—his watch—an antique Cartier—his pretentious pinky ring, but still the diamond was a decent carat weight and had good light.

She'd taken the time to search through the apartment, take valuables easily transported. On a whim she'd taken a Hermès tie.

She'd dispose of everything but the

tie—that would go in her collection. She did enjoy her little souvenirs.

And the police would, at least initially, look at the murder as a robbery gone bad.

But Capelli was dead because she'd made him dead, and because he hadn't located the egg, as promised, and Oliver Archer had.

No one would miss him until the following Monday, which gave her plenty of time to locate Archer and his bitch.

She'd tracked them this far, hadn't she? She'd been right to pay—at her own expense—for rooms where she could keep watch on Archer's New York loft. And she'd been lucky to have seen the limo, seen him leave with a suitcase.

But luck meant nothing without skill. Trailing him to the airport, finessing the flight data—that had taken skill. And had satisfied her employer enough for him to arrange for her flight to Florence on one of his jets.

A little vacation, she assumed, after death. Some friends to share it with. They'd be unaware they remained in her cross-hairs, and all the more careless.

A man like Archer, with his money,

would stay at a grand hotel, or lease a grand private accommodation. They would visit typical tourist attractions—art would play a part.

Now that she'd dispatched the package, she could begin the hunt.

And the hunt would be followed by the kill. She was looking forward to it.

She slid the knife into the custom-made case that carried her sharps, folded it neatly. She intended to use several of them on the bitch who'd bloodied her lip.

They celebrated, raising sparkling drinks at a sidewalk table while Florence streamed by.

Jai Maddok didn't go by, Lila thought as she stayed alert, scanning faces even as she talked wedding venues, flowers.

"I get it." Lila tapped a finger on the table. "You want simple elegance with a big side of fun. The ritual, and all it stands for, followed by a rocking party."

"That sums it up." Julie smiled at Luke. "Does that sum it up for you?"

"You sum it up for me."

"Aww. You're racking up such major

points," Lila said when Julie leaned over for a kiss. "I'm glad I've got my sunglasses on because the glow you two are beaming out is blinding. Maybe we should have sunglasses as guest favors. I'm making a note."

"She's kidding," Julie said.

"Maybe. I'm definitely not kidding about scoping out some of the shops for the single most important element—the wedding dress. If we have time we should take a look right here in Florence."

"You read my mind."

Lila gave Ash a poke. "You're very quiet."

"Men, in my experience, have little to do with wedding plans and execution. They show up, and their job is done."

"Think again. I'm going to have a list for you, Mr. Best Man. You can start another famous spreadsheet. I think—"

She broke off as his phone signaled.

He answered, "Archer . . . Yes . . . Okay . . . No name? . . . No, that's exactly right, thanks. . . . Yes, that's fine. Thanks again."

He ended the call, lifted his glass again. "A woman called the hotel, asking to be connected to my room. As I requested, the desk told her I wasn't registered. And neither were you," he told Lila, "when she asked."

"She's making the rounds."

"And if you hadn't seen her, I wouldn't have told the desk to tell any and all callers or visitors we aren't registered."

"And she'd know where we're staying. So that's major points for me."

"Spotting her and running after her are different things. But I'm mellowing. Let's get another round, and you can entertain yourself trying to find her in the crowd."

"I was being subtle about it."

He only smiled, signaled the waiter.

Twenty-four

She wore the white dress and the new shoes, and had to admit Julie—as always—had hit a bull's-eye. A classy and classic summer look, she decided, and finished it off by braiding her hair and rolling it into a loose knot at her nape.

Nobody would suspect, if it mattered, it was her first non-job-related visit to an Italian villa.

"You look almost perfect," Ash commented when he walked into the bedroom.

"Almost?"

"Almost." He opened the top drawer of the dresser, took out a box. "Try this."

Delighted, she lifted the top of the box, then stared at the case inside. Casual souvenir necklaces didn't come in leather cases.

"Problem?"

"No." Stupid to feel nervous over a gift. "I'm building anticipation." She took out the case, unfolded it.

The teardrop pendant glowed a soft lavender blue in a thin frame of tiny diamonds. It hung from two chains, delicate as spiderwebs, where more little diamonds sparkled like drops of dew.

"It's . . . it's beautiful. It's a moonstone."

"It seemed appropriate for a woman who essentially finished her third book about werewolves. Here."

He unclasped it himself, slid it out of the case, then around her neck. After securing it, he stood behind her, studied the results in the mirror they faced.

"Now you're perfect."

"It's gorgeous." But she looked at him, into his eyes. "Appropriate's the wrong word. Appropriate is just manners. This is thoughtful in a way that means you thought of something that would mean something specifically to me. I love it, not just because it's gorgeous, but because it's thoughtful. Thank you. I don't know what to say."

"You just said it. We were right to take the day yesterday, to celebrate with Luke and Julie. This celebrates what you've done."

She turned, pressed her cheek to his. "It's the most beautiful thing anyone's ever given me, and it means the most."

He eased her back, stroking lightly at her shoulders as he studied her face. "There are things we need to talk about once we're back in New York."

"That we can't talk about in Italy?"

"Today's the reason we came, so we need to deal with that. In fact, we should go. I'll call Lanzo."

"I just need my bag. I'm ready."

When he stepped out, she turned back to the mirror, brushed her fingers over the stone. And glanced at the binoculars she'd put by the window.

Wasn't it strange they'd led to this? And what was she going to do about this feeling of sliding down a long, long tunnel into love?

No foothold, she thought, no handy ledge to crawl onto to catch her breath, slow her speed. As exhilarating as the drop was, she didn't have a clue how to handle the landing.

A day at a time? she asked herself as she picked up her bag. Do what they'd come to do, then do what came next. It was the only way she knew.

But she looked in the mirror one last time, at the necklace. He'd known her, understood what would matter to her. And that, she understood, was as beautiful as the stone itself.

Lila would think of the drive into the Tuscan countryside in colors. Blue skies, yellow sunflowers dancing in fields along the roadside. The dusky green of hills, of olive groves, of the conical cypress, all the citrus hues of lemons, limes, oranges dripping from trees, and the deep purple of grapes thick on the vine.

Gardens blazing with hot reds and purples, or flames of yellow and orange shimmered in the sunlight against the baked white walls of houses or sturdy brick walls. Miles, it seemed, of vineyards stepped their way up terraced hills or blanketed fields in tidy rows.

If she could paint like Ash, she thought, she would paint this—all the color steeped in luminous sun.

Lanzo peppered the drive with snippets of local gossip, or questions about America, where he vowed to travel one day. As Ash had about the flight, she thought the drive a kind of limbo, as if they were traveling through paintings, from landscape to landscape.

Dusky and dusty one moment, then vivid with bold colors the next. Beauty to beauty, all saturated with heroic light.

They turned off the road onto a steep, narrow gravel track rising up through olive groves.

She saw rough steps hacked out of the hillside, as if some ancient giant had cut them out of the long drop. Wildflowers forced their way through the cracks to drink the sun just below a small flat area with an iron bench.

To sit there, she thought, was to see everything.

"This is the estate Bastone," Lanzo told

them. "Giovanni Bastone, you go to see him, has the important villa. His sister and his mother live also on the estate in a very fine house. His brother, he lives in Roma, and sees to their . . . what is it? . . . interests there. Still one sister more who lives in Milan. She sings the opera, and is known as a fine soprano. There was another brother, but he died young, in a car crash."

He made a gentle turn toward iron gates connecting white walls.

"The security, you understand. They expect you, **sì**, and my car is known."

Even as he spoke, the gates opened.

Groves of trees, a manicured terrace of gardens guided the way to the glamour of the villa.

It managed to present both the majestic and the soft with tall arched windows, the curves of porticoes and flowing terraces. Without the softer lines, the charm of vines spilling from those terraces, it would have dominated the landscape. Instead, to Lila's eye, it married it.

The red-tile roof rose, jutted, slanted above pale yellow walls. The drive circled around a central fountain where water flowed whimsically from the cupped hands of a mermaid perched on a tumble of rocks.

"I wonder if they ever need a house-sitter."

Julie rolled her eyes. "You would."

Lanzo popped out to open the door of the car just as a man in buff pants and a white shirt stepped out of the entrance.

His hair was white, dramatically streaked with black to match thick, arched eyebrows. He had a well-fed look, still shy of portly, and tawny eyes that blazed against a sharp-featured, tanned face.

"Welcome! You are welcome. I am Giovanni Bastone." He extended his hand to Ash. "I see some of your father in you."

"Signor Bastone, thank you for your hospitality."

"Of course, of course, this is delightful."

"These are my friends, Lila Emerson, Julie Bryant and Luke Talbot."

"Such a pleasure." He kissed Lila's hand, Julie's, shook Luke's. "Come in, out of the sun. Lanzo, Marietta has something special for you in the kitchen."

"Ah, grazie, Signor Bastone."

"Prego."

"Your home looks like it grew here under the sunlight hundreds of years ago."

Bastone beamed at Lila. "That is an excellent compliment. Two hundred years—the original part, you understand." Already charmed, he drew Lila's arm through his, led the way inside. "My grandfather expanded. An ambitious man, and canny in business."

He guided them into a wide foyer with golden sand tiles, creamy walls and dark beams above. The staircase curved, that softening line again, with archways wide enough for four abreast flowing room to room. Art, framed in old burnished gold, ran from Tuscan landscapes to portraits to still lifes.

"We must talk art," Bastone said. "A passion of mine. But first we'll have a drink, yes? There must always be wine for friends. Your father is well, I hope."

"He is, thank you, and sends you his best."

"Our paths haven't crossed in some time. I have met your mother, as well. More recently."

"I didn't realize."

"**Una bella donna.**" He kissed his fingers.

"Yes, she is."

"And an exceptional woman."

He led them out to a terrace under a pergola mad with bougainvillea. Flowers tumbled and speared out of waist-high terra-cotta pots; a yellow dog napped in the shade. And the Tuscan hills and fields and groves spread out like a gift beyond.

"You must get drunk every time you step outside. The view," Lila said quickly, when he furrowed his brow. "It's heady."

"Ah, yes. Heady as wine. You're clever, a writer, yes?"

"Yes."

"Please to sit." He gestured. A table already held wine, glasses, colorful trays of fruit, cheese, breads, olives.

"You must try our local cheese. It is very special. Ah, here is my wife now. Gina, our friends from America."

A slender woman with sun-streaked hair, deep, dark eyes, came out at a brisk pace. "Please, excuse me for not greeting you." She rattled something to her husband in Italian, made him laugh a little. "I explain to Giovanni, my sister on the telephone. Some small family drama, so I was delayed."

Her husband made introductions, served the wine himself.

"You had a good journey?" Gina asked.

"The drive from Florence was lovely," Julie told her.

"And you enjoy Florence? Such food, the shops, the art."

"All of it."

They settled into small talk, but the lively sort, in Lila's estimation. Watching the Bastones, she saw two people who'd lived a lifetime together, and still enjoyed it, treasured it.

"You met my husband's **amante**," she said to Lila.

Bastone chuckled, cast his eyes to the sky. "Ah, the young American girl. We had such passion, such urgency. Her father did not approve, so it was only more passionate, more urgent. I wrote her odes and sonnets, composed songs to her. Such is the pain and joy of first love. Then she was gone." He flicked his fingers. "Like a dream."

He picked up his wife's hand, kissed it. "Then there was the beautiful Tuscan woman, who spurned me, brushed me aside so I would curse her, beg her, court her until she took pity on me. With her, I lived the odes and sonnets, the song."

"How long have you been married?" Lila wondered.

"Twenty-six years."

"And it's still a song."

"Every day. Some days, the music is not in tune, but it's always a song worth singing."

"That's the best description of a good marriage I've ever heard," Lila decided. "Remember to sing," she told Julie and Luke. "They're engaged—as of yesterday."

Gina clapped her hands, and as women will, leaned over to study Julie's ring.

Bastone lifted his glass. "May your music be sweet. **Salute.**"

Gradually Ash guided the conversation back. "It was interesting meeting Miranda. Both Lila and I found the story about your grandfather and the poker game with Jonas Martin fascinating."

"They stayed friends, though rarely saw each other when my grandfather came home to work the business. Jonas Martin loved to gamble, so my grandfather said, and almost always gambled poorly. They called him, ah . . ."

"Hard Luck Jonnie," Ash supplied.

"Yes, yes."

"And betting a family treasure? Was that his usual way?"

"Not unusual, you understand. He was, ah . . . spoiled, is the word. Young, you see, and a bit wild in his youth, so my grandfather told us. My grandfather said the father of Martin was very angry about this bet, but a wager is a wager. You have interest in writing about this time?"

"I'm very interested," Lila answered. "Miranda didn't know what the bet was—what family heirloom was lost. Can you tell me?"

"I can do more. I can show you. You would enjoy to see?"

Lila's heart rammed into her throat. She managed to nod, swallow it down. "I'd love to."

"Please come." He rose, gestured to all. "Bring your wine. My grandfather loved the travel and art. He would travel on business, you see, what we would call networking now."

He led them back, over travertine tiles, under archways.

"He would search for art, something intriguing, wherever he went. This interest he passed on to my father, and so my father to me."

"You have a wonderful collection," Julie commented. "This." She paused a moment by a portrait of a woman—dreamy and romantic. "Is this an early Umberto Boccioni?"

"It is indeed."

"And this." Julie shifted to a painting of deep, rich colors, mixed shapes, which Lila realized were people. "One of his later works, when he'd embraced the Italian Futurist movement. Both are glorious. I love that you display them together, to show the evolution and the exploration of the artist."

"You're knowledgeable." He slid her hand in his arm as he'd done with Lila's earlier. "You have an art gallery."

"I manage one."

"A good manager has an ownership. I think you are a good manager."

When they passed through the next archway, Julie stopped dead.

It wouldn't be called a sitting room, Lila thought. That was much too ordinary and casual a term. "Salon," maybe. But "gallery" wouldn't have been wrong.

Chairs, sofas in quiet colors providing seating. Tables, cabinets, commodes from the simple to the ornate gleamed with age. A small fireplace filled with a display of bright orange lilies was framed with malachite.

And everywhere was art.

Paintings from faded religious icons to old masters to contemporary filled the walls. Sculptures, smooth marble, polished wood, rough stone, stood on pedestals or tables.

Objets d'art glittered and glowed in displays or on shelves.

"Oh." Julie laid a hand on her breast. "My heart."

Bastone chuckled, drew her in.

"Art is another song that must be sung. You agree, Ashton? Whether the song is of woe or joy, of love or despair, of war or serenity, it must be sung."

"Art demands it. And here, you have an opera."

"Three generations. Lovers of art, and not one artist among us. So we must be patrons and not creators."

"There's art without patrons," Ash commented, "but the artist rarely thrives without their generosity and vision."

"I must view your work when we are next in New York. I was intrigued by what I saw on the Internet, and some made Gina sigh. Which was the one, **cara**, you wished for?"

"**The Woods**. In the painting the trees are women, and at first you think, oh, they are captured, under a spell. But no, you see when you look deep, they are . . ." She fumbled, spoke to Bastone in Italian. "Yes, yes, the casters, the magic themselves. They are the woods. It's powerful, and ah, feminist. Is that correct?"

"There's no wrong, but you saw what I did, and that's a great compliment."

"You may pay me the great compliment of painting my daughters."

"Ah, Gina."

She brushed her husband aside. "Giovanni says I shouldn't ask, but if you don't, how can you get what you want?" She winked at Ash. "We will talk."

"But you're here to see the gaming prize."

He led them to a painted vitrine with serpentine-fronted shelves and a collection of jeweled and enameled boxes.

He lifted one out. "A lovely piece. The

cigarette case is gold-mounted, enameled citrine, fluted, with the cabochon sapphire as the thumb piece. You will see it carries the initial of Fabergé workmaster Michael Perchin. A great loss for the Martins."

"It's beautiful." Lila looked up from it, into Bastone's eyes.

"And the cause of a feud between the families, so I have no American wife." He winked at Gina.

"Signor Bastone." Lila laid a hand on his. "Sometimes you have to trust." She shifted, just a little, looked at Ash. "You have to trust. Signor Bastone, do you know a man named Nicholas Vasin?"

Though his face stayed completely composed, she felt his hand flinch under hers. And saw the color drop out of Gina's cheeks.

"The name is not familiar. So." He placed the case down carefully. "We have so enjoyed your company," he began.

"Signor Bastone—"

"We appreciate your hospitality," Ash cut in. "We should make our way back to Florence. Before we do, you should know my brother Oliver acquired certain documents and an objet d'art while working on Miranda

Swanson's estate sale, her father's property—her grandfather's before him. My brother acquired this object for himself, not for the uncle, the company he worked for."

Ash paused only a moment, noting the hard lines in Bastone's face.

"At one time the Martin family owned, privately, two of the lost Imperial eggs. One was lost in a poker game, the other my brother acquired as Miranda, it appears, had no knowledge or interest in what she had. My brother, the uncle he worked for and the woman he lived with are all dead."

"I'm very sorry."

"The documents, now in my possession, clearly describe the egg wagered and lost in a poker game to Antonio Bastone. The Nécessaire."

"I don't have what you're looking for."

"Your wife knew the name Nicholas Vasin. She fears it. With good reason. I believe he had my brother killed because Oliver had the second egg—the Cherub with Chariot—and foolishly tried to negotiate for more money. He was reckless, but he was my brother."

"You have suffered a tragedy. My condolences."

"You know my father, my mother. You would have done due diligence on all of us before you allowed us into your home, knowing we had an interest in that long-ago wager. Believe me when I tell you I did the same on you and yours before I brought my friends here."

"We're pleased to offer you hospitality, but we know nothing of this."

"The woman Jai Maddok kills for Nicholas Vasin. She put a knife in the side of the woman I care about." He glanced at Lila. "And got punched in the face for it. We're going to fight back, Signor Bastone. The police, in New York and internationally, are aware of her, and of Vasin. They're going to pay for what they've done to my family. Will you help me?"

"I don't have what you seek," he began, only to be interrupted by his wife. She spoke in rapid and fierce Italian, her face lit, her eyes fired.

As they argued, those hot eyes sheened with tears, but her voice remained strong, furiously so, until Bastone took her hands, gripped them, brought them to his lips. He murmured to her now, nodded.

"Family," he said, "is all. My Gina reminds

me of this. You came here for yours. I've done what I've done for mine. I need air. Come."

He strode out, circling back the way they'd come.

The table had been cleared in their absence. He strode past it to the end of the terrace, which overlooked the glory of the Tuscan summer.

"We knew the Martins had two eggs, as my grandfather had seen both. Jonas offered him his choice of them for the wager. My grandfather was young when he won the Nécessaire, not yet schooled in such things. But he learned quickly—his first piece of art, you see, and his first love of it. The feud grew. A wager is a wager, yes, but this was not the boy's to bet or lose. But my grandfather would not return it, even when offered double the wager. It became a thing of pride and principle, and it's not for me to say now who was right or wrong. It became ours. My grandfather kept it in his own room. This he would not share. My father stood with his when his time came. So it came down to me. It had been ours, a private thing, like the art, for three generations."

"The beginning," Lila said. "The rest, his love of art, his careful collecting of it, came from that one piece."

"Yes. After my father's death, after some time passed and my own children began to grow, I thought of this. Do I pass this down to my sons and daughters, then to theirs? Gina and I talked, many times. And we decided this was not a private thing. It belonged once to another family, and was taken from them like their lives. We thought to arrange for it to be donated to a museum—loaned perhaps in the name of our family and the Martins. The story is good, the young men, the poker. We must decide how this is to be done, which museum. And we think, after all this time, are we certain? We must have the egg authenticated—discreetly, privately."

"Frederick Capelli," Lila said, and he turned to her sharply.

"How do you know this?"

"He was killed yesterday, by the same woman who killed the others."

"Good." Gina lifted her chin in defiance. "He betrayed us. His own greed caused his death. He told this Vasin of the Nécessaire. Vasin sent this woman to us, first with an offer to buy the egg. We had decided to do what we felt right and good, so we would not sell. She came back to offer more, and to threaten."

"My wife, my children, my grandchildren," Bastone continued. "Were any of their lives worth this one thing—this thing we would be paid handsomely for? I ordered her away, told her I would go to the authorities. That night she called. She had our grandson. She had gone into my daughter's home, taken her youngest child while they slept. Our Antonio, only four years old. She let me hear him call for his mother, for me, promised she would kill him, causing him great pain if we did not give her the egg. She would take another child, kill, until we did what she wanted. She invited us to contact the authorities. She would simply gut the boy and move on, and come back another time for the next."

Julie stepped over to Gina, offered her a tissue as tears fell down her cheeks. "You gave her the egg. There was no other choice."

"A business venture, she called it. **Puttana.**" Bastone spat it out. "They gave half the offer they had made."

"We told them to keep their money, to choke on it, but she said if we didn't take it, sign the bill of sale, she would come back for another." Gina crossed her hands over her heart. "Our babies."

"It was business, she said. Only business. Antonio had bruises where she'd pinched him, but he was safe. Before morning, he was home again, and safe. And they had the cursed egg."

"You did what you needed to do," Luke said. "You protected your family. If this Capelli went to Vasin, he must have known the story—the poker game."

"Yes, we told him all we knew."

"Which must have led Vasin to Miranda—and she'd sold the second egg to Oliver. When did all this happen?" Lila asked.

"June the eighteenth. I will never forget the night she took him."

"From here to New York." Lila looked at Ash. "The timing works. It would've been clear Miranda didn't know what the egg was, and she would've said she sold it. Maybe Capelli tried to broker the deal with Oliver."

"And Jai stepped in, working on the girlfriend. They set a price, then Oliver pulled back, tried to squeeze out more. Did you go to the police, **signore**?"

"They have what they want. They have no reason to hurt my children."

"I would kill him if I could." Gina fisted her hands, lifted them. "Him and his bitch. She put bruises on our baby, took the little lamb he slept with. He cried for it until we found another."

"She likes her souvenirs," Ash muttered.

"Ashton, I will speak to you as I would my own son." Bastone laid a hand on his arm. "Your brother is gone. Give them what they want. It's an object. Your life, your lady's, your family's—they are more important."

"If I thought that would be the end of it, I'd consider it. She didn't have to hurt your grandchild. She put bruises on him because she enjoyed it. She failed to get the egg from Oliver, and now from me. That will require payment. The only way to end it is to stop her. To bring both her and this Vasin to justice."

"Is it justice you want or revenge?"

"It's both."

Bastone sighed, nodded. "I understand this. I fear you will find Vasin impenetrable."

"Nothing and no one is. You just have to find the weak spot."

Lila spent most of the drive back to Florence scribbling in a notebook. The minute she walked back into the suite, she headed for her temporary office and laptop.

She was still working away when Ash came in with a tall glass of the sparkling juice she enjoyed.

"Thanks. I'm putting everything on paper—sort of like an outline. Characters, what we know about all of them, events, time lines, the connections. It helps me to organize it."

"Your version of a spreadsheet."

"Yeah, I guess." She sipped the juice, watching him as he sat on the side of the bed. "Julie and I aren't going to have time to look at wedding dresses in Florence."

"I'm sorry."

"No, don't be. I'd already figured the same. And God, Ash, we've had a couple of amazing days—wonderful days, productive days. Are we leaving tonight? She wouldn't expect that. We'd be back in New York while she's still looking for us here. It would give us some room."

"We can leave in three hours if that's enough time."

"Packing up is one of my specialties."

"We'll come back, after this is finished."

"I won't say no as I now have a mission to spend a night hunting for these secret bakeries Luke told me about. And he was right. The Bastones did what they had to do to protect their family. If she'd hurt a little boy . . ."

"I'm going to say this even knowing your answer. But I'm going to say it, and I need you to think before you answer. I can get you somewhere safe, somewhere they won't find you. If I could believe making a deal with Vasin would end it, I'd make the deal."

"But you don't believe it, and neither do I."

"No, I don't believe it." And that clawed at him. "She understood the Bastones' weak spot, and she hit it. I think she understands mine."

"Your family. But—"

"No. She's already killed two of my family, or had a part in it. That didn't work out for her. You're my weak spot, Lila."

"You don't have to worry about me. I can—"

He took her hands, squeezed them to stop her words. "She hasn't come after me directly. It's not how she works. With Oliver, she used Sage. With the Bastones, their grandson. She's gone after you once already."

Lila lifted her fist. "That didn't work out for her either."

"You're my weak spot," he repeated. "I asked myself why was it I wanted to paint you the first time I saw you. Needed to, even with everything else going on, I needed it. Why is it every time I think of starting a new work, it's you."

"People in intense situations—"

"It's you. Your face, your body, your voice in my head. The feel of you, the sound of you. Your sense of right and wrong, your wariness of saying too much about yourself, and the fascination of peeling those layers back to reveal them myself. Even the baffling way you figure out how to fix things. All that makes it you. You're my weak spot because I love you."

Now something squeezed at her heart,

a mix of fear and joy she couldn't decipher. "Ash, I . . ."

"It worries you. It's easier if it stays with affection and sex and figuring out something that involves us both. Love leaves a mark that doesn't erase easily. More, given my family history, I promised myself a long time ago if and when I finally got there, I'd make it permanent. And that really worries you."

"We really can't think about any of that now." Panic climbed up her throat, clouded her mind. "Not now when we're in the middle of . . . a thing."

"If I can't tell you I love you in the middle of 'a thing,' when? Maybe a perfect moment will happen by, but the odds are slim, especially since I'm dealing with a woman afraid of commitment."

"I'm not afraid of commitment."

"Yes, you are, but we'll make it 'resistant to' if that's better for you."

"Now you're being annoying."

"Let's add to the annoyance and get it done."

He brought her hands up, kissed them. Lowered them again.

"I'll get what I want because nothing I've ever wanted matters a fraction of what you matter. So I'll get what I want. Meanwhile I can put you somewhere safe, somewhere out of all of it—even this. That'll give you time to think."

"I'm not going to be tucked away like the helpless damsel in the tower."

"Okay."

"And I'm not going to be manipulated so—"

He cut her off, just leaned forward, yanking her toward him and closing his mouth over hers. "I love you," he said again when he let her go, when he rose. "You're going to have to deal with it. I'm going to pack."

He walked out, leaving her staring after him.

What the hell was wrong with him? Who couched being in love like some sort of threat? And why the hell couldn't she stop this slide, even being pissed?

What the hell was wrong with **her**?

Twenty-five

He woke in New York, at some ungodly hour thanks to a body clock completely skewed from the time change from one continent to another and back again.

The dark, the relative quiet, told him he wouldn't like what he saw on his watch.

Right on both counts, Ash decided when he picked it up from the nightstand, squinted at the luminous dial. Four-thirty-five in the morning was ungodly, and he didn't like it.

He might have put the ungodly hour to good use, but it appeared Lila was not only awake, but up—and somewhere else.

It hadn't taken much to convince her

that staying in his loft made more sense than crowding in with Julie and Luke, or into a hotel room, until her next job.

He'd put her on edge, telling her he loved her, intended to dig in for the long haul. But he didn't mind that. He preferred laying things out clearly, whenever possible. And she needed to get used to it.

He understood perfectly well that laying it out, then letting it lie, threw her off. He didn't mind that either. He'd found that exact approach with the myriad members of his family usually bore satisfactory fruit. He had no intention of pushing—too much, too soon. A goal, one worth reaching, took certain . . . strategies and tactics.

And a woman, a woman worth having, took the same.

He'd need to outline his, but the most important thing right here and now was keeping her safe. In order to keep her safe, Jai Maddok and Nicholas Vasin had to be stopped.

The key to that goal was hidden away in the old stables in the family compound.

Since sleep was done, he needed two things. To find Lila, and coffee.

He made his way downstairs, heard music. No, singing, he realized. Lila singing . . . rolling, rolling and doggies? Baffled, he paused a minute, scrubbed his hands over his face.

Rain and wind and . . . "Rawhide," he thought. She was in his kitchen, in the middle of the night, singing "Rawhide" in a pretty admirable voice.

Why would anyone sing about herding cattle at four-thirty in the morning?

He stepped in while she was moving them on, heading them out. She sat on the kitchen counter in a short, thin robe covered with images of shoes that hiked high on her thighs. Her bare legs swung to the beat of her song. Her toes were painted a Caribbean blue, and she'd bundled her hair up in a messy knot.

Even without coffee he thought he'd be absolutely content to find her just like this— every morning for the rest of his life.

"What are you doing?"

She jumped a little, lowered the multitool she was gripping. "I'm going to buy you a collar with a bell on it. I had this weird dream my father, in full uniform, insisted I had to learn how to fly-fish, so we were standing knee-deep in this fast-moving stream, and fish were . . ."

She waved her arms up and down in the air to indicate jumping fish. "But they were cartoon fish, which was another layer of weird. One was smoking a cigar."

He just stared at her.

"What?"

"That's what I said. My dad used to watch old westerns on some old-western station. Now 'Rawhide' is stuck in my head because I had to learn how to fly-fish. Help me."

"I got 'Rawhide.'" As far as the dream went, he couldn't begin to understand. "What are you doing with that tool at four-thirty in the morning?"

"Some of the cabinet doors are a little loose—makes me crazy. I'm just tightening them up. And the pantry door squeaks a little—or did. I couldn't find any WD-40 in your utility closet, so had to get mine. You can't live in the world without WD-40, Ash. And duct tape. Plus super-glue."

"I'll make a note of it."

"Seriously. I wrote the manufacturers once—of WD-40—to thank them for making a travel size. I carry some in my purse because you never know."

He walked over, laid a hand on the counter on either side of her hips. "It's four-thirty in the morning."

"I couldn't sleep—cranky body clock and cigar-smoking cartoon fish. And I can't work because I have mushy travel brain. So, just a little household maintenance. We can consider it payment for the lodging."

"Payment's not required."

"For me it is. I feel better about it. I do it for Julie."

"Fine." He lifted her up, plucked her off, set her down.

"I wasn't quite finished."

"You're blocking the coffee."

"Oh. I had two cups back-to-back. I know better, and now I'm a little hyper."

"Really?" He checked the level of beans, saw she'd refilled it. "I hadn't noticed."

"Even mushy travel brain recognizes sarcasm. Have you considered painting the powder room down here? I was thinking about all those beautiful buildings, the old walls in Florence. There's this faux technique that looks like old plaster. It would be great as a background for art. I think I could do it, and doing the powder room means it's a small space if I mess it up."

He just stared at her while his machine ground the beans and began to brew. "Rawhide" to WD-40 to painting bathrooms.

Why did coffee take so long?

"What? It's the middle of the night, and you're thinking about painting the bathroom? Why?"

"Because I've essentially finished my book, my next job doesn't start for nearly two weeks, and I've had two cups of coffee. If I don't keep busy I get even more hyper."

"Don't you think outwitting a professional assassin and her lunatic boss is enough busywork?"

She'd been trying not to think about that. "Keeping busy helps me cope with the fact that I even know an assassin well enough to have punched her in the face. It's only the second time I've punched someone in the face."

"What was the other time?"

"Oh, Trent Vance. We were thirteen, and I thought I liked him until he pushed me up against a tree and grabbed my breasts. I

didn't really have any, but still, he just—"
She held her cupped hands up. "So I
punched him."

Ash let his not-yet-caffeinated brain
absorb the image. "In both cases, face-
punching was completely warranted."

"You'd say that as you've also punched
faces. And still, I agree. Anyway, if I cope
with the current aspect of punching, just
keep busy, I can think clearly about what
we might do, should do, shouldn't do."

"Painting the bathroom will do all that?"

"It's possible."

"Go for it." He gulped down coffee,
praised the Lord.

"Really?"

"You'll look at it or use it as much—
probably more—than I will since you'll be
living here between jobs."

"I never said I'd—"

"Play with the bathroom," he interrupted.
"And we'll both see how we feel about it."

"And in the meantime?"

"In the meantime, since the cops haven't
given us any more, I'm going to contact
Vasin directly."

"Directly? How?"

"If we're going to have an actual conversation, I want actual food." He opened the refrigerator, stared at the very limited contents. Opened the freezer. "I have frozen waffles."

"Sold. He's a recluse, and we can't even be sure where he is. What if he's in Luxembourg? And you're going to say we'll just hop on your handy private plane and go to Luxembourg. I'm never going to get used to that."

"It's not mine, specifically. It's the family's."

"Or that either. With that kind of wealth, he'd have all kinds of walls around him. Metaphorically."

"Metaphoric walls usually consist of people—lawyers, accountants, bodyguards. People clean his homes, cook his meals. He has doctors. He collects art, so someone arranges for that. He has plenty of staff."

"Including his personal hit woman."

"Including," Ash agreed as he dropped two frozen waffles into the toaster. "I only need one person to start."

Her heart gave a hard little skip. "You're not thinking of using his hired gun."

"She'd be the most direct. But since she's probably still in Italy, I think we start with the lawyers. He has business in New York, property in New York, he'll have lawyers in New York."

He rooted through a cabinet—with a newly tightened door—came up with syrup.

Lila eyed the bottle warily. "How long has that been in there?"

"It's basically tree sap, what difference does it make?"

He plucked the waffles out when they popped, tossed one on each plate, dumped syrup over both. And handed her one.

She frowned at the underdone waffle drowning in a lake of questionable syrup. "You always had cooks, didn't you?"

"Yes. I also know people on Long Island who have cooks, so that might be an avenue." He grabbed a couple of knives and forks, passed hers to her and, standing at the counter, cut into his own waffle. "But the lawyer's more direct. Our lawyers contact his lawyers, inform them I want to have a conversation. Then we see what happens next."

"He wouldn't expect the contact. It could piss him off or intrigue him. Maybe both."

"Both is fine," Ash decided. "Both is better."

Understanding she'd need something to wash the soggy waffles down, she opened the fridge.

"You have V8 Fusion. The mango blend." Her morning favorite, she thought as she took the still unopened bottle out, shook it.

He paid attention, and that—to her—was more romantic than roses and poetry.

"You should drink some, too. It's good for you."

When he only grunted, she got down two juice glasses. "Back to possibly Luxembourg. Vasin's not going to admit he had anything to do with what happened to Oliver. He'd be crazy to."

"He's a recluse who hires killers to get his hands on objets d'art he can't show to anyone. I think we've already established crazy."

"Point taken." She set a glass of juice on the counter beside him.

"But I just need him to make an offer on the egg. We can't bluff we have the second one, because we know he does. So we use what we know. Having one is an enormous prize—a big accomplishment for a collector."

"And having two is beyond." The waffle wasn't as bad as it looked, she decided. But if she stayed any amount of time, she was definitely taking charge of the shopping. "What good does having him make you an offer do? There's nothing illegal about that—you have a bill of sale, so it's a legitimate deal."

"I'll refuse it. Make it clear there's only one thing I want in exchange for it. Maddok."

"His HAG? Why would he give her over—why would she let herself be traded that way?"

"First part first. She's an employee—almost certainly a valuable one, but paid help."

"She's a person," Lila objected. "A horrible person, but a person."

"You're not thinking like a man who'd kill for a gold egg."

"You're right." She let her own sensibilities and morals go for a moment, tried to think, to feel, like Vasin might think or feel. "She's a means to an end, a tool."

"Exactly. Frederick Capelli worked for him, at least must have taken a fee. Vasin didn't have a problem disposing of him."

"All right, I'll agree the egg's worth more to him than a human being. But he can't risk turning her over, Ash. She'd flip on him, she'd make a deal, tell the police chapter and verse. Or he'd certainly have to weigh that in."

Because it was right there, he sampled the juice, found it surprisingly good. "I'm not interested in giving her to the cops, letting her make a deal. Why would I take a chance of her getting immunity, or witness protection?"

"Well, what else?"

He set the glass down with a snap. "I want revenge, I want her to fucking pay. I'm going to **make** her fucking pay. The bitch killed my brother. She spilled my family's blood, now I want to spill hers."

Her heart gave that hard kick again, then shuddered. "You can't possibly mean—you don't. You wouldn't."

"For a second you thought I might." He gestured with his fork, stabbed another bite of syrup-soaked waffle. "You should know me a lot better than he would or could, and you nearly believed it. He'll believe me. He'll believe me," Ash repeated, "because there's a part of me that means it."

"Even if he did believe you, and even if he said, 'Hey, let's shake on it,' she wouldn't go along. She killed two trained agents when they got too close."

"That's his problem. You want the egg, give me the bitch who killed my brother. It's all I want. Otherwise I'll destroy it."

"He'd never believe you could do that."

"The hell I couldn't." He shoved back from the counter so violently she jerked back, braced. "That thing took the lives of two people in my family. Their blood's on it. I've had enough of being hounded—by the police, by him and his hired killers. All over some frivolous toy some dead tsar had made for his pampered wife? Fuck that. This is about family. I'm not Oliver, and I don't give a damn about money. She killed my brother, now I kill her or take a hammer to the egg."

"Okay. Okay." She lifted her coffee cup with a trembling hand, took another jolt. "That was convincing. You scared the crap out of me."

"I mean some of that, too." He leaned back against the counter, rubbed at his eyes. "I don't give a damn about the egg, and I haven't since she cut you."

"Oh, Ash, it was just—"

"Don't tell me it was just a scratch. Fuck that, too, Lila. Given the opportunity, she would kill you in a heartbeat. And you know it. Don't push that button when I'm already wound up. I want—need—the people responsible for Oliver and Vinnie, even the woman I never met, punished. Put away. The egg matters for what it is, what it stands for, what it means to the art world. It belongs in a museum, and I'll see it goes where it belongs. Because Vinnie would've wanted it. If not for that, I would take a hammer to it."

His eyes flashed to hers, sharp, intense, as they did when he painted her. "I'd take a hammer to it, Lila, because you mean a hell of a lot more."

"I don't know what to do or say." How could she when everything inside her trembled and ached? "No one's ever felt about me the way you do. No one's ever made me feel the way you make me feel."

"You could try taking it."

"I've never had anything solid I didn't get for myself. It's just the way it was. I've never let myself hold on to anything too tight because I might have to leave it behind. When it means too much it hurts too much."

"This is solid." He took her hand, closed it into a fist, laid it on his heart. "You got it for yourself."

She felt his heartbeat—strong, steady, and hers if she could take it. "I can't figure out how."

"You got me when you reached out, gave me something to hold on to when you didn't even know me. So let me do the holding on to for a while."

To demonstrate, he drew her against him. "We're not going to leave anything behind. You'll paint the bathroom, I'll call lawyers. You'll do your work, I'll do mine. And I'll hold on until you're ready to."

She closed her eyes, steadied herself. She'd take what he offered, accept what she felt. For right now.

Prepping the powder room, doing more research on the technique, buying the supplies, agreeing on the base color—and she should have known the artist would have firm and definite ideas there—kept her occupied. She made herself take an additional day to let the process circle around in her head, and took the time to sit down, start polishing up the book.

Then she let **that** process circle, shoved up her sleeves and dived in with brush and roller.

Ash spent most of his days in the studio. She expected him to tell her he needed her to sit again, but it didn't come up. She imagined he had enough on his plate, talking to the lawyers, trying to set the stage for the showdown with Vasin.

She didn't bring any of it up again. She could plot a half dozen scenarios in her mind—and did—but none of them worked without the first step. So Ash would set things up, then she'd step in, add her weight, her thoughts—like a final polish.

She had plenty on her plate, too, with her feelings and his as the main course. Could she push the plate aside—no thanks, it looks great but? Did she want to? Could she sample a little then say thanks, that's enough? Or could she settle in, eat hearty?

But if you settled in, wouldn't the plate eventually be empty? Or was it a loaves-and-fishes sort of thing?

"Stop it," she ordered herself. "Just stop it."

"If you stop now, nobody can use the room."

She glanced over her shoulder.

There he was, the center of her thoughts, glorious black hair tousled, gorgeous face scruffed from his aversion to daily shaving, excellent body in jeans—with a faint streak of crimson paint at the left hip—and a black T-shirt.

He looked like an artist, and every time he did, he stirred all her juices.

He hooked his thumbs in his front pockets, studying her as she studied him. "What?"

"I'm wondering why men are sexy when they're scruffy, and women are just un-kempt or sloppy. I guess we'll blame it on Eve—she gets blamed for everything any-way."

"Eve who?"

"As in Adam. Anyway, I'm not stopping the painting—just some head games I have to quit. Don't frown."

She gestured, a little dangerously, with her coated roller. "This is just the base coat. The Venetian plaster technique has many steps. Go away."

"I'm about to do just that. I have to go out, get some supplies. Need anything?"

"No, I—" Reconsidering, she pressed a free hand to her stomach. "I could be hungry later. Are you interested in splitting a calzone? I'll be done with the base by the time you get back."

"I could be interested in a calzone, but I want my own."

"I can't eat a whole one."

"I can."

"Never mind, get me half a cold-cut sub. Turkey and provolone, and whatever. Load it up—but just half."

"I can do that." He leaned in, kissed her. And eyed the wall she was painting again.

"You do understand the concept of base coat?"

"As it happens, I do." He also understood the concept of paint in the hands of an amateur. Just a bathroom, he reminded himself, and one he rarely used anyway.

"Keep the door locked, don't go out, and stay out of my studio."

"If I need to—"

"I won't be long." He kissed her again.

"You're going out alone," she called after him. "Maybe you need to wait until I grab a kitchen knife and come with you."

He only glanced back, smiled. "I won't be long."

"I won't be long," she muttered, and went back to painting to work off steam. "Lock the door, stay inside. Stay out of the studio. I haven't even thought about going up there till he told me not to."

She glanced up at the ceiling. It would serve him right if she went straight up there, poked all around.

Except her work ethics bled over. You stay out of personal spaces, respect the boundaries.

Besides, she wanted to finish the base coat, and rework a scene from the book in her head. It might work better from an alternate point of view.

She entertained herself with roller and brush—and yes, definitely a POV switch. She'd change gears and hit the keyboard right after the lunch break.

She stepped back, studied the walls. A nice warm Tuscan yellow—subtle, with some orange notes to enrich it. Now she had to wait a good twenty-four hours before she started brushing on the plaster color—a deeper, richer cardamom. That would begin the more interesting, less pedestrian part of the process.

Until then, she needed to clean up—her brushes and rollers, and herself.

Still studying her work, she pulled her phone out of her pocket to answer its throbbing ringtone. "Hi, it's Lila."

"Did you enjoy your Italian holiday?"

The voice froze her blood. She hated knowing her first reaction came as white-knuckled fear. "I did, very much." She looked around wildly as she spoke—door, windows—half expecting to see that stunning, exotic face through the glass.

"I'm sure. Private plane, fine hotels. You've landed a big, shiny fish, haven't you?"

Lila bit back the spike of temper, of insult, even managed a little laugh. "And such a great-looking one. Did you enjoy your Italian holiday? I saw you in the Piazza della Signoria. You looked like you had somewhere important to go."

The brief pause told her she'd scored a

point, and it helped ease the thunder of her heartbeat. And calmer, she remembered her record app.

"I still like your shoes," she said quickly, swiping back to the recording app, engaging it. "I bought several pairs while we were there."

"It's a pity I didn't see you."

"Well, you were preoccupied. Places to go, art dealers to murder." Her throat, brutally dry, begged for water—but she couldn't quite make her legs move. "Who do you think tipped the cops, Jai?"

Second point, Lila thought. Terrified, yes, but not helpless—not stupid.

"The police don't worry me, **biao zi**. And they won't help you. You won't see me next time. You won't see the knife, not until I make you feel it."

She closed her eyes, leaned weakly against the doorjamb, but forced bravado into her voice. "You and your knife didn't do the trick last time. How's the lip? All healed up? Or do you need to cover it up with the lipstick you stole from Julie?"

"You'll beg me to kill you. The Fabergé is a job, but you, **bi**? You'll be a pleasure."

"Does your employer know you're

contacting me, talking trash? I bet he wouldn't like it."

"Every time you close your eyes, you'll know I might be there when you open them again. Enjoy your life while you can for life is short, but death, **biao zi**, it's very, very long. I look forward to showing you how long. **Ciao.**"

Lila pressed the phone to her racing heart. She managed to stumble into the powder room, splash cold water on her clammy face, then simply slid to the floor when her legs gave way.

She needed to call the police—for whatever good that could do—as soon as she stopped shaking.

But she'd held her own, hadn't she? How many people could say they'd held their own with a vengeful professional assassin? **And** had the wits to get that holding her own on record?

It was probably a pretty short list.

And this was personal, she thought. This went back to a punch in the face.

"Okay." She drew in a breath, let it out, lowered her head to her drawn-up knees. "Better. Just call the cops, and—" No, she realized. Ash.

She hadn't called him in Florence, and she'd been wrong. She'd held her own, but it didn't mean she had to stand—or sit—on her own.

She lowered the phone, studied her hand to make sure it remained steady.

And dropped it into her lap when the front door buzzer sounded.

She snatched it up again, surged to her feet, stared at the door. Secured, of course—even if she hadn't turned the internal lock after Ash went out. But windows were glass, and vulnerable.

Her first thought was defense—a weapon. With her eyes locked on the door, she began to ease her way toward the kitchen. A kitchen held countless weapons.

The buzzer sounded again, and she jerked again.

The buzzer, she thought. **You won't see me or the knife.** A woman bent on murder didn't ring the damn buzzer.

Stupid, she told herself, just stupid to jump just because someone was at the door.

"Just see who it is," she whispered. "Just walk over and see who it is instead of standing here shaking."

She made herself walk over, open the cabinet where—with Ash's go-ahead—she'd moved the monitor. And recognizing the visitor, thought she'd almost rather have the murderous intentions.

"Damn, hell, crap." After shoving the phone back in her pocket, she pressed her hands to her face, fought back tears of relief.

No one was here to try to kill her. The visitor might want her winked out of existence, but not dead in a pool of her own blood.

Still.

She tugged the ball cap tighter over her bundled-up hair. Why would Ash's father come now? Why couldn't he wait until Ash was here—and she wasn't?

Why did he have to show up when she was a basket case of nerves and panic?

And did he just have to drop by when she had the single shirt, the single pair of shorts she'd kept out of the ragbag for scut work?

"Crap, crap, crap." She wanted to ignore the buzzer, the visitor, but couldn't allow herself to be quite that rude—or, she ad-

mitted, quite that alone when even someone who detested her was company.

She squared her shoulders, strode to
the door. Deal with it, she ordered herself,
and unlocked it.

"Mr. Archer." She didn't bother to fake a
smile. Manners were one thing, hypocrisy
another. "I'm sorry it took me so long. I
was painting."

"You're a painter now?"

"Walls, not canvases. I'm sorry, Ash isn't
here. He had some errands. Do you want
to come in, wait for him?"

Rather than answer, he simply stepped
inside. "I take it you've moved in."

"No. I'm staying here until I start my next
job. Can I get you something to drink?"

"Staying here," he repeated, "after a
whirlwind trip to Italy."

"Yes, we went to Italy. I'm happy to get
you a drink, or I'm sure you know your way
around if you'd rather just help yourself. I
really need to clean my tools."

"I want to know what's going on."

She saw some of Ash in him, and oddly
some of her own father in him.

Authority, she realized. A man who had

it, a man who used it, and expected others to fall in line.

She wouldn't.

"I'm painting the powder room using a Venetian plaster technique."

It wasn't the first time someone had looked down his nose at her, Lila thought, but Spence Archer had one of the best techniques.

"Don't be stupid."

"I'm not. I'm trying to remember that whatever you think of me, you're Ash's father."

"As his father, I want to know what's going on."

"Then you'll have to be more specific."

"I want to know why you paid a visit to Giovanni Bastone. And since you've managed to insert yourself into my son's life, in his home, so quickly, I want to know how far you intend to take this."

Her head began to throb, a steady beat-beat-bang in her temples, at the base of her skull. "You should ask Ashton the first question. As to the second, I don't owe you an answer. You may want to ask your son how far he intends to take it as it's his life and his home. As you are his father and obviously don't want me here, I'll leave until you and Ash talk."

She grabbed the spare keys from the bowl in the same cabinet as the monitor, marched straight to the door, yanked it open.

And pulled up short when Ash started up the short flight of steps outside.

Twenty-six

"What part of 'Don't go out' confused you?" he wondered. Then his eyes narrowed on her face. "What's wrong?"

"Nothing. I want some air. Your father's here."

Before she could walk by him, Ash simply took her arm, turned her around.

"I don't want to be here—and you're about to become the third person I've punched in the face."

"I'm sorry, and do what you have to do. But he's not chasing you off. That needs to be made clear to both of you."

"I'm going for a damn walk."

"We'll take one later." He pulled her back inside. "Dad." With a nod, he carried the bags he was holding to a table, set them down.

"I want to talk to you, Ashton. Alone."

"We're not alone. It occurs to me, though you met, I never introduced you. Lila, this is my father, Spence Archer. Dad, this is Lila Emerson, the woman I love. You're both going to have to get used to it. Anybody want a beer?"

"You barely know her," Spence began.

"No, you barely know her because you choose to believe she's after my money—which would come under the heading of 'my business.'"

His tone, so brutally cool, had Lila fighting off a shudder. She'd rather face the fire any day, any time.

"You choose to believe that she's after your money," Ash continued, "which is your business, but entirely without merit. And you choose to believe she's after the cachet of the Archer name, which is ludicrous. In reality she doesn't care about any of those things. In fact, they seem to be points against me, which is pretty damn annoying. But I'm working on that since I intend to spend my life with her."

"I never said I—"

He just shot Lila a look so cold it burned. "Be quiet."

When sheer shock had her closing her mouth, he turned back to his father.

"She's done nothing to earn your attitude toward her or your treatment of her. On the contrary, you should be grateful she offered one of your sons compassion and generosity while he coped with the death of another of your sons."

"I came here to speak with you, Ashton, not be lectured."

"My house," Ash said simply. "My rules. As to my plans regarding Lila? They're long-term. Unlike you, this is something I plan to do only once. I've been more careful than you might think because it's a one-time deal for me. Lila hasn't done anything to deserve your behavior toward her, which is nothing but a reflection of some of your own experiences. You need to stop using them to measure my life and choices. I love you, but if you can't show Lila reasonable courtesy—the basic rules of behavior you expect from me, from everyone else—you won't be welcome here."

"Don't. Don't do that." The tears that stung her eyes appalled her nearly as much as Ashton's words. "Don't speak like that to your father."

"Do you think I won't stand up for you?" Some of the hot, ripe temper bubbling under the chill lashed out now. "Or is that something else no one else is allowed to do?"

"No, it's not—Ash, he's your father. Please don't say that to him. It's not right. We can just stay out of each other's way, can't we?" She appealed to Spence. "Can't we just agree to avoid each other? I can't be responsible for causing a rift between you. I won't be."

"You're not responsible, and everyone in this room knows it. Don't we?" Ash said to his father.

"As long as I'm head of the family, I have an obligation to look after the interests of the family."

"If you mean financial interests, do whatever you think best there. You won't get an argument. But this is my personal life, and you've no right to interfere. I never interfered in yours."

"Do you want to make the same mistakes I did?"

"I don't. Why do you think I waited? Still, whatever mistakes I make are mine. Lila's not one of them. You can back off, have a beer, or not."

After a lifetime in business, Spence knew how to change tack. "I want to know why you went to Italy to see Giovanni Bastone."

"It has to do with what happened to Oliver, and it's complicated. I'm handling it. You don't want the details, Dad, any more than you wanted the details of Oliver snorting his trust fund up his nose or gulping it down in pills and alcohol."

Some bitterness there, Ash realized, and not completely fair. He'd often wished to Christ he'd been spared Oliver's details.

"Oliver aside, there are plenty of stains on the family linen. There are too many of us for it to be otherwise. I handle what I can when I can. I wish I'd done a better job of it with Oliver when I had the chance."

Spence swallowed what Lila thought

might be a combination of pride and grief. The dregs of it roughened his voice. "What happened to Oliver isn't your fault. It's his own, and maybe partially mine."

"It doesn't much matter at this point."

"Let me help you with whatever you're trying to do. Let me do that much. Personal disagreement aside, you're my son. For God's sake, Ashton, I don't want to lose another son."

"You did help. I used the plane to get to Bastone, and used your name. You told me ahead of time what you knew and thought of him. It got me in."

"If he's involved in Oliver's murder—"

"No. I promise you he's not."

"Why won't you tell him?" Lila demanded. "Oliver was his. It's wrong not to tell him what you know, and at least partially because you're mad at him about me. You're wrong, Ashton. Both of you are wrong and stupid and too stubborn to get out of your own way. I'm going upstairs."

Ash thought about telling her to stay, then let her go. She'd been shoved into the middle long enough.

"She says what she thinks," Spence commented.

"Most of the time." And he realized he'd be sharing that calzone after all. "Let's have that beer, and unless you've eaten, you can split my calzone. We'll talk."

Nearly an hour later, Ash went upstairs. He knew women—he should, with lovers and sisters, stepmothers and the other females who'd been part of his life. So he knew when a little fussing was in order.

He put her sandwich on a plate—linen-napkin time. Added a glass of wine, and laid a flower on the tray from the arrangement she'd picked up for the living room.

He found her working on her laptop at the desk in one of the guest rooms. "Take a break."

She didn't stop or glance back. "I'm on a roll here."

"It's after two. You haven't eaten since early this morning. Take a break, Lila." He leaned down, kissed the top of her head. "You were right. I was wrong."

"About what, exactly?"

"About talking to my father about some of this. I didn't tell him everything, every detail, but I told him enough."

"Good. That's good."

"It wasn't easy for him to hear it, but you were right. He needed to. He deserved to know why he lost a son."

"I'm sorry." With her hands gripped together in her lap, she stared at her laptop screen, seeing nothing.

Ash set the tray on the bed, went back to her. "Please. Take a break."

"When I'm upset, I either stuff sweets down my throat or I can't eat at all. I'm upset."

"I know it."

He picked her up out of the chair, stepped over, set her down on the bed. With the tray between them, he sat cross-legged facing her.

"You have a habit of just putting people where you want them."

"I know that, too."

"It's an annoying habit."

"Yeah, but it saves time. He knows he was wrong, Lila. He apologized to me— and not just for form. I know when it's for form's sake. He's not ready to apologize to you, except for form. You won't want that."

"No. I don't want that."

"But he'll apologize and mean it if you

give him a little more time. You stood up for him. You have no idea how completely unexpected that was for him. He's feeling a little ashamed, and that's a tough swallow for Spence Archer."

"I can't be a wedge between you. I can't live with that."

"I think we took care of that issue today." Reaching over, he rubbed her knee. "Can you give him some time to apologize, make some amends?"

"Yes, of course. I'm not the issue. I don't want to be the issue."

"He's blaming himself for Oliver, a large part of it. He let go, Lila. He didn't want to hear any more, see any more. It got easier to just wire some money and not think about where it was going. He knows that, feels that."

Ash raked both hands through his hair. "I understand that because I'd hit pretty much the same line with Oliver."

"Your father was right when he said it wasn't your fault. It's not his either, Ash. Oliver made his choices, as hard as that is, he made his own choices."

"I know it, but—"

"He was your brother."

"Yeah, and my father's son. I think he jumped all over you because, by God, he wasn't going to have another son go down the wrong path. And I'm his first," Ash added. "The one who was supposed to follow in his footsteps and didn't even come close. It's no excuse, but I think it's part of the reason."

"He's not disappointed in you. You're wrong again if you think that. He's afraid for you, and he's still grieving for Oliver. I don't know what it's like to lose someone so close, but I know what it's like to be afraid you will. Every time my father was deployed . . . Anyway, we'll say emotions ran high. And I don't need everyone to like me."

"He already does." Ash rubbed her knee again. "He just doesn't want to."

Possibly true, but she didn't want that, or herself, to stay at the center.

"You told him about the egg, about Vasin?"

"Enough, yeah. Now I can leave it to him to make arrangements for the Fabergé to go to the Met when it's time."

Giving him part of it, Lila thought, instead of shutting him out.

"But you didn't tell him you intend to face off with Nicholas Vasin?"

"I told him enough," Ash repeated. "Are we okay here, you and me?"

She poked at the sub. "You told me to be quiet."

"Did I? It won't be the last time. You can tell me the same when you need to."

"You manhandled me."

"I don't think so." Eyes narrowed, he angled his head. "Eat that sub, then I'll show you what it's like to be manhandled."

She sniffed, deliberately, wished she didn't want to smile. Instead she just looked into his eyes. So much there she wanted, she realized, and the more she wanted, the more it scared her.

"I don't know if I can give you what you want, if I can be what you want."

"You already are what I want. As long as you're what and who you are, I'm good."

"You were talking about lifetimes, long term and—"

"I love you." He touched a hand to her cheek. "Why would I settle for less? You love me—it's all over you, Lila. You love me, so why would you settle for less?"

"I don't know whether to eat what's on the plate in a few big bites, or just nibble away at it. And what happens when it's gone? How can you know it's going to just **be** there?"

He studied her a moment. Obviously she didn't mean this plate, but some imaginary plate—holding love, he assumed, promises, commitments.

"I think the more you feed on it, the more there is, especially when you share it. Speaking of, I had to split the damn calzone after all. Are you going to eat all that sub?"

She stared back at him. After a moment, she took her multi-tool out of her pocket, selected the knife. With care she began to cut the sub in half.

"I knew you'd figure it out."

"I'm going to try. If I mess it all up, you'll have no one but yourself to blame."

She picked up half the sub, held it out to him.

"My lawyer called while I was out."

"What did he or she say?"

"He, in this case, said he'd found and contacted Vasin's lawyers in New York, relayed that I'd like to meet with Vasin about mutual business."

"But with a lot of lawyerly words."

"No question. Vasin's lawyer, in lawyerly words, agreed to contact his client."

A step, she thought, to whatever happened next. "Now we wait for an answer."

"I don't think it'll take long."

"No, he wants the egg. But you used the wrong pronoun. Not **I** but **we** want to meet with Vasin."

"There's no need for you—"

"You really don't want to finish that sentence."

Reboot, he decided. "You need to consider who he is, his background. He'd be more inclined to deal with a man."

"He has a woman doing his wet work."

"Wet work." Ash picked up her wine, sipped it. He shifted strategy to simple truth. "He could hurt you, Lila, a deliberate way to pressure me to turn over what he wants. That's what it looks like the idea was with Oliver and his girlfriend."

"I'd think a man like that wouldn't repeat the same mistake. Of course, he could hurt you to pressure me."

She bit into the sandwich, gave a decisive nod. "I'll go, you stay."

"Are you being obstinate or just trying to piss me off?"

"Neither one. You want me to sit back and wait while you go into the lion's den alone. Are you trying to piss me off?" She took the wine from him, drank. "You can't talk about lifetimes and commitments, then put me aside. We both go. Ash, if I commit to you, to anyone, I can't do it without knowing it's a full partnership."

She hesitated a moment, then brought it back to herself. "My mother waited. No one could ever say she was anything but a good, strong military wife. But I know how hard it was for her to wait. However proud of him she was, however steadfast, it was so hard for her to wait. I'm not my mother."

"We go together. With insurance."

"What insurance?"

"If you're . . . if either one of us," he corrected, "is harmed in any way, we've left instructions for the egg to be destroyed."

"Not bad—a classic for a reason, but . . . I'm wondering about the break-the-egg idea. Not that you wouldn't be convincing. I saw the rehearsal. But spoiled children would rather see a toy broken than share it, wouldn't they? He might have that impulse."

"Go ahead and break it," Ash considered. "If I can't have it, nobody can. I hadn't thought of that."

"What about if either of us is harmed, we've left instructions for an immediate announcement to the media about the discovery. And the egg is to be immediately turned over to an undisclosed museum and its security. Details to follow."

"Threatening to destroy it is so much more satisfying, but you've got a point. More than insurance," he decided, and took the wine back, sharing it as they shared the sub. "Truth. We'll set it up just that way."

"We will?"

He set the wine back on the tray, took her face in his hands. "You don't want to hear it, but I won't let anything happen to you. I'll do whatever it takes to keep you safe, whether you want me to or not. If anything happens, if I think anything's going to happen to you, I push that button."

"I want the same option, with you."

"Okay."

"Whose button is it?"

He rose, wandered the room. It should have been Vinnie's, he thought. It should have been. "Alexi's, from my family compound. Believe me, it can be arranged there—my father can make it happen. And it's as secure as it gets."

"It's a good idea. It's a smart idea. But how do we push the button?"

"We'll work it out." He stopped, looked out the window. "We have to end this, Lila."

"I know."

"I want a life with you." When she said nothing, he glanced back. "I'm going to get it, but we can't really start on it until this is done. Whatever happens with Vasin, we end it."

"What do you mean, exactly?"

"We don't go in bluffing about Maddok. We push the button if he refuses to trade her, get the hell out. And the rest is up to the cops."

"We both know if she's free she'll come after us. That's been part of the point."

"She has to find us. You can write anywhere. I can paint anywhere. We'll go anywhere. You like to travel. We'll go from anywhere to anywhere. I saw the gypsy in you the first time I met you. We'll be gypsies."

"You don't want that."

"I want you. We'll rent a cottage in Ireland, a villa in Provence, a château in Switzerland. Lots of new spaces for you, lots of new canvases to paint for me."

And her, he thought, in the kitchen every morning. A short thin robe and a multi-tool.

"They'll put her away or put her down eventually," he said. "But until then, if this doesn't work out our way, we have another option. See the world with me, Lila."

"I . . ." The little bubble of panic fizzed in her throat. "I have a business."

"We can start that way. Keep it that way if you want. But away from New York, as soon as we can manage it. Think about it," he suggested. "It's a big world. I'm going to contact Alexi, start setting things up, then get another hour or two in my studio. Why don't we see if Luke and Julie want to meet us for dinner later? Get out of here for a while?"

"Getting out's good. You're not worried about it?"

"Interested in it, on a couple levels. No reason to send his bitch after us if he's considering meeting with me, seeing what I'm offering. Eight work for you?"

"Eight's fine. I think it would— Oh God." She pressed her fingers to her eyes. "His bitch."

"What now?"

"Don't get mad—you're a little scary when you're mad. Then I'll get mad, and I can be a little scary. And it was already scary."

"What the hell are you talking about?"

"She called. Jai Maddok called me—my cell phone. She called me."

The amused exasperation flipped directly to cold fury. "When?"

"After you left. But a while after, so I don't think she was just waiting for me to be alone. I don't think that mattered."

"Why the hell didn't you tell me? God-damn it, Lila."

"I would have, was going to. I was . . . I had the phone in my hand to call you, then the buzzer—your father. And he wasn't re-ally happy to see me, then you came and— Damn it back, Ashton, it's been nothing but drama. It went out of my head with all the rest. Plus I **am** telling you. It's not like I'm keeping it a secret. I was—"

He sat again, put his hands firmly on her shoulders. "Stop. Breathe."

She drew air in, stared into his eyes as he rubbed her shoulders. And felt the little bubbles of hysteria in her throat pop and dissolve. "I'd just finished the base coat. My phone rang, and it was her. She meant to scare me, and she did. I'm glad we weren't Skyping so she couldn't see my face. She asked if I enjoyed Italy. I tried to pull a little Kaylee—you know, give as good as you get. I asked if she had, and I brought up the art dealer. Maybe I shouldn't have, but it gave her a bad moment, I could tell."

"Let me have your phone."

"My— Oh, stupid. I didn't even check the number. It all happened so fast. But I recorded most of it. I remembered my recording app."

"Of course you did," he replied. "And of course you have a recording app."

"Because you never know, right? The buzzer sounded right after she hung up, and then everything just rolled."

She handed him the phone.

"Private caller," he read when he scrolled her incomings.

"I don't think she wanted me to call back and chat. It'll be a drop phone. Everybody who reads popular fiction or watches TV knows that. Untraceable drop phone. She just wanted to spook me. She did."

"Tell me what she said to you."

"It's there. You can listen."

"Tell me first, then I'll listen."

"A lot about killing me, and it came through loud and clear we were right. I'm pretty sure she called me a couple of very nasty names in Chinese, which I'll need to look up. It's not the job to her, not now. I screwed things up for her, and I punched her—and I reminded her of that because she scared me. I was going to call you, I promise, and the police, but then your father was here, and I was in my scut clothes, so that couldn't have been worse."

"Your scut clothes? What does that have to do with it?"

"Every woman in the world would understand how that was worse."

"Okay."

Some tears had trickled through. He brushed them away with his thumbs, laid his lips lightly on hers.

He looked down at her phone. "Where's the app?"

"Here, let me do it." She brought it up, tapped play.

Refused to shudder when she heard Jai's voice, when she heard the words again. She saw the fire rekindle in his eyes, saw it burn there when the recording ended and those eyes looked into hers.

"I gave her a couple of bad moments right back. I didn't sound terrified or panicked. But—"

He wrapped around her when she threw her arms around him.

"I was. I admit it, I was. It got real. Really real—her voice on the phone, knowing she wants to kill me. She wanted to taunt me, but there was this rage under it. So much rage I could feel it as much as hear it."

"We'll go." He drew her back. "Anywhere you want. Tonight. Nothing else matters."

"No, no, no. We can't live like that—I can't. We can't just walk away from it. It didn't work for Jason Bourne either. You know, you know." Now she had to struggle not to babble as bafflement joined the fire in his eyes. "The books, the movies. Matt Damon."

"I know." Her mind, he thought, stroking her hair, was a wonderful thing. "Okay."

"This is all the more reason to finish it. She can't get away with turning me into a tremble puddle on the floor. She can't be allowed to dictate how either of us lives. It got real, Ash, and I'm not going to let her turn me into someone I don't like or recognize. Don't ask me to do that."

He pressed his lips to her forehead. "I'll call Fine." He looked at Lila's phone again. "I'll take care of it."

"I need my phone. Half my life's on that phone."

"I'll get it back to you." He stroked a hand down her hair one more time, rose. "You were heading out of the house when I walked up. Alone."

"I was mad, insulted. Stupid. God, I didn't even take my purse."

"As long as you recognize the stupid, and don't do it again. I'll go call Fine, fill her in. Are you all right up here?"

"Yeah. I'm okay now. I need to go back to the book—I can dump myself in it, let this go."

"Do that, then. I'm downstairs or in the studio. I'm here," he said. "I'm going to be right here."

"Ash." She slid off the bed, onto her feet. Because her stomach quivered, she started fast. "My father's a really good man."

"I'm sure he is." Something here, he thought, and brushed her hair back from her face.

"He's a military man. It wasn't that he put his duty before his family. But that duty came first. I'd never blame him for that because it makes him what he is. And he's a good man. But he wasn't there, a lot. He couldn't be."

"That was hard for you."

"It was, sometimes, but I understood his service to country. My mom's great. She made her life without him when he couldn't be there, set it aside without a blink when he could be. She can really cook—I didn't get much of her skill there. She could, and can, juggle a dozen things at once, which I'm pretty good at, too. She couldn't change a lightbulb. Okay, that's an exaggeration, but not by much."

"So you learned to fix things."

"Someone had to—and I liked it. Figuring out how to fix things. And it made him proud. 'Give it to Lila,' he'd say. 'She'll figure out how to fix it, or it can't be fixed.' That meant so much. At the same time, when he was home, he ruled. He was used to giving orders."

"And you didn't like taking them."

"You cope with the changes, being the new kid—again—finding your rhythm in a new place—again. You get self-sufficient. He liked that I could handle myself—and he taught me how to. How to fire a weapon, clean it, respect it, basic self-defense, first aid, all of that. But yeah, we did rub up against each other when it came to doing it because I said to do it. You're a little like him there, but you're more subtle about it. The Lieutenant Colonel is very direct."

"People who don't rub up against each other from time to time probably get very bored."

She laughed. "They probably do. But the point is, I love him. You love your father, too. I could see it, even though you were really angry, even disappointed in him. You let him think he's the head of the family when he's not—not really. You are. But you let him have that because you love him. I accept that my father couldn't be there for prom night or high school graduation. I love him, even though the times—a lot of times I really needed it—he couldn't say, 'I'm here.'"

And there, he understood, was the center of it.

"But I will be."

"I don't know what to do when someone sticks, when I start wanting them to."

"You'll get used to it." He trailed a finger down her cheek. "I'd like to meet them, your parents."

Not quite panic, she thought, but a clutch in the belly. "Oh. Well. Alaska."

"I have a private plane. Whenever you're ready. Dump it into the work," he said. "And I am here, Lila. You can count on it, and eventually you will."

Alone, she told herself to go back to work, just go back into the book and not think about anything else.

What kind of man offered to leave everything, travel the world with you to keep you safe and give you new spaces? He saw her as a gypsy—and she often thought of herself that way. On the move.

Why not just do it, then? Pack up and go, as she had countless times, only now with someone she wanted to be with? She could take it a day, a place, an adventure at a time.

She should jump at it, she realized, gradually shift her house-sitting business international. Or give it a rest, just write and travel.

Why wasn't she jumping at it?

And more, could she really get used to—let herself get used to—counting on someone when she knew herself well enough to understand she worked it the other way? She was the one people counted on.

With their homes, their pets, their plants, their things. She was the one who tended, who could be relied on to be there—until she wasn't needed.

Too much on her mind, she told herself. They needed to deal with what was—the egg, Vasin, Maddok. No time to be building pretty fantasies.

Reality came first.

She went back to her desk, read over the last page she'd worked on.

But kept thinking of traveling wherever she wanted. And couldn't quite see it.

Twenty-seven

Ash asked Fine and Waterstone to come to his loft—a deliberate move. If Vasin still had eyes on the loft, the claim of police harassment would hold more weight.

He gave them credit for listening to what he'd done and planned to do—and to Lila for recording the phone call from Jai Maddok.

"I made a copy." Lila offered Waterstone a memory card she'd put in a small baggie, labeled. "I don't know if you can use it, but I thought you might need to have it. For your files. It's legal to record a phone conversation, right, since I was one of the parties? I looked it up."

He took it, slipped it into the pocket of his sport coat. "I'd say you're clear on it."

Fine leaned forward, gave Ash what he'd come to think of as her hard-line cop stare.

"Nicholas Vasin is suspected of international crimes, including murder-for-hire."

"I'm aware, since my brother was one of his victims."

"His hired gun made personal contact with you. Twice," she said to Lila. "Personal's what it is now."

"I know. That's really clear. Um. **Biao zi** is Mandarin for 'bitch,' which is pretty tame. **Bi** is . . ."—she winced because she hated saying it out loud—"cunt. That's really ugly, and I consider that a lot more personal."

"And yet the two of you come up with some scheme to take Vasin on yourselves."

"To have a meeting," Ash corrected. "One we've got a good chance of getting. You don't."

"And what do you think you'll accomplish—if he doesn't have the two of you disposed of on the spot? You think he'll just turn over Maddok? He'd just hand over one of his major assets?"

"I know about men with wealth and power," Ash said easily. "My father's one of them. A man in Vasin's position can always buy another asset, that's the point, for some, of wealth and power. He wants the egg, something I have—we have," he corrected. "Maddok's an employee, and likely a valued one. But the egg's worth more to him. It's a very good deal, and he's a businessman. He'd recognize that."

"You really think he'd agree to a trade?"

"It's business. And my terms don't cost him a nickel. No employee's indispensable, and up against the Fabergé? Yeah, she'll come up well short."

"You're not cops." Fine began ticking off negatives with her fingers. "You have no training. You have no experience. You can't even be wired as he'd check."

Waterstone scratched his cheek. "That could be an advantage."

Fine stared at him. "What the fuck, Harry?"

"I'm not saying it's a crowd-pleaser, but we can't get near him. These two maybe can. They're not cops, they won't be wired. Couple of chickens to pluck, from his way of thinking, if you ask me."

"Because they are."

"But the chickens have the golden egg. The question is, how bad does he want it?"

"Four people are dead—including the art dealer in Florence," Lila pointed out. "That indicates really bad on my scale. And the way she came after me? She had something to prove. Her job performance hasn't been stellar on this assignment. Trading her for the egg seems like a deal to me."

"Maybe a deal," Fine agreed, "until you factor in what Maddok knows about him, what she could tell us."

"But we're not giving her to you," Lila reminded her. "At least that's what we'll tell him."

"Why would he believe that someone who's never killed before intends to, and you'd go along with it?"

"He will. First, because that's his solution to getting what he wants, and second, because Ash is pretty scary when he cuts it loose. Me?" She shrugged. "I just looked out the window. I just want it done. I've caught a really shiny fish here, in Ashton Archer. I want to start reaping those benefits without being worried someone wants to kill me."

Ash cocked a brow. "Shiny fish?"

"That's what Jai called you, and I can play on that. Rich, important name, renowned artist. A big haul for a military brat who lives in other people's houses, and has a moderately successful young adult novel under her belt. Think what hooking up with Ashton Archer could do for my publishing career. Pretty sweet."

He smirked at her. "You've been doing some thinking."

"Trying to think like a businessman **and** a soulless killer. Plus, it's all true, factually accurate. It just leaves out feelings. She doesn't have any. He can't have any or he wouldn't pay her to kill people. If you don't have feelings, you can't understand them, can you? You get revenge, I get the shiny fish, and Vasin gets the golden egg."

"Then what?" Fine demanded. "If you're not dead five minutes after meeting with him—if you get that far—if he says, 'Sure, let's make a deal,' then what?"

"Then we agree on when and where to

make the exchange. Or for our representatives to make the exchange." Because, Ash thought, he wanted Lila nowhere near that part. "And you take it from there. We're just making the contact, making the deal. If he agrees, it's conspiracy to murder on his part. And you have him with our testimony. You have her because he'll at least pretend to deliver her. And the egg goes where it belongs. In a museum."

"And if he doesn't agree? If he tells you, 'Give me the egg or I'll have your girlfriend raped, tortured and shot in the head'?"

"As I told you, he'll already know if he does anything to either of us, the announcement goes out publicly, and the egg moves out of his reach. Unless he plans to try to steal it from the Met. Possible," he said before Fine could speak. "But he hasn't tried to have any of the Imperial eggs stolen from museums or private collections."

"That we know of."

"Okay, that's a factor. But it's a hell of a lot easier, cleaner and immediate to make the deal."

"He could threaten your family as you say he threatened Bastone's."

"He could, but while we're meeting with

him, my family will be inside our compound. Again, I'm making him a straightforward deal where he pays nothing for what he wants. He just trades an asset that hasn't been paying dividends."

"It could work," Waterstone mused. "We've used civilians before."

"Wired, protected."

"Maybe we work something out there. We talk to Tech—see what they've got. See what the Feds got."

"We're meeting with him," Ash pointed out. "With or without you. We'd rather with you."

"You're handing him two hostages," Fine pointed out. "If you're going to do this, you go in, she stays out."

"Good luck with that," Ash commented.

"We both go." Lila met Fine's eye with the same hard look she received. "Not negotiable. Plus it's more likely he'd consider one of us a hostage, and the other—me—forced to turn over the egg if I was still outside. What have I got if my shiny fish is gutted?"

"Think of another metaphor," Ash advised.

"He's unlikely to agree to a meeting," Fine pointed out. "He's known for doing everything by remote. At best, you may end up talking to one of his lawyers or assistants."

"My terms are set. We meet with him, or there's no negotiation." He glanced at his phone when it signaled. "That's my lawyer, so we might have an answer. Give me a minute."

Rising, he took the phone with him, walked to the other end of the living room.

"Talk him out of this." Fine shifted that hard stare to Lila again.

"I couldn't, and at this point I can't try. This gives him—us—a good chance to end it. We have to end it, and it doesn't end, not for Ash, if he doesn't get some justice for his brother and his uncle. He'll feel responsible for what happened to them for the rest of his life without that."

"I don't think you understand the risk you're taking."

"Detective Fine, I feel I'm taking a risk every time I walk out the door. How long could you live with that? The woman wants us dead—whether her boss does or not. I saw it, I felt it. We want a chance to live our lives, to see what happens next. That's worth the risk."

"Tomorrow." Ash walked back, laid the phone on the table again. "Two o'clock, at his Long Island estate."

"There goes Luxembourg," Lila said, and made Ash smile at her.

"Less than twenty-four hours?" Waterstone shook his head. "That's cutting it damn thin."

"I think that's part of the point, and why I agreed. It should tell him I want this done, and now."

"He thinks you'll ask for millions," Lila pointed out. "What you will ask is going to take him by surprise. And it's going to intrigue him."

He crouched down beside her chair. "Go to the compound. Let me do this."

She took his face in her hands. "No."

"Argue that later," Waterstone advised. "We're going to talk about what you'll do, won't do, and if it gets that far, the where and when for the trade." He glanced at Fine. "You better call the boss, see about a way to keep them wired in, if there is one, and how we set it up from our end."

"I don't like any of it." She rose. "I like you, both of you. I wish to hell I didn't." She took out her phone, walked away to call her lieutenant.

The minute they were alone, Lila let out a huge, huffing breath. "God, all that fried my brain. Checkpoints and code words and procedures. I'm going to do the next coat on the powder room—manual labor helps fried brains—before the FBI tech guys get here. We're going undercover for the FBI. I really need to get a book out of this. If I don't, someone else will, and I'm not going to let that happen."

She pushed out of the chair. "What do you say we just order pizza later? Pizza's food you don't have to think about when your brain's tired."

"Lila. I love you."

She stopped, looked at him, felt that now familiar lift and squeeze of her heart. "Don't use that to try to persuade me to stay behind. I'm not going to be stubborn, not going to wave my feminist flag—though I could. The fact that I'm going, absolutely need to go, should tell you something about what I feel for you."

"What do you feel for me?"

"I'm figuring it out, but I know there's no one else I'd do this for or with. No one else. Do you remember that scene from **Return of the Jedi**?"

"What?"

She closed her eyes. "Please don't say you haven't seen the movies. Everything falls apart if you haven't seen Star Wars."

"Sure I've seen the movies."

"Thank you, God," she murmured, opened her eyes again. "The scene," she continued, "on the forest moon of Endor. They've got Leia and Han pinned down outside the storm trooper compound. It looks bad. And he glances down, she shows him her weapon, then he looks at her and says he loves her. She says—she smiles and says—'I know.' She didn't say it back. Okay, she said it first in **The Empire Strikes Back** before Jabba the Hutt had him frozen in carbonite, but taking just that scene on Endor, it showed they were in it together—win or lose."

"How many times have you seen those movies?"

"That's irrelevant," she said, a bit primly.

"That many. So you're Princess Leia and I'm Han Solo."

"For the purposes of this illustration. He loved her. She knew it, and vice versa. It made them both braver. It made them stronger. I feel stronger knowing you love me. I never expected to. I'm trying to get used to it—just like you asked."

She slid her arms around him, swayed a little. "When I say it to you, you'll know I mean it, would mean it even, maybe especially, if we were pinned down by storm troopers on the forest moon of Endor with only a single blaster between us."

"And somehow I find that the most touching thing anyone's ever said to me."

"The fact you do . . . I'm trying to get used to knowing you understand me, and love me anyway."

"I'd rather be Han Solo than a shiny fish."

She laughed, drew back to look up at him. "I'd rather be Leia than someone who's looking to hook one. So I'm going to go back to faux painting the powder room, work with the FBI, then eat pizza. We're leading fascinating lives right now, Ash— and yes, we want the middle part of that done and over. But I'm a big believer in making the most out of where you are while you're there. And"—she gave him a squeeze before stepping back—"it's going to work. Just like it worked for Leia and Han."

"You won't have . . . What was her weapon again?"

"I can see you need a Star Wars marathon evening, as a refresher. A blaster."

"You won't have one of those."

"I have something else she had. I have good instincts, and I have my own Han Solo."

He let her go because part of him thought she was right. They'd be stronger together. Thinking of that, of her, he went up to his studio to finish her portrait.

Lila made a point of going to the gallery the next morning. Ash insisted on going with her, then peeled off to give her and Julie time alone in Julie's office.

"You're going to tell me something I don't want to hear."

"Probably. Ash is going to the bakery to talk to Luke. You're my closest friend in the world, so I need to tell you, and I need to ask you."

"You're going to see Vasin."

"Today."

"Today? But it's too fast." Alarmed, she reached out, grabbed Lila's hands. "You can't be ready. You can't—"

"It's all set. Let me explain."

She took Julie through all the steps, the plans, the fail-safe options.

"Lila, I wish you wouldn't do this. I wish you'd go, just go with Ash anywhere, even if it meant I'd never see you again. I know you won't. I know you, and know you can't, but I wish you would."

"I thought about it. I really thought about it last night. Middle of the night, going over and over everything in my head. And because I tried to find a way to do it, I realized it had stopped being about sex and fun and affection. I guess it never was just about that. But wherever we went, it would still be a kind of house arrest. We'd never be really sure, really safe."

"But more sure. More safe."

"I don't think so. I started playing what if. What if when she can't find us, she goes after our family? Our friends? She could find my parents, Julie, hurt them. She could hurt you. I can't live with those what ifs."

"I know you can't, but I can wish you would."

"We're working with the police, the FBI. We'll have these awesome micro-recorders. Plus, the biggest plus, Ash is offering him exactly what he wants. There's no reason to hurt us if we're agreeing to give him what he wants. All we have to do is convince him to make the deal. Then we walk away and the police take over."

"You can't believe it'll be that simple. You can't think this is some sort of adventure."

"Not an adventure, a necessary and calculated step. I don't know what it's going to be, but it's worth the risk, Julie, to have a real life again. It's worth the risk so the next time my head won't turn off in the middle of the night, it's because I'm thinking about what I want with Ash. What I can give, what I can take."

"Do you love him?"

"He thinks I do."

"That doesn't answer the question."

"I think I do. And wow." She rubbed her knuckles between her breasts. "That's a lot to think for me. But I don't know what that means for either of us until this is over. And it's going to be over. Then I'm going to help you plan your wedding to your once-and-future husband. I'm going to figure out my own life. I'm going to finish this book all the way instead of essentially."

"What time today?"

"We're meeting him at two. Julie, I believe we're going to go there, make the deal, walk out, just the way I explained it. But if something goes wrong, I wrote a letter to my parents. It's in my travel kit, in the top right drawer of Ash's dresser. I need you to get it to them."

"Don't even think that." Grabbing Lila's hands, she squeezed hard enough to hurt. "Don't."

"I have to think. I don't believe, but I have to think. I let a lot of things slide with my parents the last few years. And these last few weeks with Ash have made me think about that, realize that. I want them to know I love them. What I believe I'm going to do is go out there, take a week, ask Ash if he wants to meet them, which is a big, giant step for me. I believe I'm going to take it. I believe I want to take it. If something happens, I need them to know that."

"You're going to take Ash to meet them, and tell them you love them yourself."

"I believe that, but I have to think. And I'm asking you to make sure they know in case of the what if."

"There won't be a what if." Eyes shimmering, Julie pressed her lips together hard. "But yes, I promise. Whatever you need."

"Thanks. It takes a weight off. The other thing is the book. I'd like a couple more weeks to shine it up, but if something happens . . ." She took a flash drive out of her pocket. "I made a copy for you to take to my editor."

"God, Lila."

"You're the only one I can ask, or would ask. I need to know you'll do those two things for me. Then I can just put them away, and I can just believe you're never going to have to do them anyway."

Julie pressed her fingers to her eyes a moment, struggled until she found her control. "You can count on me. You won't have to, but you can count on me."

"That's all I need. Let's have a celebration dinner tomorrow night, the four of us. Tonight's going to be too crazy, I think."

Nodding quickly, Julie grabbed tissues

out of the box on her desk. "Now you're talking."

"The Italian place the four of us went the first time. I think we should make that our spot anyway."

"I'll make reservations. We'll meet you there. Seven-thirty?"

"Perfect." She stepped over, gave Julie a hug. "I'll see you tomorrow night—and I'll call you tonight. I promise."

And if she didn't, she'd left a letter for Julie in the same drawer with the one for her parents.

Twenty-eight

Lila decided the blue dress Ash had given her after their first sitting would serve as a good-luck charm. She wore it with the moonstone necklace from Florence, deciding both would be good mojo.

She spent considerable time on her makeup. It wasn't every day you had a business meeting with an international criminal who hired killers to do his bidding.

She checked the contents of her purse—as the special agent in charge had told her, Vasin's security would. She decided to leave all her usual supplies in place. Wouldn't that seem more normal?

She turned in the mirror, looked at Ash.

Clean-shaven, hair more or less tamed, and a steel-gray suit that murmured power—because power didn't have to shout—in every line.

"I'm too casual. You're wearing a suit."

"Serious meeting, serious suit." He knotted a tie the color of a good cabernet perfectly, flicked a glance at her in the mirror. Then let it linger. "You look great."

"Too casual," she repeated. "But my serious suit is boring. Which is why it's at Julie's, because I only wear it on boring occasions, which this isn't. And I swear I'm not going to babble like this much longer."

She rooted through her little section of closet, tried out the cropped white jacket Julie had talked her into. "This is better. Is it better?"

He crossed to her, took her face, kissed her. "It's going to be fine."

"I know. I'm in full believe-it mode. But I want to look appropriate. I need to be dressed correctly to start the takedown of thieves and murderers. I'm nervous," she admitted. "But I'd be crazy not to be. I don't want him to think I'm crazy. Greedy or slutty or vengeful. But not crazy."

"Sorry, you look fresh, and pretty, and appropriately on edge."

"That'll have to do. We need to go, don't we?"

"Yeah. I'm going to go get the car, then I'll come back, pick you up. No reason for you to walk in those shoes," he pointed out. "If anyone's watching the loft, they'd think the same. Twenty minutes."

It gave her time to pace, to practice cool, an-eye-for-an-eye stares in the mirror. And to ask herself one last time if she could just walk away.

She opened the dresser drawer she'd taken as her own, then the travel kit she'd put inside. She brushed a finger over the letters she'd tucked into it.

Better to believe they'd never be opened, that she'd come back with Ash, both safe and sound and done. She'd tear them up, and she'd say what she'd written in them, face-to-face, because some words shouldn't go unsaid.

But she felt better knowing she'd written them, knowing the written word had power, and love would shine through it.

When Ash pulled the car in front of the lot, she stepped out.

The answer was no. She couldn't walk away.

In her mind she imagined the FBI tracking them through downtown traffic. Vasin might have them tracked as well. She'd be glad when she could feel alone again, really alone.

"Should we practice?" she asked him.

"Do you need to go over it again?"

"No, not really, and I know it'll seem rehearsed and staged if we go over it all again and again."

"Just remember. We have what he wants."

"And let you take the lead because that's what he expects. It's a little annoying."

He touched a hand to hers briefly. "Be yourself. Engage him. It's what you do."

"I can do that." She closed her eyes a moment. "Yes, I can do that."

She wanted to say more, found she had all sorts of personal things to tell him. But besides tracking them, the authorities would be listening.

So she kept the words in her head, in her heart, as they drove across the East River.

"After you kill her, we should go somewhere fabulous. I'm in character," she said when he glanced at her.

"Okay. How about Bali?"

"Bali?" She straightened in her seat. "Really? I've never been there."

"Neither have I, so we'll be even."

"Bali. Indonesia. I love the food. I think they have elephants." She dug out her phone to look it up, stopped. "Are you in character or do you actually want to go to Bali?"

"It can be both."

"Maybe over the winter sometime. My house-sitting business slows down in February. That's not in character—what do I care about house-sitting when I've got the shiny fish? House-sitting is so over. Bali in the winter—with maybe a trip to Switzerland for some skiing. I'll need to be outfitted, of course, for both. You'll take care of that for me, won't you, baby?"

"Anything you need, sugar."

"I hope you'd really hate having a woman say that, but reverting to character, if you could arrange a credit line for me at Barneys, maybe Bergdorf's, too, I could surprise you. A girl wants to give her man a few surprises."

"You're good at this."

"I'm channeling an adult Sasha—my

spoiled, greedy werewolf girl. Kaylee's nemesis. She'd take you for everything she could, get bored, then rip your throat out. If I can think like her, I can pull this off."

Lila huffed out a breath. "I can think like her. I created her. I can pull this off. You'll be like you are when you're really pissed off, and we'll rock this meeting."

"Lila, I am really pissed off."

She gave him a sidelong look. "You seem really calm."

"I can be both. Just like Bali."

He drove along a high stone wall, and she caught the blink of the red eye of security cameras. "This is it, isn't it?"

"The gate's just ahead. You'll do fine, Sasha."

"Too bad it's not a full moon."

The gate spanned wide enough for two cars to pass through and gleamed silver in the afternoon sun. A bas-relief of a griffin with sword and shield centered the gate.

The moment they stopped, two men stepped out of a doorway in the thick brick columns that flanked the gate.

Here we go, Lila thought as Ash rolled down his window.

"Step out of the car, please, Mr. Archer, Ms. Emerson, for a security check."

"Security check?" Lila tried for a sulky look as one of the guards opened her door. On a little huff of breath, she slid out.

They checked the car top to bottom, running scanners over it, then running what she thought must be a camera on a pole under it.

They opened the hood, the trunk.

"You're cleared to enter."

Lila slid back in, thought like Sasha. She took out a purse mirror and freshened her lip gloss. But she watched over the glass as she caught glimpses of the house through thick groves of trees.

Then the long drive turned, and she saw it in full.

It was massive and gorgeous, a wide U of golden stone, with its center curve rising above the legs. Windows that shot back beams of sun, giving no hint of what lay behind them. A trio of onion domes topped it, their bases ringed with circular balconies.

A rose garden, with its thorny bushes of abundant blooms, ran in rows of military precision while the vast lawn rolled, green and lush.

A pair of stone griffins with sword and shield guarded the carved double doors of the entrance. Their eyes, like the light of the cameras, gleamed red. Two more security men stood in front of statues, still as the stone itself. Lila clearly saw the sidearm of the one who stepped to the car.

"Step out of the car, please, and follow me."

They crossed golden pavers to what she'd taken as an elaborate garden shed. Inside, another man studied an array of monitors.

Security station, she realized, and goggled—at least internally—at the gadgetry. She'd have given a lot to play with it.

"I'll need to inspect the contents of your bag, Ms. Emerson."

She clutched it to her, put on a look of irritation.

"We require you both to be scanned and wanded before entering the house. Are you carrying any weapons or recording devices?"

"No."

The man nodded, held out a hand for Lila's bag. She surrendered it with a show of reluctance as a woman stepped out of another doorway with something similar to the wands used at airport security.

"Raise your arms, please."

"This is just silly," Lila grumbled, but obeyed. "What are you doing," she demanded when the man removed her multi-tool, her mini can of first-aid spray, WD-40 and her lighter from her bag.

"These items are restricted." He opened the box where she kept her tapes—double-sided, duct, packing and Scotch. Closed it again. "They'll be returned to you when you leave."

"Underwire bra," the woman announced. "Step over here for a manual check."

"A what? Ash."

"You can wait outside, Lila, if you don't want to go through security."

"For God's sake. It's a bra."

They'd warned her, she thought, but now that it was happening as predicted she felt her heart hammering. She pressed her lips together, looked deliberately at the wall as the woman ran her hands briskly along the wire supports of her bra.

"Next it'll be a strip search."

"Not necessary. She's clear," the woman said, and walked to Ash.

"Ms. Emerson, considering the numerous items in your bag on our restricted list, we'll keep your bag, and contents, in our safe here until you leave."

When Lila began to protest, the security woman called out, "Recorder," and removed the pen from Ash's pocket. She smirked a little as she tossed it on a tray.

"It's a pen," Lila said, and frowned at it, but Ash shrugged.

"I wanted some backup."

"Oh! Is it like a spy thing?" Lila reached for it, scowling as the woman drew the tray out of reach. "I just wanted to see."

"It will be returned to you at your departure. You're cleared to enter the house. Please follow me."

He led them out, circled around to the main entrance.

The double doors opened from inside. A woman in a severe black uniform nodded. "Thank you, William. I have it from here. Mr. Archer, Ms. Emerson." She stepped back into a kind of foyer where glass walls closed it off from a wide entrance hall with soaring ceilings and a central staircase at least fifteen feet wide with the fluid curve of banisters gleaming like mirrors.

And a world of paintings and sculpture.

"I'm Carlyle. Have either of you engaged in the use of tobacco products in the last twenty-four hours?"

"No," Ash told her.

"Have you been in contact with any animals in the last twenty-four hours?"

"No."

"Any illnesses in the past week, treated or not treated by a medical professional?"

"No."

"Contact with children under the age of twelve?"

"Seriously." Lila rolled her eyes, and this time answered herself. "No. But we have had contact with human beings, including each other. Is a blood test next?"

Saying nothing, the woman took a small spray bottle out of her pocket. "Please hold out your hands, palms up. This is an antiseptic product. It's perfectly safe. Mr. Vasin will not shake hands," she continued as she sprayed their hands. "Please turn your hands over. Do not approach him beyond the point you're given. Please be respectful and touch as little as possible on the premises, and nothing without Mr. Vasin's permission. Please come with me."

When she turned, the glass panels opened. She walked across tiles, golden like the stones, with a central tile rug depicting the Romanov coat of arms.

They walked up the stairs—in the center where no one's hands could reach the rich gleam of the railings.

Art filled the walls on the second floor as it had on the first. Every door they passed remained tightly shut, and each had a security swipe.

Here, there was no open, airy feel, but a carefully restricted one. A museum, she thought, to hold his collection. A home by default.

At the final door, Carlyle took out a swipe card, then leaned forward to put her eye to a little scanner. How paranoid was a man, Lila thought, to require a retinal scan to enter a room in his own home?

"Please sit in these two chairs." She indicated two high-backed armchairs in merlot leather. "And remain seated. You'll be served a light refreshment, and Mr. Vasin will join you shortly."

Lila scanned the room. Russian nesting dolls—old and elaborate—filled a display case. Painted lacquer boxes another.

Windows tinted pale gold let in soft light and views of a grove of what she thought were pear and apple trees.

The sad eyes of somber portraits stared sorrowfully at the visitors, surely a deliberate arrangement. She couldn't deny they made her feel uncomfortable, and a little depressed.

Central to the room stood a large chair. Its leather gleamed a few shades deeper than the other seating, its back rose higher and boasted a thick frame of carved wood. It sat higher as well, she noted, on legs formed into the griffin.

His throne, she thought, giving him the position of power. But she only said, "This is an amazing house. It's even bigger than your family's in Connecticut."

"He's playing it for all it's worth. Making us wait."

"Now, Ash, don't lose your temper. You promised."

"I don't like games," he muttered, seconds before the door opened. Carlyle came in leading another uniformed woman who wheeled in a tray holding a pretty tea service of cobalt blue painted on white, with a plate of cookies decorated with tiny bits of fruit, a bowl of glossy green grapes. Rather than napkins, a glass bowl held individual wipes with the griffin seal.

"The tea is a jasmine blend, made for Mr. Vasin. You'll find it refreshing. The grapes are grown here on the estate, organically. The cookies are traditional **pryaniki**, or spice cookies. Please enjoy. Mr. Vasin will be with you momentarily."

"They look delicious. The tea set's so pretty."

Carlyle didn't crack a smile. "It's Russian porcelain, very old."

"Oh. I'll be careful." She waited until Carlyle and the server left to roll her eyes. "You shouldn't put things out, then make people feel intimidated to use them." As she spoke she laid the tea strainers over the cups, lifted the pot to pour.

"I don't want any damn tea."

"Well, I do. It smells nice. It's going to be worth the wait, Ash, you'll see. And when you get rid of the stupid egg that's caused all these problems, we can go on our trip."

She sent him a wicked smile. "That will definitely be worth the wait. Relax, baby. Have a cookie."

When he shook his head, scowled at her offer, she only shrugged, nibbled on one herself. "I'd better keep it to one if I'm going to look good in the new bikinis I'm going to buy. Can we rent a yacht? You always see pictures of celebrities and royalty hanging out on some big white yacht. I'd love to do that. Can we?"

"Whatever you want."

Though the boredom in his tone was heavy as a brick, she beamed. "You're so good to me. As soon as we get back home, I'll be good to you. Why don't we—"

She broke off as a section of the wall opened. Hidden door, she realized, cleverly concealed with molding.

She got her first look at Nicholas Vasin.

Gaunt was her first thought. Remnants of the film-star handsome remained, but had been hollowed out to a husk. He wore his hair in a white mane, too thick and full for his emaciated face so it seemed the weight of it should bend the thin neck to breaking. The eyes above the sunken cheeks burned black, a hard light against skin so pale it nearly glowed.

Like Ash, he wore a suit, his in a buff

color, with a vest and tie all exactly the same hue.

The result was colorless, but for the black shards of his eyes—and, Lila thought, very deliberate.

A griffin pin accented with diamonds sparkled on the lapel. A gold watch circled his thin, bony wrist.

"Ms. Emerson, Mr. Archer, welcome. Forgive me for not shaking hands."

His voice, like the whisper of spider legs over silk, sent a chill up Lila's spine.

Yes, all very deliberate.

He sat, laid his hands on the thick arms of his chair. "Our cook always made **pryaniki** for tea when I was a child."

"They're delicious." Lila lifted the plate. "Would you like one?"

He waved it away. "For myself, I use a macrobiotic diet. Guests, of course, should be indulged."

"Thank you," Lila responded when Ash sat in stony silence. "You have an incredible home, and so many beautiful things, even in just the little of it we've seen. You collect nesting dolls. They're so charming."

"Matryoshki," he corrected. "An old tradition. We must always honor our roots."

"I love things that open up into something else. Finding out what the something else is."

"I started the collection as a child. These and the lacquer boxes are the first of my collections, so I keep them in my private sitting room."

"They're the most personal. Am I allowed a closer look?"

He gestured magnanimously.

She rose, walked closer. "I've never seen . . . **matryoshki** so intricately made. Of course, most of what I've seen have been in souvenir shops, but . . . Oh!" She glanced back, pointed, being careful not to touch the glass. "Is it the royal family? Nicholas, Alexandra, the children?"

"Yes. You have an intelligent eye."

"Such a terrible thing. So brutal, especially the children. I had the impression they'd all been lined up and shot, which is horrible enough, but after Ash found . . . That is, recently I read more about what happened. I don't understand how anyone could have been so cruel and brutal to children."

"Their blood was royal. That was enough for the Bolsheviks."

"They might have played with dolls like these—the children. Collected them as you did. It's another bond between you."

"That's correct. For you it's stones."

"I'm sorry?"

"A stone from everywhere you travel, since childhood. A pebble?"

"I . . . yes. It was my way of taking something with me when we had to move again. My mother keeps them in a jar now. How did you know?"

"I make it my business to know my guests and their interests. For you," he said to Ash, "it's always been art. Perhaps the cars and dolls boys play with as a child, but these things aren't worth the keeping. But art—your own, or others that draw a response from you—that's worth the collecting to you."

He laced his long, bony fingers together for a moment as Ash remained silent.

"I have some of your work in my collection. An early piece called **The Storm**. A cityscape, with a tower rising high above the rest, and in the topmost window stands a woman."

He tapped his fingers together, a precise steeple, as he spoke. "The storm rages—I found the colors extraordinary in violence and depth, clouds illuminated by lightning so it became alien, unearthly. Such movement. At first look you might think the woman, a great beauty in virgin white, is trapped in that tower, a victim of the storm. Then, look closer, you see she rules the storm."

"No. She is the storm."

"Ah." A smile flitted around Vasin's mouth. "Your appreciation of the female form—body, mind, spirit—fascinates me. I have a second piece, more recently acquired. A charcoal, with a mood that strikes as joyful—a joy in power as a woman stands in a moonstruck field playing a violin. Who—or what—I wonder, will her music call?"

The portrait from Oliver's apartment, Lila thought, and went very still.

"Only she knows," Ash said coolly. "That's the point. Discussing my work won't get you what you want."

"Yet it's entertaining. I have few visitors, fewer yet who truly share my interests."

"A mutual interest is a different thing."

"A subtle distinction. But we also share an understanding of the importance of bloodlines, how they must be honored, revered, preserved."

"Families and bloodlines are different things."

Vasin spread his hands. "You have a unique familial . . . situation. For many of us, for me, family is bloodline. We understand tragedy, loss, the need to balance the scales, you could say. My family was murdered simply for being superior. For being born into power. Power and privilege will always be attacked by smaller men who claim they have a cause. But the cause is always avarice. Whatever lofty excuse men use for war or revolution, it's always because they want the power another holds."

"So you lock yourself in this fortress to protect yourself from avaricious men?"

"Your woman was wise to stay in her tower."

"But lonely," Lila put in. "To be removed from the world? To see it, but not be part of it? It would be crushingly lonely."

"You're a romantic under it all," Vasin decided. "There is so much more than people for companionship. As I said, I have few

visitors. I'll show you some of my most treasured companions. Then we can discuss
business."

He rose, then held up a hand. "A moment, please."

He stepped back to the hidden door.
Another iris scan, Lila realized. She hadn't
noticed it within the molding.

"Few visitors," Vasin said, "and fewer
still who ever step beyond this door. But I
think we'll understand each other, and the
business at hand, much better when you
do." He stepped to the side of the door,
gestured.

"Please, after you."

Ash walked to the door, carefully blocking Lila from going through until he saw
what lay beyond. Then with a glance at
Vasin's satisfied face, Ash took Lila's arm,
went in with her.

Tinted windows let in gold light. A rich
and liquid light to serve his collection. Inside glass islands, towers and walls the
glitter and gleam and glow of Fabergé lived.

Cases for clocks, others for boxes, for
jewelry, for bowls, for flasks. Each meticu-
lously arranged according to category.

She saw no door but the one they'd come

through, and though the ceilings were high, the floors a brilliantly white marble, she saw it as a gilded and soulless Aladdin's cave.

"Of all my collections, this is my biggest triumph. If not for the Romanovs, Fabergé might have remained limited to creating for the highborn or wealthy, even the hoi polloi. The artist, of course—Fabergé himself—and the great workmaster Perchin deserve all credit for vision, for skill, even for the risks taken to turn a reasonably success-ful jewelry business into an empire of art. But without the patronage of the tsars, the Romanovs, so much of this would never have been created. Much that was would be a mere footnote in the art world."

Hundreds of pieces—hundreds of hun-dreds, Lila thought. From the tiny, festive jelly bean eggs to an elaborate tea ser-vice, what she realized was a picnic set, presentation trophies, vases, another case that held only animal figurines.

"This is amazing. I see the scope of vi-sion and craftsmanship—so much variety in one place. It's amazing," Lila repeated. "It must have taken years to collect so many pieces."

"Since childhood," Vasin agreed. "You enjoy the clocks," he commented. He crossed to her, but kept a full arm span between them. "This fan shape, so suited to a desk or mantel, and the translucence of the enamel, the soft yet rich orange color. The details—the gold rosettes in the lower corners, the rose cut of the diamond border. And here, the same workmaster—Perchin—the exquisitely simple circular clock, pale blue with reed-and-tie rim."

"They're all beautiful." And trapped, she thought, as art should never be, for his eyes alone—or those he allowed into his sanctum.

"Are they all antiques? Some look so contemporary."

"All are old. I've no wish to own here what any man can have by offering a credit card."

"They're all set to midnight."

"Midnight, when the assassins gathered the royal family together. What would have been the end, if not for Anastasia's escape."

She gave him wide eyes. "But I thought they'd proven she died, too, with her family. DNA tests, and—"

"They lie." He sliced a hand through the air like an ax. "As the Bolsheviks lied. I'm the last of the Romanovs—the last to carry the blood of Nicholas and Alexandra, through their daughter, to my father, and last to me. And what belonged to them is mine by right."

"Why here?" Ash demanded. "Why not house your collection in Russia?"

"Russia isn't what it was, and will never be what it was. I create my world, and live in it as I choose."

He walked on. "Here is what I think of as practical luxuries. These, gold and diamond opera glasses, or the jasper match holder chased in gold, the enameled bookmark—perfection in its shape, the deep green enamel. And of course the perfume bottles here. Each one a feast of art."

"You know each piece?" Lila wondered. "With so many, I'd lose track."

"I know what's mine," he said coldly. "A man can own with ignorance, but can't possess without knowledge. I know what's mine."

He turned abruptly, walked to the center of the room and a freestanding glass case. Inside stood eight white pedestals. One held what Lila recognized from the descriptions as the Nécessaire. Gold, sparkling, exquisite—and opened to reveal the diamond-encrusted manicure set inside.

She reached for Ash's hand, curled her fingers into his as she looked over into Vasin's eyes. "The lost Imperial eggs. You have three."

"Soon I'll have four. One day, I'll have all."

Twenty-nine

"The Hen with Sapphire Pendant," Vasin began. Like a prayer, worship whispered through his voice. "From 1886. The gold hen, decorated with rose-cut diamonds, holds the sapphire egg—the pendant—in her beak, just taken, it appears, from the nest. The surprise, as you see, is a small gold-and-diamond chick, freshly hatched."

"It's stunning." Easy to say, Lila thought, as she meant it. "Down to the tiniest detail."

"The egg itself," he said, his dark eyes riveted on his treasure. "Not merely a shape, but a symbol. Of life, of rebirth."

"So the tradition of decorating eggs for Easter, to celebrate the Resurrection."

"Charming, true, but this anyone can do. It was the Romanovs—my blood—who turned this simple tradition into great art."

"You leave out the artist," Ash pointed out.

"No, no. But as I said, it required the vision and the patronage of the tsars for the artist to create. This, all of this, is owed to my family."

"Every piece is amazing. Even the hinges are perfect. Which is this?" Lila asked, carefully gesturing to the second egg. "I don't recognize it."

"The Mauve, from the following year. Again rose-cut diamonds, pearls along with emeralds and rubies. This to accent the surprise, the heart-shaped frame in red, green and white enamel accented with pearls and more rose-cut diamonds. You see it open here into its three-leaf-clover shape. Each leaf with a miniature watercolor portrait on ivory. Nicholas, Alexandra and Olga, their first child."

"And the Nécessaire. I studied up," Lila said. "It is a manicure set. Everything I read was just speculation. But . . . nothing you can read comes close to the reality."

"Who did you kill to get them?" Ash demanded.

Vasin only smiled. "I've never found it necessary to kill. The hen was stolen, then used to secure passage out of Poland, a bribe to escape Hitler's holocaust. But the family of the thief was still sent to the camps, and died there."

"That's horrible," Lila said softly.

"History is written in blood," Vasin said simply. "The man who took it and betrayed them was persuaded to sell it to me rather than be exposed.

"The Mauve, more thieves. Fortune had blessed them, but the generations that passed couldn't wash the thievery away. Bloodlines," he said. "Their fortunes changed when their only son met with a tragic accident, and they were persuaded to sell the egg to me, to rid themselves of the stain."

"You had him killed," Ash said. "It's no different than killing him yourself."

Vasin's face remained impassive, perhaps faintly amused. "One pays for a meal in a fine restaurant, but isn't responsible for the dish."

Lila laid a hand on Ash's arm, as if to soothe away any spike of temper. In reality she needed the contact.

"The Nécessaire, stolen, was bought by a man who recognized beauty, then was lost through carelessness to another. I acquired it through persuasion again, and fair payment."

He studied the eggs, shifted to scan the room with a look of hot satisfaction. "We'll go back, and discuss fair payment."

"I don't want your money."

"Even a wealthy man has room for more."

"My brother's dead."

"It's unfortunate," Vasin said, and took a step back. "Please understand if you approach me, make any threatening moves?" He drew a small Taser from his pocket. "I'll protect myself. More, this room is under surveillance. Men armed with more . . . permanent weapons will move in at any perceived threat."

"I'm not here to threaten you. I'm not here for money."

"Let's sit, like civilized men, and discuss what you are here for."

"Come on, Ash, let's go sit down." Crooning a little, Lila stroked a hand on Ash's arm. "It doesn't do any good to get upset. We'll go talk. It's why we're here. You and me and Bali, okay? Okay?"

For a moment she thought he meant to jerk away from her, turn on Vasin and be done with it. Then he nodded, went with her.

She let out a breath of relief as they passed back into the sitting room.

Someone had cleared the tea, the trays. In their place was an opened bottle of Barolo and two glasses.

"Please, help yourself." Vasin sat again as the door to the collection room closed. "You may or may not be aware that your brother—or half brother, to be accurate— sat where you are now a few months ago. We talked extensively, and came to what I believed was an understanding."

With his hands on his knees, Vasin leaned forward, cold fury twisting his face. "We had an agreement."

Then he sat back again, his face smoothed out. "I made him the offer I'll make to you now—and at that time he accepted it. It was a serious disappointment to me when he attempted to extort a larger payment from me. It shouldn't have come as a surprise to me, I admit that. He wasn't the most reliable of men, you must agree. But I was enthusiastic, perhaps overly so, at the prospect of acquiring the Cherub with Chariot."

"And the Nécessaire," Ash said. "He told you he could get you both. He changed the deal, Vasin, but so did you when you used Capelli to get the Nécessaire."

Sitting back, Vasin steepled his fingers again. Tap, tap, tap as his raven's eyes stared ahead. "The information on the Nécessaire came shortly after our meeting. I saw no reason to use a middleman when I could arrange the deal myself. The payment for the Cherub remained firm."

"You cut him out, so he upped the ante. And the woman? His woman? Collateral damage?"

"They were partners, so they both said. As it appears you are. What happened to them is tragic. It was, from what I've heard, drug- and alcohol-induced. Perhaps an argument taken to extremes by whoever provided him with the pills he was unfortunately careless with."

"And Vinnie?"

"Ah, the uncle. Again, tragic. An innocent, by all accounts. His death wasteful and unnecessary. It should be clear to you their deaths gained me nothing. I'm a businessman, and I do nothing without an eye to gain or profit."

Ash leaned forward. "Jai Maddok."

There was a flicker in Vasin's eyes, but Lila couldn't be sure if it was surprise or annoyance. "You'll need to be more specific."

"She killed Sage Kendall, my brother, Vinnie and, just days ago, Capelli."

"What has that to do with me?"

"She's yours. I'm here on your turf," Ash snapped before Vasin could speak. "I have what you want. You won't get it by lying to me, by insulting me."

"I can assure you I gave no one orders to kill your brother, his woman or his uncle."

"And Capelli."

"He's nothing to you, and nothing to me. I offered Oliver forty million dollars for the delivery of the two eggs, twenty each. As I acquired one myself, the twenty stood. He required a down payment—ten percent. I gave him this in good faith. He made the deal, took the down payment, then tried to double his asking price. Greed killed him, Mr. Archer. I did not."

"Jai Maddok killed him. She's on your payroll."

"I have hundreds on various payrolls. I can hardly be held responsible for their crimes and indiscretions."

"You sent her after Vinnie."

"Assigning her to talk to Vincent Tartelli, to ascertain whether or not he knew the location of my property—**my** property—is hardly sending her after anyone."

"Yet he's dead, and the Fabergé box she took from his shop sits in your collection room."

"A gift from an employee. I'm not responsible for how it was acquired."

"She went after Lila, threatened her with a knife. Cut her."

That was a surprise, Lila realized, as Vasin's mouth tightened. So Maddok hadn't told her employer every detail.

"I'm sorry to hear that. Some employees are overenthusiastic. I trust you weren't seriously injured."

"More scared than hurt." But Lila allowed her voice to tremble a bit. "If I hadn't been able to break away and run . . . She's dangerous, Mr. Vasin. She thought I knew where the egg was, and I really didn't. She said no one had to know I told her. She'd just take it and disappear, but I was afraid she was going to kill me. Ash."

"It's okay." Now he put a hand over hers. "She's never going to touch you again."

"I still get the shakes when I think about it." She poured a glass of wine, made sure he could see the tremor of her hand. "Ash took me to Italy for a few days, but I still get spooked just going out of the house. Even in the house . . . She called and threatened me. I'm scared to answer my phone now because she said she was going to kill me. That it was personal, not a job anymore."

"I promised you, we're going to end it."

"Your difficulties with someone in my employ are unfortunate." A little color had come into his face, a rise of faint pink, of anger. "But again, I'm not responsible. To the goal of ending it, I'll offer you exactly what I offered Oliver. Twenty million."

"You could offer me ten times that, I wouldn't take it."

"Ash, maybe we could—"

"No." He rounded on her. "It's my way. That's it, Lila. My way on this."

"What is your way?" Vasin asked.

"Let me make something clear. If we don't walk out of here unharmed and with a deal, my representative is authorized to make an announcement. Those wheels are in motion, and in fact, with the time we've wasted, if he doesn't hear from me in"—he checked his watch—"twenty-two minutes, they'll roll."

"What announcement?"

"The discovery of one of the lost Imperial eggs, acquired by my brother on behalf of Vincent Tartelli. Already authenticated by leading experts and documented. The egg will be immediately transferred to a secure location, and donated to the Metropolitan Museum of Art—on permanent loan from the Archer family.

"I don't want the damn thing." Ash whipped the words out. "As far as I'm concerned it's cursed. You want it, you deal. Otherwise, go ahead and try to get it out of the Met. It won't be my problem either way."

"And what do you want if not money?"

"Jai Maddok."

Vasin let out a quick chuckle. "Do you think you can turn her over to the police? That she can be pressured to give evidence against me?"

"I don't want her in prison. I want her dead."

"Oh, Ash."

"Stop it. We've been over this. As long as she's alive, she's a threat. She said it herself, didn't she, it's personal with her. She's a paid murderer, and she intends to kill you. She killed my brother." He turned, furious, to Vasin. "And what have the cops done? Hounded me, harassed Lila. First it's murder-suicide, then a drug deal gone bad. My family's suffering over this. Then it's Vinnie, who never hurt anyone. And the cops? They try to tie me into it, tie both of us into it. So screw the cops. You want the egg, you've got it. All I want is Jai Maddok."

"You expect me to believe you'd commit cold-blooded murder?"

"Cold-blooded justice. I protect what's mine. My family, Lila. She'll pay for putting her hands on my woman, and she won't have a chance to do it again."

"Oh, baby." This time Lila tried for thrill,

poorly masked. "You make me feel so safe, so special."

"Nobody touches what's mine," Ash said flatly. "And I'll get justice for my family. It costs you nothing."

"On the contrary. It would cost me a very valuable employee."

"You've got hundreds," Ash reminded him. "You can get more. One woman," he continued, and went with Lila's improv, "who would've taken the egg for herself if Lila had known where I put it."

Ash drew a photo from his pocket, set it on the table between them. "That was taken in my loft—I imagine you can verify that easily enough as your bitch has been inside. It's not there anymore, and it's where you'll never get it. Clock's ticking, Vasin. Make the deal, or we walk away. You can see the egg at the Metropolitan Museum of Art like any tourist. It'll never be in your collection."

Vasin drew thin white gloves from his pocket, put them on before picking up the photo.

Color flooded into his face, a kind of quick, wild joy as he studied the photograph of the Cherub with Chariot.

"The detail. Do you see the detail?"

Ash tossed down another photo. "Surprise."

"Ah! The clock. Yes, yes, just as I thought. More than exquisite. A miracle of art. This was made for my blood. It belongs to me."

"Give me the woman, and it will. I have all the money I need. I have work that fulfills me. I have a woman. I don't have justice. It's what I want. Give me what I want, I give you what you want. She fucked up. If she hadn't fucked it up with Oliver, you'd have it already. You'd have it for the down payment. Instead the cops have her on Vinnie's surveillance, and have Lila's statement about the attack. They'll tie her to you, if they haven't already. She pays for my brother, or you get nothing. I'll take a hammer to the fucking thing before you get it."

"Ash, stop. You promised you wouldn't. He won't." As if panicked, Lila held out her hands in appeal to Vasin. "He won't. He's just upset. He blames himself for Oliver."

"Damn it, Lila."

"He needs to understand, that's all, baby. He needs to end it, and fix it. And—"

"And you, Ms. Emerson. You condone his brand of justice?"

"I . . ." She bit her lip. "He needs to be at peace," she said, obviously reaching. "I . . . I can't live always being scared she's going to be there. Every time I close my eyes . . . Then we're going away. First to Bali, then, maybe, I don't know . . . wherever we want. But he needs to be at peace, and I need to feel safe."

Shiny fish, she reminded herself, and reached for Ash's hand. "I want whatever Ash wants. And he wants what I want. I mean, I have a career, and he believes in me. Right, baby? He's going to make an investment in me, and maybe I can get a film deal. **Moon Rise** could be the next **Twilight** or **Hunger Games**."

"There'd be blood on your hands."

"No." She jerked straight, eyes wide. "I wouldn't do anything. I'm just . . . I'm with Ash. She hurt me. I don't want to live closed up in the loft anymore. No offense, but I don't want to live the way you do, Mr. Vasin, where we can't go out and have fun and see people, go places. You'd have what you want, Ash would have what he needs. We'd all just . . . be happy."

"If I agreed, how would you do it?"

Ash looked down at his hands—strong,

artist's hands—then back into Vasin's eyes, the implication clear. Lila immediately looked away.

"Please, I don't want to know. Ash promised we'd never have to talk about it again after this. I just want to put it all out of my mind."

"Bloodlines," Ash said simply. "What would you do to the men who killed your ancestors if you had the chance?"

"I'd kill them, as brutally as they did mine. I'd kill their families, their friends."

"I'm just interested in one. I don't care about her family, if she has one. Just her. Yes or no, Vasin. Time's running out. Once it does, neither of us gets what we want."

"You propose an exchange. Value for value. When?"

"As soon as possible."

"Such an interesting proposition." He reached under the arm of the chair. In seconds the door opened to Carlyle.

"Sir?"

"Have Jai brought in."

"Right away."

"Oh." Lila cringed back in her chair.

"She won't touch you," Ash promised.

"You have my word on it. A guest must

never be harmed in the host's home. It's not only bad manners, but bad luck. I will tell you, if this deal is struck and you, like your brother, aren't true to your word, Ms. Emerson will be more than harmed."

Ash bared his teeth. "Threaten my woman, Vasin, and you'll never fill your trophy case."

"Terms, not threats. You should understand what happens to those who renege on a deal, or provide unsatisfactory service. Come," he said at the brisk knock on the door.

Jai wore black—snug pants, fitted shirt, tailored jacket. Her eyes gleamed at Lila. "How interesting to see you here. Both of you. Mr. Vasin told me you were visiting today. Should I show them . . . out, sir?"

"We haven't quite finished. I'm told you and Ms. Emerson have met."

"A brief encounter in the market." Jai skimmed her gaze down. "You're wearing better shoes today."

"And again, another encounter you didn't include in your report. Where was this, Ms. Emerson?"

Lila only shook her head, stared at the floor.

"In Chelsea," Ash said. "A couple of blocks from the gallery that shows my work. You held her at knifepoint."

"She exaggerates."

"You failed to mention this encounter to me."

"It was so inconsequential."

"I hit you. I punched you in the face." Lila let the show of bravery dissolve as Jai stared at her. "Ash."

"I count on details, Jai."

"My apologies, sir. An oversight."

"Yes, an oversight. As your phone call to Ms. Emerson was, I'm sure, an oversight. Mr. Archer and I have reached an agreement as regards my property. Your assignment in this regard has concluded."

"As you wish, Mr. Vasin."

"You failed to do as I wished, Jai. This is very disappointing."

He drew out the Taser. Her reaction was swift, the weapon under her jacket nearly in her hand. But the shock hit, and shuddering with it, she fell. From his seat, he gave her a second jolt, then with absolute calm pressed under the chair arm again.

Carlyle opened the door. Her gaze flicked down to Jai, rose again impassively. "Have her taken out and secured. Be certain she's relieved of all weapons."

"Of course."

"I'll show our guests out. Ms. Emerson, Mr. Archer." Lila's legs wobbled. She felt as if she was walking over a layer of mud as they crossed the pristine floor, descended the graceful curve of stairs.

"Tonight would be best," Vasin said conversationally. "We'll say two A.M. A quiet spot, don't you agree? Considering Jai's skills, the sooner the exchange is made, the better for all."

"Your time, my place. My representatives meet yours, two A.M., Bryant Park."

"Considering the value, it's best if you make the exchange personally. The temptation for a hireling to walk away with the prize would be great."

"Maddok's of equal value to me. Will you bring her, personally?"

"Her only use to me now is your desire for her."

"The egg's only use to me is yours for it," Ash countered. "It's down to business, nothing more. Once I have what I want, I intend to forget you and the egg exist. You'd be wise to do the same about me and mine." Ash checked his watch again. "You're cutting it close, Vasin."

"Two A.M., Bryant Park. My representative will contact me at two-oh-five. If the egg isn't delivered, as agreed, it won't go well for you. Or yours."

"Bring Maddok, and it's done."

He took Lila's arm, walked out. One of the security guards stood beside his car. He handed Lila her purse, opened the passenger door and remained silent as Lila got in.

She didn't speak, barely breathed, until they were through the gates and speeding along the road beside the high wall.

"You need to make that call, and I . . . Could you pull over for a minute? I feel a little sick."

When he veered to the shoulder, she shoved the door open, stumbled out. She bent over, closed her eyes as her head spun—and felt his hand on the small of her back.

"Take it easy."

"Just need some air." Something fresh, something clean. "He's worse than she is.

I didn't think there could be anything worse, but he is. I don't think I could've stood another five minutes in that room, in that place. It was like suffocating."

"You could've fooled me." But he could see it now that she'd let down her guard. The light tremors running through her body, the pallor of her face when she lifted it.

"He would have killed her himself, right there, right in front of us, if it would've gotten him the egg. And he could've walked away, snapped a finger for some servant to clean up the mess."

"She's the least of my worries."

"We would never have walked out of there if you didn't have what he wants. I know that. I know that."

"He'll keep his word. For now."

"For now," she agreed. "Did you see his face when you showed him the pictures? He might've been looking at God."

"It's one of his."

She let herself lean against him, closed her eyes again. "You're right. He's not crazy, not the way I imagined, anyway. He believes everything he said, about the Romanovs and bloodlines. All those beautiful things, placed so precisely behind glass. Just for him. Just to own. Like the house, his castle, where he can be tsar, surrounded by people who'll do whatever he tells them to do. Any one of those pretty boxes means more to him than the people who do his bidding. And the eggs, they matter most of all."

"We'll finish it, and he'll have nothing."

"That would be worse than death for him. I'm glad. I'm glad it'll be worse for him. When he put on those stupid gloves, I wanted to lean over and sneeze in his face, just to get a reaction. Except I was afraid someone would come in and shoot me."

"You're feeling better."

"Much."

"I'm going to call Alexi, just in case the cops didn't get the transmission."

"Okay, I'm going to check my purse, the car. They had plenty of time to install a bug or a LoJack."

She found the tiny listening device inside the glove compartment, showed it to Ash.

Saying nothing, he took it, dropped it, crushed it under his heel.

"Oh! I wanted to play with it."

"I'll buy you another."

"Not the same," she muttered, then dug a mirror out of her purse. She crouched beside the car, angled the mirror. "If I trusted absolutely no one, and someone had one of my gods, I'd . . . and there it is."

"There what is?"

"The tracker. A LoJack. I just need to . . . I told Julie white's not practical." She stripped off the jacket, tossed it inside the car. "Have you got a blanket in the trunk? I really like this dress."

Fascinated, he got the old bath sheet he kept in the trunk for emergencies, watched her spread it, then, armed with her multitool, scoot under the car.

"Seriously?"

"I'm just going to disable it. They won't be sure what happened, right? Later, I can take it off, see how it works. It looks like a really good one to me. They work differently—or have different ones for classic cars like this. I'd say Vasin's security team's ready for anything."

"You want to change the oil while you're at it?"

"Some other time. There, that did it."

She scooted out again, sat up, looked at him. "He thinks we're stupid."

"We're not only not stupid, but I'm smart enough to have a woman with her own tools who knows how to use them." Taking her hand, he pulled her to her feet. "Marry me."

She started to laugh, then revisited the head spinning when she realized he was serious. "Oh, God."

"Think about it." He caught her face in his hands, kissed her. "Let's go home."

Just an impulse of the moment, Lila assured herself. A man didn't propose to a woman who'd just disabled a LoJack planted by an obsessed criminal with delusions of tsarist grandeur.

An impulse, she thought again, because their part in this whole convoluted, bloody and surreal nightmare was essentially done.

Undercover agents would keep the rendezvous in Bryant Park. As they took Jai Maddok and Vasin's "representatives" into custody, Fine and Waterstone, in conjunction with a joint task force with the FBI, would arrest Vasin. Conspiracy to murder, murder for hire topped the bill.

They'd managed to bring down an international crime organization, with hardly more than a scratch.

Who wouldn't feel a little giddy?

And nervous, she admitted, pacing the bedroom when she should've been checking her web page, working on her book, updating her blog. But she just couldn't settle down.

People just didn't go from meeting—and under horrible circumstances—to mutual interest, to sex, to love, to marriage all within a matter of weeks.

But then, people didn't generally work to solve murders, discover priceless objets d'art, fly off to Italy and back, and step into a vicious spider's web to trap him in it.

All while essentially finishing a book, creating paintings, having really great sex. And faux painting a bathroom.

But then, she liked to keep busy.

How would they deal together when things slowed down to normal? When they could just work and live and be?

Then he walked in. He'd taken off his suit jacket and tie, rolled up the sleeves of his shirt. Tousled hair and those X-ray eyes. He looked the artist again. The artist—what he was—who made her yearn for things she'd never believed she wanted.

"It's set," he told her.

"It's set?"

"They have the warrants. They're going to wait until the scheduled meeting time, then move in simultaneously. The transmission was a little patchy in places, but they got enough."

"The bra transmitter was so totally Q."

"Q?"

"We're definitely scheduling a movie marathon. Bond, James Bond. You know, Q."

"Oh, right. Q. You're not still wearing it, are you?"

"No. I took it off, but I'm sort of hoping they forget to ask for it back. I'd love to play with it. The obvious pen recorder was a good distraction, but I really thought the glad-hand woman was going to cop to the wire when she was copping a feel."

"Even if she had, we'd still get Maddok. He was done with her."

As much as she despised the woman, Lila felt her belly clutch. "I know. He was done as soon as I told him she'd attacked me, called me—and didn't tell him."

"The ad lib about her hoping to snag the egg for herself didn't hurt."

"I got caught up. He'd have killed her, so we're actually doing her a favor. Yes, that's reaching," she admitted. "But I honestly can't wish Vasin on anyone. Even her."

"She made her choices, Lila. The cops want our full statements tomorrow. Even if Maddok doesn't turn on Vasin, they have enough to charge him. For Oliver, for Vinnie, for Oliver's girlfriend. Fine says the authorities are talking to Bastone."

"Good, that's all good. I really liked them. I like knowing they'll get justice, too."

"Alexi's staying at the compound tonight. The Cherub with Chariot goes to the Met tomorrow. We'll hold the announcement until the cops clear it, but it'll be where it belongs. Where it's safe."

So straightforward now, she thought. All the steps neatly in place. "It's really done."

"Essentially," he said, and made her smile. "They asked if we'd stay in tonight, stay low in case Vasin's still having us watched. It might look off for us to go out."

"I guess that's right, considering. I'm too wired—ha ha—anyway."

"We'll have that celebration with Luke

and Julie tomorrow, as planned." He crossed over to take her hands. "Anywhere you want to go."

Anywhere, she thought, and he meant it literally.

"Why?"

"I'd say because we earned it."

"No, why? Why did you ask me what you asked me? We'd just spent an hour pretending to be people we aren't, and the stress of that had me so twisted up I was afraid I'd lose it all over your classic car. Then I'm under your car, for God's sake, because Vasin would probably be just as happy to see us dead—the people we are or the people we pretended to be. I don't think it matters."

"That's a good part of the reason."

"It doesn't make sense. We didn't even know each other existed on the Fourth of July, and it's barely Labor Day and you're talking about . . ."

"You can say it. It won't burn your tongue."

"I don't know how this happened. I'm good at figuring out how things work, but I don't know how this happened."

"Love's not a faulty toaster. You can't take it apart and study the pieces, replace a part and figure out how it all fits back together. You just feel it."

"But what if—"

"Try what **is** instead," he suggested. "You crawled under the car in your blue dress. When I was grieving you gave me comfort. You told my father to go to hell when he was unpardonably rude to you."

"I didn't exactly—"

"Close enough. You fix cabinets, paint bathrooms, ask the doorman about his family and smile at waiters. When I touch you, the rest of the world goes away. When I look at you, I see the rest of my life. I'm going to marry you, Lila. I'm just giving you time to get used to it."

Everything that had softened while he spoke stiffened again. "You can't just say 'I'm going to marry you' like 'I'm going out for Chinese.' Maybe I don't want Chinese. Maybe I'm allergic. Maybe I don't trust egg rolls."

"Then we'll get pork-fried rice. You'd better come with me."

"I'm not finished," she said when he pulled her from the room.

"I am. The painting. I think you need to see it."

She stopped trying to tug free. "You finished the painting? You didn't tell me."

"I'm telling you now. I'm not going to pull the 'Picture's worth a thousand words' to a writer, but you need to see it."

"I'm dying to see it, but you banned me from your studio. I don't know how you finished it when I haven't sat for you in days. How did you—"

She stopped, words and motion, in the doorway of his studio.

The painting stood on its easel, facing her, centered in the long ribbon of windows with the early-evening light washing over it.

Thirty

She walked toward it slowly. She understood art was subjective, that it could—and should—reflect the vision of the artist and the observer.

So it lived and changed from eye to eye, mind to mind.

From Julie she'd learned to recognize and appreciate technique and form, balance or the deliberate lack of it.

But all that went out the window, whisked away on emotion, on amazement.

She didn't know how he'd made the night sky so luminous, how he could create the light of his perfect moon against the dark. Or how the campfire seemed to snap with heat and energy.

She didn't know how he could see her this way, so vibrant, so beautiful, caught in that spin, the red dress flaring out, the colors of the underskirt defiant against her bare leg.

Bracelets jangling at her wrists—she could almost hear them—hoops flashing at her ears while her hair flew free. Rather than the chains she'd posed in, she wore the moonstone. The one he'd given her. The one she wore even now.

Just above her lifted hands floated a crystal ball, one full of light and shadows.

She understood it. It was the future. She held the future in her hands.

"It's . . . it's alive. I expect to see myself finish that spin. It's magnificent, Ashton. It's breathtaking. You made me beautiful."

"I paint what I see. I saw you like this almost from the beginning. What do you see?"

"Joy. Sexuality, but a delight in it rather than, I don't know, smoldering. Freedom, and power. She's happy, confident. She knows who she is, and what she wants. And in her crystal, everything that can be."

"What does she want?"

"It's your painting, Ash."

"It's you," he corrected. "Your face—your eyes, your lips. The gypsy is a story, the setting, the costume. Dancing around the fire, the men watching her, wanting her. Wanting that joy, that beauty, that power, if only for a night. But she doesn't look at them—she performs for them, but doesn't see them. She doesn't look in the crystal, but holds it aloft."

"Because knowing isn't the power. Choosing is."

"And she only looks at one man, one choice. Your face, Lila, your eyes, your lips. It's love that lights it. It's in your eyes, in the curve of your lips, the tilt of your head. Love, the joy and power and freedom that comes from it. I've seen it on your face, for me."

He turned her. "I know infatuation, lust, flirtation, calculation. I've seen all of it go in and out of my parents' lives. And I know love. Do you think I'll let it go, that I'll let you hide from it because you, who's anything but a coward, is afraid of what ifs?"

"I don't know what to do about it, with it, for it. For you."

"Figure it out."

He lifted her to her toes, took her mouth with his in a long, smoldering kiss suited to campfires and moonlit nights.

He ran his hands, molded them from her hips, up her torso, to her shoulders, before easing away.

"You're good at figuring things out."

"It's not a faulty toaster."

He smiled at the use of his own argument. "I love you. If you had a dozen or so siblings you'd find it easier to say, and to feel, under every possible circumstance. But this is you and me. It's you," he said, shifting her to face the painting again. "You'll figure it out."

He touched his lips to the top of her head. "I'll go pick up some dinner. I feel like Chinese."

She tilted her head to look over her shoulder, sent him a look martini-dry. "Really?"

"Yeah, really. I'll stop by the bakery, check in with Luke if he's around. Either way, I'll buy you a cupcake."

When she said nothing, he gave her shoulders a squeeze. "Do you want to come with me, get out, take a walk?"

"Actually, that would be great, but I think

I should start figuring things out. And maybe try to sneak in some work."

"Fair enough." He started out. "I told Fine to call, no matter what time it was, when they have them both in custody. Then you'll be able to sleep."

He knew her, she thought, and for that she could be grateful. "When she calls, when they're in custody, prepare to be ridden like a wild stallion."

"That's a definite date. I won't be long—an hour tops."

She walked to the door of the studio, just to watch him walk down.

He'd get his keys, check his wallet, she thought, and his phone. Then he'd walk to the bakery first, talk things over with Luke. He'd call in the dinner order so it would be waiting when he got there, but he'd take a few minutes, talk to the owners, the delivery guy if he was there.

She walked back to the painting. Her face—her eyes, her lips. But when she looked in the mirror, she didn't see the brilliance.

Wasn't it amazing he did?

She understood now why he'd waited to

paint her face, her features. He'd needed to see this look on it—and he had.

He painted what he saw.

She glanced at another easel and, surprised, went over for a closer look. He'd pinned dozens of sketches to it—all of her.

The faerie in the bower, sleeping, waking, the goddess by the water—wearing a diadem and thin white robes. She rode a winged horse over the city—Florence, she realized—legs bare, one arm raised high. And over her upturned palm a ball of fire shimmered.

He gave her power, she realized, and courage, and beauty. He put the future in her hands.

She laughed at sketches of her at her keyboard, eyes intense, hair tumbled—and best of all her body caught in mid transformation to sleek wolf.

"He has to give me one of these."

She wished she could draw so she could draw him as she saw him, give him that gift. Inspired, she ran downstairs, into the little bedroom. She couldn't draw, but she damn well knew how to paint with words.

A knight, she decided. Not in shining

armor because he used it—not tarnished because he tended it. Tall in stature and demeanor. Both honorable and fierce.

A short story, she mused—something fun and romantic.

She set it in the mythical world of Korweny—he'd enjoy the anagram—a world where dragons flew and wolves ran free. And he, warrior prince, defended home and family above all. He gave his heart to a gypsy who rode beside him and spoke the language of wolves. Add the evil tyrant seeking to steal the magic dragon's egg and usurp the throne, the dark sorceress who did his bidding—she could have something.

A couple pages in, she backtracked, began a new opening. She realized she could write a novella instead of a short story. And she realized she'd gone from a character sketch to short story to novella in about twenty minutes.

"Give me an hour, I'll start thinking novel. And, hey, maybe."

Considering just that, she decided to go down, get a tall glass of lemon water, take a few minutes to think it through.

"Just a few rough pages," she promised

herself. "I have to focus on the book, but a few rough pages—for fun."

She started out, imagining a battle—the clang of swords and ax, and the morning mists rising from the blood-soaked ground.

She smiled as she heard the front door open. "Did I lose track of the time? I was just—"

She broke off, froze at the top of the steps as Jai shut the door behind her.

Purpling bruises marred her extraordinary face under her right eye, along her jawline. The tailored black shirt showed a rip in the shoulder seam.

Baring her teeth, she drew a gun from the waistband at the small of her back, said, "Bitch."

Lila ran, choking out a scream when she heard the slap of a bullet hit the wall. She flew into the bedroom, slammed the door, fumbled with the lock.

Call the police, she ordered herself, then clearly saw her phone sitting beside her keyboard in the little bedroom.

No way to call for help. She bolted toward the window, wasted time trying to shove it open before remembering the lock, and heard the solid kick hit the door.

She needed a weapon.

She grabbed her purse, dumped everything out, pawed through it.

"Think, think, think!" she chanted as she heard wood splinter.

She grabbed the can of pepper spray, sent by her mother a year before and never used. Prayed it worked. She closed her fist around her Leatherman—a solid weight in her fist. Hearing the door give, she ran, put her back to the wall beside it.

Be strong, be smart, be fast, she told herself, repeating it over and over like a mantra as the door crashed open. Biting back a fresh scream as a swath of bullets swept through the doorway.

She held her breath, shifted and aimed for the eyes as Jai stepped in. The scream ripped like a scalpel. Thinking only of escape, Lila punched out with her weighted hand, glanced a blow off Jai's shoulder, followed it with a shove. With Jai firing blindly, Lila ran.

Get down, get out.

She was nearly halfway down when she heard running footsteps. She glanced back, braced for a bullet, saw the blur of Jai leaping.

The force knocked her off her feet, stole even the thought of breath. As the world spun, pain shot into her shoulder, her hip, her head as they fell down the steps, rolling like dice from a shaken cup.

She tasted blood, watched streaks of light spear across her vision. She kicked weakly, tried to crawl as nausea churned up from belly to throat. Her own scream tore free as hands dragged her back. Pulling on her strength, she kicked again, felt the blow land. She gained her hands and knees, sucked in a breath to shove to her feet, and tumbled back, the streaks bursting into stars when the fist caught the side of her jaw.

Then Jai was on her, a hand clamped around her throat.

No beauty now. Eyes red, leaking, face splotched, bruised, bloodied. But the hand cutting off Lila's air weighed like iron.

"Do you know how many I've killed? You're nothing. You're just the next. And when your man comes back, **biao zi**, I'll gut him and watch him bleed out. You're nothing, and I'll make you less."

No breath, a red mist crawling over her eyes.

She saw Ash at his easel, saw him eating waffles, laughing into her eyes at a sun-washed café.

She saw him—them—traveling together, being home together, living their lives together.

The future in her hands.

Ash. She'd kill Ash.

Adrenaline surged, an electric jolt. She bucked, but the grip on her throat only tightened. She struck out, saw Jai's lips peel back in a terrible smile.

Weight in her hand, she realized. She still had the tool; she hadn't dropped the tool. Frantic, she fought to open it one-handed.

"Egg." She croaked it out.

"You think I care about the fucking egg?"

"Here. Egg. Here."

The vicious grip loosened a fraction. Air seared Lila's throat as she gulped it in.

"Where?"

"I'll give it to you. To you. Please."

"Tell me where it is."

"Please."

"Tell me or die."

"In . . ." She garbled the rest on a fit of

coughing that had tears streaming down her cheeks.

Jai slapped her. "Where. Is. The. Egg," she demanded, slapping Lila between each word.

"In the . . ." she whispered, hoarse, breathless. And Jai leaned closer.

In her head, she screamed, but her abused throat only released a screeching wheeze as she plunged the knife into Jai's cheek. Weight shifted off her chest, for just an instant. She bucked, kicked, stabbed out again. Pain radiated down her arm as Jai twisted her wrist, pulled the knife from her.

"My face! My face! I'm going to carve you up."

Spent, defeated, Lila prepared to die.

Ash carried Chinese takeout, a small bakery box and a bouquet of gerbera daisies bright as candy.

They'd make her smile.

He imagined them opening a bottle of wine, sharing the meal, sharing the bed. Keeping each other distracted until the call finally came, and they knew it was over, it was finished.

Then they'd get on with the business of their lives.

He thought of her reaction to his proposal by the side of the road. He hadn't meant to ask her then and there, but it had been the moment for him. The way she'd looked, the way she was—the way they'd read each other's every cue during the charade with Vasin.

What they had together was a rare thing. He knew it. Now he had to make her believe it.

They could travel wherever she wanted as long as she wanted. The where didn't matter to him. They could use the loft as a base until she was ready to put down roots.

And she would be, he thought, once she really believed, once she trusted what they had together.

As far as he was concerned, they had all the time in the world.

He shifted bags to pull out his keys as he started up the steps.

He noticed that the lights on the alarm, on the camera he'd had installed, were off.

They'd been on, hadn't they, when he left? Had he checked?

The hairs on the back of his neck rose when he saw the scratches on the locks, the slight gap in the way the door fit.

He'd already dropped the bags when he heard the scream.

He charged the door. It creaked, groaned, but held. Rearing back, he threw his body, his rage against it.

It crashed open, showed him his worst nightmare.

He didn't know if she was dead or alive, all he saw was the blood—her blood, her limp body and glassy eyes. And Maddok straddling her, the knife poised to strike.

Fury snapped through him, a lightning charge that boiled the blood, burned the bones. He rushed her, never slowing as she sprang up, never feeling the bite of the knife as she sliced it down.

He simply picked her up bodily, heaved her aside. He stood between her and Lila, not daring to look down, bracing instead to attack, to defend.

She didn't spring to her feet this time but heaved herself up to a crouch from the rubble of what had been his grandmother's

Pembroke table. Blood ran down her cheek in a river, leaked out of her nose. Somewhere in the back of his mind he wondered if that's why she wept. Her eyes were red, swollen, running with tears.

He charged her again, would have rammed her like a bull, but she managed a staggering dance aside, a shaky pivot, and an underhand strike with the knife that missed by a whisper.

He grabbed her knife hand by the wrist, twisted, imagined snapping the bone like a dry twig. In panic and pain, she swept a leg out, nearly took him down, but he held on, used the momentum to take her back, around.

And he saw Lila swaying like a drunk, her face fierce, and a lamp in her hands like a bat or a sword. Relief and rage churned together. "Run," he ordered, but she kept coming.

Jai fought against his hold. Blood-slick skin nearly allowed her to slip free. He tore his gaze from Lila, looked into Jai's eyes.

And for the first time in his life, he balled his fist and punched a woman in the face. Not once, but twice.

The knife fell to the floor with a single

hard bang. When Jai's knees buckled he let her drop. He scooped up the bloodied tool, managed to get an arm around Lila as she pitched forward.

"Is she dead? Is she dead?"

"No. How bad are you hurt? Let me see."

"I don't know. You're bleeding. Your arm is bleeding."

"It's okay. I'm going to call the police. Can you go in the kitchen, in the utility closet. There's some cord."

"Cord. We have to tie her up."

"I can't leave you alone with her and get it myself. Can you get it?"

"Yes." She handed him the lamp. "I broke the plug when I pulled it out of the wall. I'll fix it. I'll get the cord first. And the first-aid kit. Your arm's bleeding."

He knew he shouldn't take the time, but he couldn't stop himself. He set the lamp aside, then he pulled her to him, gently, gently. "I thought you were dead."

"So did I. But we're not." She moved her hands over his face as if memorizing the shape. "We're not. Don't let her wake up. You have to hit her again if she starts to wake up. I'll be right back."

He took out his phone, watched his hand shake as he called the police.

It took hours, and felt like days. Uniformed police, paramedics, Fine and Waterstone, the FBI. People in and out, in and out. Then a doctor, shining lights in her eyes, poking, prodding, asking her who was president. Even through the glaze of shock she wondered at a doctor making an emergency house call.

"What kind of a doctor are you?" she asked him.

"A good one."

"I mean what kind of doctor makes house calls?"

"A really good one. And I'm a friend of Ash's."

"She stabbed him—or it looked like more of a slice. I just fell down the stairs."

"You're a lucky woman. You took some hard knocks, but nothing's broken. Throat's pretty sore, I bet."

"It feels like I've been drinking glass chips. Ash needs to go to the hospital for that arm. So much blood . . ."

"I can stitch him up."

"Here?"

"It's what I do. Do you remember my name?"

"Jud."

"Good. You've got a mild concussion, some heroic bruising—that's a medical term," he added, and made her smile. "It wouldn't hurt for you to spend the night in the hospital, just for observation."

"I'd rather just have a shower. Can I just take a shower? She's all over me."

"Not by yourself."

"I really don't think I'm up to sex in the shower just now."

He laughed, gave her hand a squeeze. "Your friend's here—Julie? How about if she helps you out?"

"That'd be great."

"I'll go down and get her. You wait, okay? Bathrooms are minefields."

"You're a good friend. I . . . Oh, I remember now. I met you at Oliver's funeral. Dr. Judson Donnelly—concierge medicine. Like the guy on TV."

"That's a good sign your brain's not overly scrambled—another fancy medical term. I'm going to leave written instructions on the medication, and I'll swing by tomorrow to take a look at both of you. Meanwhile, rest, use the cold packs on the bruises and skip the shower sex for the next twenty-four hours."

"I can do that."

He packed up his bag, then paused on his way out to look back at her. "Ash said you were an amazing woman. He's not wrong."

Her eyes welled up, but she fought the tears back. She wouldn't break down, just couldn't. She feared if she did, even for a moment, she'd never stop.

So she had what passed for a smile when Julie rushed in.

"Oh, Lila."

"Not looking my best, and it's worse under what's left of this dress. But I have some very nice pills, courtesy of Jud, so I really do feel better than I look. How's Ash?"

Sitting on the side of the bed, Julie took her hand. "He was talking to some of the crime scene people, but the doctor dragged him off to take care of him. Luke's with him. Luke's going to stay with him."

"Good. Luke's really good in a crisis. I really like Luke."

"You scared the crap out of us."

"Join the team. Are you up for standing by while I take a shower? I need to . . . I have to . . ."

The pressure dropped into her chest, stealing her breath.

Hands around her throat, squeezing, squeezing.

"She ruined my dress." She felt herself gasping, couldn't stop. "It was Prada."

"I know, sweetie." Julie just gathered her up when she broke, rocked her like a baby when she sobbed.

After the shower, after the pain pill kicked in, it didn't take much for Julie to persuade her to lie down. When she woke, the light was on low, and her head was pillowed on Ash's shoulder.

She sat up—and the twinges woke her fully. "Ash."

"Right here. Do you need another pill? It's about time."

"Yes. No. Yes. What time is it? It's after midnight. Your arm."

"It's okay."

But despite the twinges, she reached over to turn up the light, see for herself. The bandage ran from shoulder to elbow.

"It's okay," he repeated at her sound of distress.

"Don't say it's just a scratch."

"It's not just a scratch, but Jud claims he sews as exquisitely as a Breton nun. I'll get your pill, and you can get some more rest."

"Not yet. I need to go downstairs. I need to see— God, you're so tired." She laid her hands on his cheeks, looked into his exhausted eyes. "I need to see it, go through it, settle it."

"Okay."

She winced as she got out of bed. "Wow, the cliché about run over by a truck is real. Believe me, I won't be shy about the drugs. I just want to see, clear head, clear eyes. Then we'll both take drugs and zone out."

"That's a deal. Julie and Luke wouldn't leave," he told her as they walked each other out. "They're in the guest room."

"Good friends are better than diamonds. I cried all over Julie—I'm going to confess that. I may cry all over you at some point, but I'm pretty steady right now."

She paused at the top of the stairs, looked down.

They'd cleaned up. The table Jai had landed on was no longer scattered in pieces on the floor. There'd been shattered pottery, glass. And blood. Hers, his, Jai's. Scrubbed away now, for the most part.

"She had a gun, there was a gun."

"They have it. You told them."

"The telling part's foggy. Did Waterstone hold my hand? I sort of remember him holding my hand."

"Yeah, he did."

"But they got the gun. They took it away?"

"Yes. It was empty. She'd run out of bullets."

Hearing the strain in his voice, she took his hand as they walked down.

"Vasin's security people underestimated her. She killed two of them, got one of their guns, got a car."

"She was hurt when she got here. That was lucky for me. I didn't bother with the internal locks. That was stupid of me."

"We were careless. I can't remember if I set the alarm when I left. She got through the system, either way. She got to you, and I wasn't here."

"We're not going to do that." She turned,

took his face again. "We're not going to do that to ourselves or each other."

He lowered his forehead to hers. "Pepper spray and a Leatherman."

"I couldn't figure out how to incorporate duct tape. I blinded her ass—well, her eyes. She should never have come here, never have tried this. She could've gotten away."

"Pride, I guess. It cost her. Fine and Waterstone came back while you were sleeping. She's not going to see daylight except through bars for the rest of her life—and she's rolling like an avalanche on Vasin. They've already picked him up."

"So it's really over." She let out a breath, realized the tears wanted to flood again.

Not yet, she told herself.

"That thing you asked me to think about, before? I have." She drew away, walked over to examine the lamp with the broken plug. Yes, she could fix that. "You saved my life tonight."

"If that idea persuades you to marry me . . . I'll take it."

She shook her head. "We fell down the steps. It's all so blurry. She was choking me, and I didn't have much left. My life didn't pass in front of my eyes—not the past stuff, like you hear about. I thought about you, and the image you have of us. I thought, I'll never have that now, that life inside the crystal ball, and all that could go with it. I wanted to give up—but she said she was going to kill you when you came back. And I found more. Not just the trusty Leatherman I'd hung on to. But more. Because I love you. Wow, give me a minute."

She held her hand up to keep him back until she got it all out. "I couldn't stand the idea of the world without you, that she could take you away, take the future away from us. So I found more—not enough, but more. Just before you came crashing in, and I thought it was over, all I could think was I never told you I love you. What an idiot. Then my knight in not-too-shiny armor saved my life. Of course, I loosened the lid."

"The lid."

"Like the pickle jar. I really softened her up for you, you have to admit."

"She was cursing your name when they took her out."

"Really?" Lila's smile was fierce. "That just makes my day."

"Make mine. Are you going to marry me?"

In her hands, she thought. She didn't have to look to know. She only had to trust—and choose.

"I have some conditions. I do want to travel, but I think it's time I stopped living out of two suitcases. I want what I was afraid to want until my possible future passed in front of my eyes. I want a home, Ash. I want one with you. I want to go places, see places—with you—but I want to make a home. I think I can make a good one. I want to work off what's on my schedule, then focus on writing. I have a new story I really want to tell."

A new story, she realized, she wanted to live.

"Maybe I'll house-sit now and again, for an established client or as a favor, but I don't want to spend my future living in someone else's space. I want to spend it living in my own. In ours."

She drew a breath. "And I want you to come to Alaska with me and meet my parents, which is a little scary since I've never taken anyone to meet my parents. And I want . . ." She swiped at her cheeks. "This isn't the time for another jag. I want a dog."

"What kind of dog?"

"I don't know, but I want one. I always wanted a dog, but we could never have one because we were always moving around. I don't want to be a gypsy anymore. I want a home and a dog and children, and you. I want you so much. So, will you marry me with all that hanging on it?"

"I have to think about it." He laughed, forgot himself long enough to grab her, yank her against him, then eased back quickly when she gasped. "Sorry. I'm sorry." He took her mouth, pressed light kisses over her face. "I accept your terms, absolutely."

"Thank God. I love you, and now that I know how good it feels to say it, I'm going to say it a lot." She ran her fingers through his hair. "But not till spring—to get married. Julie and Luke come first."

"Next spring. It's a date."

"We got through it. All of it." She rested her head on his shoulder. "We're where we're supposed to be—like the golden egg." Turning her head, she pressed her lips to his throat. "How can I hurt all over and still feel so wonderful?"

"Let's get those drugs, then you'll just feel wonderful."

"You read my mind." Arms around each other's waist, they started upstairs.

"Oh, one more thing I want? I want to paint the master bath. I have this idea I want to try."

"We'll talk about it."

They would, she thought as they helped each other upstairs. They'd talk about all sorts of things. They had plenty of time.